A SHORT WAIT
BETWEEN TRAINS

A SHORT WAIT
BETWEEN TRAINS

·

An Anthology of
War Short Stories
by American Writers

Edited by Robert Benard
Introduction by Knox Burger

Delacorte
Press

141316

Published by
Delacorte Press
Bantam Doubleday Dell Publishing Group, Inc.
666 Fifth Avenue
New York, New York 10103

The Acknowledgments on pages vii–viii constitute an extension of the
copyright page.

Library of Congress Cataloging in Publication Data

A Short wait between trains / edited by Robert Benard ; introduction
by Knox Burger.
p.   cm.
Summary: Twenty-two stories of war, from the Civil War to the
Vietnam War. Includes authors such as Eudora Welty, Stephen Crane,
James Jones, Ralph Ellison, and Bernard Malamud.
ISBN 0-385-30486-2
1. War stories, American. [1. War—Fiction. 2. Short stories.]
I. Benard, Robert.
PS648.W34S5   1991
813′.0108358—dc20
[Fic]   91-15882   CIP   AC

Designed by GDS/Jeffrey L. Ward

Manufactured in the United States of America

November 1991

10 9 8 7 6 5 4 3 2 1

BVG

For Gregg Mitchell
Ever valiant,
Ever beloved

Acknowledgments

I thank Richard Walton for his help in assembling permissions; Knox Burger, Gregg Mitchell, and Ivan Webster for suggesting stories; E. J. McCarthy and George Nicholson for their editorial faith and support; and, once more, Knox Burger for his perspicacious introduction.

CONTENTS

CONTENTS

INTRODUCTION

·

by Knox Burger

My qualifications to be the master of ceremonies for this collection of war stories are fairly broad, if not very deep. I am not a writer by trade, or a literary critic, nor did I spend much time in combat. And besides, don't all stories speak for themselves? With these disclaimers in mind, I will say that as a magazine and book editor after World War II and latterly a literary agent, I've spent a professional lifetime presuming to judge the literary and popular worth of narrative prose, and continue to find the process involving.

As it happened, I was an English major in college during the early 1940s, when I read several of these stories for the first time. A few years later, as a corporal in the Air Force, I found myself in a B-29 squadron on the island of Saipan. While not an aircrew member, I was subjected to a couple of bombing and strafing runs by Japanese planes, and I did volunteer to fly as an observer on a number of bombing missions over Japan. This was in order to write articles for *Yank, The Army Weekly,* for which I was then a part-time free lance. I was regarded as something of a fool by my fellow groundlings, and as an interloper and dilettante by most of the crewmen, whose tours ran thirty-five missions. I had flown on three, and was ordered by the squadron sergeant major to cancel my participation in a fourth so that I might serve my turn as kitchen policeman, a chore I'd been weaseling out of for weeks.

The aircraft in which I was to have flown was the same one I'd flown in during the very first B-29 raid on Japan from the Marianas, and I'd made good friends among the crew. That day I pulled K.P., the plane ditched in the ocean on the way up to the target. Three survivors out of the eleven-man crew were picked up by a Navy Dumbo seaplane—two gunners and the navigator.

As the enlisted man assigned to write up recommendations for medals for conspicuous acts of bravery, I was ordered by the C.O. of the squadron to recommend the pilot for a posthumous award. The C.O. was Lt. Col. Robert K. Morgan, who had been the pilot of the B-17 bomber *Memphis Belle,* the subject of a justly famed wartime documentary made by William Wyler, and, in 1990, of a feature film.

The pilot of the downed bomber had been in Morgan's squadron in the E.T.O., and Morgan took his loss hard. In what amounted to a paroxysm of honest (and rare) emotion, he directed me to come up with evidence to warrant the nation's highest award, the Congressional Medal of Honor. He probably should have known better, but he didn't want to. He assumed the memorial stance, the sacred view of battle: heroism transcendent over death.

At the base hospital, I visited the navigator. He'd been seated in the forward section of the aircraft, and was the only surviving witness to the pilot's actions. He was the spitting image of a cartoon accident victim—head swathed in bandages, one arm strapped across his chest, one leg in a cast, raised in traction. To my question about the pilot's heroism, he gave succinct response: "Congressional Medal? If he'd have lived, I'd testify to get the son of a bitch court-martialed." He then listed all the things the pilot had done wrong, after a fire had broken out in one engine, to worsen the disaster. So much for the Medal of Honor. Morgan had to settle for one more cluster on the pilot's Distinguished Flying Cross. If Morgan stood for the sacred, the navigator represented the profane, the subversive truth. His bitterness was palpable, and that is the posture of most of the writers of these stories. The basic dichotomy between the two views is what gives most war fiction its surface tension.

I did fly on a couple missions later on. During the great March 9, 1945 incendiary bombing of Tokyo, the aircraft on which I was a passenger feathered a propellor just before reaching the target. The loss of the engine retarded our progress home considerably, inducing a slow but steady decline in altitude. We were out of radio contact with the base, and some two hours overdue. The people on Saipan had to believe we had been shot down over the target or had ditched somewhere in the 1500 miles of ocean between Japan and the Marianas. Sitting there in the dawn sky on the edge of my seat as our height above the ocean kept diminishing, I thought of my good friend and tentmate Jack Duffy, whom—even now as we dawdled toward home—I could envision rifling my footlocker, probably with a tear in his eye, for he was not without sentiment. In addition to useful items like socks and cigarettes, he would find the letters (to be mailed in the event . . .) that I'd written to my parents and girlfriend before taking off. Hail and farewell. Inevitably, war sharpens any instinct one may have to write.

My volunteerism was a passing phase, a function of hormones. When you're twenty-two, it is a well-established fact that bad things happen to other people. I now think back on the bravado that led me to volunteer to fly on missions that seemed as if they might be particularly newsworthy, with a shudder of alarm. The characters in most of the stories in this volume are in their early twenties. Patriotism has been said to be the last refuge of scoundrels—perhaps also of old politicians, it might be added, and of kids too young to know any better. What short memories we have, and what wretched powers of prognostication when it comes to war.

The early stories in this volume deal with the Civil War. In "The Burning," by Eudora Welty, we have a modern writer looking back through legend, hearsay, folk wisdom, and folk hatred to the Civil War, and how it tore the fabric of social life in the South. The story is Grand Guignol, almost grotesque in its depiction of the horrors visited on two genteel Southern ladies. It opens with a Yankee soldier entering their house on horseback. He has come to burn down the house and to strangle the peacocks that strut under the pecan trees. The writing is deceptively simple, almost homey, the ensuing events are never made quite explicit; the writer nibbles at the edges and glances off what actually happened, as if she cannot bear to describe it straight out. Sherman's march through Georgia seems to be in her very bones a century after the event.

The Caroline Gordon story, "The Forest of the South," is also about a time and a circumstance she can only have imagined. Her Civil War story is about officers and gentlemen from North and South, and a chilling act of revenge—masquerading as Southern good manners—visited on a Union officer. Gordon's memory is as long as Welty's.

"One of the Missing," the Ambrose Bierce story, deals with actual combat, and takes on timeless and sacred themes, including suicidal sacrifice for one's fellow soldiers. A curious mixture, it has a "modern" feel of immediacy and irony, and yet it's also a story of old-fashioned gallantry.

Stephen Crane's "The Open Boat" takes place after a steamship sinking off the American coast. It is about men struggling against the sea, and the persistence of hope. Crane himself survived a ship sinking while covering an arms-smuggling expedition during the Spanish-American War in 1898; and if that circumstance contributes to this story's unmistakable air of authenticity, how then do we account for the fact that his great Civil War novel, *The Red Badge of Courage,* reads like the most unsparing and meticulous reportage, when Crane never experienced combat?

Except for the Civil War, our battles have been fought abroad, and in some of these stories we witness a character's first encounter with a foreign land. William Faulkner got no farther than Canada as an air cadet, but in "Victory" he chose to imagine what it was like to grow up in a Scottish shipbuilding town, and later, in the trenches of France. So here we have a young American of rather parochial background electing to write a novelette about the rise and fall of a Scottish boy of humble origins who becomes a celebrated British war hero; his horizons thus expanded, he uncertainly takes on some of the trappings and attitudes of a gentleman. Faulkner's interest in heroism seems akin to that of Joseph Conrad (whose novel bearing the same title he had surely read). The story is an early example of Faulkner's abiding interest in caste and class. It seems a singularly nineteenth-century sort of piece to have come from the man who was to become America's greatest prose innovator. Reading it is a little like looking at an early Picasso picture, painted before he began experimenting with perspective.

The character in Hemingway's "In Another Country" is evidently a victim of a kind of shell shock—what we now call Post Traumatic Stress Disorder—before the syndrome was acknowledged and discussed. The author's just-developing style seems exactly adapted to reveal the bleak outlook of the central figure, just returned from the First World War, and "interested in what was the matter." Narrative and viewpoint seem felicitously wedded, seem to shadow each other. It is low-key, relatively unmannered Hemingway, a bit self-conscious perhaps, but free of the posturing that sometimes marred his later work. It seems honest and understated, seems to have been set down at the time it depicts, without retrospection, the war still an unhealed wound in the memory of the protagonist.

United States involvement in World War I was relatively brief, and not many Americans were actually involved in combat. It produced correspondingly little American fiction. Both Faulkner and Hemingway volunteered their services to foreign governments before the United States entered the war. Judging from their writing about that time in their lives, Hemingway's view of combat was better informed and certainly more jaundiced and closer to the modern outlook than Faulkner's, which —in other fiction dealing with the war—tended to romanticize it shamelessly.

World War II was the first war in which deliberate, wide-scale killing and terrorizing of civilians became a matter of policy, and thus taken for granted. Kay Boyle's story examines what it's like to be defeated, and the occupied French reaction to the occupying Germans. It's almost a treatise on the psychology of losing.

War can anesthetize. Regard the James Jones story, "Greater Love," set in the South Pacific, where he served. I first encountered it when I published it in *Collier's* magazine, of which I was fiction editor in the late 1940s. Jones's protagonist simply cannot face the fact of men falling around him, killed or wounded. His mind rationalizes the fallen as men taking unwarranted breaks from the action, as cowards. If he were to succumb to the objective reality, that all had been hit, he simply could not have plodded on through the gunfire, hunting down the enemy. (The ignoble side of that coin is the "I'm all right, Jack" syndrome, evident in other stories in this volume: If a man beside you falls, or an aircraft on your wing goes down, some feeling of relief, of gratitude that it's not you, is inescapable—mixed in, of course, with whatever sense of loss and guilt your psyche has provided you with the capacity to feel.)

Evan S. Connell's "The Marine" has to do with a grisly activity not uncommonly performed on the corpses of Japanese soldiers in the early days of the Pacific war. War has frequently ennobled men with a more profound sense of humanity and self-sacrifice than had animated them before; but just as likely is the situation exemplified here. All the humanity has been pounded out of this boy, this child, by his experiences in the field. He's been robotized. Again, war is seen as nature's novocaine.

Since war is mostly waiting, a lot of war stories inevitably deal with the lulls, the long dips between the high points. Irwin Shaw's "Gunners' Passage" takes place in such a backwater time, aircrewmen waiting shipment from one theater of war to another. His fine ear for the speech of men of action is apparent.

The Phillip Roth story "Defender of the Faith," deservedly famous, is introspective and controversial. It's about Jews, and is almost bursting with exasperation, understanding, and—almost reluctantly—love. Like many Irwin Shaw stories, it has a deracinated Jewish male as its protagonist. He is a combat veteran, now back in the States, and the ace pitcher on the training camp cadre's ball team. Jews evading combat have been a staple of barracks slander for centuries. This story deals with this folklore, assumes it might have occasional basis in fact, and performs a marvelous flip-flop. Had Roth not been Jewish, he could not have gotten away with the story; had his hero not been Jewish, the story would have no ironic punch and would have been two-dimensional and ugly.

"A Short Wait Between Trains," the McLaughlin story,

springs from a breathtakingly simple premise. It is quietly told, deceptively mild in tone, like the preponderance of *New Yorker* stories that appeared forty and fifty years ago. It reflected actual events, things-as-they-were in those days, and caused a real stir when it first appeared. It brings the segregation of the races in the armed forces into sharp and absurd relief. The Negroes' (approved W.W.-II designation) reaction to the story's small central event seems strangely muted by the standards of what would happen today in the face of such a skewed idea of who's Us and who's Them.

Ralph Ellison's "Flying Home" also deals with race. It is about a student pilot breaking his leg while crash-landing during a training flight in the American South. The pilot is an educated (and unusual) black cadet; the first person who comes upon him is a rural black sharecropper, amazed at this young brother having emerged from the cockpit of this flying machine. A Caucasian authority figure (read bigoted white farmer) enters the scene, and there ensues the kind of racial confrontation almost inevitable under the circumstances. The story was written while the war was going on, and despite some awkwardness, is obviously deeply felt.

I gave James Ross's story its first publication, and I confess to a particular affection for the story and for its late author. It is called "Zone of Interior," an army locution for the United States, though the story takes place at a replacement depot in France, after the war has ended and everybody wants to go home. It is about a phenomenon common to all armies, and indeed to all other bureaucracies: a lower ranking man happening to be more sophisticated and manipulative than his nominal superior. Sergeant Fat Otis knows just how things work in the military, and sadistically employs the knowledge to subject a brave and well-meaning—if not too bright—lieutenant to acute mental torture. Ross, a Southern newspaperman, will probably be an unfamiliar name to readers. He published only a few other stories in his lifetime, but his rural North Carolina novel *They Don't Dance Much,* written when he was still in his twenties, is a minor classic.

"The Ram in the Thicket" is a home-front story, dealing with a couple whose only son is a war casualty. The woman is a gold-star mother—with a vengeance. It's about how she reacts to her loss, and about the debasement of your basic American marriage.

Miller Harris's name is even less well-known than that of James Ross. He has published only two short stories (though he collaborated on a lot of sparkling ad copy for Eagle Shirtmakers, of which he was C.E.O. for many years). He was a first sergeant with the 69th Infantry Division, which participated in the Battle of the Bulge. He chose to write about an encounter altogether different from his own war experiences. Popular magazines like *Collier's* and *The Saturday Evening Post* went out of their way not to disturb their readers (and advertisers), and this story was regarded as too downbeat to be acceptable by the publisher for whom I worked. I suggested to Harris, whom I'd known in college, that he try it on the *Atlantic,* which published it. The grisly subtext—a marine sergeant back in the zone of interior from the Pacific to accompany the corpse of a fellow marine on its last train ride—is papered over by a wry little boy-meets-girl situation comedy.

The stories that came out of the Vietnam war are generally more cynical, more bitter, more horrific than stories from earlier conflicts. Certainly they are more profane, in both the larger and the lesser sense of the word.

The experience of combat, real or imagined, in certain stories seems to serve as a kind of prism, concentrating light to burn intense, specific moments into the memory of the writer forever. Such a story is "The Village," which after a minute-to-minute account of miserable heat, leeches, mosquitoes—all strands threaded through the story's basic fabric of fear—ends in one breathtaking anticlimactic mistake. No one could ever catalogue the number and magnitude and tragic aftermaths of mistakes that happen in wars.

Tim O'Brien's "The Ghost Soldiers" is a character study, a story of relationships, hung on the structure of a sadistically elaborate practical joke played on one of their colleagues by two grunts up on the line. It is perhaps worth noting, as an indication of the pervasiveness of pop culture, that O'Brien shows us characters who, upon being wounded, hark back to remembered reactions of movie stars to make-believe bullets in old war movies.

O'Brien has written: "If a story is moral, do not believe it. A true war story is never moral. If at the end of a war story, you feel uplifted, or if you feel that some small bit of rectitude has been salvaged from a larger waste, then you have been made the victim of a very old and terrible lie. There is no rectitude whatsoever. There is no virtue . . . a true war story bears an absolute and uncompromising allegiance to obscenity and evil."

Far be it from me to argue the point. And yet, and yet . . . as someone whose very calling involves assessing and being moved by language, I find it hard sometimes to resist the words of great leaders of righteous causes, or of great poets, exhorting us against the enemy, or celebrating the heroism of fighting men. Lincoln during the Civil War, certainly our most eloquent leader, whose words almost literally held the country together; Roosevelt intoning his "day of infamy" speech after the Japanese attacked Pearl Harbor; Churchill ("We shall fight on the beaches, we shall fight on the landing grounds, we shall fight in the fields and in the streets, we shall fight in the hills, we shall never surrender"); Shakespeare's Henry IV predicting everlasting glory to the happy few, the band of brothers whom he inspires on the eve of Agincourt ("He that outlives this day and comes safe home will stand a tiptoe when this day is named. . . .").

Stunning language is, of course, a hallmark of great writers, and of many great leaders of men. While their exhortations may not stand up well in hindsight, or submit to nuclear logic, they can stir men in primeval ways even now.

So let these stories serve as antidotes to propaganda. The sentiments they express are more appropriate for our time than the high-flown rhetoric. In every war, the reality of what happens seems to give the lie to the anticipation; retrospective memory plays tricks. The further behind us we put a war, the more bad things we seem to forget, until war recedes to the status of nostalgia. It is good to have these stories to edify the young and to help set our collective memory straight.

ONE OF THE MISSING

.

by *Ambrose Bierce*

Jerome Searing, a private soldier of General Sherman's army, then confronting the enemy at and about Kenesaw Mountain, Georgia, turned his back upon a small group of officers, with whom he had been talking in low tones, stepped across a light line of earthworks, and disappeared in a forest. None of the men in line behind the works had said a word to him, nor had he so much as nodded to them in passing, but all who saw understood that this brave man had been intrusted with some perilous duty. Jerome Searing, though a private, did not serve in the ranks; he was detailed for service at division headquarters, being borne upon the rolls as an orderly. "Orderly" is a word covering a multitude of duties. An orderly may be a messenger, a clerk, an officer's servant—anything. He may perform services for which no provision is made in orders and army regulations. Their nature may depend upon his aptitude, upon favor, upon accident. Private Searing, an incomparable marksman, young—it is surprising how young we all were in those days—hardy, intelligent, and insensible to fear, was a scout. The general commanding his division was not content to obey orders blindly without knowing what was in his front, even when his command was not on detached service, but formed a fraction of the line of the army; nor was he satisfied to receive his knowledge of his *vis-à-vis* through the customary channels; he wanted to know more than he was apprised of by the corps commander and the collisions of pickets and skirmishers. Hence Jerome Searing—with his extraordinary daring, his woodcraft, his sharp eyes and truthful tongue. On this occasion his instructions were simple: to get as near the enemy's lines as possible and learn all that he could.

In a few moments he had arrived at the picket line, the men on duty there lying in groups of from two to four behind little banks of earth scooped out of the slight depression in which they lay, their rifles protruding from the green boughs with which they had masked their small defenses. The forest extended without a break toward the front, so solemn and silent that only by an effort of the imagination could it be conceived as populous with armed men, alert and vigilant—a forest formidable with possibilities of battle. Pausing a moment in one of the rifle pits to apprise the men of his intention, Searing crept stealthily forward on his hands and knees and was soon lost to view in a dense thicket of underbrush.

"That is the last of him," said one of the men; "I wish I had his rifle; those fellows will hurt some of us with it."

Searing crept on, taking advantage of every accident of ground and growth to give himself better cover. His eyes penetrated everywhere, his ears took note of every sound. He stilled his breathing, and at the cracking of a twig beneath his knee stopped his progress and hugged the earth. It was slow work, but not tedious; the danger made it exciting, but by no physical signs was the excitement manifest. His pulse was as regular, his nerves were as steady, as if he were trying to trap a sparrow.

"It seems a long time," he thought, "but I cannot have come very far; I am still alive."

He smiled at his own method of estimating distance, and crept forward. A moment later he suddenly flattened himself upon the earth and lay motionless, minute after minute. Through a narrow opening in the bushes he had caught sight of a small mound of yellow clay—one of the enemy's rifle pits. After some little time he cautiously raised his head, inch by inch, then his body upon his hands, spread out on each side of him, all the while intently regarding the hillock of clay. In another moment he was upon his feet, rifle in hand, striding rapidly forward with little attempt at concealment. He had rightly interpreted the signs, whatever they were; the enemy was gone.

To assure himself beyond a doubt before going back to report upon so important a matter, Searing pushed forward across the line of abandoned pits, running from cover to cover in the more open forest, his eyes vigilant to discover possible stragglers. He came to the edge of a plantation—one of those forlorn, deserted homesteads of the last years of the war, upgrown with brambles, ugly with broken fences, and desolate with vacant buildings having blank apertures in place of doors and windows. After a keen reconnaissance from the safe seclusion of a clump of young pines, Searing ran lightly across a field and through an orchard to a small structure which stood apart from the other farm buildings, on a slight elevation, which he thought would enable him to overlook a large scope of country in the direction that he supposed the enemy to have taken in withdrawing. This building, which had originally consisted of a single room, elevated upon four posts about ten feet high, was now little more than a roof; the floor had fallen away, the joists and planks loosely piled on the ground below or resting on end at various angles, not wholly torn from their fastenings above. The supporting posts were themselves no longer vertical. It looked as if the whole edifice would go down at the touch of a finger. Concealing himself in the debris of joists and flooring, Searing looked across the open ground between his point of view and a spur of Kenesaw Mountain, a half mile away. A road leading up and across this spur was crowded with troops—the rear guard of the retiring enemy, their gun barrels gleaming in the morning sunlight.

Searing had now learned all that he could hope to know. It was his duty to return to his own command with all possible speed and report his discovery. But the gray column of infantry toiling up the mountain road was singularly tempting. His rifle—an ordinary Springfield, but fitted with a globe sight and hair trigger—would easily send its ounce and a quarter of lead hissing into their midst. That would probably not affect the duration and result of the war, but it is the business of a soldier to kill. It is also his pleasure if he is a good soldier. Searing cocked his rifle and "set" the trigger.

But it was decreed from the beginning of time that Private Searing was not to murder anybody that bright summer morning, nor was the Confederate retreat to be announced by him. For countless ages events had been so matching themselves together in that wondrous mosaic to some parts of which, dimly discernible, we give the name of history, that the acts which he had in will would have marred the harmony of the pattern.

Some twenty-five years previously the Power charged with the execution of the work according to the design had provided against that mischance by causing the birth of a certain male child in a little village at the foot of the Carpathian Mountains, had carefully reared it, supervised its education, directed its desires into a military channel, and in due time made it an officer of artillery. By the concurrence of an infinite number of favoring influences and their preponderance over an infinite number of opposing ones, this officer of artillery had been made to commit a breach of discipline and fly from his native country to avoid punishment. He had been directed to New Orleans (instead of New York), where a recruiting officer awaited him on the wharf. He was enlisted and promoted, and things were so ordered that he now commanded a Confederate battery some three miles along the line from where Jerome Searing, the Federal scout, stood cocking his rifle. Nothing had been neglected—at every step in the progress of both these men's lives, and in the lives of their ancestors and contemporaries, and of the lives of the contemporaries of their ancestors —the right thing had been done to bring about the desired result. Had anything in all this vast concatenation been overlooked, Private Searing might have fired on the retreating Confederates that morning, and would perhaps have missed. As it fell out, a captain of artillery, having nothing better to do while awaiting his turn to pull out and be off, amused himself by sighting a field piece obliquely to his right at what he took to be some Federal officers on the crest of a hill, and discharged it. The shot flew high of its mark.

As Jerome Searing drew back the hammer of his rifle, and, with his eyes upon the distant Confederates, considered where he could plant his shot with the best hope of making a widow or an orphan or a childless mother—perhaps all three, for Private Searing, although he had repeatedly refused promotion, was not without a certain kind of ambition—he heard a rushing sound in the air, like that made by the wings of a great bird swooping down upon its prey. More quickly than he could apprehend the gradation, it increased to a hoarse and horrible roar, as the missile that made it sprang at him out of the sky, striking with a deafening impact one of the posts supporting the confusion of timbers above him, smashing it into matchwood, and bringing down the crazy edifice with a loud clatter, in clouds of blinding dust!

* * *

Lieutenant Adrian Searing, in command of the picket guard on that part of the line through which his brother Jerome had passed on his mission, sat with attentive ears in his breastwork behind the line. Not the faintest sound escaped him; the cry of a bird, the barking of a squirrel, the noise of the wind among the pines—all were anxiously noted by his overstrained sense. Suddenly, directly in front of his line, he heard a faint, confused rumble, like the clatter of a falling building translated by distance. At the same moment an officer approached him on foot from the rear and saluted.

"Lieutenant," said the aide, "the colonel directs you to move forward your line and feel the enemy if you find him. If not, continue the advance until directed to halt. There is reason to think that the enemy has retreated."

The lieutenant nodded and said nothing; the other officer retired. In a moment the men, apprised of their duty by the non-commissioned officers in low tones, had deployed from their rifle pits and were moving forward in skirmishing order, with set teeth and beating hearts. The lieutenant mechanically looked at his watch. Six o'clock and eighteen minutes.

When Jerome Searing recovered consciousness, he did not at once understand what had occurred. It was, indeed, some time before he opened his eyes. For a while he believed that he had died and been buried, and he tried to recall some portions of the burial service. He thought that his wife was kneeling upon his grave, adding her weight to that of the earth upon his breast. The two of them, widow and earth, had crushed his coffin. Unless the children should persuade her to go home, he would not much longer be able to breathe. He felt a sense of wrong. "I cannot speak to her," he thought; "the dead have no voice; and if I open my eyes I shall get them full of earth."

He opened his eyes—a great expanse of blue sky, rising from a fringe of the tops of trees. In the foreground, shutting out some of the trees, a high, dun mound, angular in outline and crossed by an intricate, patternless system of straight lines; in the center a bright ring of metal—the whole an immeasurable distance away—a distance so inconceivably great that it fatigued him, and he closed his eyes. The moment that he did so he was conscious of an insufferable light. A sound was in his ears like the low, rhythmic thunder of a distant sea breaking in successive waves upon the beach, and out of this noise, seeming a part of it, or possibly coming from beyond it, and intermingled with its ceaseless undertone, came the articulate words: "Jerome Searing, you are caught like a rat in a trap—in a trap, trap, trap."

Suddenly there fell a great silence, a black darkness, an infinite tranquillity, and Jerome Searing, perfectly conscious of his rathood, and well assured of the trap that he was in, remembered all, and, nowise alarmed, again opened his eyes to reconnoiter, to note the strength of his enemy, to plan his defense.

He was caught in a reclining posture, his back firmly supported by a solid beam. Another lay across his breast, but he had been able to shrink a little way from it so that it no longer oppressed him though it was immovable. A brace joining it at an angle had wedged him against a pile of boards on his left, fastening the arm on that side. His legs, slightly parted and straight along the ground, were covered upward to the knees with a mass of debris which towered above his narrow horizon. His head was as rigidly fixed as in a vise; he could move his eyes, his chin—no more. Only his right arm was partly free. "You must help us out of this," he said to it. But he could not get it from under the heavy timber athwart his chest, nor move it outward more than six inches at the elbow.

Searing was not seriously injured, nor did he suffer pain. A smart rap on the head from a flying fragment of the splintered post, incurred simultaneously with the frightfully sudden shock to the nervous system, had momentarily dazed him. His term of unconsciousness, including the period of recovery, during which he had had the strange fancies, had probably not exceeded a few seconds, for the dust of the wreck had not wholly cleared away as he began an intelligent survey of the situation.

With his partly free right hand he now tried to get hold of the beam which lay across, but not quite against, his breast. In no way could he do so. He was unable to depress the shoulder so as to push the elbow beyond that edge of the timber which was nearest his knees; failing in that, he could not raise the forearm and hand to grasp the beam. The brace that made an angle with it downward and backward prevented him from doing anything in that direction, and between it and his body the space was not half as wide as the length of his forearm. Obviously he could not get his hand under the beam nor over it; he could not, in fact, touch it at all. Having demonstrated his inability, he desisted, and began to think if he could reach any of the debris piled upon his legs.

In surveying the mass with a view to determining that point, his attention was arrested by what seemed to be a ring of shining metal immediately in front of his eyes. It appeared to him at first to surround some perfectly black substance, and it was somewhat more than a half inch in diameter. It suddenly occurred to his mind that the blackness was simply shadow, and that the ring was in fact the muzzle of his rifle protruding from the pile of debris. He was not long in satisfying himself that this was so—if it was a satisfaction. By closing either eye he could look a little way along the barrel—to the point where it was hidden by the rubbish that held it. He could see the one side, with the corresponding eye, at apparently the same angle as the other side with the other eye. Looking with the right eye, the weapon seemed to be directed at a point to the left of his head, and *vice versa*. He was unable to see the upper surface of the barrel, but could see the under surface of the stock at a slight angle. The piece was, in fact, aimed at the exact center of his forehead.

In the perception of this circumstance, in the recollection that just previously to the mischance of which this uncomfortable situation was the result, he had cocked the gun and set the trigger so that a touch would discharge it, Private Searing was affected with a feeling of uneasiness. But that was as far as possible from fear; he was a brave man, somewhat familiar with the aspect of rifles from that point of view, and of cannon, too; and now he recalled, with something like amusement, an incident of his experience at the storming of Missionary Ridge, where, walking up to one of the enemy's embrasures from which he had seen a heavy gun throw charge after charge of grape among the assailants, he thought for a moment that the piece had been withdrawn; he could see nothing in the opening but a brazen circle. What that was he had understood just in time to step aside as it pitched another peck of iron down that swarming slope. To face firearms is one of the commonest incidents in a soldier's life—firearms, too, with malevolent eyes blazing behind them. That is what a soldier is for. Still, Private Searing did not altogether relish the situation, and turned away his eyes.

After groping, aimless, with his right hand for a time, he made an ineffectual attempt to release his left. Then he tried to disengage his head, the fixity of which was the more annoying from his ignorance of what held it. Next he tried to free his feet, but while exerting the powerful muscles of his legs for that purpose it occurred to him that a disturbance of the rubbish which held them might discharge the rifle; how it could have endured what had already befallen it he could not understand, although memory assisted him with various instances in point. One in particular he recalled, in which, in a moment of mental abstraction, he had clubbed his rifle and beaten out another gentleman's brains, observing afterward that the weapon which he had been diligently swinging by the muzzle was loaded, capped, and at full cock—knowledge of which circumstance would doubtless have cheered his antagonist to longer endurance. He had always smiled in recalling that blunder of his "green and salad days" as a soldier, but now he did not smile. He turned his eyes again to the muzzle of the gun, and for a moment fancied that it had moved; it seemed somewhat nearer.

Again he looked away. The tops of the distant trees beyond the bounds of the plantation interested him; he had not before observed how light and feathery they seemed, nor how darkly blue the sky was, even among their branches, where they somewhat paled it with their green; above him it appeared almost black. "It will be uncomfortably hot here," he thought, "as the day advances. I wonder which way I am looking."

Judging by such shadows as he could see, he decided that his face was due north; he would at least not have the sun in his eyes, and north—well, that was toward his wife and children.

"Bah!" he exclaimed aloud, "what have they to do with it?"

He closed his eyes. "As I can't get out, I may as well go to sleep. The rebels are gone, and some of our fellows are sure to stray out here foraging. They'll find me."

But he did not sleep. Gradually he became sensible of a pain in his forehead—a dull ache, hardly perceptible at first, but growing more and more uncomfortable. He opened his eyes and it was gone—closed them and it returned. "The devil!" he said irrelevantly, and stared again at the sky. He heard the singing of birds, the strange metallic note of the meadow lark, suggesting the clash of vibrant blades. He fell into pleasant memories of his childhood, played again with his brother and sister, raced across the fields, shouting to alarm the sedentary larks, entered the somber forest beyond, and with timid steps followed the faint path to Ghost Rock, standing at last with audible heart-throbs before the Dead Man's Cave and seeking to penetrate its awful mystery. For the first time he observed that the opening of the haunted cavern was encircled by a ring of metal. Then all else vanished, and left him gazing into the barrel of his rifle as before. But whereas before it had seemed nearer, it now seemed an inconceivable distance away, and all the more sinister for that. He cried out, and, startled by something in his own voice—the note of fear—lied to himself in denial: "If I don't sing out I may stay here till I die."

He now made no further attempt to evade the menacing stare of the gun barrel. If he turned away his eyes an instant it was to look for assistance (although he could not see the ground on either side the ruin), and he permitted them to return, obedient to the imperative fascination. If he closed them, it was from weariness, and instantly the poignant pain in his forehead—the prophecy and menace of the bullet—forced him to reopen them.

The tension of nerve and brain was too severe; nature came to his relief with intervals of unconsciousness. Reviving from one of these, he became sensible of a sharp, smarting pain in his right hand, and when he worked his fingers together, or rubbed his palm with them, he could feel that they were wet and slippery. He could not see the hand, but he knew the sensation; it was running blood. In his delirium he had beaten it against the jagged fragments of the wreck, had clutched it full of splinters. He resolved that he would meet his fate more manly. He was a plain, common soldier, had no religion and not much philosophy; he could not die like a hero, with great and wise last words, even if there were someone to hear them, but he could die "game," and he would. But if he could only know when to expect the shot!

Some rats which had probably inhabited the shed came

sneaking and scampering about. One of them mounted the pile of debris that held the rifle; another followed, and another. Searing regarded them at first with indifference, then with friendly interest; then, as the thought flashed into his bewildered mind that they might touch the trigger of his rifle, he screamed at them to go away. "It is no business of yours," he cried.

The creatures left; they would return later, attack his face, gnaw his nose, cut his throat—he knew that, but he hoped by that time to be dead.

Nothing could now unfix his gaze from the little ring of metal with its black interior. The pain in his forehead was fierce and constant. He felt it gradually penetrating the brain more and more deeply, until at last its progress was arrested by the wood at the back of his head. It grew momentarily more insufferable; he began wantonly beating his lacerated hand against the splinters again to counteract that horrible ache. It seemed to throb with a slow, regular recurrence, each pulsation sharper than the preceding, and sometimes he cried out, thinking he felt the fatal bullet. No thoughts of home, of wife and children, of country, of glory. The whole record of memory was effaced. The world had passed away—not a vestige remained. Here, in this confusion of timbers and boards, is the sole universe. Here is immortality in time—each pain an everlasting life. The throbs tick off eternities.

Jerome Searing, the man of courage, the formidable enemy, the strong, resolute warrior, was as pale as a ghost. His jaw was fallen; his eyes protruded; he trembled in every fibre; a cold sweat bathed his entire body; he screamed with fear. He was not insane—he was terrified.

In groping about with his torn and bleeding hand he seized at last a strip of board, and, pulling, felt it give way. It lay parallel with his body, and by bending his elbow as much as the contracted space would permit, he could draw it a few inches at a time. Finally it was altogether loosened from the wreckage covering his legs; he could lift it clear of the ground its whole length. A great hope came into his mind: perhaps he could work it upward, that is to say backward, far enough to lift the end and push aside the rifle; or, if that were too tightly wedged, so hold the strip of board as to deflect the bullet. With this object he passed it backward inch by inch, hardly daring to breath, lest that act somehow defeat his intent, and more than ever unable to remove his eyes from the rifle, which might perhaps now hasten to improve its waning opportunity. Something at least had been gained; in the occupation of his mind in this attempt at self-defense he was less sensible of the pain in his head and had ceased to scream. But he was still dreadfully frightened, and his teeth rattled like castanets.

The strip of board ceased to move to the suasion of his hand. He tugged at it with all his strength, changed the direction of its length all he could, but it had met some extended obstruction behind him, and the end in front was still too far away to clear the pile of debris and reach the muzzle of the gun. It extended, indeed, nearly as far as the trigger-guard, which, uncovered by the rubbish, he could imperfectly see with his right eye. He tried to break the strip with his hand, but had no leverage. Perceiving his defeat, all his terror returned, augmented tenfold. The black aperture of the rifle appeared to threaten a sharper and more imminent death in punishment of his rebellion. The track of the bullet through his head ached with an intenser anguish. He began to tremble again.

Suddenly he became composed. His tremor subsided. He clinched his teeth and drew down his eyebrows. He had not exhausted his means of defense; a new design had shaped itself in his mind—another plan of battle. Raising the front end of the strip of board, he carefully pushed it forward through the wreckage at the side of the rifle until it pressed against the trigger guard. Then he moved the end slowly outward until he could feel that it had cleared it, then, closing his eyes, thrust it against the trigger with all his strength! There was no explosion; the rifle had been discharged as it dropped from his hand when the building fell. But Jerome Searing was dead.

* * *

A line of Federal skirmishers swept across the plantation toward the mountain. They passed on both sides of the wrecked building, observing nothing. At a short distance in their rear came their commander, Lieutenant Adrian Searing. He casts his eyes curiously upon the ruin and sees a dead body half buried in boards and timbers. It is so covered with dust that its clothing is Confederate gray. Its face is yellowish white; the cheeks are fallen in, the temples sunken, too, with sharp ridges about them, making the forehead forbiddingly narrow; the upper lip, slightly lifted, shows the white teeth, rigidly clinched. The hair is heavy with moisture, the face as wet as the dewy grass all about. From his point of view the officer does not observe the rifle; the man was apparently killed by the fall of the building.

"Dead a week," said the officer curtly, moving on, mechanically pulling out his watch as if to verify his estimate of time. Six o'clock and forty minutes.

THE FOREST OF THE SOUTH

·

by Caroline Gordon

I

Major Reilly and Lieutenant Munford stood on the upper gallery of Villa Rose and watched the blowing up of Clifton. They knew the time it was to happen, knew the hour, even the minute. An orderly had ridden out from Natchez that morning with the news. A fort was to be built. Its line would cut through the mansion of Clifton. The house and its garden were to be blown up within the hour.

Major Reilly and Lieutenant Munford were in the major's office at Villa Rose, making out reports—there had been a brush with Confederate cavalry over near Lake St. John the night before. One of Reilly's men had been killed, another wounded. He was glad to be back at this old house with the rest of his squadron safe.

He read the papers the orderly brought. When the soldier

had left the room he turned to John Munford. His dark mustache lifted to disclose gleaming teeth.

"Mr. Surget of Clifton would never make a diplomat."

John Munford turned serious blue eyes on his chief. "A diplomat?"

The major leaned back in his chair. "Mr. Surget of Clifton has given a series of dinners for Federal officers. But he has never had the wit to invite the Chief Engineer."

John Munford said, "Ah!" and tried to look knowing. But he still did not understand. "Do you mean, sir, that the Chief Engineer is going to blow the place up because he was not invited to dinner?"

"He is going to blow it clean to hell," the major said. He looked at his watch. "In about three minutes, I should say. Come on, boy, we might as well see the explosion."

They went out through the hall and up the winding stairway into an upper hall and then up another short flight of steps and emerged on a balcony. John Munford had stepped out on this balcony before and always with astonishment. Villa Rose, a squat house built in the old manorial style, stood on a hill high for that part of the country. Below them on the right lay the Mississippi and four or five miles away as the crow flies was the town. Munford's eyes sought and found the tall spire of St. Mary's Cathedral, white in the morning sun, then moved on. There was the river again and, dark against it, masses of green: the famous gardens of Clifton. His eye roved on. More white. That would be the columns of the house or perhaps one of the pavilions. It was hard to tell at this distance just where the house stood.

He summoned up the picture of the house as he had seen it two days before when he had gone in to town with a message from Major Reilly. The Indiana colonel whom he was seeking was an ardent botanist. He had been told to look for him in the gardens of Clifton. He had traversed graveled walks, between box hedges, through scented arbors, and at last had found the colonel standing with Mr. Surget beside a great star-shaped flower bed. There had been an expanse of placid water beyond them with, as he lived, swans floating upon it. Returning through a vine-hung pavilion he had had to put up his hand to brush away masses of bloom. He had made a mental note of the lake, of the swans, of the oleanders for the letter he wrote home each week.

Major Reilly drew in his breath with a whistle. "There she goes!"

A great column of smoke rose and wavered over the trees. A few seconds later they heard the detonation. It jarred the earth beneath them and rattled against the distant woods. Reilly was turning away. John Munford followed him down the stairs. In his mind was a dull wonder. The flowers and the fountains he had seen two days before, the camellias, the Cape jessamines, the late roses, the marble of the grottoes and the pavilions—all those shining, rose-colored things had vanished in that plume of dull smoke!

In the hall below, the two men faced each other a second, then crossed the gallery and went out into the garden. Major Reilly was breathing hard as if to clear his lungs. "A great pity, Munford. As handsome a gentleman's estate as I've seen, here or in the old country." He had found his cigars at last and was offering Munford one. He drew on his cigar and suddenly was himself again. He remembered an engagement in town. "I'll let you finish up those requisitions by yourself, boy. You can manage, eh?"

John said that he could. The major motioned to an orderly to bring his horse, and strode toward the gate. Halfway there he turned. "You'd better look in on the old lady. See if she wants anything."

John said, "Yes, sir," again. After the major had ridden off he stood there a few minutes, the unlit cigar in his hand. There was an acrid smell of smoke in the air but the garden—this garden in which he stood—was just as it had been when he came out on the gallery into the fresh morning air an hour ago. The walks, branching out from the graveled circular drive, straggled off into dense greenery. The greenery was starred here and there with the pink of japonicas and off to the right a low hedge of Cape jessamine was popcorn-white with bloom.

His thoughts went to his Connecticut home. He had had a letter that morning from his sister, Eunice. She reported that the first big snow of the winter had come the night before. She was driving in to Danbury that afternoon, but she would have to go by sleigh, and over the winter road. Snow was drifted five feet deep between their house and the Robinsons'.

A hummingbird was hovering over a vine nearby. Munford watched the tiny wings which never for a second stopped their beating, then raised his eyes. Everywhere about him light fell, on glossy green leaves, on a scarlet flower, on the scarlet of the bird's breast. The fancy came to him that this light might have been filtered through the wings of birds, so shimmering it was, so iridescent. Off toward the stables some men were shouting to each other but their distant voices only served to emphasize the quiet of the garden. He had never known it so quiet before. But the stillness was oppressive and the landscape, he thought suddenly, too bright. This shining air held a menace.

A soldier came down the steps and made off toward the stables. Munford, recalled to his duty, followed the man around to the back of the house. A wide gallery ran the length of the ell. At the end of the ell up a short flight of steps there was a little room. It had been the overseer's room, originally. Now Mrs. Mazereau and her daughter, the owners of the house, lived in it.

In the shadow of one of the columns a soldier sat in a low, split-bottomed chair picking a chicken. Munford paused beside him a second to watch how deftly he was pulling the pinfeathers out from the wings. A good forager, Bill Morehouse. A good man at everything. Munford wished that Morehouse had the job of looking after the old lady instead of himself.

He went up the short flight of steps and knocked at the door. There was the sound of footsteps. The door opened a little way. He put the palm of his hand against it and pushed. It opened a little wider. He stepped inside the room. The blinds were drawn and the air was oppressive with stale odors. A young woman confronted him. She stood erect at first, then shrank a little back. Her hands came up in front of her face. She did not speak.

Impatience and embarrassment made his voice brusque. He said: "It is Lieutenant Munford, Miss Mazereau. Major Reilly's compliments. He wants to know how your mother is this morning."

The girl, still moving backwards, let her hands drop to her sides. "She didn't sleep," she said in a low voice.

He glanced toward the closed blinds. "Perhaps if you had more light . . ."

She halted at that. "I had the blinds open when we first got up but she saw some men going by. . . ." Suddenly she was coming toward him. He could not be sure in that half light but he thought that there was a smile on her face. "She thinks she's a girl," she said. "And I'm another girl. We're on our way to her old home . . . to the Green Springs, in Virginia. . . ." Damn it, she was laughing! Laughing at her old mother for being crazy. He would have to tell Reilly that.

A harsh voice came from the bed in the corner. "Eugénie!"

"Yes, Mama!"

The old woman was out of the bed and was coming toward them. A fierce, incredibly fat white cockatoo. The quilt from the bed was half hanging from her shoulders. She wore a nightgown which he, John Munford, had bought for her in a shop in Natchez-under-the-Hill. Clutching the quilt about her as if it had been a bed gown, she fixed him with her bloodshot blue eyes. "Young man, where are you going?"

Munford bowed his fair head. He said patiently, "I wasn't going anywhere this morning, ma'am. Major Reilly has gone to town and has left me in command."

She said, *"Major!"* She closed her eyes, pursed her lips. *"Soldiers,"* she whispered. She leaned forward, so close that her foul breath fanned his cheek. She went on whispering. "Two women in distress . . . trying to find our way home . . . I knew this country well once but it has changed. . . . So many roads . . . and the people . . ." Her voice sank lower. Her lower lip was wry with cunning. "I will give you a barrel of flour if you will conduct us to our home. It is in the Green Springs. . . ."

"We haven't any barrel of flour, Mama!"

Munford felt the girl's eyes upon him. He bowed and said, "I am sorry, ma'am, but I don't know the country. I can't conduct you to your home." He went out, shutting the door behind him.

As he reached the foot of the stairs a cur pup, the soldiers' pet, came scampering toward him, then fell on her back with her habitual gesture of outstretched paws. He thrust out his toe to poke her gently in the belly and then withdrew his foot, frowning. "Get up!" he said harshly.

He walked the length of the gallery and entered the wide front hall. At the far end the open door disclosed vistas of green. Patches of quivering light fell on the broad boards. There was one place where the oak was discolored in a great splotch. Munford, as he approached it, slowed his steps. Always when he passed this spot he had to stop and look down. Colonel Mazereau's blood, gushing from his cloven chest, had made that dark, greasy-looking place there by the newel post.

Munford's thoughts went to that night. He had had the story from Major Reilly, who in turn had had it from Eugénie Mazereau. Reilly, when he told it to Munford, had used what must have been the girl's words.

"The Negroes all ran away. Then the soldiers came. Mama said not to worry. She talked to the captain and she said he was a gentleman. But he rode off somewhere. He left three or four soldiers. There was one kept walking through the house. He came and looked in the library where we were. Mama said not to notice. We worked on our embroidery.

"Then we heard somebody step up on the porch. Mama said, 'Eugénie, it's your father.'

"I went to the door. I could see the soldier hiding there by the post and I could see Papa. He had on a long cloak and he was all splashed with mud. He stood there and he kept calling: 'Josephine! Eugénie! Josephine!'

"I went back into the room. I said, 'Mama, Papa is there and he keeps calling.'

"She went to the door. She said, 'Arsène, for God's sake . . . Arsène,' she said, 'I beg of you. For God's sake, go away!'

"He didn't listen. He started toward her. He got as far as the post. The soldier came up from behind. He had the axe in his hand." Major Reilly, telling the story, would put his hand to his breast. "It was like felling an ox. He went back, very slow, on his heels. Then he was standing straight and then he fell over. The blood was on the floor even before he fell."

John Munford had wanted to know what the women did then.

Colonel Mazereau, the major reported, had lived for several hours, until nearly sundown. "The thing that worried the girl most was that her mother kept trying to get the cloth out of the wound. The cloth of his uniform, Munford, was driven down into his breastbone and he was spouting blood like a whale. Unconscious, of course, from the moment of the blow. Finally, toward sundown, they were convinced that he was dead. The old lady was all for getting him buried before the soldiers came back. She made the girl go out and dig the grave. The girl said she dug all over the garden, but the ground was too hard. At last she persuaded the old lady to bury him temporarily under a pile of rotting leaves. Just as they finished Slocomb's men came back. The women ran and hid in the overseer's room and stayed there till those damned Dutchmen set the house on fire.

"I found them wandering around in the yard after the fire was put out and Slocomb's men had gone. The old lady was perfectly quiet then. It was the girl that was hard to handle. She kept coming up to me and saying they wouldn't do any harm and when I said I didn't expect them to she kept thanking me. I said, 'My God, madam, the exigencies of war have made it necessary for me to commandeer your house but you needn't be grateful to me. . . .' A queer girl, Munford. I wonder what she'd be like in other circumstances."

It was a subject that Major Reilly often speculated on: the character and personality of Miss Eugénie Mazereau. "In my opinion she's loonier than the old lady." Or "She's still scared out of her wits. You ought to do something about that, Munford. Take her for a buggy ride. Convince her we're not ogres."

John Munford, following the major's suggestion, had invited Miss Mazereau to walk with him in the garden and had even taken her driving several times in a trap that had been found in the stables. She came with him whenever he invited her, wearing always the same black dress and a voluminous black shawl that must have been her mother's. She never wore a bonnet. She had been bareheaded when she escaped from the house.

She talked to him as they drove along the river road. "Yes, Lieutenant Munford, the weather has been delightful for the

past week . . . You say your home is in Connecticut . . .
No, I have never been farther north than Memphis . . ."

Once he halted his horse before a gate set in a tall hedge. He
motioned with his whip. "All those people who lived here.
What has become of them?"

"They have all gone away, Lieutenant Munford."

But as they drove on she had turned to look back at the
gate. "The Macrae place," she said. "That is the Macrae
place." Her tone struck Munford as strange. It was the tone
that might have been used by a traveler returning to his old
haunts after years of absence.

He went now through the hall and turned right, into the
great room that was used as an office for the cavalry squadron.
It was barely furnished: two field desks, six or seven pine
chairs, and an old sofa in one corner where Major Reilly sometimes napped. The major had a grudge against the officer
whom he had relieved. Once, walking in the garden with Munford, Reilly had kicked at the charred pieces of a mahogany
dining table. "Those damned Dutchmen! They might at least
have left that for the officers to eat on."

Young Slater was pushing a sheaf of requisition blanks toward Munford. He took them and began signing them
mechanically. They worked for two hours. At twelve o'clock
Munford put his pen down and went out on the gallery. Young
Slater stood with him for a few minutes, then went back into
the house. Munford began pacing up and down the gallery.
Once he stopped to stare into the windows that ran on each
side of the doorway. The glass was full of imperfections; some
of the whorls had opalescent tints. When he was a child he
used to press his nose against just such cloudy panes of glass—
in his grandfather's house at Danbury. A white house with a
steep, gabled roof, twin "bride" trees—elms—on each side of
the stoop. He could see it all clearly but it seemed unreal, like
something he had seen in a picture rather than something he

remembered. He fell to pacing again and as he went was conscious of greenery pressing in there beyond the graveled walks, of sunshine on the gravel, of pink and white blossoms. And yet it was a hushed landscape. Moving about these grounds he had sometimes the feeling that he imagined a man might have on a desert island. Here in this smiling land he was lonely. It came to him that there was one person lonelier than he. That girl in the little back room. There was not, he supposed, anybody in the world lonelier than she. Colonel Mazereau, before he was killed, had quarreled with all his relations, Reilly said. The girl's mother, her companion in misfortune, had deserted her to wander in memory along the road that led to the Green Springs in Virginia. Yes, she was quite alone, that girl.

The call for mess sounded. Young Slater spoke to him from the doorway. He told the boy that he was coming, but before he went into the mess hall he turned back into the office. Sitting down at his desk, he drew a sheet of paper toward him and wrote a note. It presented Lieutenant Munford's compliments to Miss Mazereau and inquired if she would drive with him that afternoon.

II

At three o'clock Lieutenant Munford and Miss Mazereau were driving north along the river road. She sat with her hands folded, one over the other, in her lap. She was wearing a pair of gloves, lace gloves or rather mitts, for they left the tips of her fingers bare. Munford wondered where in the world she had got them. Some old trunk, probably, that had escaped Slocomb's men.

He stared ahead of him. The bit of road visible between the horse's forward-pricked ears was not unlike a stretch of road on the way to Gaylordsville with the dark trees and that old rail fence riding against the skyline. He had driven young ladies along that road often enough—in sleighs at this time of year. That New Year's party at the Robinsons'. He had escorted Jane Scoville, and Sam Dillon and Roberta Jennings had been in the back seat. He was not in love with Jane Scoville now but he would like to have her beside him with her furs and her perfume and her chatter. Well, he was on pleasure bent this afternoon, with a pretty girl beside him. He had always flattered himself that he could keep a pretty girl entertained, but how could you make yourself agreeable to a girl when you were occupying the house that by rights should have been hers?

By rights? His thoughts went, as they often did these days, to the conflict in which he was engaged. Major Reilly said that he himself was not opposed to slavery. Certain types of civilization, he said, were always founded on slavery, and he had cited ancient Athens and God knows what other countries— the major was a graduate of the University of Dublin. Well, he, John Munford, was not a highly educated man. But he knew right from wrong. He would do it all over again, to strike the shackles from the wrists of slaves. And yet it was all so different from what he had pictured.

The girl was turning toward him. Her eyes—unusually large, luminous eyes—were the color of the chestnuts that used to fall from the great tree in his grandfather's yard. The lids were heavy, so heavy that they dimmed the brilliance of her glance. And the lids themselves had a peculiar pallor. Wax-white, like the petals of the magnolia blossom. When he had first come into this country he had gathered one of those creamy blossoms only to see it turn brown in his grasp. She was saying something about a letter. ". . . It may be we can leave."

He said, *"Leave* Villa Rose?"

She nodded, still with those large strange-colored eyes fixed on his. "My cousin in Kentucky says we can come there."

He said, "I should not think you would want to go to Kentucky, Miss Mazereau. They are fighting there too."

She did not answer. As they drove on he considered what she had said. If he or Major Reilly went away—and they might be ordered away at any time—what would become of this girl and her mother? He turned to her abruptly. "Perhaps you would be better advised to go to Kentucky—if you can get through the lines."

She looked up at him, then suddenly shrank back as, he thought savagely, she might have done if he had menaced her with the whip he held in his hand. "I don't want to go where they're fighting."

He compressed his lips, feeling the angry blood surge to his forehead. "I don't know where you'll go then," he said curtly.

She did not answer.

They were at the top of a little rise, descending toward a stream. The horse's hooves splashed little drops of water in their faces as they crossed it. And now they were on a rise again. He looked at the pines crowding close on each side of the road and wondered if they would come to any hilltop which would command a view. "What is the name of that stream we have just crossed?" he asked.

"Sand Creek," she said.

He checked the horse. Before them was the tall hedge and the gate where they had paused the other day. She was looking about her with more animation than he had ever seen her display. On an impulse he pulled the horse up short and motioned with his whip at the gate. "Shall we go in there?"

"Yes," she said.

He got down and opened the gate; then, as she did not pick up the reins from where he had hung them over the dashboard, he led the horse through. He closed the gate and went up to the trap. "Shall we hitch the horse and walk for a little?"

"Yes," she said.

He assisted her down, then turned the trap about and hitched the horse to one of the bars of the gate. They started up the avenue. It was broader than the one at Villa Rose and lined on each side with live oaks. At the end of the avenue a square gray structure with a dilapidated double gallery was visible through the drooping wreaths of Spanish moss. They paused beside the carriage block to look up at it.

"A dreary place," Munford said.

She did not say anything.

"What is the name of the family that lived here?"

"Macrae," she said dreamily. Suddenly she took a few steps away from him, then looked back over her shoulder. "There is a fountain over here in the shrubbery," she said.

He followed her silently between the unclipped hedges into an abandoned garden. Once she had to stand aside while he dragged away a great, fallen branch. Suddenly the path widened and they emerged into what had once been a circle of flower beds. In the center was a fountain, a great basin, and standing beside it the marble figure of a woman. The woman was bending a little forward. Water from the pitcher which she carried had once run into the basin but no water had run there for a long time now. The basin was green with moss up to its rim.

The girl had walked over and was standing beside the fountain in much the same attitude as that of the marble figure. He studied the pale, down-bent face, wondering wherein lay its attraction. For it had come to that. She was the most attractive woman he had ever seen. The conviction had been growing on him for months. He remembered now his first sight of her, the day after he had been transferred to Reilly's squadron. A small figure in black, hurrying around the corner of the house—she had been gathering chips and was carrying them in her up-turned skirt. He had thought that she must be the wife of one of the soldiers or perhaps a camp follower—Reilly was lenient with them. Then he had seen slim ankles swinging out from under a ragged petticoat and the thought had come to him that she might be a lady. A lady! He had not seen a woman—a respectable woman—in weeks. He hurried on and caught up with her. She had looked up at him just as she had looked at him a moment ago, but he had insisted on gathering some more wood for her and had carried it up to the little room. He had followed her at first because he had been attracted by the sight of a woman. After he caught up with her he was repelled by her manner—the slight favor he proposed doing her did not deserve such effusive thanks. He had gone on, however, finding the wood for her, showing her all the courtesy he would have shown any respectable woman. He might never have thought of her again if Reilly had not told him her story that night.

He had seen her often since, and though he felt that he understood her better he still found her manner strange. He thought of another girl, a girl he had seen for one brief evening only, in Tennessee. When she was asked to play the piano for some Federal officers she had asked to be excused for a moment and had returned to the parlor with an axe. She had hurled it high above her head and had brought it down on the keyboard, saying she would make matchwood of the instrument before it should play a tune for despised "Yankees." . . . The word "Yankee" was never on Eugénie Mazereau's lips. She seemed to have no concern for the Confederate cause, and yet, he thought, she might be patriotic, and proud too, in other circumstances. . . .

She had put out her hand and with the tip of her index finger was tracking the rim of the basin. Her head, with its smoothly banded black hair, was still down-bent. There was a faint, mysterious smile on her lips.

Munford found this smile maddening. He took two steps and was beside her. "Why are you doing that?"

She looked up. Her eyes were blue! He had thought them

brown. That was because of the stain of light brown about the iris but the eye itself was blue. Blue, that is, if you stood there and looked into her eyes but if you stepped back a few paces you would say, "This girl's eyes are brown, pale brown," and you would say, too, "She looks at me but she never sees me." Why should an eye look out and not see? Does it look within? Has it seen something it cannot look away from?

She had not spoken. He laid his finger on that part of the marble her finger had touched.

She smiled. "The fountain? You mean why did I touch the fountain?"

He said hoarsely, "Miss Mazereau . . . Eugénie . . . you must know my sentiments."

She gazed at him, still smiling. He could not tell whether she had heard what he said.

A sudden thought turned him scarlet. He took a turn around the fountain and came back. He bowed. "I have the honor to ask for your hand in marriage."

She said, "My hand!" and moved a little away so that a tuft of long grass she had been standing on sprang up between them.

"I would have spoken to your mother," he said stiffly, "if circumstances had been different."

"No," she whispered. "Don't speak to my mother."

"I understand that," he said. "The point is . . . will you marry me? I . . . Is the prospect agreeable to you, Miss Mazereau?"

"Agreeable?" she said.

He stammered, "Eugénie. *Look* at me!"

She put out a hand and fearfully touched his face. He seized her. He kissed her lips, her brow, her throat, her lips again. "I will send you home," he whispered. "To my people. To Connecticut."

She drew back at that. "Connecticut? Is it a long way?"

"Yes," he said impatiently, and went on to tell her that his mother would welcome her as a daughter. His sister, Eunice, would be a sister to her, for there was a special bond of affection between him and his sister. In place of the family she had lost she should have his family. He swore that he would make her so happy that she would forget everything that had happened.

She did not say anything, only put up her hand again and touched his cheek. They went over and sat down on a bench near the fountain. Munford's arm was about her waist. She allowed her head to rest on his shoulder. All around them was a tangle of green but they could see rising about the hedge a slanting roof, a red chimney.

"What is that?" he asked.

"The old schoolhouse."

"Did you go to school there?"

"Yes, with the Macrae children."

He had been thinking that very soon, in a few days at most, he would have to send her North. Yes, three days at most, and he did not know how she had looked as a child, what nickname she had had, what paths she had taken when she came here to school. He was even curious about the Macraes, the departed owners of this place. "How many children were there?" he asked.

"Mary and Ellen. And there was Frank."

Some impulse made him repeat the name he was never afterwards to forget. "Frank . . . ?"

She tilted her head away from his caressing hand. The strange eyes gleamed under the heavy lids. "Frank . . . He was always playing jokes. He put Cousin Maria's crinoline on that statue there and he put a bonnet on it and painted its face with pokeberry juice and put a prayer book in its hand. He said she was going to church."

He laughed. "Where is Frank now?"

"He joined the army. . . ."

The shadows were getting longer. He roused himself and said that they must go back. They walked slowly along the path past the fountain. Munford smiled, seeing a mischievous boy coming through the hedge, his arms heaped with women's wear. The boy's eyes were gray and lively. He was laughing as he went up to the statue. Suddenly Munford was jealous of that boy who had played here in this garden. He stopped and, taking Eugénie's face between his hands, looked deep into her eyes before he kissed her.

"Say you love me."

"I love you," she said.

III

Major Reilly was silent when Munford told him of his engagement. Finally he shook his head. "You are a rash man. You seem to forget that Miss Mazereau's father was killed here in this hall. Her brothers, if she has any, certainly many of her cousins, are in the Confederate service."

"I shall be able to answer for my wife's loyalty," Munford said stiffly.

The major's brown face broke up into crisscross lines as it did when he laughed, and yet he wasn't laughing. "I wasn't thinking of her loyalty," he said.

Munford left the room. Later that night, lying on his cot in the officers' quarters, he thought of the expression that had been on Reilly's face. Yet Reilly, on the whole, had been as sympathetic, as considerate as a man could be. Munford and Eugénie Mazereau were to be married in Reilly's office tomorrow afternoon at four o'clock—Reilly had already sent a message to the chaplain. It would be all right for Eugénie to stay at Villa Rose a few days, Reilly said, but it could be only a few days. She and her mother ought to be on their way north as soon as the trip could be arranged for. Munford wondered what his mother and sister would think when they were confronted with the old woman and had to listen to her ravings. Would it not perhaps be better to let the two women stay in the South; if not at Villa Rose, at some safe quarters nearby?

His head felt hot. There was little air in the room. He got up and went to the open window. There was a full moon over the garden. In its light every leaf, every twig stood out as bright as if in noonday light. "Too bright, too light," he thought irritably. He stayed at the window long enough to smoke a cigar, then went back to bed and finally slept.

Major Reilly rode off to town early the next morning and Munford was again left in command. He was engaged with Ralph Slater in making out company reports when the guard at the door suddenly advanced into the room and told him that Miss Mazereau wanted to see him on business.

He told young Slater he would be gone for a little while and went, half smiling at the word "business," through the hall and out onto the back gallery. Eugénie Mazereau was waiting for him there. She had her black shawl drawn close about her shoulders. Her face was pale. Her eyes had a curious, intent look.

She came up to him, whispering, "Could you come with me a minute?"

He had given a cautious glance over his shoulder and, seeing that no one was in sight, was about to lean over to kiss her when something in her expression checked him. "Yes," he said quietly, and followed her down the steps and out through the yard. They passed through a side gate and took a path through the woods. They had progressed some distance along it before Munford saw the gray outline of a house through the trees and realized that this was a shortcut to the Macrae place.

The girl walked on before him in silence. And yet when they had stopped there in the woods a moment ago she had yielded herself to his embraces more freely than at any time yesterday. She had even put her arm up about his neck to draw his head down to hers. He had thought when they first started out that she had changed her mind about their engagement and was bringing him back to the same place they had visited yesterday to tell him that she would not marry him. He smiled. If that was the case he would be able to persuade her to change her mind back to what it had been yesterday. They were entering the ground by a side entrance. She did not go toward the garden but walked instead toward the house. On the gallery she paused a moment, then slipped quietly inside the half-open door, motioning to him to follow her. He hesitated a second. He was armed but he was only one man. But he put the thought of ambush away from him and walked resolutely after her.

The hall smelled musty. The blinds at both ends were drawn. What light there was came from a window high on the landing. Munford's eyes went to this window and then to the stairs below. The steps were thick with dust. He stiffened suddenly as he saw places where that dust had been disturbed, by boot soles. At the same moment there was the sound of steps above him. A face appeared over the railing.

Munford drew back, his hand on his revolver. But the girl was already starting up the steps. She looked back at him over her shoulder. "You can come," she said; "he's alone."

Munford drew his revolver. He pushed past her and went up, taking the stairs two at a time. The best way, he told himself mechanically. To rush the man was the only chance now. He came to the landing, made the turn, and stopped dead still. A man in a Federal uniform stood at the head of the stairs.

Eugénie had come up behind him. She stretched out her hand. "Lieutenant Munford, this is my cousin, Captain

Macrae," she said, calmly, as if she were making an introduction in a drawing room.

Frank Macrae stood on the top step, staring down at them. He looked exactly as Munford had pictured him. Blond, with a handsome, well-fleshed face, made red by exposure to wind and weather, an aquiline nose, steady gray eyes set under fair brows.

He did not seem to see Munford. He was staring at the girl. "Eugénie," he said in a low voice, "have you gone crazy?"

Her laugh rang out. "It's Mama . . . She thinks she's a girl and she thinks she's back in the Green Springs. . . . Ever since Papa was killed."

Munford said stiffly, "I regret to say that Mrs. Mazereau suffers from hallucinations . . ."

Eugénie interrupted him. "He came in the hall and a soldier killed him, with an axe." She looked at her cousin. "The blood was all over everything, Frank."

Frank Macrae, as if suddenly recollecting himself, took a step backwards. He looked at Munford, then stood aside while the other two ascended the stairs. Munford, his revolver cocked, went up to Macrae, laid his hand on his arm. "Captain Macrae, you are my prisoner," he said sternly. He paused a moment, then added, "It is unfortunate that you are in Federal uniform."

Frank Macrae laughed. "It is indeed unfortunate," he said. But he did not start down the stairs. Instead he turned into one of the great dim rooms opening off the upper hall. Munford, a little bewildered, followed him. The girl came too. She advanced toward her cousin but he motioned her back. "Go over there and stand by the window, Eugénie," he said curtly.

She went obediently and stood in the place he had indicated. The two men confronted each other. Macrae was very pale and his brows were drawn. He had been staring at the girl and now he still kept glancing at her though he had turned to

Munford. Absentmindedly, in the manner of a man making conversation, he asked Munford some questions about recent movements of the Federal squadron. Munford answered them. But he was conscious that time was passing. Perhaps he was in a trap. The Confederate officer might be trying to delay him until help came. He was about to speak when Macrae gave a long sigh.

"Well, we had better get on with it . . . Lieutenant, before your court meets there is a matter I must attend to."

Munford bowed. "I am at your service, Captain."

"Will you secure for me a license and the services of a chaplain? I want to go through a marriage ceremony with my cousin. I . . . there is certain property that will then be automatically at her disposal!"

Munford lifted his fair head haughtily. "That is impossible, Captain. Your cousin has promised to marry me."

Macrae stared. "You are engaged to marry my cousin?"

Munford bowed again.

There was a long silence. The girl laughed suddenly, left the window, and started toward the two men. Macrae lifted his hand, gently, in the gesture he might have used to a child or a puppy. "Stay where you are, Eugénie." He turned to Munford. "Lieutenant Munford, I know you by reputation. I believe you to be a man of honor. I do not envy you the privilege of marrying my cousin. . . . Do you fully understand the responsibilities you assume?"

The two men gazed at each other. Macrae's eyes were gray and hard as steel. It came to Munford that in a few hours this man would be dead, hanged as a spy. He looked away, to where the girl was standing beside the open window. Her strange, incurious eyes were fixed upon him, Munford. There was a smile on her lips. It was the smile that had so wrought upon him in the garden. It was not mysterious now. He averted his gaze. The window frame was dark and gauzy with cobwebs but beyond stretched a green meadow. Light played everywhere upon it, the same luminous, quivering light that yesterday at this hour had struck through the leaves at Villa Rose.

He withdrew his eyes from the scene. When he lifted them it was to meet the prisoner's hard, victorious glance.

"Yes," he said dully, "I understand."

THE BURNING

·

by Eudora Welty

Delilah was dancing up to the front with a message; that was how she happened to be the one to see. A horse was coming in the house, by the front door. The door had been shoved wide open. And all behind the horse, a crowd with a long tail of dust was coming after, all the way up their road from the gate between the cedar trees.

She ran on into the parlor, where they were. They were standing up before the fireplace, their white sewing dropped over their feet, their backs turned, both ladies. Miss Theo had eyes in the back of her head.

"Back you go, Delilah," she said.

"It ain't me, it's them," cried Delilah, and now there were running feet to answer all over the downstairs; Ophelia and all had heard. Outside the dogs were thundering. Miss Theo and Miss Myra, keeping their backs turned to whatever shape or ghost Commotion would take when it came—as long as it was still in the yard, mounting the steps, crossing the porch, or even, with a smell of animal sudden as the smell of snake, planting itself in the front hall—they still had to see it if it came in the parlor, the white horse. It drew up just over the ledge of the double doors Delilah had pushed open, and the ladies lifted their heads together and looked in the mirror over the fireplace, the one called the Venetian mirror, and there it was.

It was a white silhouette, like something cut out of the room's dark. July was so bright outside, and the parlor so dark for coolness, that at first nobody but Delilah could see. Then Miss Myra's racing speech interrupted everything.

"Will you take me on the horse? Please take me first."

It was a towering, sweating, grimacing, uneasy white horse. It had brought in two soldiers with red eyes and clawed, mosquito-racked faces—one a rider, hang-jawed and head-hanging, and the other walking by its side, all breathing in here now as loud as trumpets.

Miss Theo with shut eyes spoke just behind Miss Myra. "Delilah, what is it you came in your dirty apron to tell me?"

The sisters turned with linked hands and faced the room.

"Come to tell you we got the eggs away from black broody hen and sure enough, they's addled," said Delilah.

She saw the blue rider drop his jaw still lower. That was his laugh. But the other soldier set his boot on the carpet and heard the creak in the floor. As if reminded by tell-tale, he took another step, and with his red eyes sticking out he went as far as Miss Myra and took her around that little bending waist. Before he knew it, he had her lifted as high as a child, she was so light. The other soldier with a grunt came down from the horse's back and went toward Miss Theo.

"Step back, Delilah, out of harm's way," said Miss Theo, in such a company-voice that Delilah thought harm was one of two men.

"Hold my horse, nigger," said the man it was.

Delilah took the bridle as if she'd always done that, and held the horse that loomed there in the mirror—she could see it there now, herself—while more blurred and blind-like in the room between it and the door the first soldier shoved the tables and chairs out of the way behind Miss Myra, who flitted when she ran, and pushed her down where she stood and dropped on top of her. There in the mirror the parlor remained, filled up with dusted pictures, and shuttered since six o'clock against the heat and that smell of smoke they were all so tired of, still glimmering with precious, breakable things white ladies were never tired of and never broke, unless they were mad at each other. Behind *her,* the bare yawn of the hall was at her back, and the front stair's shadow, big as a tree and empty. Nobody went up there without being seen, and nobody was supposed to come down. Only if a cup or a silver spoon or a little string of spools on a blue ribbon came hopping down the steps like a frog, sometimes Delilah was the one to pick it up and run back up with it. Outside the mirror's frame, the flat of Miss Theo's hand came down on mankind with a boisterous sound.

Then Miss Theo lifted Miss Myra without speaking to her; Miss Myra closed her eyes but was not asleep. Her bands of black hair awry, her clothes rustling stiffly as clothes through winter quiet, Miss Theo strode half-carrying Miss Myra to the chair in the mirror, and put her down. It was the red, rubbed velvet, pretty chair like Miss Myra's ringbox. Miss Myra threw her head back, face up to the little plaster flowers going around the ceiling. She was asleep somewhere, if not in her eyes.

One of the men's voices spoke out, all gone with righteousness. "We just come in to inspect."

"You presume, you dare," said Miss Theo. Her hand came down to stroke Miss Myra's back-flung head in a strong, forbidding rhythm. From upstairs, Phinny threw down his breakfast plate, but Delilah did not move. Miss Myra's hair streamed loose behind her, bright gold, with the combs caught like leaves in it. Maybe it was to keep her like this, asleep in the heart, that Miss Theo stroked her on and on, too hard.

"It's orders to inspect beforehand," said the soldier.

"Then inspect," said Miss Theo. "No one in the house to prevent it. Brother—no word. Father—dead. Mercifully so—" She spoke in an almost rough-and-tumble kind of way used by ladies who didn't like company—never did like company, for anybody.

Phinny threw down his cup. The horse, shivering, nudged Delilah who was holding him there, a good obedient slave in her fresh-ironed candy-stripe dress beneath her black apron. She would have had her turban tied on, had she known all this ahead, like Miss Theo. "Never is Phinny away. Phinny here. He a he," she said.

Miss Myra's face was turned up as if she were dead, or as if she were a fierce and hungry little bird. Miss Theo rested her hand for a moment in the air above her head.

"Is it shame that's stopping your inspection?" Miss Theo asked. "I'm afraid you found the ladies of this house a trifle out of your element. My sister's the more delicate one, as you see. May I offer you this young kitchen Negro, as I've always understood—"

That Northerner gave Miss Theo a serious, recording look as though she had given away what day the mail came in.

"My poor little sister," Miss Theo went on to Miss Myra, "don't mind what you hear. Don't mind this old world." But Miss Myra knocked back the stroking hand. Kitty came picking her way into the room and sat between the horse's front feet; Friendly was her name.

One soldier rolled his head toward the other. "What was you saying to me when we come in, Virge?"

"I was saying I opined they wasn't gone yet."

"*Wasn't* they?"

Suddenly both of them laughed, jolting each other so hard that for a second it looked like a fight. Then one said with straight face, "We come with orders to set the house afire, ma'am," and the other one said, "General Sherman."

"I hear you."

"Don't you think we're going to do it? We done just burnt up Jackson twice," said the first soldier with his eye on Miss Myra. His voice made a man's big echo in the hall, like a long time ago. The horse whinnied and moved his head and feet.

"Like I was telling you, you ladies ought to been out. You didn't get no word here we was coming?" The other soldier pointed one finger at Miss Theo. She shut her eyes.

"Lady, they told you." Miss Myra's soldier looked hard at Miss Myra there. "And when your own people tell you something's coming to burn your house down, the business-like thing to do is get out of the way. And the right thing. I ain't beholden to tell you no more times now."

"Then go."

"Burning up *people's* further'n I go yet."

Miss Theo stared him down. "I see no degree."

So it was Miss Myra's soldier that jerked Delilah's hand from the bridle and turned her around, and cursed the Bedlam-like horse which began to beat the hall floor behind. Delilah listened, but Phinny did not throw anything more down; maybe he had crept to the landing, and now looked over. He was scared, if not of horses, then of men. He didn't know anything about them. The horse did get loose; he took a clattering trip through the hall and dining room and library, until at last his rider caught him. Then Delilah was set on his back.

She looked back over her shoulder through the doorway, and saw Miss Theo shake Miss Myra and catch the peaked face with its purple eyes and slap it.

"Myra," she said, "collect your senses. We have to go out in front of them."

Miss Myra slowly lifted her white arm, like a lady who has been asked to dance, and called, "Delilah!" Because that was the one she saw being lifted onto the horse's hilly back and ridden off through the front door. Skittering among the iron shoes, Kitty came after, trotting fast as a little horse herself, and ran ahead to the woods, where she was never seen again; but Delilah, from where she was set up on the horse and then dragged down on the grass, never called after her.

She might have been saving her breath for the screams that soon took over the outdoors and circled that house they were going to finish for sure now. She screamed, young and strong, for them all—for everybody that wanted her to scream for them, for everybody that didn't; and sometimes it seemed to her that she was screaming her loudest for Delilah, who was lost now—carried out of the house, not knowing how to get back.

*   *   *

Still inside, the ladies kept them waiting.

Miss Theo finally brought Miss Myra out through that wide-open front door and across the porch with the still perfect and motionless vine shadows. There were some catcalls and owl hoots from under the trees.

"Now hold back, boys. They's too ladylike for you."

"Ladies must needs take their time."

"And then they're no damn good at it!" came a clear, youthful voice, and under the branches somewhere a banjo was stroked to call up the campfires further on, later in the evening, when all this would be over and done.

The sisters showed no surprise to see soldiers and Negroes alike (old Ophelia in the way, talking, talking) strike into and out of the doors of the house, the front now the same as the back, to carry off beds, tables, candlesticks, washstands, cedar buckets, china pitchers, with their backs bent double; or the horses ready to go; or the food of the kitchen bolted down—

and so much of it thrown away, this must be a second dinner; or the unsilenceable dogs, the old pack mixed with the strangers and fighting with all their hearts over bones. The last skinny sacks were thrown on the wagons—the last flour, the last scraping and clearing from Ophelia's shelves, even her pepper-grinder. The silver Delilah could count was counted on strange blankets and then, knocking against the teapot, rolled together, tied up like a bag of bones. A drummer boy with his drum around his neck caught both Miss Theo's peacocks, Marco and Polo, and wrung their necks in the yard. Nobody could look at those bird-corpses; nobody did.

The sisters left the porch like one, and in step, hands linked, came through the high grass in their crushed and only dresses, and walked under the trees. They came to a stop as if it was moonlight under the leafy frame of the big tree with the swing, without any despising left in their faces which were the same as one, as one face that didn't belong to anybody. This one clarified face, looking both left and right, could make out every one of those men through the bushes and tree trunks, and mark every looting slave also, as all stood momently fixed like serenaders by the light of a moon. Only old Ophelia was talking all the time, all the time, telling everybody in her own way about the trouble here, but of course nobody could understand a thing that day anywhere in the world.

"What are they fixing to do now, Theo?" asked Miss Myra, with a frown about to burn into her too-white forehead.

"What they want to," Miss Theo said, folding her arms.

To Delilah that house they were carrying the torches to was like one just now coming into being—like the showboat that slowly came through the trees just once in her time, at the peak of high water—bursting with the unknown, sparking in ruddy light, with a minute to go before that ear-aching cry of the calliope.

When it came—but it was a bellowing like a bull, that came

from inside—Delilah drew close, with Miss Theo's skirt to
peep around, and Miss Theo's face looked down like death
itself and said, "Remember this. You black monkeys," as the
blaze outdid them all.

* * *

A while after the burning, when everybody had gone away,
Miss Theo and Miss Myra, finding and taking hold of Delilah,
who was face-down in a ditch with her eyes scorched open, did
at last go beyond the tramped-down gate and away through
the grand worthless fields they themselves had burned long
before.

It was a hot afternoon, hot out here in the open, and it
played a trick on them with a smell and prophecy of fall—it
was the burning. The brown wet standing among the stumps
in the cracked cup of the pond tasted as hot as coffee and as
bitter. There was still and always smoke between them and the
sun.

After all the July miles, there Jackson stood, burned twice,
or who knew if it was a hundred times, facing them in the
road. Delilah could see through Jackson like a haunt, it was all
chimneys, all scooped out. There were soldiers with guns
among the ashes, but these ashes were cold. Soon even these
two ladies, who had been everywhere and once knew their
way, told each other they were lost. While some soldiers
looked them over, they pointed at what they couldn't see,
traced gone-away spires, while a horse without his rider passed
brushing his side against them and ran down a black alley
softly, and did not return.

They walked here and there, sometimes over the same track,
holding hands all three, like the timeless time it snowed, and
white and black went to play together in hushed woods. They
turned loose only to point and name.

"The State House."—"The school."
"The Blind School."—"The penitentiary!"

"The big stable."—"The Deaf-and-Dumb."

"Oh! Remember when we passed three of *them,* sitting on a hill?" They went on matching each other, naming and claiming ruin for ruin.

"The lunatic asylum!"—"The State House."

"No, I said that. Now where are we? That's surely Captain Jack Calloway's hitching post."

"But why would the hitching post be standing and the rest not?"

"And ours not."

"I think I should have told you, Myra—"

"Tell me now."

"Word *was* sent to us to get out when it was sent to the rest on Vicksburg Road. Two days' warning. I believe it was a message from General Pemberton."

"Don't worry about it now. Oh no, of course we couldn't leave," said Miss Myra. A soldier watched her in the distance, and she recited:

> "There was a man in our town
> And he was wondrous wise.
> He jumped into a bramble bush
> And scratched out both his eyes."

She stopped, looking at the soldier.

"He sent word," Miss Theo went on, "General Pemberton sent word, for us all to get out ahead of what was coming. You were in the summerhouse when it came. It was two days' warning—but I couldn't bring myself to call and tell you, Myra. I suppose I couldn't convince myself—couldn't quite *believe* that they meant to come and visit that destruction on us."

"Poor Theo. I could have."

"No you couldn't. I couldn't *understand* that message, any

more than Delilah here could have. I can reproach myself now, of course, with everything." And they began to walk boldly through and boldly out of the burnt town, single file.

"Not everything, Theo. Who had Phinny? Remember?" cried Miss Myra ardently.

"Hush."

"If I hadn't had Phinny, that would've made it all right. Then Phinny wouldn't have—"

"Hush, dearest, that wasn't *your* baby, you know. It was Brother Benton's baby. I won't have your nonsense now." Miss Theo led the way through the ashes, marching in front. Delilah was in danger of getting left behind.

"—perished. Dear Benton. So good. Nobody else would have felt so *bound,*" Miss Myra said.

"Not after I told him what he owed a little life! Each little life is a *man's* fault. Oh, who'll ever forget that awful day?"

"Benton's forgotten, if he's dead. He was so good after that too, never married."

"Stayed home, took care of his sisters. Only wanted to be forgiven."

"There has to be somebody to take care of everybody."

"I told him, he must never dream he was *inflicting* his sisters. That's what we're for."

"And it never would have inflicted us. We could have lived and died. Until *they* came."

"In at the front door on the back of a horse," said Miss Theo. "If Benton had been there!"

"I'll never know what possessed them, riding in like that," said Miss Myra almost mischievously; and Miss Theo turned.

"And *you said—*"

"I said something wrong," said Miss Myra quickly. "I apologize, Theo."

"No, I blame only myself. That I let you remain one hour in

that house after it was doomed. I thought I was equal to it, and I proved I was, but not you."

"Oh, to my shame you saw me, dear! Why do you say it wasn't my baby?"

"Now don't start that nonsense over again," said Miss Theo, going around a hole.

"I had Phinny. When we were all at home and happy together. Are you going to take Phinny away from me now?"

Miss Theo pressed her cheeks with her palms and showed her pressed, pensive smile as she looked back over her shoulder.

Miss Myra said, "Oh, don't *I* know who it really belonged to, who it loved the best, that baby?"

"I won't have you misrepresenting yourself."

"It's never what I intended."

"Then reason dictates you hush."

Both ladies sighed, and so did Delilah; they were tired of going on. Miss Theo still walked in front but she was looking behind her through the eyes in the back of her head.

"You hide him if you want to," said Miss Myra. "Let Papa shut up all upstairs. I had him, dear. It was an officer, no, one of our beaux that used to come out and hunt with Benton. It's because I was always the impetuous one, highstrung and so easily carried away. . . . And if Phinny *was* mine—"

"Don't you know he's black?" Miss Theo blocked the path.

"He *was* white." Then, "He's black *now,*" whispered Miss Myra, darting forward and taking her sister's hands. Their shoulders were pressed together, as if they were laughing or waiting for something more to fall.

"If I only had something to eat!" sobbed Miss Myra, and once more let herself be embraced. One eye showed over the tall shoulder. "Oh, Delilah!"

"Could be he got out," called Delilah in a high voice. "He strong, he."

"Who?"

"Could be Phinny's out loose. Don't cry."

"Look yonder. What do I see? I see the Dicksons' perfectly good hammock still under the old pecan trees," Miss Theo said to Miss Myra, and spread her hand.

* * *

There was some little round silver cup, familiar to the ladies, in the hammock when they came to it down in the grove. Lying on its side with a few drops in it, it made them smile.

The yard was charged with butterflies. Miss Myra, as if she could wait no longer, climbed into the hammock and lay down with ankles crossed. She took up the cup like a story book she'd begun and left there yesterday, holding it before her eyes in those freckling fingers, slowly picking out the ants.

"So still out here and all," Miss Myra said. "Such a big sky. Can you get used to that? And all the figs dried up. I wish it would rain."

"Won't rain till Saturday," said Delilah.

"Delilah, don't go 'way."

"Don't you try, Delilah," said Miss Theo.

"No'm."

Miss Theo sat down, rested a while, though she did not know how to sit on the ground and was afraid of grasshoppers, and then she stood up, shook out her skirt, and cried out to Delilah, who had backed off far to one side, where some chickens were running around loose with nobody to catch them.

"Come back here, Delilah! Too late for that!" She said to Miss Myra, "The Lord will provide. We've still got Delilah, and as long as we've got her we'll use her, my dearie."

Miss Myra "let the cat die" in the hammock. Then she gave her hand to climb out, Miss Theo helped her, and without needing any help for herself Miss Theo untied the hammock from the pecan trees. She was long bent over it, and Miss Myra studied the butterflies. She had left the cup sitting on the ground in the shade of the tree. At last Miss Theo held up two lengths of cotton rope, the red and the white strands untwisted from each other, bent like the hair of ladies taken out of plaits in the morning.

Delilah, given the signal, darted up the tree and hooking her toes made the ropes fast to the two branches a sociable distance apart, where Miss Theo pointed. When she slid down, she stood waiting while they settled it, until Miss Myra repeated enough times, in a spoiled sweet way, "I bid to be first." It was what Miss Theo wanted all the time. Then Delilah had to squat and make a basket with her fingers, and Miss Myra tucked up her skirts and stepped her ashy shoe in the black hands.

"Tuck under, Delilah."

Miss Myra, who had ordered that, stepped over Delilah's head and stood on her back, and Delilah felt her presence tugging there as intimately as a fish's on a line, each longing Miss Myra had to draw away from Miss Theo, draw away from Delilah, away from that tree.

Delilah rolled her eyes around. The noose was being tied by Miss Theo's puckered hands like a bonnet on a windy day, and Miss Myra's young, lifted face was looking out.

"I learned as a child how to tie, from a picture book in Papa's library—not that I ever was called on," Miss Theo said. "I guess I was always something of a tomboy." She kissed Miss Myra's hand and at almost the same instant Delilah was seized by the ribs and dragged giggling backward, out from under—not soon enough, for Miss Myra kicked her in the head—a bad kick, almost as if that were Miss Theo or a man up in the tree, who meant what he was doing.

Miss Theo stood holding Delilah and looking up—helping herself to grief. No wonder Miss Myra used to hide in the summerhouse with her reading, screaming sometimes when there was nothing but Delilah throwing the dishwater out on the ground.

"I've proved," said Miss Theo to Delilah, dragging her by more than main force back to the tree, "what I've always suspicioned: that I'm brave as a lion. That's right: look at me. If I ordered you back up that tree to help my sister down to the grass and shade, you'd turn and run: I know your minds. You'd desert me with your work half done. So I haven't said a word about it. About mercy. As soon as you're through, you can go, and leave us where you've put us, unspared, just alike. And that's the way they'll find us. The sight will be good for them for what they've done," and she pushed Delilah down and walked up on her shoulders, weighting her down like a rock.

Miss Theo looped her own knot up there; there was no mirror or sister to guide her. Yet she was quicker this time than last time, but Delilah was quicker too. She rolled over in a ball, and then she was up running, looking backward, crying. Behind her Miss Theo came sailing down from the tree. She was always too powerful for a lady. Even those hens went flying up with a shriek, as if they felt her shadow on their backs. Now she reached in the grass.

There was nothing for Delilah to do but hide, down in the jungly grass choked with bitterweed and black-eyed susans, wild to the pricking skin, with many heads nodding, cauldrons of ants, with butterflies riding them, grasshoppers hopping them, mosquitoes making the air alive, down in the loud and lonesome grass that was rank enough almost to matt the sky over. Once, stung all over and wild to her hair's ends, she ran back and asked Miss Theo, "What must I do now? Where must I go?" But Miss Theo, whose eyes from the ground were looking straight up at her, wouldn't tell. Delilah danced away from her, back to her distance, and crouched down. She believed Miss Theo twisted in the grass like a dead snake until the sun went down. She herself held still like a mantis until the grass had folded and spread apart at the falling of dew. This was after the chickens had gone to roost in a strange uneasy tree against the cloud where the guns still boomed and the way from Vicksburg was red. Then Delilah could find her feet.

She knew where Miss Theo was. She could see the last white of Miss Myra, the stockings. Later, down by the swamp, in a wading bird tucked in its wing for sleep, she saw Miss Myra's ghost.

*   *   *

After being lost a day and a night or more, crouching awhile, stealing awhile through the solitudes of briar bushes, she came again to Rose Hill. She knew it by the chimneys and by the crape myrtle off to the side, where the bottom of the summerhouse stood empty as an egg basket. Some of the flowers looked tasty, like chicken legs fried a little black.

Going around the house, climbing over the barrier of the stepless back doorsill, and wading into ashes, she was lost still, inside that house. She found an iron pot and a man's long boot, a doorknob and a little book fluttering, its leaves spotted and fluffed like guinea feathers. She took up the book and read out from it, "Ba-ba-ba-ba-ba—trash." She was being Miss Theo taking away Miss Myra's reading. Then she saw the Venetian mirror down in the chimney's craw, flat and face-up in the cinders.

Behind her the one standing wall of the house held notched and listening like the big ear of King Solomon into which poured the repeated asking of birds. The tree stood and flowered. What must she do? Crouching suddenly to the ground, she heard the solid cannon, the galloping, the low fast drum of burning. Crawling on her knees she went to the glass and rubbed it with spit and leaned over it and saw a face all neck and ears, then gone. Before it she opened and spread her arms;

she had seen Miss Myra do that, try that. But its gleam was addled.

Though the mirror did not know Delilah, Delilah would have known that mirror anywhere, because it was set between black men. Their arms were raised to hold up the mirror's roof, which now the swollen mirror brimmed, among gold leaves and gold heads—black men dressed in gold, looking almost into the glass themselves, as if to look back through a door, men now half-split away, flattened with fire, bearded, noseless as the moss that hung from swamp trees.

Where the mirror did not cloud like the horse-trampled spring, gold gathered itself from the winding water, and honey under water started to flow, and then the gold fields were there, hardening gold. Through the water, gold and honey twisted up into houses, trembling. She saw people walking the bridges in early light with hives of houses on their heads, men in dresses, some with red birds; and monkeys in velvet; and ladies with masks laid over their faces looking from pointed windows. Delilah supposed that was Jackson before Sherman came. Then it was gone. In this noon quiet, here where all had passed by, unless indeed it had gone in, she waited on her knees.

The mirror's cloudy bottom sent up minnows of light to the brim where now a face pure as a water-lily shadow was floating. Almost too small and deep down to see, they were quivering, leaping to life, fighting, aping old things Delilah had seen done in this world already, sometimes what men had done to Miss Theo and Miss Myra and the peacocks and to slaves, and sometimes what a slave had done and what anybody now could do to anybody. Under the flicker of the sun's licks, then under its whole blow and blare, like an unheard scream, like an act of mercy gone, as the wall-less light and July blaze struck through from the opened sky, the mirror felled her flat.

She put her arms over her head and waited, for they would

all be coming again, gathering under her and above her, bees saddled like horses out of the air, butterflies harnessed to one another, bats with masks on, birds together, all with their weapons bared. She listened for the blows, and dreaded that whole army of wings—of flies, birds, serpents, their glowing enemy faces and bright kings' dresses, that banner of colors forked out, all this world that was flying, striking, stricken, falling, gilded or blackened, mortally splitting and falling apart, proud turbans unwinding, turning like the spotted dying leaves of fall, spiraling down to bottomless ash; she dreaded the fury of all the butterflies and dragonflies in the world riding, blades unconcealed and at point—descending, and rising again from the waters below, down under, one whale made of his own grave, opening his mouth to swallow Jonah one more time.

Jonah!—a homely face to her, that could still look back from the red lane he'd gone down, even if it was too late to speak. He was her Jonah, her Phinny, her black monkey; she worshiped him still, though it was long ago he was taken from her the first time.

Stiffly, Delilah got to her feet. She cocked her head, looked sharp into the mirror, and caught the motherly image—head wagging in the flayed forehead of a horse with ears and crest up stiff, the shield and the drum of big swamp birdskins, the horns of deer sharpened to cut and kill with. She showed her teeth. Then she looked in the feathery ashes and found Phinny's bones. She ripped a square from her manifold fullness of skirts and tied up the bones in it.

She set foot in the road then, walking stilted in Miss Myra's shoes and carrying Miss Theo's shoes tied together around her neck, her train in the road behind her. She wore Miss Myra's willing rings—had filled up two fingers—but she had had at last to give up the puzzle of Miss Theo's bracelet with the chain. They were two stones now, scalding-white. When the combs were being lifted from her hair, Miss Myra had come down too, beside her sister.

Light on Delilah's head the Jubilee cup was set. She paused now and then to lick the rim and taste again the ghost of sweet that could still make her tongue start clinging—some sweet lapped up greedily long ago, only a mystery now when or who by. She carried her own black locust stick to drive the snakes.

Following the smell of horses and fire, to men, she kept in the wheel tracks till they broke down at the river. In the shade underneath the burned and fallen bridge she sat on a stump and chewed for a while, without dreams, the comb of a dirtdauber. Then once more kneeling, she took a drink from the Big Black, and pulled the shoes off her feet and waded in.

Submerged to the waist, to the breast, stretching her throat like a sunflower stalk above the river's opaque skin, she kept on, her treasure stacked on the roof of her head, hands laced upon it. She had forgotten how or when she knew, and she did not know what day this was, but she knew—it would not rain, the river would not rise, until Saturday.

THE OPEN BOAT

A Tale Intended to Be After the Fact: Being the Experience of Four Men from the Sunk Steamer *Commodore*

·

by Stephen Crane

None of them knew the color of the sky. Their eyes glanced level, and were fastened upon the waves that swept toward them. These waves were of the hue of slate, save for the tops, which were of foaming white, and all of the men knew the colors of the sea. The horizon narrowed and widened, and dipped and rose, and at all times its edge was jagged with waves that seemed thrust up in points like rocks.

Many a man ought to have a bathtub larger than the boat which here rode upon the sea. These waves were most wrongfully and barbarously abrupt and tall, and each froth-top was a problem in small-boat navigation.

The cook squatted in the bottom, and looked with both eyes at the six inches of gunwale which separated him from the ocean. His sleeves were rolled over his fat forearms, and the two flaps of his unbuttoned vest dangled as he bent to bail out the boat. Often he said, "Gawd! that was a narrow clip." As he remarked it he invariably gazed eastward over the broken sea.

The oiler, steering with one of the two oars in the boat, sometimes raised himself suddenly to keep clear of water that swirled in over the stern. It was a thin little oar, and it seemed often ready to snap.

The correspondent, pulling at the other oar, watched the waves and wondered why he was there.

The injured captain, lying in the bow, was at this time buried in that profound dejection and indifference which comes, temporarily at least, to even the bravest and most enduring when, willy-nilly, the firm fails, the army loses, the ship goes down. The mind of the master of a vessel is rooted deep in the timbers of her, though he command for a day or a decade; and this captain had on him the stern impression of a scene in the grays of dawn of seven turned faces, and later a stump of a topmast with a white ball on it, that slashed to and fro at the waves, went low and lower, and down. Thereafter there was something strange in his voice. Although steady, it was deep with mourning, and of a quality beyond oration or tears.

"Keep'er a little more south, Billie," said he.

"A little more south, sir," said the oiler in the stern.

A seat in this boat was not unlike a seat upon a bucking broncho, and by the same token a broncho is not much smaller. The craft pranced and reared and plunged like an animal. As each wave came, and she rose for it, she seemed like a horse making at a fence outrageously high. The manner of her scramble over these walls of water is a mystic thing, and, moreover, at the top of them were ordinarily these problems in white water, the foam racing down from the summit of each wave requiring a new leap, and a leap from the air. Then, after scornfully bumping a crest, she would slide and race and splash down a long incline, and arrive bobbing and nodding in front of the next menace.

A singular disadvantage of the sea lies in the fact that after successfully surmounting one wave you discover that there is another behind it just as important and just as nervously anxious to do something effective in the way of swamping boats. In a ten-foot dinghy one can get an idea of the resources of the sea in the line of waves that is not probable to the average experience, which is never at sea in a dinghy. As each slaty wall of water approached, it shut all else from the view of the men in the boat and it was not difficult to imagine that this particular wave was the final outburst of the ocean, the last effort of the grim water. There was a terrible grace in the move of the waves, and they came in silence, save for the snarling of the crests.

In the wan light the faces of the men must have been gray. Their eyes must have glinted in strange ways as they gazed steadily astern. Viewed from a balcony, the whole thing would doubtless have been weirdly picturesque. But the men in the boat had no time to see it, and if they had had leisure, there were other things to occupy their minds. The sun swung steadily up the sky, and they knew it was broad day because the color of the sea changed from slate to emerald-green streaked with amber lights, and the foam was like tumbling snow. The process of the breaking day was unknown to them. They were aware only of this effect upon the color of the waves that rolled toward them.

In disjointed sentences the cook and the correspondent argued as to the difference between a lifesaving station and a house of refuge. The cook had said: "There's a house of refuge just north of the Mosquito Inlet Light, and as soon as they see us they'll come off in their boat and pick us up."

"As soon as who see us?" said the correspondent.

"The crew," said the cook.

"Houses of refuge don't have crews," said the correspondent. "As I understand them, they are only places where clothes and grub are stored for the benefit of shipwrecked people. They don't carry crews."

"Oh, yes, they do," said the cook.

"No, they don't," said the correspondent.

"Well, we're not there yet, anyhow," said the oiler, in the stern.

"Well," said the cook, "perhaps it's not a house of refuge that I'm thinking of as being near Mosquito Inlet Light; perhaps it's a lifesaving station."

"We're not there yet," said the oiler in the stern.

II

As the boat bounced from the top of each wave the wind tore through the hair of the hatless men, and as the craft plopped her stern down again the spray splashed past them. The crest of each of these waves was a hill, from the top of which the men surveyed for a moment a broad tumultuous expanse, shining and wind-driven. It was probably splendid, it was probably glorious, this play of the free sea, wild with lights of emerald and white and amber.

"Bully good thing it's an onshore wind," said the cook. "If not, where would we be? Wouldn't have a show."

"That's right," said the correspondent.

The busy oiler nodded his assent.

Then the captain, in the bow, chuckled in a way that expressed humor, contempt, tragedy, all in one. "Do you think we've got much of a show now, boys?" said he.

Whereupon the three were silent, save for a trifle of hemming and hawing. To express any particular optimism at this time they felt to be childish and stupid, but they all doubtless possessed this sense of the situation in their minds. A young man thinks doggedly at such times. On the other hand, the ethics of their condition were decidedly against any open suggestion of hopelessness. So they were silent.

"Oh, well," said the captain, soothing his children, "we'll get ashore all right."

But there was that in his tone which made them think; so the oiler quoth, "Yes! if this wind holds."

The cook was bailing. "Yes! if we don't catch hell in the surf."

Canton-flannel gulls flew near and far. Sometimes they sat down on the sea, near patches of brown seaweed that rolled over the waves with a movement like carpets on a line in a gale. The birds sat comfortably in groups, and they were envied by some in the dinghy, for the wrath of the sea was no more to them than it was to a covey of prairie chickens a thousand miles inland. Often they came very close and stared at the men with black bead-like eyes. At these times they were uncanny and sinister in their unblinking scrutiny, and the men hooted angrily at them, telling them to be gone. One came, and evidently decided to alight on the top of the captain's head. The bird flew parallel to the boat and did not circle, but made short sidelong jumps in the air in chicken fashion. His black eyes were wistfully fixed upon the captain's head. "Ugly brute," said the oiler to the bird. "You look as if you were made with a jackknife." The cook and the correspondent swore darkly at the creature. The captain naturally wished to knock it away with the end of the heavy painter, but he did not dare do it, because anything resembling an emphatic gesture would have capsized this freighted boat; and so, with his open hand, the captain gently and carefully waved the gull away. After it had been discouraged from the pursuit the captain breathed easier on account of his hair, and others breathed easier because the bird struck their minds at this time as being somehow gruesome and ominous.

In the meantime the oiler and the correspondent rowed. And also they rowed. They sat together in the same seat, and each rowed an oar. Then the oiler took both oars; then the correspondent took both oars; then the oiler; then the correspondent. They rowed and they rowed. The very ticklish part of the business was when the time came for the reclining one in the stern to take his turn at the oars. By the very last star of truth, it is easier to steal eggs from under a hen than it was to change seats in the dinghy. First the man in the stern slid his hand along the thwart and moved with care, as if he were of Sevres. Then the man in the rowing-seat slid his hand along the other thwart. It was all done with the most extraordinary care. As the two sidled past each other, the whole party kept watchful eyes on the coming wave, and the captain cried: "Look out, now! Steady, there!"

The brown mats of seaweed that appeared from time to time were like islands, bits of earth. They were traveling, apparently, neither one way nor the other. They were, to all intents, stationary. They informed the men in the boat that it was making progress slowly toward the land.

The captain, rearing cautiously in the bow after the dinghy soared on a great swell, said that he had seen the lighthouse at Mosquito Inlet. Presently the cook remarked that he had seen it. The correspondent was at the oars then, and for some reason he too wished to look at the lighthouse; but his back was toward the far shore, and the waves were important, and for some time he could not seize an opportunity to turn his head. But at last there came a wave more gentle than the others, and when at the crest of it he swiftly scoured the western horizon.

"See it?" said the captain.

"No," said the correspondent, slowly; "I didn't see anything."

"Look again," said the captain. He pointed. "It's exactly in that direction."

At the top of another wave the correspondent did as he was bid, and this time his eyes chanced on a small, still thing on the edge of the swaying horizon. It was precisely like the point of a pin. It took an anxious eye to find a lighthouse so tiny.

"Think we'll make it, Captain?"

"If this wind holds and the boat don't swamp, we can't do much else," said the captain.

The little boat, lifted by each towering sea and splashed viciously by the crests, made progress that in the absence of seaweed was not apparent to those in her. She seemed just a wee thing wallowing, miraculously top up, at the mercy of five oceans. Occasionally a great spread of water, like white flames, swarmed into her.

"Bail her, cook," said the captain, serenely.

"All right, Captain," said the cheerful cook.

III

It would be difficult to describe the subtle brotherhood of men that was here established on the seas. No one said that it was so. No one mentioned it. But it dwelt in the boat, and each man felt it warm him. They were a captain, an oiler, a cook, and a correspondent, and they were friends—friends in a more curiously ironbound degree than may be common. The hurt captain, lying against the water jar in the bow, spoke always in a low voice and calmly; but he could never command a more ready and swiftly obedient crew than the motley three of the dinghy. It was more than a mere recognition of what was best for the common safety. There was surely in it a quality that was personal and heartfelt. And after this devotion to the commander of the boat, there was this comradeship, that the correspondent, for instance, who had been taught to be cynical of men, knew even at the time was the best experience of his life. But no one said that it was so. No one mentioned it.

"I wish we had a sail," remarked the captain. "We might try my overcoat on the end of an oar, and give you two boys a chance to rest." So the cook and the correspondent held the mast and spread wide the overcoat; the oiler steered; and the little boat made good way with her new rig. Sometimes the oiler had to scull sharply to keep a sea from breaking into the boat, but otherwise sailing was a success.

Meanwhile the lighthouse had been growing slowly larger. It had now almost assumed color, and appeared like a little gray shadow on the sky. The man at the oars could not be prevented from turning his head rather often to try for a glimpse of this little gray shadow.

At last, from the top of each wave, the men in the tossing boat could see land. Even as the lighthouse was an upright shadow on the sky, this land seemed but a long black shadow on the sea. It certainly was thinner than paper. "We must be about opposite New Smyrna," said the cook, who had coasted this shore often in schooners. "Captain, by the way, I believe they abandoned that lifesaving station there about a year ago."

"Did they?" said the captain.

The wind slowly died away. The cook and the correspondent were not now obliged to slave in order to hold high the oar. But the waves continued their old impetuous swooping at the dinghy, and the little craft, no longer under way, struggled woundily over them. The oiler or the correspondent took the oars again.

Shipwrecks are *apropos* of nothing. If men could only train for them and have them occur when the men had reached pink condition, there would be less drowning at sea. Of the four in the dinghy none had slept any time worth mentioning for two days and two nights previous to embarking in the dinghy, and in the excitement of clambering about the deck of a foundering ship they had also forgotten to eat heartily.

For these reasons, and for others, neither the oiler nor the correspondent was fond of rowing at this time. The correspondent wondered ingenuously how in the name of all that was sane could there be people who thought it amusing to row a boat. It was not an amusement; it was a diabolical punishment, and even a genius of mental aberrations could never conclude that it was anything but a horror to the muscles and a crime against the back. He mentioned to the boat in general how the amusement of rowing struck him, and the weary-faced oiler smiled in full sympathy. Previously to the foundering, by the way, the oiler had worked a double watch in the engine room of the ship.

"Take her easy now, boys," said the captain. "Don't spend yourselves. If we have to run a surf you'll need all your strength, because we'll sure have to swim for it. Take your time."

Slowly the land arose from the sea. From a black line it became a line of black and a line of white—trees and sand. Finally the captain said that he could make out a house on the shore. "That's the house of refuge, sure," said the cook. "They'll see us before long, and come out after us."

The distant lighthouse reared high. "The keeper ought to be able to make us out now, if he's looking through a glass," said the captain. "He'll notify the lifesaving people."

"None of those other boats could have got ashore to give word of this wreck," said the oiler, in a low voice, "else the lifeboat would be out hunting us."

Slowly and beautifully the land loomed out of the sea. The wind came again. It had veered from the northeast to the southeast. Finally a new sound struck the ears of the men in the boat. It was the low thunder of the surf on the shore. "We'll never be able to make the lighthouse now," said the captain. "Swing her head a little more north, Billie."

"A little more north, sir," said the oiler.

Whereupon the little boat turned her nose once more down the wind, and all but the oarsman watched the shore grow. Under the influence of this expansion doubt and direful apprehension were leaving the minds of the men. The management of the boat was still most absorbing, but it could not prevent a quiet cheerfulness. In an hour, perhaps, they would be ashore.

Their backbones had become thoroughly used to balancing in the boat, and they now rode this wild colt of a dinghy like circus men. The correspondent thought that he had been drenched to the skin, but happening to feel in the top pocket of his coat, he found therein eight cigars. Four of them were soaked with seawater; four were perfectly scatheless. After a search, somebody produced three dry matches; and thereupon the four waifs rode impudently in their little boat and, with an assurance of an impending rescue shining in their eyes, puffed at the big cigars, and judged well and ill of all men. Everybody took a drink of water.

IV

"Cook," remarked the captain, "there don't seem to be any signs of life about your house of refuge."

"No," replied the cook. "Funny they don't see us!"

A broad stretch of lowly coast lay before the eyes of the men. It was of low dunes topped with dark vegetation. The roar of the surf was plain, and sometimes they could see the white lip of a wave as it spun up the beach. A tiny house was blocked out black upon the sky. Southward, the slim light-house lifted its little gray length.

Tide, wind, and waves were swinging the dinghy northward. "Funny they don't see us," said the men.

The surf's roar was here dulled, but its tone was nevertheless thunderous and mighty. As the boat swam over the great rollers the men sat listening to this roar. "We'll swamp sure," said everybody.

It is fair to say here that there was not a lifesaving station within twenty miles in either direction; but the men did not

know this fact, and in consequence they made dark and oppro-
brious remarks concerning the eyesight of the nation's lifesav-
ers. Four scowling men sat in the dinghy and surpassed
records in the invention of epithets.

"Funny they don't see us."

The light-heartedness of a former time had completely
faded. To their sharpened minds it was easy to conjure pictures
of all kinds of incompetency and blindness and, indeed, cow-
ardice. There was the shore of the populous land, and it was
bitter and bitter to them that from it came no sign.

"Well," said the captain, ultimately, "I suppose we'll have to
make a try for ourselves. If we stay out here too long, we'll
none of us have strength left to swim after the boat swamps."

And so the oiler, who was at the oars, turned the boat
straight for the shore. There was a sudden tightening of muscles. There was some thinking.

"If we don't all get ashore," said the captain—"if we don't
all get ashore, I suppose you fellows know where to send news
of my finish?"

They then briefly exchanged some addresses and admoni-
tions. As for the reflections of the men, there was a great deal
of rage in them. Perchance they might be formulated thus: "If
I am going to be drowned—if I am going to be drowned—if I
am going to be drowned, why, in the name of the seven mad
gods who rule the sea, was I allowed to come thus far and
contemplate sand and trees? Was I brought here merely to
have my nose dragged away as I was about to nibble the sacred
cheese of life? It is preposterous. If this old ninny-woman,
Fate, cannot do better than this, she should be deprived of the
management of men's fortunes. She is an old hen who knows
not her intention. If she has decided to drown me, why did she
not do it in the beginning and save me all this trouble? The
whole affair is absurd . . . But no; she cannot mean to drown
me. She dare not drown me. She cannot drown me. Not after

all this work." Afterward the man might have had an impulse to shake his fist at the clouds. "Just you drown me, now, and then hear what I call you!"

The billows that came at this time were more formidable. They seemed always just about to break and roll over the little boat in a turmoil of foam. There was a preparatory and long growl in the speech of them. No mind unused to the sea would have concluded that the dinghy could ascend these sheer heights in time. The shore was still afar. The oiler was a wily surfman. "Boys," he said swiftly, "she won't live three minutes more, and we're too far out to swim. Shall I take her to sea again, Captain?"

"Yes; go ahead!" said the captain.

This oiler, by a series of quick miracles and fast and steady oarsmanship, turned the boat in the middle of the surf and took her safely to sea again.

There was a considerable silence as the boat bumped over the furrowed sea to deeper water. Then somebody in gloom spoke: "Well, anyhow, they must have seen us from the shore by now."

The gulls went in slanting flight up the wind toward the gray, desolate east. A squall, marked by dingy clouds and clouds brick-red, like smoke from a burning building, appeared from the southeast.

"What do you think of those lifesaving people? Ain't they peaches?"

"Funny they haven't seen us."

"Maybe they think we're out here for sport! Maybe they think we're fishin'. Maybe they think we're damned fools."

It was a long afternoon. A changed tide tried to force them southward, but wind and wave said northward. Far ahead, where coastline, sea, and sky formed their mighty angle, there were little dots which seemed to indicate a city on the shore.

"St. Augustine?"

The captain shook his head. "Too near Mosquito Inlet."

And the oiler rowed, and then the correspondent rowed; then the oiler rowed. It was a weary business. The human back can become the seat of more aches and pains than are registered in books for the composite anatomy of a regiment. It is limited area, but it can become the theater of innumerable muscular conflicts, tangles, wrenches, knots, and other comforts.

"Did you ever like to row, Billie?" asked the correspondent.

"No," said the oiler; "hang it!"

When one exchanged the rowing-seat for a place in the bottom of the boat, he suffered a bodily depression that caused him to be careless of everything save an obligation to wiggle one finger. There was cold seawater swashing to and fro in the boat, and he lay in it. His head, pillowed on a thwart, was within an inch of the swirl of a wave-crest, and sometimes a particularly obstreperous sea came inboard and drenched him once more. But these matters did not annoy him. It is almost certain that if the boat had capsized he would have tumbled comfortably out upon the ocean as if he felt sure that it was a great soft mattress.

"Look! There's a man on the shore!"

"Where?"

"There! See 'im? See 'im?"

"Yes, sure! He's walking along."

"Now he's stopped. Look! He's facing us!"

"He's waving at us!"

"So he is! By thunder!"

"Ah, now we're all right! Now we're all right! There'll be a boat out here for us in half an hour."

"He's going on. He's running. He's going up to that house there."

The remote beach seemed lower than the sea, and it required a searching glance to discern the little black figure. The captain saw a floating stick and they rowed to it. A bath towel was by some weird chance in the boat, and, tying this on the stick, the captain waved it. The oarsman did not dare turn his head, so he was obliged to ask questions.

"What's he doing now?"

"He's standing still again. He's looking, I think . . . There he goes again—toward the house . . . Now he's stopped again."

"Is he waving at us?"

"No, not now; he was, though."

"Look! There comes another man!"

"He's running."

"Look at him go, would you!"

"Why, he's on a bicycle. Now he's met the other man. They're both waving at us. Look!"

"There comes something up the beach."

"What the devil is that thing?"

"Why, it looks like a boat."

"Why, certainly, it's a boat."

"No; it's on wheels."

"Yes, so it is. Well, that must be the lifeboat. They drag them along shore on a wagon."

"That's the lifeboat, sure."

"No, by God, it's—it's an omnibus."

"I tell you it's a lifeboat."

"It is not! It's an omnibus. I can see it plain. See? One of these big hotel omnibuses."

"By thunder, you're right. It's an omnibus, sure as fate. What do you suppose they are doing with an omnibus? Maybe they are going around collecting the life-crew, hey?"

"That's it, likely. Look! There's a fellow waving a little black flag. He's standing on the steps of the omnibus. There come those other two fellows. Now they're all talking together. Look at the fellow with the flag. Maybe he ain't waving it!"

"That ain't a flag, is it? That's his coat. Why, certainly, that's his coat."

"So it is; it's his coat. He's taken it off and is waving it around his head. But would you look at him swing it!"

"Oh, say, there isn't any lifesaving station there. That's just a winter-resort hotel omnibus that has brought over some of the boarders to see us drown."

"What's that idiot with the coat mean? What's he signaling, anyhow?"

"It looks as if he were trying to tell us to go north. There must be a lifesaving station up there."

"No; he thinks we're fishing. Just giving us a merry hand. See? Ah, there, Willie!"

"Well, I wish I could make something out of those signals. What do you suppose he means?"

"He don't mean anything; he's just playing."

"Well, if he'd just signal us to try the surf again, or to go to sea and wait, or go north, or go south, or go to hell, there would be some reason in it. But look at him! He just stands there and keeps his coat revolving like a wheel. The ass!"

"There come more people."

"Now there's quite a mob. Look! Isn't that a boat?"

"Where? Oh, I see where you mean. No, that's no boat."

"That fellow is still waving his coat."

"He must think we like to see him do that. Why don't he quit it? It don't mean anything."

"I don't know. I think he is trying to make us go north. It must be that there's a lifesaving station there somewhere."

"Say, he ain't tired yet. Look at 'im wave!"

"Wonder how long he can keep that up. He's been revolving his coat ever since he caught sight of us. He's an idiot. Why aren't they getting men to bring a boat out? A fishing boat—

one of those big yawls—could come out here all right. Why don't he do something?"

"Oh, it's all right now."

"They'll have a boat out here for us in less than no time, now that they've seen us."

A faint yellow tone came into the sky over the low land. The shadows on the sea slowly deepened. The wind bore coldness with it, and the men began to shiver.

"Holy smoke!" said one, allowing his voice to express his impious mood, "if we keep on monkeying out here! If we've got to flounder out here all night!"

"Oh, we'll never have to stay here all night! Don't you worry. They've seen us now, and it won't be long before they'll come chasing out after us."

The shore grew dusky. The man waving a coat blended gradually into this gloom, and it swallowed in the same manner the omnibus and the group of people. The spray, when it dashed uproariously over the side, made the voyagers shrink and swear like men who were being branded.

"I'd like to catch the chump who waved the coat. I feel like socking him one, just for luck."

"Why? What did he do?"

"Oh, nothing, but then he seemed so damned cheerful."

In the meantime the oiler rowed, and then the correspondent rowed, and then the oiler rowed. Gray-faced and bowed forward, they mechanically, turn by turn, plied the leaden oars. The form of the lighthouse had vanished from the southern horizon, but finally a pale star appeared, just lifting from the sea. The streaked saffron in the west passed before the all-merging darkness, and the sea to the east was black. The land had vanished, and was expressed only by the low and drear thunder of the surf.

"If I am going to be drowned—if I am going to be drowned —if I am going to be drowned, why, in the name of the seven mad gods who rule the sea, was I allowed to come thus far and contemplate sand and trees? Was I brought here merely to have my nose dragged away as I was about to nibble the sacred cheese of life?"

The patient captain, drooped over the water jar, was sometimes obliged to speak to the oarsman.

"Keep her head up! Keep her head up!"

"Keep her head up, sir." The voices were weary and low.

This was surely a quiet evening. All save the oarsman lay heavily and listlessly in the boat's bottom. As for him, his eyes were just capable of noting the tall black waves that swept forward in a most sinister silence, save for an occasional subdued growl of a crest.

The cook's head was on a thwart, and he looked without interest at the water under his nose. He was deep in other scenes. Finally he spoke. "Billie," he murmured, dreamfully, "what kind of pie do you like best?"

V

"Pie!" said the oiler and the correspondent, agitatedly. "Don't talk about those things, blast you!"

"Well," said the cook, "I was just thinking about ham sandwiches, and—"

A night on the sea in an open boat is a long night. As darkness settled finally, the shine of the light, lifting from the sea in the south, changed to full gold. On the northern horizon a new light appeared, a small bluish gleam on the edge of the waters. These two lights were the furniture of the world. Otherwise there was nothing but waves.

Two men huddled in the stern, and distances were so magnificent in the dinghy that the rower was enabled to keep his feet partly warm by thrusting them under his companions. Their legs indeed extended far under the rowing-seat until they touched the feet of the captain forward. Sometimes, despite the efforts of the tired oarsman, a wave came piling into the boat, an icy wave of the night, and the chilling water soaked them anew. They would twist their bodies for a moment and groan, and sleep the dead sleep once more, while the water in the boat gurgled about them as the craft rocked.

The plan of the oiler and the correspondent was for one to row until he lost the ability, and then arouse the other from his sea-water couch in the bottom of the boat.

The oiler plied the oars until his head drooped forward and the overpowering sleep blinded him; and he rowed yet afterward. Then he touched a man in the bottom of the boat, and called his name. "Will you spell me for a little while?" he said meekly.

"Sure, Billie," said the correspondent, awaking and dragging himself to a sitting position. They exchanged places carefully, and the oiler, cuddling down in the seawater at the cook's side, seemed to go to sleep instantly.

The particular violence of the sea had ceased. The waves came without snarling. The obligation of the man at the oars was to keep the boat headed so that the tilt of the rollers would not capsize her, and to preserve her from filling when the crests rushed past. The black waves were silent and hard to be seen in the darkness. Often one was almost upon the boat before the oarsman was aware.

In a low voice the correspondent addressed the captain. He was not sure that the captain was awake, although this iron man seemed to be always awake. "Captain, shall I keep her making for that light north, sir?"

The same steady voice answered him. "Yes. Keep it about two points off the port bow."

The cook had tied a lifebelt around himself in order to get even the warmth which this clumsy cork contrivance could donate, and he seemed almost stove-like when a rower, whose teeth invariably chattered wildly as soon as he ceased his labor, dropped down to sleep.

The correspondent, as he rowed, looked down at the two men sleeping underfoot. The cook's arm was around the oiler's shoulder, and, with their fragmentary clothing and haggard faces, they were the babes of the sea—a grotesque rendering of the old babes in the wood.

Later he must have grown stupid at his work, for suddenly there was a growling of water, and a crest came with a roar and a swash into the boat, and it was a wonder that it did not set the cook afloat in his lifebelt. The cook continued to sleep, but the oiler sat up, blinking his eyes and shaking with the new cold.

"Oh, I'm awful sorry, Billie," said the correspondent, contritely.

"That's all right, old boy," said the oiler, and lay down again and was asleep.

Presently it seemed that even the captain dozed, and the correspondent thought that he was the one man afloat on all the oceans. The wind had a voice as it came over the waves, and it was sadder than the end.

There was a long, loud swishing astern of the boat, and a gleaming trail of phosphorescence, like blue flame, was furrowed on the black waters. It might have been made by a monstrous knife.

Then there came a stillness, while the correspondent breathed with open mouth and looked at the sea.

Suddenly there was another swish and another long flash of bluish light, and this time it was alongside the boat, and might almost have been reached with an oar. The correspondent saw an enormous fin speed like a shadow through the water, hurling the crystalline spray and leaving the long glowing trail.

The correspondent looked over his shoulder at the captain. His face was hidden, and he seemed to be asleep. He looked at the babes of the sea. They certainly were asleep. So, being bereft of sympathy, he leaned a little way to one side and swore softly into the sea.

But the thing did not then leave the vicinity of the boat. Ahead or astern, on one side of the other, at intervals long or short, fled the long sparkling streak, and there was to be heard the *whirroo* of the dark fin. The speed and power of the thing was greatly to be admired. It cut the water like a gigantic and keen projectile.

The presence of this biding thing did not affect the man with the same horror that it would if he had been a picnicker. He simply looked at the sea dully and swore in an undertone.

Nevertheless, it is true that he did not wish to be alone with the thing. He wished one of his companions to awake by chance and keep him company with it. But the captain hung motionless over the water jar, and the oiler and the cook in the bottom of the boat were plunged in slumber.

VI

"If I am going to be drowned—if I am going to be drowned—if I am going to be drowned, why, in the name of the seven mad gods who rule the sea, was I allowed to come thus far and contemplate sand and trees?"

During this dismal night, it may be remarked that a man would conclude that it was really the intention of the seven gods to drown him, despite the abominable injustice of it. For it was certainly an abominable injustice to drown a man who had worked so hard, so hard. The man felt it would be a crime most unnatural. Other people had drowned at sea since galleys swarmed with painted sails, but still—

When it occurs to a man that nature does not regard him as important, and that she feels she would not maim the universe by disposing of him, he at first wishes to throw bricks at the temple, and he hates deeply the fact that there was no bricks and no temples. Any visible expression of nature would surely be pelleted with his jeers.

Then, if there be no tangible thing to hoot, he feels, perhaps, the desire to confront a personification and indulge in pleas, bowed to one knee, and with hands supplicant, saying, "Yes, but I love myself."

A high cold star on a winter's night is the word he feels that she says to him. Thereafter he knows the pathos of his situation.

The men in the dinghy had not discussed these matters, but each had, no doubt, reflected upon them in silence and according to his mind. There was seldom any expression upon their faces save the general one of complete weariness. Speech was devoted to the business of the boat.

To chime the notes of his emotion, a verse mysteriously entered the correspondent's head. He had even forgotten that he had forgotten this verse, but it suddenly was in his mind.

A soldier of the Legion lay dying in Algiers;
There was lack of woman's nursing, there was dearth of
    woman's tears;
But a comrade stood beside him, and he took that comrade's
    hand,
And he said, "I never more shall see my own, my native
    land."

In his childhood the correspondent had been made acquainted with the fact that a soldier of the Legion lay dying in Algiers, but he had never regarded the fact as important. Myriads of his schoolfellows had informed him of the soldier's plight, but the dinning had naturally ended by making him perfectly indifferent. He had never considered it his affair that a soldier of the Legion lay dying in Algiers, nor had it appeared to him as a matter for sorrow. It was less to him than the breaking of a pencil's point.

Now, however, it quaintly came to him as a human, living thing. It was no longer merely a picture of a few throes in the breast of a poet, meanwhile drinking tea and warming his feet at the grate; it was an actuality—stern, mournful, and fine.

The correspondent plainly saw the soldier. He lay on the sand with his feet out straight and still. While his pale left hand was upon his chest in an attempt to thwart the going of his life, the blood came between his fingers. In the far Algerian distance, a city of low square forms was set against a sky that was faint with the last sunset hues. The correspondent, plying the oars and dreaming of the slow and slower movements of the lips of the soldier, was moved by a profound and perfectly impersonal comprehension. He was sorry for the soldier of the Legion who lay dying in Algiers.

The thing which had followed the boat and waited had evidently grown bored at the delay. There was no longer to be heard the slash of the cut-water, and there was no longer the flame of the long trail. The light in the north still glimmered, but it was apparently no nearer to the boat. Sometimes the boom of the surf rang in the correspondent's ears, and he turned the craft seaward then and rowed harder. Southward, someone had evidently built a watch fire on the beach. It was too low and too far to be seen, but it made a shimmering, roseate reflection upon the bluff in back of it, and this could be discerned from the boat. The wind came stronger, and sometimes a wave suddenly raged out like a mountain cat, and there was to be seen the sheen and sparkle of a broken crest.

The captain, in the bow, moved on his water jar and sat erect. "Pretty long night," he observed to the correspondent. He looked at the shore. "Those lifesaving people take their time."

"Did you see that shark playing around?"

"Yes, I saw him. He was a big fellow, all right."

"Wish I had known you were awake."

Later the correspondent spoke into the bottom of the boat. "Billie!" There was a slow and gradual disentanglement. "Billie, will you spell me?"

"Sure," said the oiler.

As soon as the correspondent touched the cold, comfortable seawater in the bottom of the boat and had huddled close to the cook's lifebelt he was deep in sleep, despite the fact that his teeth played all the popular airs. This sleep was so good to him that it was but a moment before he heard a voice call his name in a tone that demonstrated the last stages of exhaustion. "Will you spell me?"

"Sure, Billie."

The light in the north had mysteriously vanished, but the correspondent took his course from the wide-awake captain.

Later in the night they took the boat farther out to sea, and the captain directed the cook to take one oar at the stern and keep the boat facing the seas. He was to call out if he should hear the thunder of the surf. This plan enabled the oiler and the correspondent to get respite together. "We'll give those boys a chance to get into shape again," said the captain. They curled down and, after a few preliminary chatterings and trembles, slept once more the dead sleep. Neither knew they had bequeathed to the cook the company of another shark, or perhaps the same shark.

As the boat caroused on the waves, spray occasionally bumped over the side and gave them a fresh soaking, but this had no power to break their repose. The ominous slash of the wind and the water affected them as it would have affected mummies.

"Boys," said the cook, with the notes of every reluctance in his voice, "she's drifted in pretty close. I guess one of you had better take her to sea again." The correspondent, aroused, heard the crash of the toppled crests.

As he was rowing, the captain gave him some whiskey-and-water, and this steadied the chills out of him. "If I ever get ashore and anybody shows me even a photograph of an oar—"

At last there was a short conversation.

"Billie! . . . Billie, will you spell me?"

"Sure," said the oiler.

VII

When the correspondent again opened his eyes, the sea and the sky were each of the gray hue of the dawning. Later, carmine and gold was painted upon the waters. The morning appeared finally, in its splendor, with a sky of pure blue, and the sunlight flamed on the tips of the waves.

On the distant dunes were set many little black cottages, and a tall white windmill reared above them. No man, nor dog, nor bicycle appeared on the beach. The cottages might have formed a deserted village.

The voyagers scanned the shore. A conference was held in the boat. "Well," said the captain, "if no help is coming, we might better try a run through the surf right away. If we stay out here much longer we will be too weak to do anything for ourselves at all." The others silently acquiesced in this reasoning. The boat was headed for the beach. The correspondent wondered if none ever ascended the tall wind-tower, and if then they never looked seaward. This tower was a giant, standing with its back to the plight of the ants. It represented in a degree, to the correspondent, the serenity of nature amid the struggles of the individual—nature in the wind, and nature in the vision of men. She did not seem cruel to him then, nor beneficent, nor treacherous, nor wise. But she was indifferent, flatly indifferent. It is, perhaps, plausible that a man in this situation, impressed with the unconcern of the universe, should see the innumerable flaws of his life, and have them taste wickedly in his mind, and wish for another chance. A distinction between right and wrong seems absurdly clear to him, then, in this new ignorance of the grave-edge, and he understands that if he were given another opportunity he would mend his conduct and his words, and be better and brighter during an introduction or at a tea.

"Now, boys," said the captain, "she is going to swamp sure. All we can do is to work her in as far as possible, and then when she swamps, pile out and scramble for the beach. Keep cool now, and don't jump until she swamps sure."

The oiler took the oars. Over his shoulders he scanned the surf. "Captain," he said, "I think I'd better bring her about and keep her head-on to the seas and back her in."

"All right, Billie," said the captain. "Back her in." The oiler swung the boat then, and, seated in the stern, the cook and the correspondent were obliged to look over their shoulders to contemplate the lonely and indifferent shore.

The monstrous inshore rollers heaved the boat high until the men were again enabled to see the white sheets of water scudding up the slanted beach. "We won't get in very close," said the captain. Each time a man could wrest his attention from the rollers, he turned his glance toward the shore, and in the expression of the eyes during this contemplation there was a singular quality. The correspondent, observing the others, knew that they were not afraid, but the full meaning of their glances was shrouded.

As for himself, he was too tired to grapple fundamentally with the fact. He tried to coerce his mind into thinking of it, but the mind was dominated at this time by the muscles, and the muscles said they did not care. It merely occurred to him that if he should drown it would be a shame.

There were no hurried words, no pallor, no plain agitation.

The men simply looked at the shore. "Now, remember to get well clear of the boat when you jump," said the captain.

Seaward the crest of a roller suddenly fell with a thunderous crash, and the long white comber came roaring down upon the boat.

"Steady now," said the captain. The men were silent. They turned their eyes from the shore to the comber and waited. The boat slid up the incline, leaped at the furious top, bounced over it, and swung down the long back of the wave. Some water had been shipped, and the cook bailed it out.

But the next crest crashed also. The tumbling, boiling flood of white water caught the boat and whirled it almost perpendicular. Water swarmed in from all sides. The correspondent had his hands on the gunwale at this time, and when the water entered at that place he swiftly withdrew his fingers, as if he objected to wetting them.

The little boat, drunken with this weight of water, reeled and snuggled deeper into the sea.

"Bail her out, cook! Bail her out!" said the captain.

"All right, Captain," said the cook.

"Now, boys, the next one will do for us sure," said the oiler. "Mind to jump clear of the boat."

The third wave moved forward, huge, furious, implacable. It fairly swallowed the dinghy, and almost simultaneously the men tumbled into the sea. A piece of lifebelt had lain in the bottom of the boat, and as the correspondent went overboard he held this to his chest with his left hand.

The January water was icy, and he reflected immediately that it was colder than he had expected to find it off the coast of Florida. This appeared to his dazed mind as a fact important enough to be noted at the time. The coldness of the water was sad; it was tragic. This fact was somehow mixed and confused with his opinion of his own situation, so that it seemed almost a proper reason for tears. The water was cold.

When he came to the surface he was conscious of little but the noisy water. Afterward he saw his companions in the sea. The oiler was ahead in the race. He was swimming strongly and rapidly. Off to the correspondent's left, the cook's great white and corked back bulged out of the water; and in the rear the captain was hanging with his one good hand to the keel of the overturned dinghy.

There is a certain immovable quality to a shore, and the correspondent wondered at it amid the confusion of the sea.

It seemed also very attractive; but the correspondent knew that it was a long journey, and he paddled leisurely. The piece of life preserver lay under him, and sometimes he whirled down the incline of a wave as if he were on a hand-sled.

But finally he arrived at a place in the sea where travel was beset with difficulty. He did not pause swimming to inquire what manner of current had caught him, but there his progress ceased. The shore was set before him like a bit of scenery on a stage, and he looked at it and understood with his eyes each detail of it.

As the cook passed, much farther to the left, the captain was calling to him, "Turn over on your back, cook! Turn over on your back and use the oar."

"All right, sir." The cook turned on his back, and, paddling with an oar, went ahead as if he were a canoe.

Presently the boat also passed to the left of the correspondent, with the captain clinging with one hand to the keel. He would have appeared like a man raising himself to look over a board fence if it were not for the extraordinary gymnastics of the boat. The correspondent marveled that the captain could still hold to it.

They passed on nearer to shore—the oiler, the cook, the captain—and following them went the water jar, bouncing gaily over the seas.

The correspondent remained in the grip of this strange new

enemy—a current. The shore, with its white slope of sand and its green bluff topped with little silent cottages, was spread like a picture before him. It was very near to him then, but he was impressed as one who, in a gallery, looks at a scene from Brittany or Algiers.

He thought: "I am going to drown? Can it be possible? Can it be possible? Can it be possible?" Perhaps an individual must consider his own death to be the final phenomenon of nature.

But later a wave perhaps whirled him out of this small deadly current, for he found suddenly that he could again make progress toward the shore. Later still he was aware that the captain, clinging with one hand to the keel of the dinghy, had his face turned away from the shore and toward him, and was calling his name. "Come to the boat! Come to the boat!"

In his struggle to reach the captain and boat, he reflected that when one gets properly wearied drowning must really be a comfortable arrangement—a cessation of hostilities accompanied by a large degree of relief; and he was glad of it, for the main thing in his mind for some moments had been horror of the temporary agony. He did not wish to be hurt.

Presently he saw a man running along the shore. He was undressing with most remarkable speed. Coat, trousers, shirt, everything flew magically off him.

"Come to the boat!" called the captain.

"All right, Captain." As the correspondent paddled, he saw the captain let himself down to bottom and leave the boat. Then the correspondent performed his one little marvel of the voyage. A large wave caught him and flung him with ease and supreme speed completely over the boat and far beyond it. It struck him even then as an event in gymnastics and a true miracle of the sea. An overturned boat in the surf is not a plaything to a swimming man.

The correspondent arrived in water that reached only to his waist, but his condition did not enable him to stand for more than a moment. Each wave knocked him into a heap, and the undertow pulled at him.

Then he saw the man who had been running and undressing, and undressing and running, come bounding into the water. He dragged ashore the cook, and then waded toward the captain; but the captain waved him away and sent him to the correspondent. He was naked—naked as a tree in winter, but a halo was about his head, and he shone like a saint. He gave a strong pull, and a long drag, and a bully heave at the correspondent's hand. The correspondent, schooled in the minor formulae, said, "Thanks, old man." But suddenly the man cried, "What's that?" He pointed a swift finger. The correspondent said, "Go."

In the shallows, face downward, lay the oiler. His forehead touched sand that was periodically, between each wave, clear of the sea.

The correspondent did not know all that transpired afterward. When he achieved safe ground he fell, striking the sand with each particular part of his body. It was as if he had dropped from a roof, but the thud was grateful to him.

It seems that instantly the beach was populated with men with blankets, clothes, and flasks, and women with coffeepots and all the remedies sacred to their minds. The welcome of the land to the men from the sea was warm and generous; but a still and dripping shape was carried slowly up the beach, and the land's welcome for it could only be the different and sinister hospitality of the grave.

When it came night, the white waves paced to and fro in the moonlight, and the wind brought the sound of the great sea's voice to the men on the shore, and they felt that they could then be interpreters.

IN ANOTHER COUNTRY

.

by *Ernest Hemingway*

In the fall the war was always there, but we did not go to it any more. It was cold in the fall in Milan and the dark came very early. Then the electric lights came on, and it was pleasant along the streets looking in the windows. There was much game hanging outside the shops, and the snow powdered in the fur of the foxes and the wind blew their tails. The deer hung stiff and heavy and empty, and small birds blew in the wind and the wind turned their feathers. It was a cold fall and the wind came down from the mountains.

We were all at the hospital every afternoon, and there were different ways of walking across the town through the dusk to the hospital. Two of the ways were alongside canals, but they were long. Always, though, you crossed a bridge across a canal to enter the hospital. There was a choice of three bridges. On one of them a woman sold roasted chestnuts. It was warm, standing in front of her charcoal fire, and the chestnuts were warm afterward in your pocket. The hospital was very old and very beautiful, and you entered through a gate and walked across a courtyard and out a gate on the other side. There were usually funerals starting from the courtyard. Beyond the old hospital were the new brick pavilions, and there we met every afternoon and were all very polite and interested in what was the matter, and sat in the machines that were to make so much difference.

The doctor came up to the machine where I was sitting and said: "What did you like best to do before the war? Did you practice a sport?"

I said: "Yes, football."

"Good," he said. "You will be able to play football again better than ever."

My knee did not bend and the leg dropped straight from the knee to the ankle without a calf, and the machine was to bend the knee and make it move as in riding a tricycle. But it did not bend yet, and instead the machine lurched when it came to the bending part. The doctor said: "That will all pass. You are a fortunate young man. You will play football again like a champion."

In the next machine was a major who had a little hand like a baby's. He winked at me when the doctor examined his hand, which was between two leather straps that bounced up and down and flapped the stiff fingers, and said: "And will I, too, play football, captain-doctor?" He had been a very great fencer, and before the war the greatest fencer in Italy.

The doctor went to his office in a back room and brought a photograph which showed a hand that had been withered almost as small as the major's, before it had taken a machine course, and after was a little larger. The major held the photograph with his good hand and looked at it very carefully. "A wound?" he asked.

"An industrial accident," the doctor said.

"Very interesting, very interesting," the major said, and handed it back to the doctor.

"You have confidence?"

"No," said the major.

There were three boys who came each day who were about the same age I was. They were all three from Milan, and one of them was to be a lawyer, and one was to be a painter, and one had intended to be a soldier, and after we were finished with the machines, sometimes we walked back together to the Café Cova, which was next door to the Scala. We walked the short way through the Communist quarter because we were four together. The people hated us because we were officers, and from a wineshop someone would call out, *"A basso gli ufficiali!"* as we passed. Another boy who walked with us sometimes and made us five wore a black silk handkerchief across his face because he had no nose then and his face was to be rebuilt. He had gone out to the front from the military academy and been wounded within an hour after he had gone into the front line for the first time. They rebuilt his face, but he came from a very old family and they could never get the nose exactly right. He went to South America and worked in a bank. But this was a long time ago, and then we did not any of us know how it was going to be afterward. We only knew then that there was always the war, but that we were not going to it any more.

We all had the same medals, except the boy with the black silk bandage across his face, and he had not been at the front long enough to get any medals. The tall boy with a very pale face who was to be a lawyer had been a lieutenant of Arditi and had three medals of the sort we each had only one of. He had lived a very long time with death and was a little detached. We were all a little detached, and there was nothing that held us together except that we met every afternoon at the hospital. Although, as we walked to the Cova through the tough part of town, walking in the dark, with light and singing coming out of the wineshops, and sometimes having to walk into the street when the men and women would crowd together on the sidewalk so that we would have had to jostle them to get by, we felt held together by there being something that had happened that they, the people who disliked us, did not understand.

We ourselves all understood the Cova, where it was rich and warm and not too brightly lighted, and noisy and smoky at certain hours, and there were always girls at the tables and the illustrated papers on a rack on the wall. The girls at the Cova were very patriotic, and I found that the most patriotic people in Italy were the café girls—and I believe they are still patriotic.

The boys at first were very polite about my medals and asked me what I had done to get them. I showed them the papers, which were written in very beautiful language and full of *fratellanza* and *abnegazione,* but which really said, with the adjectives removed, that I had been given the medals because I was an American. After that their manner changed a little toward me, although I was their friend against outsiders. I was a friend, but I was never really one of them after they had read the citations, because it had been different with them and they had done very different things to get their medals. I had been wounded, it was true; but we all knew that being wounded, after all, was really an accident. I was never ashamed of the ribbons, though, and sometimes, after the cocktail hour, I would imagine myself having done all the things they had done to get their medals; but walking home at night through the empty streets with the cold wind and all the shops closed, trying to keep near the streetlights, I knew that I would never have done such things, and I was very much afraid to die, and often lay in bed at night by myself, afraid to die and wondering how I would be when I went back to the front again.

The three with the medals were like hunting-hawks; and I was not a hawk, although I might seem a hawk to those who had never hunted; they, the three, knew better and so we drifted apart. But I stayed good friends with the boy who had been wounded his first day at the front, because he would never know now how he would have turned out; so he could never be accepted either, and I liked him because I thought perhaps he would not have turned out to be a hawk either.

The major, who had been the great fencer, did not believe in bravery and spent much time while we sat in the machines correcting my grammar. He had complimented me on how I spoke Italian, and we talked together very easily. One day I had said that Italian seemed such an easy language to me that I could not take a great interest in it; everything was so easy to say. "Ah, yes," the major said. "Why, then, do you not take up the use of grammar?" So we took up the use of grammar, and soon Italian was such a difficult language that I was afraid to talk to him until I had the grammar straight in my mind.

The major came very regularly to the hospital. I do not think he ever missed a day, although I am sure he did not believe in the machines. There was a time when none of us believed in the machines, and one day the major said it was all nonsense. The machines were new then and it was we who were to prove them. It was an idiotic idea, he said, "a theory, like another." I had not learned my grammar, and he said I was a stupid impossible disgrace, and he was a fool to have bothered with me. He was a small man and he sat straight up in his chair with his right hand thrust into the machine and looked straight ahead at the wall while the straps thumped up and down with his fingers in them.

"What will you do when the war is over if it is over?" he asked me. "Speak grammatically!"

"I will go to the States."

"Are you married?"

"No, but I hope to be."

"The more of a fool you are," he said. He seemed very angry. "A man must not marry."

"Why, Signor Maggiore?"

"Don't call me 'Signor Maggiore.' "

"Why must not a man marry?"

"He cannot marry. He cannot marry," he said angrily. "If he is to lose everything, he should not place himself in a position to lose that. He should not place himself in a position to lose. He should find things he cannot lose."

He spoke very angrily and bitterly, and looked straight ahead while he talked.

"But why should he necessarily lose it?"

"He'll lose it," the major said. He was looking at the wall. Then he looked down at the machine and jerked his little hand out from between the straps and slapped it hard against his thigh. "He'll lose it," he almost shouted. "Don't argue with me!" Then he called to the attendant who ran the machines. "Come and turn this damned thing off."

He went back into the other room for the light treatment and the massage. Then I heard him ask the doctor if he might use his telephone and he shut the door. When he came back into the room, I was sitting in another machine. He was wearing his cape and had his cap on, and he came directly toward my machine and put his arm on my shoulder.

"I am so sorry," he said, and patted me on the shoulder with his good hand. "I would not be rude. My wife has just died. You must forgive me."

"Oh—" I said, feeling sick for him. "I am so sorry."

He stood there, biting his lower lip. "It is very difficult," he said. "I cannot resign myself."

He looked straight past me and out through the window. Then he began to cry. "I am utterly unable to resign myself," he said and choked. And then crying, his head up looking at nothing, carrying himself straight and soldierly, with tears on both his cheeks and biting his lips, he walked past the machines and out the door.

The doctor told me that the major's wife, who was very young and whom he had not married until he was definitely invalided out of the war, had died of pneumonia. She had been sick only a few days. No one expected her to die. The major did not come to the hospital for three days. Then he came at the usual hour, wearing a black band on the sleeve of his uniform. When he came back, there were large framed photographs around the wall, of all sorts of wounds before and after they had been cured by the machines. In front of the machine the major used were three photographs of hands like his that were completely restored. I do not know where the doctor got them. I always understood we were the first to use the machines. The photographs did not make much difference to the major because he only looked out of the window.

VICTORY

.

by William Faulkner

I

Those who saw him descend from the Marseilles express in the
Gare de Lyon on that damp morning saw a tall man, a little
stiff, with a bronze face and spike-ended moustaches and almost white hair. "A milord," they said, remarking his sober,
correct suit, his correct stick correctly carried, his sparse baggage; "a milord military. But there is something the matter
with his eyes." But there was something the matter with the
eyes of so many people, men and women too, in Europe since
four years now. So they watched him go on, a half head above
the French people, with his gaunt, strained eyes, his air
strained, purposeful, and at the same time assured, and vanish
into a cab, thinking, if they thought about him any more at all:
"You will see him in the Legation offices or at a table on the
Boulevards, or in a carriage with the fine English ladies in the
Bois." That was all.

And those who saw him descend from the same cab at the Gare du Nord, they thought: "This milord returns home by haste"; the porter who took his bag wished him good morning in fair English and told him that he was going to England, receiving for reply the English glare which the porter perhaps expected, and put him into a first-class carriage of the boat train. And that was all, too. That was all right, too, even when he got down at Amiens. English milords even did that. It was only at Rozières that they began to look at him and after him when he had passed.

In a hired car he jounced through a gutted street between gutted walls rising undoored and unwindowed in jagged shards in the dusk. The street was partially blocked now and then by toppled walls, with masses of masonry in the cracks of which a thin grass sprouted, passing empty and ruined courtyards, in one of which a tank, mute and tilted, rusted among rank weeds. This was Rozières, but he didn't stop there because no one lived there and there was no place to stop.

So the car jounced and crept on out of the ruin. The muddy and unpaved street entered a village of harsh new brick and sheet iron and tarred paper roofs made in America, and halted before the tallest house. It was flush with the street: a brick wall with a door and one window of American glass bearing the word RESTAURANT. "Here you are, sir," the driver said.

The passenger descended, with his bag, his ulster, his correct stick. He entered a biggish, bare room chill with new plaster. It contained a billiard table at which three men played. One of the men looked over his shoulder and said,

"Bonjour, monsieur."

The newcomer did not reply at all. He crossed the room, passing the new zinc bar, and approached an open door beyond which a woman of any age around forty looked at him above the sewing on her lap.

"Bong jour, madame," he said. "Dormie, madame?"

The woman gave him a single glance, brief, still. "C'est ça, monsieur," she said, rising.

"Dormie, madame?" he said, raising his voice a little, his spiked moustache beaded a little with rain, dampness beneath his strained yet assured eyes. "Dormie, madame?"

"Bon, monsieur," the woman said. "Bon. Bon."

"Dor—" the newcomer essayed again. Someone touched his arm. It was the man who had spoken from the billiard table when he entered.

"Regardez, Monsieur l'Anglais," the man said. He took the bag from the newcomer and swept his other arm toward the ceiling. "La chambre." He touched the traveler again; he laid his face upon his palm and closed his eyes; he gestured again toward the ceiling and went on across the room toward a wooden stair without balustrade. As he passed the bar he took a candle stub from it and lit the candle (the big room and the room beyond the door where the woman sat were lighted by single bulbs hanging naked on cords from the ceiling) at the foot of the stair.

They mounted, thrusting their fitful shadows before them, into a corridor narrow, chill, and damp as a tomb. The walls were of rough plaster not yet dried. The floor was of pine, without carpet or paint. Cheap metal doorknobs glinted symmetrically. The sluggish air lay like a hand upon the very candle. They entered a room, smelling too of wet plaster, and even colder than the corridor; a sluggish chill almost substantial, as though the atmosphere between the dead and recent walls were congealing, like a patent three-minute dessert. The room contained a bed, a dresser, a chair, a washstand; the bowl, pitcher, and slop basin were of American enamel. When the traveler touched the bed the linen was soundless under his hand, coarse as sacking, clinging damply to the hand in the dead air in which their two breathings vaporized in the faint candle.

The host set the candle on the dresser. "Dîner, monsieur?" he said. The traveler stared down at the host, incongruous in his correct clothes, with that strained air. His waxed moustaches gleamed like faint bayonets above a cravat striped with what the host could not have known was the patterned coloring of a Scottish regiment. "Manger?" the host shouted. He chewed violently in pantomime. "Manger?" he roared, his shadow aping his gesture as he pointed toward the floor.

"Yes," the traveler shouted in reply, their faces not a yard apart. "Yes. Yes."

The host nodded violently, pointed toward the floor and then at the door, nodded again, went out.

He returned below stairs. He found the woman now in the kitchen, at the stove. "He will eat," the host said.

"I knew that," the woman said.

"You would think that they would stay at home," the host said. "I'm glad I was not born of a race doomed to a place too small to hold all of us at one time."

"Perhaps he has come to look at the war," the woman said.

"Of course he has," the host said. "But he should have come four years ago. That was when we needed Englishmen to look at the war."

"He was too old to come then," the woman said. "Didn't you see his hair?"

"Then let him stay at home now," the host said. "He is no younger."

"He may have come to look at the grave of his son," the woman said.

"Him?" the host said. "That one? He is too cold to ever have had a son."

"Perhaps you are right," the woman said. "After all, that is his affair. It is our affair only that he has money."

"That's right," the host said. "A man in this business, he cannot pick and choose."

"He can pick, though," the woman said.

"Good!" the host said. "Very good! Pick! That is worth telling to the English himself."

"Why not let him find it out when he leaves?"

"Good!" the host said. "Better still. Good! Oh, good!"

"Attention," the woman said. "Here he comes."

They listened to the traveler's steady tramp, then he appeared in the door. Against the lesser light of the bigger room, his dark face and his white hair looked like a Kodak negative.

The table was set for two, a carafe of red wine at each place. As the traveller seated himself, the other guest entered and took the other place—a small, rat-faced man who appeared at first glance to have no eyelashes at all. He tucked his napkin into the top of his vest and took up the soup ladle (the tureen sat between them in the center of the table) and offered it to the other. "Faites-moi l'honneur, monsieur," he said. The other bowed stiffly, accepting the ladle. The small man lifted the cover from the tureen. "Vous venez examiner ce scène de nos victoires, monsieur?" he said, helping himself in turn. The other looked at him. "Monsieur l'Anglais a peut-être beaucoup des amis qui sont tombés en voisinage."

"A speak no French," the other said, eating.

The little man did not eat. He held his yet unwetted spoon above his bowl. "What agreeable for me. I speak the Engleesh. I am Suisse, me. I speak all langue." The other did not reply. He ate steadily, not fast. "You ave return to see the grave of your galant countreemans, eh? You ave son here, perhaps, eh?"

"No," the other said. He did not cease to eat.

"No?" The other finished his soup and set the bowl aside. He drank some wine. "What deplorable, that man who ave," the Swiss said. "But it is finish now. Not?" Again the other said nothing. He was not looking at the Swiss. He did not seem to be looking at anything, with his gaunt eyes, his rigid moustaches upon his rigid face. "Me, I suffer too. All suffer. But I tell myself, What would you? It is war."

Still the other did not answer. He ate steadily, deliberately, and finished his meal and rose and left the room. He lit his candle at the bar, where the host, leaning beside a second man in a corduroy coat, lifted a glass slightly to him. "Au bon dormir, monsieur," the host said.

The traveler looked at the host, his face gaunt in the candle, his waxed moustaches rigid, his eyes in shadow. "What?" he said. "Yes. Yes." He turned and went toward the stairs. The two men at the bar watched him, his stiff, deliberate back.

Ever since the train left Arras, the two women had been watching the other occupant of the carriage. It was a third-class carriage because no first-class trains ran on this line, and they sat with their shawled heads and the thick, still hands of peasants folded upon closed baskets on their laps, watching the man sitting opposite them—the white distinction of the hair against the bronze, gaunt face, the needles of the moustaches, the foreign-made suit and the stick—on a worn and greasy wooden seat, looking out the window. At first they had just looked, ready to avert their gaze, but as the man did not seem to be aware of them, they began to whisper quietly to one another behind their hands. But the man did not seem to notice this, so they soon were talking in undertone, watching with bright, alert, curious eyes the stiff, incongruous figure leaning a little forward on the stick, looking out a foul window beyond which there was nothing to see save an occasional shattered road and man-high stump of shattered tree breaking small patches of tilled land whorled with apparent unreason about islands of earth indicated by low signboards painted red, the islands inscrutable, desolate above the destruction which they wombed. Then the train, slowing, ran suddenly among tumbled brick, out of which rose a small house of corrugated iron bearing a name in big letters; they watched the man lean forward.

"See!" one of the women said. "His mouth. He is reading the name. What did I tell you? It is as I said. His son fell here."

"Then he had lots of sons," the other woman said. "He has read the name each time since we left Arras. Eh! Eh! Him a son? That cold?"

"They do get children, though."

"That is why they drink whisky. Otherwise . . ."

"That's so. They think of nothing save money and eating, the English."

Presently they got out; the train went on. Then others entered the carriage, other peasants with muddy boots, carrying baskets or live or dead beasts; they in turn watched the rigid, motionless figure leaning at the window while the train ran across the ruined land and past the brick or iron stations among the tumbled ruins, watching his lips move as he read the names. "Let him look at the war, about which he has apparently heard at last," they told one another. "Then he can go home. It was not in his barnyard that it was fought."

"Nor in his house," a woman said.

II

The battalion stands at ease in the rain. It has been in rest billets two days, equipment has been replaced and cleaned, vacancies have been filled and the ranks closed up, and it now stands at ease with the stupid docility of sheep in the ceaseless rain, facing the streaming shape of the sergeant-major.

Presently the colonel emerges from a door across the square. He stands in the door a moment, fastening his trench coat, then, followed by two A.D.C.'s, he steps gingerly into the mud in polished boots and approaches.

"Para-a-a-de—'Shun!" the sergeant-major shouts. The battalion clashes, a single muffled, sullen sound. The sergeant-major turns, takes a pace toward the officers, and salutes, his stick beneath his armpit. The colonel jerks his stick toward his cap peak.

"Stand at ease, men," he says. Again the battalion clashes, a single sluggish, trickling sound. The officers approach the guide file of the first platoon, the sergeant-major falling in behind the last officer. The sergeant of the first platoon takes a pace forward and salutes. The colonel does not respond at all. The sergeant falls in behind the sergeant-major, and the five of them pass down the company front, staring in turn at each rigid, forward-staring face as they pass it. First Company.

The sergeant salutes the colonel's back and returns to his original position and comes to attention. The sergeant of the second company has stepped forward, saluted, is ignored, and falls in behind the sergeant-major, and they pass down the second company front. The colonel's trench coat sheathes water onto his polished boots. Mud from the earth creeps up his boots and meets the water and is channelled by the water as the mud creeps up the polished boots again.

Third Company. The colonel stops before a soldier, his trench coat hunched about his shoulders where the rain trickles from the back of his cap, so that he looks somehow like a choleric and outraged bird. The other two officers, the sergeant-major and the sergeant halt in turn, and the five of them glare at the five soldiers whom they are facing. The five soldiers stare rigid and unwinking straight before them, their faces like wooden faces, their eyes like wooden eyes.

"Sergeant," the colonel says in his pettish voice, "has this man shaved today?"

"Sir!" the sergeant says in a ringing voice; the sergeant-major says:

"Did this man shave today, Sergeant?" and all five of them

glare now at the soldier, whose rigid gaze seems to pass through and beyond them, as if they were not there. "Take a pace forward when you speak in ranks!" the sergeant-major says.

The soldier, who has not spoken, steps out of ranks, splashing a jet of mud yet higher up the colonel's boots.

"What is your name?" the colonel says.

"024186 Gray," the soldier raps out glibly. The company, the battalion, stares straight ahead.

"Sir!" the sergeant-major thunders.

"Sir-r," the soldier says.

"Did you shave this morning?" the colonel says.

"Nae, sir-r."

"Why not?"

"A dinna shave, sir-r."

"You don't shave?"

"A am nae auld enough tae shave."

"Sir!" the sergeant-major thunders.

"Sir-r," the soldier says.

"You are not . . ." The colonel's voice dies somewhere behind his choleric glare, the trickling water from his cap peak. "Take his name, Sergeant-major," he says, passing on.

The battalion stares rigidly ahead. Presently it sees the colonel, the two officers and the sergeant-major reappear in single file. At the proper place the sergeant-major halts and salutes the colonel's back. The colonel jerks his stick hand again and goes on, followed by the two officers, at a trot toward the door from which he had emerged.

The sergeant-major faces the battalion again. "Para-a-a-de—" he shouts. An indistinguishable movement passes from rank to rank, an indistinguishable precursor of that damp and sullen clash which dies borning. The sergeant-major's stick has come down from his armpit; he now leans on it, as officers do. For a time his eye roves along the battalion front.

"Sergeant Cunninghame!" he says at last.

"Sir!"

"Did you take that man's name?"

There is silence for a moment—a little more than a short moment, a little less than a long one. Then the sergeant says: "What man, sir?"

"You, soldier!" the sergeant-major says.

The battalion stands rigid. The rain lances quietly into the mud between it and the sergeant-major as though it were too spent to either hurry or cease.

"You soldier that don't shave!" the sergeant-major says.

"Gray, sir!" the sergeant says.

"Gray. Double out 'ere."

The man Gray appears without haste and tramps stolidly before the battalion, his kilts dark and damp and heavy as a wet horse-blanket. He halts, facing the sergeant-major.

"Why didn't you shave this morning?" the sergeant-major says.

"A am nae auld enough tae shave," Gray says.

"Sir!" the sergeant-major says.

Gray stares rigidly beyond the sergeant-major's shoulder.

"Say *sir* when addressing a first-class warrant officer!" the sergeant-major says. Gray stares doggedly past his shoulder, his face beneath his visorless bonnet as oblivious of the cold lances of rain as though it were granite. The sergeant-major raises his voice:

"Sergeant Cunninghame!"

"Sir!"

"Take this man's name for insubordination also."

"Very good, sir!"

The sergeant-major looks at Gray again. "And I'll see that you get the penal battalion, my man. Fall in!"

Gray turns without haste and returns to his place in ranks,

the sergeant-major watching him. The sergeant-major raises his voice again:

"Sergeant Cunninghame!"

"Sir!"

"You did not take that man's name when ordered. Let that happen again and you'll be for it yourself."

"Very good, sir!"

"Carry on!" the sergeant-major says.

"But why did ye no shave?" the corporal asked him. They were back in billets: a stone barn with leprous walls, where no light entered, squatting in the ammoniac air on wet straw about a reeking brazier. "Ye kenned we were for inspection thae mor-rn."

"A am nae auld enough tae shave," Gray said.

"But ye kenned thae colonel would mar-rk ye on parade."

"A am nae auld enough tae shave," Gray repeated doggedly and without heat.

III

"For two hundred years," Matthew Gray said, "there's never a day, except Sunday, has passed but there is a hull rising on Clyde or a hull going out of Clydemouth with a Gray-driven nail in it." He looked at young Alec across his steel spectacles, his neck bowed. "And not excepting their godless Sabbath hammering and sawing either. Because if a hull could be built in a day, Grays could build it," he added with dour pride. "And now, when you are big enough to go down to the yards with your grandadder and me and take a man's place among men, to be trusted manlike with hammer and saw yersel."

"Whisht, Matthew," old Alec said. "The lad can saw as

straight a line and drive as mony a nail a day as yersel or even me."

Matthew paid his father no attention. He continued to speak his slow, considered words, watching his oldest son across the spectacles. "And with John Wesley not old enough by two years, and wee Matthew by ten, and your grandfather an auld man will soon be—"

"Whisht," old Alec said. "I'm no but sixty-eight. Will you be telling the lad he'll make his bit journey to London and come back to find me in the parish house, mayhap? 'Twill be over by Christmastide."

"Christmastide or no," Matthew said, "a Gray, a ship-wright, has no business at an English war."

"Whisht ye," old Alec said. He rose and went to the chimney cupboard and returned, carrying a box. It was of wood, dark and polished with age, the corners bound with iron, and fitted with an enormous iron lock which any child with a hair-pin could have solved. From his pocket he took an iron key almost as big as the lock. He opened the box and lifted care-fully out a small velvet-covered jeweler's box and opened it in turn. On the satin lining lay a medal, a bit of bronze on a crimson ribbon: a Victoria Cross. "I kept the hulls going out of Clydemouth while your uncle Simon was getting this bit of brass from the Queen," old Alec said. "I heard naught of com-plaint. And if need be, I'll keep them going out while Alec serves the Queen a bit himsel. Let the lad go," he said. He put the medal back into the wooden box and locked it. "A bit fighting winna hurt the lad. If I were his age, or yours either, for that matter, I'd gang mysel. Alec, lad, hark ye. Ye'll see if they'll no take a hale lad of sixty-eight and I'll gang wi ye and leave the auld folk like Matthew to do the best they can. Nay, Matthew; dinna ye thwart the lad; have no the Grays ever served the Queen in her need?"

So young Alec went to enlist, descending the hill on a weekday in his Sunday clothes, with a New Testament and a loaf of homebaked bread tied in a handkerchief. And this was the last day's work which old Alec ever did, for soon after that, one morning Matthew descended the hill to the shipyard alone, leaving old Alec at home. And after that, on the sunny days (and sometimes on the bad days too, until his daughter-in-law found him and drove him back into the house) he would sit shawled in a chair on the porch, gazing south and eastward, calling now and then to his son's wife within the house: "Hark now. Do you hear them? The guns."

"I hear nothing," the daughter-in-law would say. "It's only the sea at Kinkeadbight. Come into the house, now. Matthew will be displeased."

"Whisht, woman. Do you think there is a Gray in the world could let off a gun and me not know the sound of it?"

*　　*　　*

They had a letter from him shortly after he enlisted, from England, in which he said that being a soldier, England, was different from being a shipwright, Clydeside, and that he would write again later. Which he did, each month or so, writing that soldiering was different from building ships and that it was still raining. Then they did not hear from him for seven months. But his mother and father continued to write him a joint letter on the first Monday of each month, letters almost identical with the previous one, the previous dozen:

We are well. Ships are going out of Clyde faster than they can sink them. You still have the Book?

This would be in his father's slow, indomitable hand. Then, in his mother's:

Are you well? Do you need anything? Jessie and I are knitting the stockings and will send them. Alec, Alec.

115

He received this one during the seven months, during his term in the penal battalion, forwarded to him by his old corporal, since he had not told his people of his changed life. He answered it, huddled among his fellow felons, squatting in the mud with newspapers buttoned inside his tunic and his head and feet wrapped in strips of torn blanket:

I am well. Yes I still have the Book (not telling them that his platoon was using it to light tobacco with and that they were now well beyond Lamentations). *It still rains. Love to Grandadder and Jessie and Matthew and John Wesley.*

Then his time in the penal battalion was up. He returned to his old company, his old platoon, finding some new faces, and a letter:

We are well. Ships are going out of Clyde yet. You have a new sister. Your Mother is well.

He folded the letter and put it away. "A see mony new faces in thae battalion," he said to the corporal. "We ha a new sairrgeant-major too, A doot not?"

"Naw," the corporal said. "'Tis the same one." He was looking at Gray, his gaze intent, speculative; his face cleared. "Ye ha shaved thae mor-rn," he said.

"Ay," Gray said. "Am auld enough tae shave noo."

That was the night on which the battalion was to go up to Arras. It was to move at midnight, so he answered the letter at once:

I am well. Love to Grandadder and Jessie and Matthew and John Wesley and the baby.

"Morning! Morning!" The General, lap-robed and hooded, leans from his motor and waves his gloved hand and shouts cheerily to them as they slog past the car on the Bapaume road, taking the ditch to pass.

"A's a cheery auld card," a voice says.

"Awfficers," a second drawls; he falls to cursing as he slips in the greaselike mud, trying to cling to the crest of the knee-deep ditch.

"Aweel," a third says, "thae awfficers wud gang tae thae war-r too, A doot not."

"Why dinna they gang then?" a fourth says. "Thae war-r is no back that way."

Platoon by platoon they slip and plunge into the ditch and drag their heavy feet out of the clinging mud and pass the halted car and crawl terrifically onto the crown of the road again: "A says tae me, A says: 'Fritz has a new gun that will carry to Par-ris,' A says, and A says tae him: ' 'Tis nawthin: A has one that will hit our Cor-rps Headquar-rters.' "

"Morning! Morning!" The General continues to wave his glove and shout cheerily as the battalion detours into the ditch and heaves itself back onto the road again.

*　　*　　*

They are in the trench. Until the first rifle explodes in their faces, not a shot has been fired. Gray is the third man. During all the while that they crept between flares from shellhole to shellhole, he has been working himself nearer to the sergeant-major and the Officer; in the glare of that first rifle he can see the gap in the wire toward which the Officer was leading them, the moiled rigid glints of the wire where bullets have nicked the mud and rust from it, and against the glare the tall, leaping shape of the sergeant-major. Then Gray, too, springs bayonet first into the trench full of grunting shouts and thudding blows.

Flares go up by dozens now; in the corpse glare Gray sees the sergeant-major methodically tossing grenades into the next traverse. He runs toward him, passing the Officer leaning, bent double, against the fire step. The sergeant-major has vanished beyond the traverse. Gray follows and comes upon the sergeant-major. Holding the burlap curtain aside with one hand, the sergeant-major is in the act of tossing a grenade into a dugout as if he might be tossing an orange hull into a cellar.

The sergeant-major turns in the rocket glare. " 'Tis you, Gray," he says. The earth-muffled bomb thuds; the sergeant-major is in the act of catching another bomb from the sack about his neck as Gray's bayonet goes into his throat. The sergeant-major is a big man. He falls backward, holding the rifle barrel with both hands against his throat, his teeth glaring, pulling Gray with him. Gray clings to the rifle. He tries to shake the speared body on the bayonet as he would shake a rat on an umbrella rib.

He frees the bayonet. The sergeant-major falls. Gray reverses the rifle and hammers its butt into the sergeant-major's face, but the trench floor is too soft to supply any resistance. He glares about. His gaze falls upon a duckboard upended in the mud. He drags it free and slips it beneath the sergeant-major's head and hammers the face with his rifle-butt. Behind him in the first traverse the Officer is shouting: "Blow your whistle, Sergeant-major!"

IV

In the citation it told how Private Gray, on a night raid, one of four survivors, following the disablement of the Officer and the death of all the N.C.O.'s, took command of the situation and (the purpose of the expedition was a quick raid for prisoners) held a foothold in the enemy's front line until a supporting attack arrived and consolidated the position. The Officer told how he ordered the men back out, ordering them to leave him and save themselves, and how Gray appeared with a German machine gun from somewhere and, while his three companions built a barricade, overcame the Officer and took from him his Very pistol and fired the colored signal which called for the attack; all so quickly that support arrived before the enemy could counterattack or put down a barrage.

It is doubtful if his people ever saw the citation at all. Anyway, the letters which he received from them during his sojourn in hospital, the tenor of them, were unchanged: "We are well. Ships are still going out."

His next letter home was once more months late. He wrote it when he was sitting up again, in London:

I have been sick but I am better now. I have a ribbon like in the box but not all red. The Queen was there. Love to Grandadder and Jessie and Matthew and John Wesley and the baby.

The reply was written on Friday:

Your mother is glad that you are better. Your grandfather is dead. The baby's name is Elizabeth. We are well. Your mother sends her love.

His next letter was three months later, in winter again:

My hurt is well. I am going to a school for officers. Love to Jessie and Matthew and John Wesley and Elizabeth.

Matthew Gray pondered over this letter for a long while; so long that the reply was a week late, written on the second Monday instead of the first. He wrote it carefully, waiting until his family was in bed. It was such a long letter, or he had been at it so long, that after a time his wife came into the room in her nightdress.

"Go back to bed," he told her. "I'll be coming soon. 'Tis something to be said to the lad."

When at last he laid the pen down and sat back to reread the letter, it was a long one, written out slowly and deliberately and without retraction or blot:

. . . your bit ribbon . . . for that way lies vainglory and pride. The pride and vainglory of going for an officer. Never miscall your birth, Alec. You are not a gentleman. You are a Scottish shipwright. If your grandfather were here he would not be last to tell you so. . . . We are glad your hurt is well. Your mother sends her love.

He sent home the medal, and his photograph in the new tunic with the pips and ribbon and the barred cuffs. But he did not go home himself. He returned to Flanders in the spring, with poppies blowing in the churned beet- and cabbage-fields. When his leaves came, he spent them in London, in the haunts of officers, not telling his people that he had any leave.

He still had the Book. Occasionally he came upon it among his effects and opened it at the jagged page where his life had changed: *. . . and a voice said, Peter, raise thyself; kill—*

Often his batman would watch him as, unawares and oblivious, he turned the Book and mused upon the jagged page—the ranker, the gaunt, lonely man with a face that belied his years or lack of them: a sobriety, a profound and mature calm, a grave and deliberate conviction of expression and gesture ("like a mout be Haig hissel," the batman said)—watching him at his clean table, writing steadily and slowly, his tongue in his cheek as a child writes:

I am well. It has not rained in a fortnight. Love to Jessie and Matthew and John Wesley and Elizabeth.

Four days ago the battalion came down from the lines. It has lost its major and two captains and most of the subalterns, so that now the remaining captain is major, and two subalterns and a sergeant have the companies. Meanwhile, replacements have come up, the ranks are filled, and the battalion is going in again tomorrow. So today K Company stands with ranks open for inspection while the subaltern-captain (his name is Gray) moves slowly along each platoon front.

He passes from man to man, slowly, thoroughly, the sergeant behind him. He stops.

"Where is your trenching tool?" he says.

"Blawn—" the soldier begins. Then he ceases, staring rigidly before him.

"Blawn out of your pack, eh?" the captain finishes for him. "Since when? What battles have ye taken par-rt in since four days?"

The soldier stares rigidly across the drowsy street. The captain moves on. "Take his name, Sergeant."

He moves on to the second platoon, to the third. He halts again. He looks the soldier up and down.

"What is your name?"

"010801 McLan, sir-r."

"Replacement?"

"Replacement, sir-r."

The captain moves on. "Take his name, Sergeant. Rifle's filthy."

*   *   *

The sun is setting. The village rises in black silhouette against the sunset; the river gleams in mirrored fire. The bridge across the river is a black arch upon which slowly and like figures cut from black paper, men are moving.

The party crouches in the roadside ditch while the captain and the sergeant peer cautiously across the parapet of the road. "Do ye make them out?" the captain says in a low voice.

"Huns, sir-r," the sergeant whispers. "A ken their-r helmets."

Presently the column has crossed the bridge. The captain and the sergeant crawl back into the ditch, where the party crouches, among them a wounded man with a bandaged head. "Keep yon man quiet, now," the captain says.

He leads the way along the ditch until they reach the out-skirts of the village. Here they are out of the sun, and here they sit quietly beneath a wall, surrounding the wounded man, while the captain and the sergeant again crawl away. They return in five minutes. "Fix bayonets," the sergeant says in a low voice. "Quiet, now."

"Wull A stay wi thae hur-rt lad, Sair-rgent?" one whispers.

"Nay," the sergeant says. "A'll tak's chance wi us. For-rard."

They steal quietly along the wall, behind the captain. The wall approaches at right angles to the street, the road which crosses the bridge. The captain raises his hand. They halt and watch him as he peers around the corner. They are opposite the bridgehead. It and the road are deserted; the village dreams quietly in the setting sun. Against the sky beyond the village the dust of the retreating column hangs, turning to rose and gold.

Then they hear a sound, a short, guttural word. Not ten yards away and behind a ruined wall leveled breast-high and facing the bridge, four men squat about a machine gun. The captain raises his hand again. They grasp their rifles: a rush of hobnails on cobblestones, a cry of astonishment cut sharply off; blows, short, hard breaths, curses; not a shot.

The man with the bandaged head begins to laugh, shrilly, until someone hushes him with a hand that tastes like brass. Under the captain's direction they bash in the door of the house and drag the gun and the four bodies into it. They hoist the gun upstairs and set it up in a window looking down upon the bridgehead. The sun sinks further, the shadows fall long and quiet across village and river. The man with the bandaged head babbles to himself.

Another column swings up the road, dogged and orderly beneath coalhod helmets. It crosses the bridge and passes on through the village. A party detaches itself from the rear of the column and splits into three squads. Two of them have machine guns, which they set up on opposite sides of the street, the near one utilizing the barricade behind which the other gun had been captured. The third squad returns to the bridge, carrying sappers' tools and explosive. The sergeant tells off six of the nineteen men, who descend the stairs silently. The captain remains with the gun in the window.

Again there is a brief rush, a scuffle, blows. From the window the captain sees the heads of the machine-gun crew across the street turn, then the muzzle of the gun swings, firing. The captain rakes them once with his gun, then he sweeps with it the party on the bridge, watching it break like a covey of quail for the nearest wall. The captain holds the gun on them. They wilt running and dot the white road and become motionless. Then he swings the gun back to the gun across the street. It ceases.

He gives another order. The remaining men, except the man with the bandage, run down the stairs. Half of them stop at the gun beneath the window and drag it around. The others dash on across the street, toward the second gun. They are halfway across when the other gun rattles. The running men plunge as one in midstep. Their kilts whip forward and bare their pale thighs. The gun rakes across the doorway where the others are freeing the first gun of bodies. As the captain sweeps his gun down again, dust puffs from the left side of the window, his gun rings metallically, something sears along his arm and across his ribs, dust puffs from the right side of the window. He rakes the other gun again. It ceases. He continues to fire into the huddled clump about it long after the gun has ceased.

The dark earth bites into the sun's rim. The street is now all in shadow; a final level ray comes into the room, and fades. Behind him in the twilight the wounded man laughs, then his laughter sinks into a quiet contented gibberish.

Just before dark another column crosses the bridge. There is still enough light for it to be seen that these troops wear khaki and that their helmets are flat. But likely there is no one to see, because when a party mounted to the second story and found the captain propped in the window beside the cold gun, they thought that he was dead.

* * *

This time Matthew Gray saw the citation. Someone clipped it from the *Gazette* and sent it to him, and he sent it in turn to his son in the hospital, with a letter:

> . . . *Since you must go to a war we are glad that you are doing well in it. Your mother thinks that you have done your part and that you should come home. But women do not understand such things. But I myself think that it is time they stopped fighting. What is the good in the high wages when food is so high that there is profit for none save the profiteers. When a war gets to where the battles do not even prosper the people who win them, it is time to stop.*

V

In the bed next his, and later in the chair next his on the long glassed veranda, there was a subaltern. They used to talk. Or rather, the subaltern talked while Gray listened. He talked of peace, of what he would do when it was over, talking as if it were about finished, as if it would not last past Christmas.

"We'll be back out there by Christmas," Gray said.

"Gas cases? They don't send gas cases out again. They have to be cured."

"We will be cured."

"But not in time. It will be over by Christmas. It can't last another year. You don't believe me, do you? Sometimes I believe you want to go back. But it will be. It will be finished by Christmas, and then I'm off. Canada. Nothing at home for us now." He looked at the other, at the gaunt, wasted figure with almost white hair, lying with closed eyes in the fall sunlight. "You'd better come with me."

"I'll meet you in Givenchy on Christmas Day," Gray said. But he didn't. He was in the hospital on the eleventh of November, hearing the bells, and he was still there on Christmas Day, where he received a letter from home:

You can come on home now. It will not be too soon now. They will need ships worse than ever now, now that the pride and the vainglory have worn themselves out.

The medical officer greeted him cheerfully. "Dammit, stuck here, when I know a place in Devon where I could hear a nightingale, by jove." He thumped Gray's chest. "Not much: just a bit of a murmur. Give you no trouble, if you'll stop away from wars from now on. Might keep you from getting in again, though." He waited for Gray to laugh, but Gray didn't laugh. "Well, it's all finished now, damn them. Sign here, will you." Gray signed. "Forget it as quickly as it began, I hope. Well—" He extended his hand, smiling his antiseptic smile. "Cheer-O, Captain. And good luck."

*   *   *

Matthew Gray, descending the hill at seven o'clock in the morning, saw the man, the tall, hospital-colored man in city clothing and carrying a stick, and stopped.

"Alec?" he said. "Alec." They shook hands. "I could not—I did not . . ." He looked at his son, at the white hair, the waxed moustaches. "You have two ribbons now for the box, you have written." Then Matthew turned back up the hill at seven o'clock in the morning. "We'll go to your mother."

Then Alec Gray reverted for an instant. Perhaps he had not progressed as far as he thought, or perhaps he had been climbing a hill, and the return was not a reversion so much as something like an avalanche waiting the pebble, momentary though it was to be. "The shipyard, Father."

His father strode firmly on, carrying his lunchpail. " 'Twill wait," he said. "We'll go to your mother."

His mother met him at the door. Behind her he saw young Matthew, a man now, and John Wesley, and Elizabeth whom he had never seen. "You did not wear your uniform home," young Matthew said.

"No," he said. "No, I—"

"Your mother had wanted to see you in your regimentals and all," his father said.

"No," his mother said. "No! Never! Never!"

"Hush, Annie," his father said. "Being a captain now, with two ribbons now for the box. This is false modesty. Ye hae shown courage; ye should have— But 'tis of no moment: the proper uniform for a Gray is an overall and a hammer."

"Ay, sir," Alec said, who had long since found out that no man has courage but that any man may blunder blindly into valor as one stumbles into an open manhole in the street.

*　　*　　*

He did not tell his father until that night, after his mother and the children had gone to bed. "I am going back to England. I have work promised there."

"Ah," his father said. "At Bristol, perhaps? They build ships there."

The lamp glowed, touching with faint gleams the black and polished surface of the box on the mantel-shelf. There was a wind getting up, hollowing out the sky like a dark bowl, carving house and hill and headland out of dark space. " 'Twill be blowing out yon the night," his father said.

"There are other things," Alec said. "I have made friends, you see."

His father removed the iron-rimmed spectacles. "You have made friends. Officers and such, I doubt not?"

"Yes, sir."

"And friends are good to have, to sit about the hearth of nights and talk with. But beyond that, only them that love you will bear your faults. You must love a man well to put up with all his trying ways, Alec."

"But they are not that sort of friends, sir. They are . . ." He ceased. He did not look at his father. Matthew sat, slowly polishing the spectacles with his thumb. They could hear the wind. "If this fails, I'll come back to the shipyard."

His father watched him gravely, polishing the spectacles slowly. "Shipwrights are not made like that, Alec. To fear God, to do your work like it was your own hull you were putting the ribs in . . ." He moved. "We'll see what the Book will say." He replaced the glasses. On the table was a heavy, brass-bound Bible. He opened it; the words seemed to him to rise to meet him from the page. Yet he read them, aloud: ". . . *and the captains of thousands and the captains of ten thousands* . . ." A paragraph of pride. He faced his son, bowing his neck to see across the glasses. "You will go to London, then?"

"Yes, sir," Alec said.

VI

His position was waiting. It was in an office. He had already had cards made: Captain A. Gray, M.C., D.S.M., and on his return to London he joined the Officers' Association, donating to the support of the widows and orphans.

He had rooms in the proper quarter, and he would walk to and from the office, with his cards and his waxed moustaches, his sober correct clothes and his stick carried in a manner inimitable, at once jaunty and unobtrusive, giving his coppers to blind and maimed in Piccadilly, asking of them the names of their regiments. Once a month he wrote home:

I am well. Love to Jessie and Matthew and John Wesley and Elizabeth.

During that first year Jessie was married. He sent her a gift of plate, stinting himself a little to do so, drawings from his savings. He was saving, not against old age; he believed too firmly in the Empire to do that, he who had surrendered completely to the Empire like a woman, a bride. He was saving against the time when he would recross the Channel among the dead scenes of his lost and found life.

That was three years later. He was already planning to ask for leave, when one day the manager broached the subject himself. With one correct bag he went to France. But he did not bear eastward at once. He went to the Riviera; for a week he lived like a gentleman, spending his money like a gentleman, lonely, alone in that bright aviary of the svelte kept women of all Europe.

That was why those who saw him descend from the Mediterranean Express that morning in Paris said, "Here is a rich milord," and why they continued to say it in the hard-benched third-class trains, as he sat leaning forward on his stick, lip-moving the names on sheet-iron stations about the battered and waking land lying now three years quiet beneath the senseless and unbroken battalions of days.

He reached London and found what he should have known before he left. His position was gone. Conditions, the manager told him, addressing him punctiliously by his rank.

What savings he had left melted slowly: he spent the last of them on a black silk dress for his mother, with the letter:

I am well. Love to Matthew and John Wesley and Elizabeth.

He called upon his friends, upon the officers whom he had known. One, the man he knew best, gave him whisky in a comfortable room with a fire: "You aren't working now? Rotten luck. By the way, you remember Whiteby? He had a company in the —th. Nice chap: no people, though. He killed himself last week. Conditions."

"Oh. Did he? Yes. I remember him. Rotten luck."

"Yes. Rotten luck. Nice chap."

He no longer gave his pennies to the blind and the maimed in Piccadilly. He needed them for papers:

Artisans needed
Become stonemason
Men to drive motorcars. War record not necessary
Shop-assistants (must be under twenty-one)
Shipwrights needed

and at last:

Gentleman with social address and connections to meet out-of-town clients. Temporary

He got the place, and with his waxed moustaches and his correct clothes he revealed the fleshpots of the West End to Birmingham and Leeds. It was temporary.

Artisans
Carpenters
Housepainters

Winter was temporary, too. In the spring he took his waxed moustaches and his ironed clothes into Surrey, with a set of books, an encyclopedia, on commission. He sold all his things save what he stood in, and gave up his rooms in town.

He still had his stick, his waxed moustaches, his cards. Surrey, gentle, green, mild. A tight little house in a tight little garden. An oldish man in a smoking jacket puttering in a flower bed: "Good day, sir. Might I—"

The man in the smoking jacket looks up. "Go to the side, can't you? Don't come this way."

He goes to the side entrance. A slatted gate, freshly white, bearing an enameled plate:

NO HAWKERS
BEGGARS

He passes through and knocks at a tidy door smug beneath a vine. "Good day, miss. May I see the—"

"Go away. Didn't you see the sign on the gate?"

"But I—"

"Go away, or I'll call the master."

In the fall he returned to London. Perhaps he could not have said why himself. Perhaps it was beyond any saying, instinct perhaps bringing him back to be present at the instant out of all time of the manifestation, apotheosis, of his life which had died again. Anyway, he was there, still with his waxed moustaches, erect, his stick clasped beneath his left armpit, among the Household troops in brass cuirasses, on dappled geldings, and Guards in scarlet tunics, and the Church militant in stole and surplice and Prince defenders of God in humble mufti, all at attention for two minutes, listening to despair. He still had thirty shillings, and he replenished his cards: Captain A. Gray, M.C., D.S.M.

* * *

It is one of those spurious, pale days like a sickly and premature child of spring while spring itself is still weeks away. In the thin sunlight buildings fade upward into misty pinks and golds. Women wear violets pinned to their furs, appearing to bloom themselves like flowers in the languorous, treacherous air.

It is the women who look twice at the man standing against the wall at a corner: a gaunt man with white hair, and moustaches twisted into frayed points, with a bleached and frayed regimental scarf in a celluloid collar, a once-good suit now threadbare yet apparently pressed within twenty-four hours, standing against the wall with closed eyes, a dilapidated hat held bottom-up before him.

He stood there for a long time, until someone touched his arm. It was a constable. "Move along, sir. Against orders." In his hat were seven pennies and three halfpence. He bought a cake of soap and a little food.

Another anniversary came and passed; he stood again, his stick at his armpit, among the bright, silent uniforms, the quiet throng in either frank or stubborn cast-offs, with patient, bewildered faces. In his eyes now is not that hopeful resignation of a beggar, but rather that bitterness, that echo as of bitter and unheard laughter of a hunchback.

* * *

A meager fire burns on the sloping cobbles. In the fitful light the damp, fungus-grown wall of the embankment and the stone arch of the bridge loom. At the foot of the cobbled slope the invisible river clucks and gurgles with the tide.

Five figures lie about the fire, some with heads covered as though in slumber, others smoking and talking. One man sits upright, his back to the wall, his hands lying beside him; he is blind: he sleeps that way. He says that he is afraid to lie down.

"Can't you tell you are lying down, without seeing you are?" another says.

"Something might happen," the blind man says.

"What? Do you think they would give you a shell, even if it would bring back your sight?"

"They'd give him the shell, all right," a third said.

"Ow. Why don't they line us all up and put down a bloody barrage on us?"

"Was that how he lost his sight?" a fourth says. "A shell?"

"Ow. He was at Mons. A dispatch rider, on a motorbike. Tell them about it, mate."

The blind man lifts his face a little. Otherwise he does not move. He speaks in a flat voice. "She had the bit of scar on her wrist. That was how I could tell. It was me put the scar on her wrist, you might say. We was working in the shop one day. I had picked up an old engine and we was fitting it onto a bike so we could—"

"What?" the fourth says. "What's he talking about?"

"Shhhh," the first says. "Not so loud. He's talking about his girl. He had a bit of a bike shop on the Brighton Road and they were going to marry." He speaks in a low tone, his voice just under the weary, monotonous voice of the blind man. "Had their picture taken and all the day he enlisted and got his uniform. He had it with him for a while, until one day he lost it. He was fair wild. So at last we got a bit of a card about the same size of the picture. 'Here's your picture, mate,' we says. 'Hold onto it this time.' So he's still got the card. Likely he'll show it to you before he's done. So don't you let on."

"No," the other says. "I shant let on."

The blind man talks. "—got them at the hospital to write her a letter, and sure enough, here she come. I could tell her by the bit of scar on her wrist. Her voice sounded different, but then everything sounded different since. But I could tell by the scar. We would sit and hold hands, and I could touch the bit of scar inside her left wrist. In the cinema too. I would touch the scar and it would be like I—"

"The cinema?" the fourth says. "Him?"

"Yes," the other says. "She would take him to the cinema, the comedies, so he could hear them laughing."

The blind man talks. "—told me how the pictures hurt her eyes, and that she would leave me at the cinema and when it was over she would come and fetch me. So I said it was all right. And the next night it was again. And I said it was all right. And the next night I told her I wouldn't go either. I said we would stop at home, at the hospital. And then she didn't say anything for a long while. I could hear her breathing. Then she said it was all right. So after that we didn't go to the cinema. We would just sit, holding hands, and me feeling the scar now and then. We couldn't talk loud in the hospital, so we would whisper. But mostly we didn't talk. We just held hands. And that was for eight nights. I counted. Then it was the eighth night. We were sitting there, with the other hand in my hand, and me touching the scar now and then. Then on a sudden the hand jerked away. I could hear her standing up. 'Listen,' she says. 'This can't go on any longer. You will have to know sometime,' she says. And I says, 'I don't want to know but one thing. What is your name?' I says. She told me her name; one of the nurses. And she says—"

"What?" the fourth says. "What is this?"

"He told you," the first said. "It was one of the nurses in the hospital. The girl had been buggering off with another fellow and left the nurse for him to hold her hand, thinking he was fooled."

"But how did he know?" the fourth says.

"Listen," the first says.

"—'and you knew all the time,' she says, 'since the first time?' 'It was the scar,' I says. 'You've got it on the wrong wrist. You've got it on your right wrist,' I says. 'And two nights ago, I lifted up the edge of it a bit. What is it,' I says. 'Courtplaster?'" The blind man sits against the wall, his face lifted a little, his hands motionless beside him. "That's how I knew, by the scar. Thinking they could fool me, when it was me put the scar on her, you might say—"

The prone figure farthest from the fire lifts its head. "Hup," he says; "ere e comes."

The others turn as one and look toward the entrance.

"Here who comes?" the blind man says. "Is it the bobbies?"

They do not answer. They watch the man who enters: a tall man with a stick. They cease to talk, save the blind man, watching the tall man come among them. "Here who comes, mates?" the blind man says. "Mates!"

The newcomer passes them, and the fire; he does not look at them. He goes on. "Watch, now," the second says. The blind man is now leaning a little forward; his hands fumble at the ground beside him as though he were preparing to rise.

"Watch who?" he says. "What do you see?"

They do not answer. They are watching the newcomer covertly, attentively, as he disrobes and then, a white shadow, a ghostly gleam in the darkness, goes down to the water and washes himself, slapping his body hard with icy and filthy handfuls of river water. He returns to the fire; they turn their faces quickly aside, save the blind man (he still sits forward, his arms propped beside him as though on the point of rising, his wan face turned toward the sound, the movement) and one other. "Yer stones is ot, sir," this one says. "I've ad them right in the blaze."

"Thanks," the newcomer says. He still appears to be utterly oblivious of them, so they watch him again, quietly, as he spreads his sorry garments on one stone and takes a second stone from the fire and irons them. While he is dressing, the man who spoke to him goes down to the water and returns with the cake of soap which he had used. Still watching, they see the newcomer rub his fingers on the cake of soap and twist his moustaches into points.

"A bit more on the left one, sir," the man holding the soap says. The newcomer soaps his fingers and twists his left moustache again, the other man watching him, his head bent and tilted a little back, in shape and attitude and dress like a caricatured scarecrow.

"Right, now?" the newcomer says.

"Right, sir," the scarecrow says. He retreats into the darkness and returns without the cake of soap, and carrying instead the hat and the stick. The newcomer takes them. From his pocket he takes a coin and puts it into the scarecrow's hand. The scarecrow touches his cap; the newcomer is gone.

They watch him, the tall shape, the erect back, the stick, until he disappears.

"What do you see, mates?" the blind man says. "Tell a man what you see."

VII

Among the demobilized officers who emigrated from England after the Armistice was a subaltern named Walkley. He went out to Canada, where he raised wheat and prospered, both in pocket and in health. So much so that, had he been walking out of the Gare de Lyon in Paris instead of in Piccadilly Circus on this first evening (it is Christmas Eve) of his first visit home, they would have said, "Here is not only a rich milord; it is a well one."

He had been in London just long enough to outfit himself with the beginning of a wardrobe, and in his new clothes (bought of a tailor which in the old days he could not have afforded) he was enjoying himself too much to even go anywhere. So he just walked the streets, among the cheerful throngs, until suddenly he stopped dead still, staring at a face. The man had almost white hair, moustaches waxed to needle points. He wore a frayed scarf in which could be barely distinguished the colors and pattern of a regiment. His threadbare clothes were freshly ironed and he carried a stick. He was standing at the curb, and he appeared to be saying something to the people who passed, and Walkley moved suddenly forward, his hand extended. But the other man only stared at him with eyes that were perfectly dead.

"Gray," Walkley said, "don't you remember me?" The other stared at him with that dead intensity. "We were in hospital together. I went out to Canada. Don't you remember?"

"Yes," the other said. "I remember you. You are Walkley." Then he quit looking at Walkley. He moved a little aside, turning to the crowd again, his hand extended; it was only then that Walkley saw that the hand contained three or four boxes of the matches which may be bought from any tobacconist for a penny a box. "Matches? Matches, sir?" he said. "Matches? Matches?"

Walkley moved also, getting again in front of the other. "Gray—" he said.

The other looked at Walkley again, this time with a kind of restrained yet raging impatience. "Let me alone, you son of a bitch!" he said, turning immediately toward the crowd again, his hand extended. "Matches! Matches, sir!" he chanted.

Walkley moved on. He paused again, half turning, looking back at the gaunt face above the waxed moustaches. Again the other looked him full in the face, but the glance passed on, as though without recognition. Walkley went on. He walked swiftly. "My God," he said. "I think I am going to vomit."

GUNNERS' PASSAGE

.

by Irwin Shaw

"In Brazil," Whitejack was saying, "the problem was girls.
American girls."

They were lying on the comfortable cots with the mosquito
netting looped gracefully over their heads and the barracks
quiet and empty except for the two of them and shaded and
cool when you remembered that outside the full sun of Africa
stared down.

"Three months in the jungle, on rice and monkey meat."
Whitejack lit a large, long, nickel cigar and puffed deeply,
squinting up at the tin roof. "When we got to Rio, we felt we
deserved an American girl. So the Lieutenant and Johnny and
myself, we got the telephone directory of the American Embassy, and we went down the list, calling up likely names—
secretaries, typists, interpreters, filing clerks. . . ." Whitejack
grinned up at the ceiling. He had a large, sunburned, rough
face, that was broken into good looks by the white teeth of his

smile, and his speech was Southern, but not the kind of Southern that puts a Northerner's teeth on edge.

"It was the Lieutenant's idea, and by the time we got to the Q's he was ready to give up but we hit pay dirt on the S's." Slowly he blew out a long draught of cigar smoke. "Uh-uh," he said, closing his eyes reflectively. "Two months and eleven days of honey and molasses. Three tender and affectionate American girls as loving as the day is long, with their own flat. Beer in the icebox from Sunday to Sunday, steaks big enough to saddle a mule with, and nothing to do, just lie on the beach in the afternoon and go swimmin' when the mood seized yuh. On per diem."

"How were the girls?" Stais asked. "Pretty?"

"Well, Sergeant," Whitejack paused and pursed his lips with thoughtful honesty. "To tell you the truth, Sergeant, the girls the Lieutenant and Johnny Moffat had were as smart and pretty as chipmunks. Mine . . ." Once more he paused. "Ordinarily, my girl would find herself hard put to collect a man in the middle of a full division of infantry soldiers. She was small and runty and she had less curves than a rifle barrel, and she wore glasses. But from the first time she looked at me, I could see she wasn't interested in Johnny or the Lieutenant. She looked at me and behind her glasses her eyes were soft and hopeful and humble and appealing." Whitejack flicked the cigar ash off into the little tin can on his bare chest he was using as an ashtray. "Sometimes," he said slowly, "a man feels mighty small if he just thinks of himself and turns down an appeal like that. Let me tell you something, Sergeant, I was in Rio two months and eleven days and I didn't look at another woman. All those dark-brown women walkin' along the beach three-quarters out of their bathing suits, just wavin' it in front of your face. . . . I didn't look at them. This runty, skinny little thing with glasses was the most lovin' and satisfactory and decent little person a man could possibly conceive of, and a man'd just have to be hog-greedy with sex to have winked an eye at another woman." Whitejack doused his cigar, took his ashtray off his chest, rolled over on his belly, adjusted the towel properly over his bare buttocks. "Now," he said, "I'm going to get myself a little sleep. . . ."

In a moment Whitejack was snoring gently, his tough mountaineer's face tucked childishly into the crook of his arm. Outside the barracks the native boy hummed low and wild to himself as he ironed a pair of suntan trousers on the shady side of the building. From the field, two hundred yards away, again and again came the sliding roar of engines climbing or descending the afternoon sky.

Stais closed his eyes wearily. Ever since he'd got into Accra he had done nothing but sleep and lie on his cot, day-dreaming, listening to Whitejack talk.

"Hi," Whitejack had said, as Stais had come slowly into the barracks two days before, "which way you going?"

"Home," Stais had said, smiling wearily as he did every time he said it. "Going home. Which way you going?"

"Not home." Whitejack had grinned a little. "Not home at all."

Stais liked to listen to Whitejack. Whitejack talked about America, about the woods of the Blue Ridge Mountains where he had been in the forestry service, about his mother's cooking and how he had owned great dogs which had been extraordinary at finding a trail and holding it, about how they had tried hunting deer in the hills from the medium bomber, no good because of the swirling winds rising from the gorges, about pleasant indiscriminate weekend parties in the woods with his friend Johnny Moffat and the girls from the mill in the next town. . . . Stais had been away from America for nineteen months now and Whitejack's talk made his native country seem present and pleasantly real to him.

"There was a man in my town by the name of Thomas

Wolfe," Whitejack had said irrelevantly that morning. "He was a great big feller and he went away to New York to be an author. Maybe you heard of him?"

"Yes," said Stais. "I read two books of his."

"Well, I read that book of his," said Whitejack, "and the people in town were yellin' to lynch him for a while, but I read that book and he got that town down fair and proper, and when they brought him back dead I came down from the hills and I went to his funeral. There were a lot of important people from New York and over to Chapel Hill down for the funeral and it was a hot day, too, and I'd never met the feller, but I felt it was only right to go to his funeral after readin' his book. And the whole town was there, very quiet, although just five years before they were yellin' to lynch him, and it was a sad and impressive sight and I'm glad I went."

And another time, the slow deep voice rolling between sleep and dreams in the shaded heat. . . . "My mother takes a quail and bones it, then she scoops out a great big sweet potato and lays some bacon on it, then she puts the quail in and cooks it slow for three hours, bastin' it with butter all the time. . . . You got to try that some time. . . ."

"Yes," said Stais, "I will."

Stais did not have a high priority number and there seemed to be a flood of colonels surging toward America, taking all the seats on the C-54's setting out westward, so he'd had to wait. It hadn't been bad. Just to lie down, stretched full-out, unbothered, these days, was holiday enough after Greece, and anyway he didn't want to arrive home, in front of his mother, until he'd stopped looking like a tired old man. And the barracks had been empty and quiet and the chow good at the transient mess and you could get Coca-Cola and chocolate milk at the PX. The rest of the enlisted men in Whitejack's crew were young and ambitious and were out swimming all day and going to the movies or playing poker in another barracks all night, and Whitejack's talk was smooth and amusing in the periods between sleep and dreams. Whitejack was an aerial photographer and gunner in a mapping-and-survey squadron and he'd been in Alaska and Brazil and back to the States and now was on his way to India, full of conversation. He was in a Mitchell squadron and the whole squadron was supposed to be on its way together, but two of the Mitchells had crashed and burned on the take-off at Natal, as Whitejack's plane had circled the field, waiting to form up. The rest of the squadron had been held at Natal and Whitejack's plane had been sent on to Accra across the ocean, by itself.

Vaguely and slowly, lying on the warm cot, with the wild song of the Negro boy outside the window, Stais thought of the two Mitchells burning between sea and jungle three thousand miles away, and other planes burning elsewhere, and what it was going to be like sitting down in the armchair in his own house and looking across the room at his mother, and the pretty Viennese girl in Jerusalem, and the DC-3 coming down slowly, like an angel in the dusk to the rough secret pasture in the Peloponnesian hills. . . .

He fell asleep. His bones knit gently into dreams on the soft cot, with the sheets, in the quiet barracks, and he was over Athens again, with the ruins pale and shining on the hills, and the fighters boring in, and Lathrop saying, over the intercom, as they persisted in to a hundred, fifty yards twisting swiftly and shiftily in the bright Greek sky, "They grounded all the students today. They have the instructors up this afternoon. . . ." And, suddenly, and wildly, fifty feet over Ploesti, with Liberators going down into the filth in dozens, flaming. . . . Then swimming off the white beach at Bengasi with the dead boys playing in the mild, tideless swell, then the parachute pulling at every muscle in his body, then the green and forest blue of Minnesota woods and his father, fat and small, sleeping on pine needles on his Sunday off, then Athens again, Athens . . .

"I don't know what's come over the Lieutenant," a new voice was saying as Stais came out of his dream. "He passes us on the field and he just don't seem to see us."

Stais opened his eyes. Novak, a farm boy from Oklahoma, was sitting on the edge of Whitejack's bed, talking. "It has all the guys real worried." He had a high, shy, rather girlish voice. "I used to think they never came better than the Lieutenant. . . . Now . . ." Novak shrugged. "If he does see you, he snaps at you like he was General George Patton."

"Maybe," Whitejack said, "maybe seeing Lieutenant Brogan go down in Natal . . . He and Brogan were friends since they were ten years old. Like as if I saw Johnny Moffat go down . . ."

"It's not that." Novak went over to his own cot and got out his writing pad. "It began back in Miami four weeks ago. Didn't you notice it?"

"I noticed it," Whitejack said slowly.

"You ought to ask him about it." Novak started writing a letter. "You and him are good friends. After all, going into combat now, it's bad, the Lieutenant just lookin' through us when he passes us on the field. You don't think he's drunk all the time, do you?"

"He's not drunk."

"You ought to ask him."

"Maybe I will." Whitejack sat up, tying the towel around his lean middle. "Maybe I will." He looked forlornly down at his stomach. "Since I got into the Army, I've turned pig-fat. On the day I took the oath, I was twenty-eight and one-half inches around the waist. Today I'm thirty-two and three-quarters, if I'm an inch. The Army . . . Maybe I shouldn't've joined. I was in a reserved profession, and I was the sole support of an ailing mother."

"Why did you join?" Stais asked.

"Oh," Whitejack smiled at him, "you're awake. Feeling any better, Sergeant?"

"Feeling fine, thanks. Why did you join?"

"Well . . ." Whitejack rubbed the side of his jaw. "Well . . . I waited and I waited. I sat up in my cabin in the hills and I tried to avoid listenin' to the radio, and I waited and I waited, and finally I went downtown to my mother and I said, 'Ma'am, I just can't wait any longer,' and I joined up."

"When was that?" Stais asked.

"Eight days . . ." Whitejack lay down again, plumping the pillow under his head. "Eight days after Pearl Harbor."

"Sergeant," Novak said, "Sergeant Stais, you don't mind if I tell my girl you're a Greek, do you?"

"No," Stais said gravely. "I don't mind. You know, I was born in Minnesota."

"I know," said Novak, writing industriously. "But your parents came from Greece. My girl'll be very interested, your parents coming from Greece and you bombing Greece and being shot down there."

"What do you mean, your girl?" Whitejack asked. "I thought you said she was going around with a technical sergeant in Flushing, Long Island."

"That's true," Novak said apologetically. "But I still like to think of her as my girl."

"It's the ones that stay at home," said Whitejack darkly, "that get all the stripes and all the girls. My motto is: Don't write to a girl once you get out of pillow-case distance from her."

"I like to write to this girl in Flushing, Long Island," Novak said, his voice shy but stubborn. Then to Stais, "How many days were you in the hills before the Greek farmers found you?"

"Fourteen," said Stais.

"And how many of you were wounded?"

"Three. Out of seven. The others were dead."

"Maybe," Whitejack said, "he doesn't like to talk about it, Charley."

"Oh, I'm sorry." Novak looked up, his young, unlined face crossed with concern.

"That's all right," Stais said. "I don't mind."

"Did you tell them you were a Greek, too?" Novak asked.

"When one finally showed up who could speak English."

"That must be funny," Novak said reflectively. "Being a Greek, bombing Greece, not speaking the language . . . Can I tell my girl they had a radio and they radioed to Cairo . . . ?"

"It's the girl of a technical sergeant in Flushing, Long Island," Whitejack chanted. "Why don't you look facts in the face?"

"I prefer it this way," Novak said with dignity.

"I guess you can tell about the radio," Stais said. "It was pretty long ago. Three days later, the DC-3 came down through a break in the clouds. It'd been raining all the time and it just stopped for about thirty minutes at dusk and that plane came down throwin' water fifteen feet in the air. . . . We cheered, but we couldn't get up from where we were sitting, any of us, because we were too weak to stand."

"I got to write that to my girl," Novak said. "Too weak to stand."

"Then it started to rain again and the field was hip-deep in mud and when we all got into the DC-3, we couldn't get it started." Stais spoke calmly and thoughtfully, as though he were alone, reciting to himself. "We were just bogged down in that Greek mud. Then the pilot got out—he was a captain— and he looked around, with the rain coming down and all those farmers just standing there, sympathizing with him, and nothing anyone could do and he just cursed for ten minutes.

He was from San Francisco and he really knew how to curse. Then everybody started breaking branches off the trees in the woods around that pasture, even two of us who couldn't stand one hour before, and we just covered that big DC-3 complete with branches and waited for the rain to stop. We just sat in the woods and prayed no German patrols would come out in weather like that. In those three days I learned five words of Greek."

"What are they?" Novak asked.

"*Vouno,*" Stais said. "That means mountain. *Vrohi:* Rains. *Theos:* God. *Avrion:* Tomorrow. And *yassov:* That means farewell."

"*Yassov,*" Novak said. "Farewell."

"Then the sun came out and the field started to steam and nobody said anything. We just sat there, watching the water dry off the grass, then the puddles started to go here and there, then the mud to cake a little. Then we got into the DC-3 and the Greeks pushed and hauled for a while and we broke loose and got out. And those farmers just standing below waving at us, as though they were seeing us off at Grand Central Station. Ten miles farther on we went right over a German camp. They fired at us a couple of times, but they didn't come anywhere close. The best moment of my whole life was getting into that hospital bed in Cairo, Egypt. I just stood there and looked at it for a whole minute, looking at the sheets. Then I got in very slow."

"Did you ever find out what happened to those Greeks?" Novak asked.

"No," said Stais. "I guess they're still there, waiting for us to come back some day."

There was silence, broken only by the slow scratching of Novak's pen. Stais thought of the thin, dark mountain faces of the men he had last seen, fading away, waving, standing in the scrub and short silver grass of the hill pasture near the Aegean

Sea. They had been cheerful and anxious to please, and there was a look on the faces that made you feel they expected to die.

"How many missions were you on?" Novak asked.

"Twenty-one and a half," Stais said. He smiled. "I count the last one as half."

"How old are you?" Novak was obviously keeping the Technical Sergeant's girl carefully posted on all points of interest.

"Nineteen."

"You look older," said Whitejack.

"Yes," said Stais.

"A lot older."

"Yes."

"Did you shoot down any planes?" Novak peered at him shyly, his red face uncertain and embarrassed, like a little boy asking a doubtful question about girls. "Personally?"

"Two," Stais said. "Personally."

"What did you feel?"

"Why don't you leave him alone?" Whitejack said. "He's too tired to keep his eyes open, as it is."

"I felt—relieved," Stais said. He tried to think of what he'd really felt when the tracers went in and the Focke-Wolfe started to smoke like a crazy smudge pot and the German pilot fought wildly for half a second with the cowling and then didn't fight wildly any more. There was no way of telling these men, no way of remembering, in words, himself. "You'll find out," he said. "Soon enough. The sky's full of Germans."

"Japs," Whitejack said. "We're going to India."

"The sky's full of Japs."

There was silence once more, with the echo of the word "Japs" rustling thinly in the long, quiet room, over the empty rows of cots. Stais felt the old waving dizziness starting behind his eyes that the doctor in Cairo had said came from shock or starvation or exposure or all of these things, and lay back, still keeping his eyes open, as it became worse and waved more violently when he closed his eyes.

"One more question," Novak said. "Are—are guys afraid?"

"You'll be afraid," Stais said.

"Do you want to send that back to your girl in Flushing?" Whitejack asked sardonically.

"No," said Novak quietly. "I wanted that for myself."

"If you want to sleep," said Whitejack, "I'll shut this farmer up."

"Oh, no," said Stais, "I'm pleased to talk."

"If you're not careful," Whitejack said, "he'll talk about his girl in Flushing."

"I'd be pleased to hear it," said Stais.

"It's only natural I should want to talk about her," Novak said defensively. "She was the best girl I ever knew in my whole life. I'd've married her if I could."

"My motto," said Whitejack, "is never marry a girl who goes to bed with you the first time out. The chances are she isn't pure. The second time—that, of course, is different." He winked at Stais.

"I was in Flushing, Long Island, taking a five-weeks course in aerial cameras," Novak said, "and I was living at the YMCA. . . ."

"This is where I leave." Whitejack got off the bed and put on his pants.

"The YMCA was very nice. There were bathrooms for every two rooms and the food was very good," said Novak, talking earnestly to Stais, "but I must confess, I was lonely in Flushing, Long Island. . . ."

"I will be back," Whitejack was buttoning up his shirt, "for the ninth installment."

"As long as you're going out," Novak said to him, "I wish you'd talk to the Lieutenant. It really makes me feel queer passing him, and him just looking through me like I was a window pane."

"Maybe I'll talk to the Lieutenant. And leave the Sergeant alone. Remember he's a tired man who's been to the war and he needs his rest." Whitejack went out.

Novak stared after him. "There's something wrong with him, too," he said. "Just lying on his back here for ten days, reading and sleeping. He never did that before. He was the liveliest man in the United States Air Force. Seeing those two planes go down . . . It's a funny thing, you fly with fellers all over the world, over America, Brazil, Alaska; you watch them shoot porpoises and sharks in gunnery practice over the Gulf Stream, you get drunk with them, go to their weddings, talk to them over the radio with their planes maybe a hundred feet away, in the air—and after all that flying, in one minute, for no reason, two planes go down. Fourteen fellers you've been livin' with for over a year. . . ." Novak shook his head. "There was a particular friend of Whitejack's in one of those planes. Frank Sloan. Just before we left Miami, they had a big fight. Frank went off and married a girl that Whitejack's been going with off and on for a year, every time we hit Miami. Whitejack told him he was crazy, half the squadron had slept with the lady, and that was true, too, and just to teach him a lesson he'd sleep with her himself after they'd been married. And he did, too. . . ." Novak sighed. "A lot of funny things happen in the Army, when fellers've been together a long time and get to know each other real well. And then, one minute, the Mitchell goes down. I guess Whitejack must've felt sort of queer, watching Frankie burn." Novak had put his writing pad down and now he screwed the top on his fountain pen. "The truth is," he said, "I don't feel so solid myself. That's why I like to talk. Especially to you . . . You've been through it. You're young, but you've been through it. But if it's any bother to you, I'll keep quiet. . . ."

"No," said Stais, still lying back, abstractedly wondering whether the waving would get worse or better, "not at all."

"This girl in Flushing, Long Island," Novak said slowly. "It's easy for Whitejack to make fun of me. The girls fall all over themselves chasing after him; he has no real conception of what it's like to be a man like me. Not very good-looking. Not much money. Not an officer. Not humorous. Shy."

Stais couldn't help grinning. "You're going to have a tough time in India."

"I know," Novak said. "I have resigned myself to not having a girl until the armistice. How did you do with the girls in the Middle East?" he asked politely.

"There was a nice Viennese girl in Jerusalem," Stais said dreamily. "But otherwise zero. You have to be very good unless you're an officer in the Middle East."

"That's what I heard," Novak said sorrowfully. "Well, it won't be so different to me from Oklahoma. That was the nice thing about this girl in Flushing, Long Island. She saw me come into the jewelry store where she worked and . . . I was in my fatigues and I was with a very smooth feller who made a date with her for that night. But she smiled at me, and I knew if I had the guts I could ask her for a date, too. But of course I didn't. But then later that night I was sitting in my room in the YMCA and my phone rang. It was this girl. The other feller had stood her up, she said, and would I take her out." Novak smiled dimly, thinking of that tremulous moment of glory in the small hotel room far away. "I got my fatigues off in one minute and shaved and showered and I picked her up. We went to Coney Island. It was the first time in my entire life I had ever seen Coney Island. It took three and a half weeks for me to finish my course and I went out with that girl every single night. Nothing like that ever happened to me before in my life—a girl who just wanted to see me every night of the week. Then the night before I was due to leave to join my squadron she told me she had got permission to take the afternoon off and she would like to see me off if I let her. I called at the jewelry shop at noon and her boss shook my hand and she had a package under her arm and we got into the subway and we rode to New York City. Then we went into a cafeteria and had a wonderful lunch and she saw me off and gave me the package. It was Schrafft's candy, and she was crying at the gate there, crying for me, and she said she would like me to write, no matter what. . . ." Novak paused and Stais could tell that the scene at the gate, the hurrying crowds, the package of Schrafft's chocolates, the weeping young girl, were as clear as the afternoon sunlight to Novak there on the coast of Africa. "So I keep writing," Novak said. "She's written me she has a technical sergeant now, but I keep writing. I haven't seen her in a year and a half and what's a girl to do? Do you blame her?"

"No," said Stais, "I don't blame her."

"I hope I haven't bored you," Novak said.

"Not at all." Stais smiled at him. Suddenly the dizziness had gone and he could close his eyes. As he drifted down into that weird and ever-present pool of sleep in which he half-lived these days, he heard Novak say, "Now I have to write my mother."

Outside, the Negro boy sang and the planes grumbled down from the Atlantic and laboriously set out across the Sahara Desert.

Dreams again. Arabs, bundled in rags, driving camels along the perimeter of the field, outlined against the parked Liberators and waiting bombs, two Mitchells still burning on the shores of Brazil and Frank Sloan burning there and circling above him, Whitejack, who had told him he'd sleep with his wife and had, the hills around Jerusalem, gnarled, rocky, dusty, with the powdered green of olive groves set on slopes here and there, clinging against the desert wind, Mitchells slamming along the gorges of the Blue Ridge Mountains, bucking in the updraughts, their guns going, hunting deer, the Mediterranean, bluer than anything in America, below them on the way home from Italy, coming down below oxygen level, with the boys singing dirty songs over the intercom and leave in Alexandria ahead of them. The girl from Flushing, Long Island, quietly going hand in hand with Novak to Coney Island on a summer's night. . . .

It was Whitejack who awakened him. He woke slowly. It was dark outside and the electric light was shining in his eyes and Whitejack was standing over him, shaking him gently.

"I thought you'd like to know," Whitejack was saying, "your name's on the bulletin board. You're leaving tonight."

"Thanks," Stais said, dimly grateful at being shaken out of the broken and somehow sorrowful dreams.

"I took the liberty of initialing it for you, opposite your name," Whitejack said. "Save you a trip up to the field."

"Thanks," said Stais. "Very kind of you."

"Also," said Whitejack, "there's fried chicken for chow."

Stais pondered over the fried chicken. He was a little hungry, but the effort of getting up and putting on his shoes and walking the hundred yards to the mess hall had to be weighed in the balance. "Thanks. I'll just lie right here," he said. "Any news of your boys?" he asked.

"Yes," said Whitejack. "The squadron came in."

"That's good."

"All except one plane." Whitejack sat down on the end of Stais' cot. His voice was soft and expressionless, under the bright electric light. "Johnny Moffat's plane."

In all the months that Stais had been in the Air Force, on fields to which planes had failed to return, he had learned that there was nothing to say, He was only nineteen years old, but he had learned that. So he lay quiet.

"They got separated in clouds on the way out of Ascension,

and they never picked them up again. There's still a chance," Whitejack said, "that they'll drop in any minute." He looked at his watch. "Still a chance for another hour and forty minutes . . ."

There was still nothing to say, so Stais lay silent.

"Johnny Moffat," said Whitejack, "at one time looked as though he was going to marry my sister. In a way, it's a good thing he didn't. It'd be a little hard, being brothers-in-law, on some of the parties the Air Force goes on in one place and another." Whitejack fell silent, looked down at his belly. Deliberately, he let his belt out a notch. He pulled it to, with a severe little click. "That fried chicken was mighty good," he said. "You sure you want to pass it up?"

"I'm saving my appetite," Stais said, "for my mother's cooking."

"My sister," said Whitejack, "was passing fond of Johnny, and I have a feeling when he gets home from the war and settles down, she's going to snag him. She came to me right before I left and she asked me if I would let her have ten acres on the north side of my property and three acres of timber to build their house. I said it was OK with me." He was silent again, thinking of the rolling ten acres of upland meadow in North Carolina and the three tall acres of standing timber, oak and pine, from which it would be possible to build a strong country house. "There's nobody in the whole world I'd rather have living on my property than Johnny Moffat. I've known him for twenty years and I've had six fist fights with him and won them all, and been alone with him in the woods for two months at a time, and I still say that. . . ." He got up and went over to his own cot, then turned and came back. "By the way," he said softly, "this is between you and me, Sergeant."

"Sure," said Stais.

"My sister said she'd murder me for my hide and taller if I ever let Johnny know what was in store for him." He grinned a little. "Women're very confident in certain fields," he said. "And I never did tell Johnny, not even when I was so drunk I was singing 'Casey Jones' naked in the middle of the city of Tampa at three o'clock in the morning." He went over to his musette bag and got out a cigar and thoughtfully lit it. "You'd be surprised," he said, "how fond you become of nickel cigars in the Army."

"I tried smoking," said Stais. "I think I'll wait until I get a little older."

Whitejack sat heavily on his own cot. "Do you think they'll send you out to fight again?" he asked.

Stais stared up at the ceiling. "I wouldn't be surprised," he said. "There's nothing really wrong with me. I'm just tired."

Whitejack nodded, smoking slowly. "By the way," he said, "you heard us talking about the Lieutenant, didn't you?"

"Yes."

"I went out to the field and had a little conversation with him. He's just been sittin' there all day and most of the night since we got here, outside the Operations room, just lookin' and starin' across at the planes comin' in. Him and me, we've been good friends for a long time and I asked him pointblank. I said, 'Freddie,' I said, 'there's a question the boys're askin' themselves these days about you.' And he said, 'What's the matter?' And I said, 'The boys're asking if you've turned bad. You pass 'em and you don't even look at them as though you recognize 'em. What is it, you turn GI after a year?' I said. He looked at me and then he looked at the ground and he didn't say anything for maybe a minute. Then he said, 'I beg your pardon, Arnold. It never occurred to me.' Then he told me what was on his mind." Whitejack looked at his watch, almost automatically, then lifted his head again. "Ever since we got the order to go overseas he's been worrying. About the waist gunner and his navigator."

"What's he worrying about?" For a moment a crazy list of

all the thousand things you can worry about in the crew of one airplane flashed through Stais' head.

"They're not fighting men," Whitejack said slowly. "They're both good fellers, you wouldn't want better, but the Lieutenant's been watchin' 'em for a long time on the ground, in the air, at their guns, and he's convinced they won't measure. And he feels he's responsible for taking the Mitchell in and getting it out with as many of us alive as possible and he feels the waist gunner and the navigator're dangerous to have in the plane. And he's making up his mind to put in a request for two new men when we get to India, and he can't bear to think of what it'll do to the gunner and the navigator when they find out he's asked to have 'em grounded and that's why he just sits there outside Operations, not even seein us when we go by. . . ." Whitejack sighed. "He's twenty-two years old, the Lieutenant. It's a strain, something like that, for a man twenty-two years old. If you see Novak, you won't tell him anything, will you?"

"No," said Stais.

"I suppose things like this come up all the time in any army."

"All the time," said Stais.

Whitejack looked at his watch. Outside there was the growing and lapsing roar of engines that had been the constant sound of both their lives for so many months.

"Ah," said Whitejack, "they should've put me in the infantry. I can hit a rabbit at three hundred yards with a rifle; they put me in the Air Force and give me a camera . . . Well, Sergeant, I think it's about time you were movin'."

Slowly, Stais got up. He put on his shoes and put his shaving kit into his musette bag and slung it over his shoulder.

"You ready?" asked Whitejack.

"Yes," said Stais.

"That all the baggage you got—that little musette bag?"

"Yes," said Stais. "I was listed as missing, presumed dead, and they sent all my stuff into the supply room and all my personal belongings home to my mother."

Stais looked around the barracks. It shone in the harsh army light of barracks at night all over the world, by now familiar, homelike, to all the men who passed through them. He had left nothing.

They walked out into the soft, engine-filled night. A beacon flashed nervously across the sky, dimming the enormous pale twinkle of Southern stars for a moment. They walked slowly, stepping cautiously over the ditches dug for the flood rains of the African West Coast.

As they passed the Operations room, Stais saw a young lieutenant slumped down in a wobbly old wicker chair, staring out across the field.

"They come yet?" Whitejack asked.

"No," said the Lieutenant, without looking up.

Stais went into the building and into the room where they had the rubber raft and the patented radio and the cloth painted blue on one side and yellow on the other. A fat middle-aged ATC captain wearily told them about ditching procedure. There were more than thirty people in the room, all passengers on Stais' plane. There were two small, yellow Chinese who were going to be airsick and five bouncing fat Red Cross women, and three sergeants with a lot of Air Force medals, trying not to seem excited about going home, and two colonels in the Engineers, looking too old for this war. Stais only half-listened as the fat captain explained how to inflate the raft, what strings to pull, what levers to move, where to find the waterproofed Bible. . . .

Whitejack was standing outside when Stais started for his plane. He gave Stais a slip of paper. "It's my home address," he said. "After the war, just come down sometime in October and I'll take you hunting."

"Thank you very much," said Stais gravely. Over Whitejack's shoulder he saw the Lieutenant, still slumped in the wicker chair, still staring fixedly and unrelievedly out across the dark field.

Whitejack walked out to the great plane with Stais, along the oil-spattered concrete of the runway, among the Chinese and loud Red Cross women and the sergeants. They stopped, without a word, at the steps going up to the doorway of the plane and the other passengers filed past them.

They stood there, silently, with the two days of random conversation behind them and Brazil and Athens behind them, and five hundred flights behind them, and Jerusalem and Miami behind them, and the girls from Vienna and the American Embassy and Flushing, Long Island, behind them, and the Greek mountaineers behind them and Thomas Wolfe's funeral, and friends burning like torches, and dogs under treed raccoons in the Blue Ridge Mountains behind them, and a desperate twenty-two-year-old Lieutenant painfully staring across a dusty airfield for ten days behind them, and the Mediterranean and the hospital bed in Cairo and Johnny Moffat wandering that night over the Southern Atlantic, with ten acres of meadow and three acres of timber for his house, and Whitejack's sister waiting for him, all behind them. And, ahead of Stais, home and a mother who had presumed him dead and wept over his personal belongings, and ahead of Whitejack the cold bitter mountains of India and China and the tearing dead sound of the fifties and the sky full of Japs. . . .

"All right, Sergeant," the voice of the Lieutenant checking the passengers. "Get on."

Stais waved, a little broken wave, at Whitejack standing there. "See you," he said, "in North Carolina."

"Some October." Whitejack smiled a little in the light of the floodlamps.

The door closed and Stais sat down in the seat in front of the two Chinese.

"I think these planes are absolutely charming," one of the Red Cross women was saying loudly. "Don't you?"

The engines started and the big plane began to roll. Stais looked out of the window. A plane was landing. It came slowly into the light of the runway lamps and set down heavily, bumping wearily. Stais stared. It was a Mitchell. Stais sighed to himself. As the big C-54 wheeled at the head of the runway, then started clumsily down, Stais put the slip of paper with Arnold Whitejack written on it, and the address, in scrawling, childlike handwriting, into his pocket. And as he saw the Mitchell pull to a stop near the Operations room, he felt for the moment a little less guilty for going home.

A SHORT WAIT BETWEEN TRAINS

·

by Robert McLaughlin

They came into Forrest Junction at eleven-thirty in the morning. Seen from the window of their coach, it wasn't much of a town. First there were the long rows of freight cars on sidings with green-painted locomotives of the Southern Railway nosing strings of them back and forth. Then they went past the sheds of cotton ginners abutting on the tracks. There were small frame houses with weed-choked lawns enclosed by broken picket fences, a block of frame stores with dingy windows and dark interiors, a small brick-and-concrete bank, and beyond that the angled roof and thin smokestacks of a textile mill.

The station was bigger than you would expect; it was of dirty brick and had a rolling, bungalow-type roof adorned with cupolas and a sort of desperate scrollwork. The grime of thousands of trains and fifty years gave it a patina suggesting such great age that it seemed to antedate the town.

Corporal Randolph, a big, sad Negro, said, "Here we is."

Private Brown, his pink-palmed hand closed over a comic book, looked out the window. "How long we here?" he asked.

"Until one o'clock," said Randolph, getting up. "Our train west is at one o'clock."

The two other privates—Butterfield and Jerdon—were taking down their barracks bags from the rack. Other passengers bunched in the aisles—two young colored girls in slacks; a fat, bespectacled mother and her brood, with the big-eyed child in her arms staring fixedly at the soldiers; tall, spare, colored farmers in blue overalls.

As they waited for the line to move, Jerdon said, "Who dat?"

Grinning, Brown answered, "Whodatsay 'Whodat?' "

Jerdon replied in a nervous quaver, "Who dat say 'Who dat?' when I say 'Who dat?' "

They both began to laugh and some of the passengers looked at them with half-smiles and uncertain eyes.

Butterfield said, "Even the kid thinks you're nuts."

The child in the fat woman's arms looked at him sharply as he spoke, then her eyes went back to Jerdon and Brown.

"You think I'm nuts, baby?" asked Jerdon. "Is it like the man say?"

The line of passengers began to move.

"That baby don't think I'm nuts," said Jerdon. "That baby is sure a smart baby."

Their coach was up by the engine, and they descended to the platform into a cloud of released steam, with the sharp pant of the engine seemingly at their shoulders.

A motor-driven baggage truck, operated by a colored man wearing an engineer's cap, plowed through them. The three privates, with their bags slung over their shoulders, stood watching the corporal. He was checking through the papers in a large manila envelope marked "War Department, Official

Business." It contained their railway tickets and their orders to report to a camp in Arizona.

"Man," said Brown, "you better not lose anything. We don't want to stay in this place."

"This don't look like any town to me, either," said Jerdon.

Butterfield, slim, somewhat lighter in complexion, and a year or two older than the others, looked around him. "Hey," he said, "look what's up there."

The others turned. Down the platform they could see two white soldiers armed with carbines and what appeared to be a group of other white soldiers in fatigues. A crowd was forming around them.

"They're prisoners of war," said Butterfield. "You want to see some Germans, Brown? You say you're going to kill a lot of them; you want to see what they look like?"

Brown said, "That what they are?"

"Sure," said Butterfield. "See what they've got on their backs? 'PW.' That means 'prisoner of war.' "

The four soldiers moved forward. They stood on the fringe of the crowd, which was mostly white, looking at the Nazi prisoners with wide-eyed curiosity. There were twenty Germans standing in a compact group, acting rather exaggeratedly unconscious of the staring crowd. A small mound of barracks bags was in the center of the group, and the eyes of the prisoners looked above and through the crowd in quick glances at the station, the train, the seedy town beyond. They were very reserved, very quiet, and their silence put a silence on the crowd.

One of the guards spoke to a prisoner in German and the prisoner gave an order to his fellows. They formed up in a rough double column and moved off.

Little boys in the crowd ran off after them and the knot of watchers broke up.

When the four soldiers were alone again, Brown said, "They don't look like much. They don't look no different."

"What did you think they'd look like?" Butterfield asked.

"I don't know," said Brown.

"Man, you just don't know nothing," said Jerdon. "You're just plain ignorant."

"Well, what did *you* think they'd look like?" Butterfield asked Jerdon.

Jerdon shifted his feet and didn't look at Butterfield or answer him directly. "That Brown, he just don't know nothing," he repeated. He and Brown began to laugh; they were always dissolving in laughter at obscure jokes of their own.

A trainman got up on the steps of one of the coaches, moved his arm in a wide arc, the pant of the locomotive changed to a short puffing, and the train jerked forward.

The colored baggageman came trundling back in his empty truck and Corporal Randolph said to him, "They any place we can leave these bags?"

The baggageman halted. "You taking the one o'clock?"

"That's right."

"Dump them on the truck. I'll keep them for you."

Randolph said, "Any place we can eat around here?"

"No, they ain't."

"Where we have to go?"

"They ain't no place," the baggageman said, looking at them as though curious to see how they'd take it.

"Man," said Jerdon, "we're hungry. We got to eat."

"Maybe you get a handout someplace," said the baggageman, "but they sure no place for colored around here."

Butterfield said sourly, "We'll just go to the USO."

"Oh, man, that's rich," Brown said, and he and Jerdon laughed.

"They got a USO in this here town?" Jerdon asked the baggageman.

"Not for you they ain't," said the baggageman.

"Man, ain't that the truth," replied Jerdon.

Randolph said stubbornly, "We got to get something to eat."

The baggageman said, "You want to walk to Rivertown you get something. That the only place, though."

"Where's Rivertown?" Butterfield asked.

"Take the main road down past the mill. It's about three, four miles."

"Hell, man," said Jerdon, "I'm hungry now. I don't have to walk no four miles to get hungry."

"You stay hungry then," said the baggageman, and went off.

"Well, ain't this just dandy?" said Brown.

The men all looked at Corporal Randolph, who transferred the manila envelope from one hand to the other, his heavy face wearing an expression of indecision.

Butterfield said, "There's a lunchroom in the station. You go tell them they've got to feed us."

Randolph said angrily, "You heard the man. You heard him say there's no place to eat."

"You're in charge of us," Butterfield said. "You've got to find us a place to eat."

"I can't find nothing that ain't there."

"You're just afraid to go to talk to them," said Butterfield. "That's all that's the matter with you."

Brown said, "Corporal, you just let Mr. Butterfield handle this. He'll make them give us something to eat." He and Jerdon began to laugh.

"O.K.," said Butterfield. "I'll do it."

Brown and Jerdon looked at Randolph.

"My God," said Butterfield, "you even afraid to come with me while I ask them?"

"You're awful loud-talking—" Randolph began, angrily but defensively.

"You coming with me or not?" Butterfield asked.

"We're coming with you," Randolph said.

The four soldiers went into the colored section of the station and walked through it and into the passage that led to the main entrance. The lunchroom was right next to the white waiting room. The four men moved up to the door, bunching a little as though they were soldiers under fire for the first time.

Butterfield opened the screen door of the lunchroom and they followed him in. There were five or six tables and a lunch counter and, although it was around twelve, only a few diners. A cashier's desk and cigarette counter was by the door, and seated behind it was a gray-haired woman, stout and firm-chinned and wearing glasses.

Butterfield went up to her, rested his hands on the edge of the counter, and then hastily removed them.

She looked up.

Butterfield said quickly, "Is there any place we could get something to eat, Ma'am?"

She looked at him steadily, then her eyes shifted to the others, who were looking elaborately and with desperation at their shoes.

"This all of you?" asked the woman.

"Yes, Ma'am, there's just us four."

"All right," she said. "Go out to the kitchen. They'll feed you."

"Thank you, Ma'am."

Butterfield, trailed by the others, started back toward the kitchen.

"Just a minute," said the woman. "Go out and around to the back."

They turned, bumping each other a little, and went back out the door.

Brown said, when they were outside, "Mr. Butterfield, he sure do it."

"That's right," said Jerdon. "You want to look out, Corporal. That Butterfield, he'll be getting your stripes."

Butterfield and Randolph didn't answer, didn't look at each other.

In the kitchen they found a thin, aged colored man in a white apron and a young, thick-bodied colored girl, who was washing dishes.

"What you want?" asked the cook.

"Something to eat."

"Man, we're hungry," Jerdon told him. "We ain't put nothing inside us since before sun-up. Ain't that right, Brown?"

"Since before sun-up *yesterday,*" said Brown.

"The lady say you come back here?" asked the cook.

"That right."

The cook took their orders and, as he worked, asked them what camp they were from, where they were going, how long they'd been in the Army. He told them about his two sons, who were in the Engineers at Fort Belvoir.

"Labor troops," said Butterfield. "A bunch of ditch diggers and road menders."

The cook stared at him. "What the matter with you, man?"

Butterfield didn't answer. He lit a cigarette and walked to the serving window, looking out at the woman at the cashier's desk.

Brown and Jerdon went over to the girl washing dishes, and Corporal Randolph, his manila envelope under his arm, listened mournfully to the cook.

Suddenly Butterfield threw away his half-smoked cigarette and called to the others, "Come here and look at this."

"What?" said Randolph.

"You come here and see this."

They all came over, the cook, the girl, the three other soldiers.

Sitting down at the tables in the lunchroom were the twenty

German prisoners. One of their guards was at the door with his carbine slung over his shoulder, the other was talking to the cashier. The other diners were staring at the Nazis in fascination. The prisoners sat relaxed and easy at the tables, lighting cigarettes, drinking water, taking rolls from the baskets on their tables, and munching them unbuttered, their eyes incurious, their attitudes casual.

"God damn! Look at that," said Butterfield. "We don't amount to as much here as the men we're supposed to fight. Look at them, sitting there like kings, and we can't get a scrap to eat in this place without bending our knee and sneaking out to the kitchen like dogs or something."

The cook said severely, "Where you from, boy?"

"He from Trenton, New Jersey," said Brown.

Butterfield stared around at them and saw that only Randolph and the cook even knew what he was talking about and that they were both looking at him with troubled disapproval. Brown and Jerdon and the girl just didn't care. He turned and crossed the kitchen and went out the back door.

The cook said to Randolph, "I'll wrap some sandwiches for him and you give them to him on the train." He shook his head. "All the white folks around here is talking about all the nigger killing they going to do after the war. That boy, he sure to be one of them."

Randolph cracked his big knuckles unhappily. "We all sure to be one of them," he said. "The Lord better have mercy on us all."

THE MARINE

.

by Evan S. Connell

In the officers' quarters of the naval hospital at Bremerton, Washington, two men lay on adjoining beds. One was a Marine captain who had been wounded in the fighting at Guadalcanal and the other was a Navy pilot with catarrhal fever who had not yet left the United States. The pilot had expected to start for his assignment in the South Pacific on the following day, but now he was delayed by the fever and was asking the marine what it was like on the front lines.

The captain, whose legs had been amputated, did not feel like talking but had answered a number of questions out of courtesy, and now was resting with his eyes shut. He had said to the pilot that many of the men under his command were very young and that many of them were volunteers, and that for the most part they were excellent shots. Some of them, the captain said, were the finest marksmen he had ever seen, although he had put in almost twenty years as a marine and had seen more good shooting than he could begin to remember.

Many of these boys had come from small towns or from farm country and had grown up with a rifle in their hand, which was the reason they were so deadly. They had been picking Jap snipers out of trees as though they were squirrels. Often the Japs tied themselves to the trunk of a palm or into the crotch where the coconuts grew, so that if they were hit they would not fall, and when they were hit sometimes it seemed as if there was an explosion among the palm fronds as the man thrashed about. Other times an arm might be seen suddenly dangling alongside the trunk while the man's weapon dropped forty feet to the ground. Or nothing at all would happen, except that no more shots came from the tree. The captain had narrated these things with no particular interest, in a courteous and tired voice.

The pilot understood that he had been too inquisitive and he had decided not to ask any more questions. He lay with his arms folded on his chest and stared out the window at the pine trees on the hill. It had been raining since dawn but occasional great columns of light thousands of feet in height burst diagonally through the clouds and illuminated the pines or some of the battleships anchored in Puget Sound. The pilot was watching this and thinking about Guadalcanal, which he might see very soon. He felt embarrassed because the captain had talked so much and he felt to blame for this. He was embarrassed, too, about the fact that he himself would recover while the captain was permanently maimed, but there was nothing he could say about that without making it worse.

Presently the captain went on in the same tired and polite voice.

Lieutenant, he said without opening his eyes, I can tell you everything you need to know about what the war is like on Guadalcanal, although I don't know about the other islands because I was only on Guadalcanal. Listen. In my company there was a boy from southern Indiana who was the best shot I believe I ever saw. I couldn't say how many Japs he killed, but he thought he knew because he would watch where they fell and keep track of them. My guess is that he accounted for at least twenty. There were times when he would get into arguments over a body we could see lying not very far away from us in the jungle. He was jealous about them. One night I observed him crawl beyond his post, which was the perimeter of our defense, and go some distance into the jungle. The night was not very dark and I observed him crawling from one body to another. I thought he was going through their wallets and pulling the rings off their fingers. The men often did that although they were not supposed to. However, I was puzzled by what this boy was doing because he made a strange motion over several of the Jap bodies. He appeared to be doing some sort of difficult work, and when he crawled back into the camp I went over to him and lay down next to him and asked what he had been doing. He told me he had been collecting gold teeth. He carried a tobacco pouch in his pocket, which he showed me. It was half-filled with gold and he told me how much gold was selling for by the ounce in the United States. He said that if he lived long enough and got onto enough islands he expected that he would be a rich man by the time the war ended. It was not uncommon to collect teeth and I had suspected he might be doing that also, but I told him I had been watching and was puzzled by the strange movements he had made over several of the bodies. He explained that he had been cutting off their heads and what I had observed was him cutting the spinal cord and the neck muscles with his knife. I asked why he had done this, if it was just for the sake of cruelty, although the men were dead, and he seemed very much surprised by this and looked at me carefully to see why I wanted to know. "They're mine, sir," he said to me. He thought that the bodies of the men he killed belonged to him. Then he said that he did not sever a head unless the man had died face down. I didn't understand what this meant. I thought perhaps it served some purpose that I knew nothing about, relating possibly to the way animals were butchered, but his explanation was so simple and so sensible that I felt foolish not to have thought of it. He reminded me that the jungle was full of snipers and that he did not want to expose himself more than necessary. In order to get at the mouths of the men who had died face down it would have been necessary to turn them over, and he did not want to risk this. A dead man is heavy and it takes a lot of work to turn him over if you yourself are lying flat, so he had severed these heads which, by themselves, could be turned over easily. You wished to know what the war is like on Guadalcanal, Lieutenant, although as I say, it may be different on other islands.

The captain had not opened his eyes while he was talking, and having said this much he cleared his throat, moved around slightly on his bed and then lay still. The pilot decided that the captain wanted to sleep, so he too lay still on his painted iron bed and listened to the rain and gazed at the fleet anchored in the sound.

There's one other thing, the captain continued. I had not known how old the boy was, except that he was very young. I thought he might be eighteen or nineteen, or twenty at the most. It's hard to tell with some of them. They look older or younger than they are. I've seen a man of twenty-six who looked no more than eighteen. At any rate this boy soon afterward was discharged from the service because he had run away from home in order to enlist and managed to get all the way to Guadalcanal before his mother, who had been trying to locate him, discovered what had happened. He was fourteen when he was sworn in and apparently he celebrated his fifteenth birthday on the island with us, telling his buddies it was his nineteenth. But finally, as I say, it caught up with him and he was sent home. His mother, I was told, was very anxious for her son to finish high school. Perhaps he's there now.

I believe what I'm going to remember longest, the captain added in a mild voice, is the moment he stared at me while we were lying side by side. We were closer than you and I. He was young enough to be my own boy, which is a thought that occurred to me at the time, although it seems irrelevant now. Be that as it may, when I looked into his eyes I couldn't see a spark of humanity. I've often thought about this without deciding what it means or where it could lead us, but you'll be shipping out presently, as soon as your fever subsides, and will experience the war yourself. Maybe you'll come to some conclusion that has escaped me.

The captain said nothing more and when the nurse came around a few minutes later, after looking at him, she held one finger to her lips because he had gone to sleep.

YOU REACH FOR YOUR HAT

.

by James Purdy

People saw her every night on the main street. She went out
just as it was getting dark, when the street lights would pop
on, one by one, and the first bats would fly out round Mrs.
Bilderbach's. That was Jennie. Now what was she up to? everyone would ask, and we all knew, in company and out. Jennie Esmond was off for her evening walk and to renew old
acquaintances. Now don't go into details, the housewives
would say over the telephone. Ain't life dreary enough without
knowing? They all knew anyhow as in a movie they had seen
five times and where the sad part makes them cry just as much
the last showing as the first.

They couldn't say too much, though. Didn't she have the
gold star in the window, meaning Lafe was dead in the service
of his country? They couldn't say too much, and, after all,
what did Jennie do when she went out? There wasn't any proof
she went the whole hog. She only went to the Mecca, which
had been a saloon in old World War days and where no ladies

went. And, after all, she simply drank a few beers and joked with the boys. Yes, and well, once they told that she played the piano there, but it was some sort of old-fashioned number and everybody clapped politely after she stopped.

She bought all her clothes at a store run by a young Syrian. Nobody liked him or his merchandise, but he did sell cheap and he had the kind of things that went with her hair, that dead-straw color people in town called angel hair. She bought all her dresses there that last fall and summer, and they said the bargain she got them for no one would ever believe.

Then a scandalous thing. She took the gold star out of the window. What could it mean? Nobody had ever dreamed of such a thing. You would have thought anyone on such shaky ground would have left it up forever. And she took it down six months after the sad news. It must mean marriage. The little foreign man. But the janitor said nobody ever called on her except Mamie Jordan and little Blake Higgins.

She went right on with her evening promenades, window-shopping the little there was to window-shop, nodding to folks in parked cars and to old married friends going in and out of the drugstore. It wasn't right for a woman like Jennie to be always walking up and down the main street night after night and acting, really acting, as if she had no home to go to. She took on in her way as bad as the loafers had in front of the courthouse before the mayor ordered the benches carried away so they couldn't sit down. Once somebody saw her in the section around the brewery and we wondered. Of course, everyone supposed the government paid her for Lafe's death; so it wasn't as if she was destitute.

Nobody ever heard her mention Lafe, but Mamie Jordan said she had a picture of him in civilian clothes in her bedroom. He wasn't even smiling. Mamie said Jennie had had such trouble getting him to go to Mr. Hart's photography studio. It was right before his induction, and Jennie had harped on it so long that Lafe finally went, but he was so mad all the time they were taking him he never smiled once; they had to finish him just looking. Mamie said Jennie never showed any interest in the picture and even had toilet articles in front of it. No crepe on it or anything.

Mamie didn't understand it at all. Right after he was reported missing in action she went down to offer her sympathy and Jennie was sitting there eating chocolates. She had come to have a good cry with her and there she was cool as a cucumber. You'd never have known a thing had happened. It made Mamie feel so bad, because she had always liked Lafe even if he never would set the world on fire, and she had burst out crying, and then after a little while Jennie cried too and they sat there together all evening weeping and hugging each other.

But even then Jennie didn't say anything about Lafe's going really meaning anything to her. It was as though he had been gone for twenty years. An old hurt. Mamie got to thinking about it and going a little deeper into such a mystery. It came back to her that Lafe had always gone to the Mecca tavern and left Jennie at home, and now here she was out there every night of her life.

Mamie thought these things over on her way to the movie that night. No one had ever mentioned Jennie's case lately to her, and, truth to tell, people were beginning to forget who Lafe was. People don't remember anymore. When she was a girl they had remembered a dead man a little longer, but today men came and went too fast; somebody went somewhere every week, and how could you keep fresh in your memory such a big list of departed ones?

She sighed. She had hoped she would run into Jennie on her way to the movie. She walked around the courthouse and past the newspaper office and she went out of her way to go by the drygoods store in hopes she would see her, but not a sign. It was double feature night; so she knew she would never get out in time to see Jennie after the show.

But the movie excited her more than ever, and she came out feeling too nervous to go home. She walked down the main street straight north, and before she knew it she was in front of the Mecca. Some laboring men were out front and she felt absolutely humiliated. She didn't know what on earth had come over her. She looked in the window and as she did so she half expected the men to make some underhanded move or say something low-down, but they hardly looked at her. She put her hands to the glass, pressing her nose flat and peering in so that she could see clear to the back of the room.

She saw Jennie all right, alone, at one of the last tables. Almost before she knew what she was doing, she was walking through the front door. She felt herself blushing the most terrible red ever, going into a saloon where there were no tables for ladies and before dozens of coarse laboring men, who were probably laughing at her.

Jennie looked up at her, but she didn't seem surprised.

"Sit down, Mamie." She acted just as cool as if they were at her apartment.

"I walked past," Mamie explained, still standing. "I couldn't help noticing you from outside."

"Sweet of you to come in," Jennie went on. Something in the dogged, weary quality of her voice gave Mamie her chance. She brought it right out: "Jennie, is it because you miss him so that you're . . . here?"

The old friend looked up quickly. "Dear Mame," she said, laughing, "that's the first time I've heard you mention him in I don't know how long."

Jennie simply kept on looking about as if she might perhaps find an explanation for not only why she was here but for the why of anything.

"I wish you would let me help you," Mamie continued. "I

don't suppose you would come home with me. I suppose it's still early for you. I know my 'Lish always said time passed so fast with beer."

Jennie kept gazing at this frowsy old widow who was in turn gazing at her even more intently. She looked like her dead mother the way she stared.

"I understand," Mamie repeated. She was always saying something like that, but Jennie didn't weigh her friend's words very carefully. She wasn't quite sure just who Mamie was or what her friendship stood for, but she somehow accepted them both tonight and brought them close to her.

"You may as well drink. May as well be sheared for a sheep as a lamb."

"I believe I will," Mamie said, a kind of belligerence coming into her faded voice.

"Charley," Jennie called, "give Mamie some bottle beer."

The "girls" sat there laughing over it all.

The smile began to fade from Jennie's mouth. She looked at her old friend again as if trying to keep fresh in her mind that she was really sitting there, that she had come especially. Mamie had that waiting look on her face that old women always have.

The younger woman pulled the tiny creased photograph from her purse. Mamie took it avidly. Yes, it was coming, she knew. At last Jennie was going to pour herself out to her. She would know everything. At last nothing would be held back. In her excitement at the thought of the revelation to come, she took several swallows of beer. "Tell me," she kept saying. "You can tell old Mamie."

"He wasn't such a bad looker," Jennie said.

The friend leaned forward eagerly. "Lafe?" she said. "Why, Lafe was handsome, honey. Didn't you know that? He was." And she held the picture farther forward and shook her head sorrowfully but admiringly.

"If he had shaved off that little mustache, he would have been better looking. I was always after him to shave it off, but somehow he wouldn't. Well, you know, his mouth was crooked. . . ."

"Oh, don't say those things," Mamie scolded. "Not about the dead." But she immediately slapped her hand against her own mouth, closing out the last word. Oh, she hadn't meant to bring that word out! We don't use that word about loved ones.

Jennie laughed a little, the laugh an older woman might have used in correcting a small girl.

"I always wondered if it hurt him much when he died," she said. "He never was a real lively one, but he had a kind of hard, enduring quality in him that must have been hard to put out. He must have died slow and hard and knowing to the end."

Mamie didn't know exactly where to take up the thread from there. She hadn't planned for this drift in the conversation. She wanted to have a sweet memory talk and she would have liked to reach for Jennie's hand to comfort her, but she couldn't do it now the talk had taken this drift. She took another long swallow of beer. It was nasty, but it calmed one a little.

"I look at his picture every night before I climb in bed," Jennie went on. "I don't know why I do. I never loved him, you know."

"Now, Jennie, dear," she began, but her protest was scarcely heard in the big room. She had meant to come forward boldly with the "You did love him, dear," but something gray and awful entered the world for her. At that moment she didn't quite believe even in the kind of love which she had seen depicted that very night in the movies and which, she knew, was the only kind that filled the bill.

"You never loved him!" Mamie repeated the words and they

echoed dully. It was a statement which did not bear repeating; she realized that as soon as it was out of her mouth.

But Jennie went right on. "No, I never did love Lafe Esmond."

"Closing time!" Charley called out.

Mamie looked around apprehensively.

"That don't apply to us," Jennie explained. "Charley lets me stay many a night until four."

It was that call of closing time that took her back to her days at the cigar factory when fellows would wait in their cars for her after work. She got to thinking of Scott Jeffreys in his new Studebaker.

She looked down at her hands to see if they were still as lovely as he had said. She couldn't tell in the dim light, and besides, well, yes, why not say it, who cared about her hands now? Who cared about any part of her now?

"My hands were lovely once," Jennie said aloud. "My mother told me they were nearly every night and it was true. Nearly every night she would come into my bedroom and say, 'Those lovely white hands should never have to work. My little girl was meant for better things.'"

Mamie swallowed the last of the bottle and nodded her head for Jennie to go on.

"But do you think Lafe ever looked at my hands? He never looked at anybody's hands. He wasn't actually interested in woman's charm. No man really is. It only suggests the other to them, the thing they want out of us and always get. They only start off by complimenting us on our figures. Lafe wasn't interested in anything I had. And I did have a lot once. My mother knew I was beautiful."

She stopped. This was all so different from anything Mamie had come for. Yes, she had come for such a different story.

"Lafe married me because he was lonesome. That's all. If it hadn't been me it would have been some other fool. Men want a place to put up. They get the roam taken out of them and they want to light. I never loved him or anything he did to me. I only pretended when we were together.

"I was never really fond of any man from the first."

Mamie pressed her finger tightly on the glass as if begging a silent power in some way to stop her.

"I was in love with a boy in the eighth grade and that was the only time. What they call puppy love. Douglas Fleetwood was only a child. I always thought of forests and shepherds when I heard his name. He had beautiful chestnut hair. He left his shirt open winter and summer and he had brown eyes like a calf's. I never hardly spoke to him all the time I went to school. He was crippled, too, poor thing, and I could have caught up with him any day on the way home, he went so slow, but I was content to just lag behind him and watch him. I can still see his crutches moving under his arms."

Mamie was beginning to weep a little, a kind of weeping that will come from disappointment and confusion, the slow heavy controlled weeping women will give when they see their ideals go down.

"He died," Jennie said.

"When Miss Matthias announced it in home economics class that awful January day, I threw up my arms and made a kind of whistling sound, and she must have thought I was sick because she said 'Jennie, you may be excused.'

"Then there were those nice boys at the cigar factory, like I told you, but it never got to be the real thing, and then Lafe came on the scene."

Here Jennie stopped suddenly and laughed rather loudly. Charley, who was at the other end of the room, took this for some friendly comment on the lateness of the hour and waved and laughed in return.

Mamie was stealthily helping herself to some beer from Jennie's bottle.

"Drink it, Mame," she said. "I bought it for you, you old toper." Mamie wiped a tear away from her left eye.

"As I said, I was tired of the cigar factory and there was Lafe every Friday at the Green Mill dance hall. We got married after the big Thanksgiving ball."

"Why, I think I remember that," Mamie brightened. "Didn't I know you then?"

But Jennie's only answer was to pour her friend another glass.

"He went to the foundry every morning after I had got up to cook his breakfast. He wouldn't go to the restaurants like other men. I always had such an ugly kimono to get breakfast in. I was a fright. He could at least have given me a good-looking wrapper to do that morning work in. Then there I was in the house from 4:30 in the A.M. till night waiting for him to come back. I thought I'd die. I was so worn out waiting for him I couldn't be civil when he come in. I was always frying chops when he come."

She took a big drink of beer.

"Everything smelled of chops in that house. He had to have them."

Charley began again calling closing time. He said everybody had to clear the place.

"It ain't four o'clock, is it?" Mamie inquired.

"No, not yet. I don't know what come over Charley tonight. He seems to want to get rid of us early. It's only one-thirty. I suppose some good-lookin' woman is waiting for him."

Yes, the Mecca was closing. Jennie thought, then, of the places she had read about in the Sunday papers, places where pleasure joints never closed, always open night and day, where you could sit right through one evening into another, drinking and forgetting, or remembering. She heard there were places like that in New Orleans where they had this life, but mixed up with colored people and foreigners. Not classy at all and nothing a girl would want to keep in her book of memories.

And here she was all alone, unless, of course, you could count Mamie.

"I was attractive once," she went on doggedly. "Men turned around every time I went to Cincinnati."

Mamie, however, was no longer listening attentively. The story had somehow got beyond her as certain movies of a sophisticated slant sometimes did with her. She was not sure at this stage what Jennie's beauty or her lack of it had to do with her life, and her life was not at all clear to her. It seemed to her in her fumy state that Jennie had had to cook entirely too many chops for her husband and that she had needed a wrapper, but beyond that she could recall only the blasphemies against love.

"My mother would have never dreamed I would come to this lonely period. My mother always said that a good-looking woman is never lonely. 'Jennie,' she used to say, 'keep your good looks if you don't do another thing.' "

The craven inattention, however, of Mamie Jordan demanded notice. Jennie considered her case for a moment. Yes, there could be no doubt about it. Mamie was hopelessly, unbelievably drunk. And she was far from sober herself.

"Mamie Jordan," she said severely, "are you going to be all right?"

The old friend looked up. Was it the accusation of drink or the tone of cruelty in the voice that made her suddenly burst into tears? She did not know, but she sat there now weeping, loudly and disconsolately.

"Don't keep it up anymore, Jennie," she said. "You've said such awful things tonight, honey. Don't do it anymore. Leave me my little mental comforts."

Jennie stared uncomprehendingly. The sobs of the old woman vaguely filled the great empty hall of the drinking men.

It was the crying, she knew, of an old woman who wanted something that was fine, something that didn't exist. It was the crying for the idea of love like in songs and books, the love that wasn't there. She wanted to comfort her. She wanted to take her in her arms and tell her everything would be all right. But she couldn't think of anything really convincing to say on that score. She looked around anxiously as if to find the answer written on a wall, but all her eyes finally came to rest on was a puddle of spilled beer with Lafe Esmond's picture swimming in the middle.

No, you can't really feel sorry for yourself when you see yourself in another, and Jennie had had what Mamie was having now too many times, the sorrow with drink as the sick day dawned.

But the peculiar sadness evinced by Mamie's tears would not go away. The sore spot deep in the folds of the flesh refused to be deadened this time, and it was this physical pang which brought her back to Lafe. She saw him as if for a few illumined seconds almost as though she had never seen him before, as though he were existing for her for the first time. She didn't see exactly how the dead could know or Lafe could be in any other world looking down on her, and yet she felt just then that some understanding had been made at last between them.

But it was soon over, the feeling of his existing at all. Lafe wasn't coming back and nobody else was coming back to her either. If she had loved him she would have had some kind of happiness in looking at his photograph and crying like Mamie wanted her to. There would be consolation in that. Or even if they had brought him home to her so she would be able to visit the grave and go through the show and motions of grief. But what was him was already scattered so far and wide they could never go fetch any part of it back.

Clasping Mamie by the arm, then, and unfolding the handkerchief to give to her, she had the feeling that she had been to see a movie all over again and that for the second time she had wept right in the same place. There isn't anything to say about such private sorrow. You just wait till the lights go on and then reach for your hat.

DEFEAT

·

by Kay Boyle

Toward the end of June that year and through July there was a sort of uncertain pause, an undetermined suspension that might properly be called neither an armistice nor a peace, and it lasted until the men began coming back from where they were. They came at intervals, trickling in twos or threes down from the north, or even one by one; some of them having been made prisoner and escaped and others merely a part of that individual retreat in which the sole destination was home. They had exchanged their uniforms for something else as they came along, corduroys or workmen's blue or whatever people might have given them in secret to get away: bearded, singularly and shabbily outfitted men getting down from a bus or off a train without so much as a knapsack in their hands, and the same bewildered, scarcely discrepant story to tell. Once they had reached the precincts of familiarity, they stood there where the vehicle had left them a moment, maybe trying to button over the jacket that didn't fit them or set the neck or shoulders right, like men who have been waiting in a court-room and have finally heard their names called and stand up to take the oath and mount the witness stand. You could see them getting the words ready, revising the very quality of truth and the look in their eyes, and then someone coming out of the local post office or crossing the station square in the heat would recognize them and go toward them with a hand out, and the testimony would begin.

They had found their way back from different places, by different means, some on bicycle, some by bus, some over the mountains on foot, coming back to the Alps from Rennes, or from Clermont-Ferrand, or from Lyon, or from any part of France (as colloquial and incongruous to modern defeat as survivors of the Confederate army might have looked trans-planted to this year and place with their spurs on still and their soft-brimmed, dust-whitened hats, limping wanly back half dazed and not yet having managed to get straight the story of what had happened). Only this time they were the men of that tragically unarmed and undirected force which had been the French army once but was no longer, returning to what ora-tors might call reconstruction but which they knew could never be the same.

Wherever they came from, they had identical evidence to give: that the German ranks had advanced bareheaded, in short-sleeved, summer shirts—young, blond-haired men with their arms linked, row on row, and their trousers immacu-lately creased; having slept all night in hotel beds and their stomachs full, advancing singing, and falling singing before the puny coughing of the French machine guns. That is, the first line of them might fall, and part of the second possibly, but never more, for just then the French ammunition would sud-denly expire and the bright-haired, blond demigods would march on singing across their dead, and then would follow all the glittering. display: the rustproof tanks and guns, the chromiumed electric kitchens, the crematoriums. Legends or truth, the stories became indistinguishable in the mouths of the Frenchmen who returned: that the Germans were dressed as if for tennis that summer, with nothing but a tune to carry in their heads, while the French crawled out from under lorries where they'd slept that night and maybe every night for a week, coming to meet them like crippled, encumbered miners emerging from the pit of a warfare fifty years interred, with thirty-five kilos of kit and a change of shoes and a tin helmet left over from 1914 breaking them in two as they met the brilliantly nickeled Nazi dawn. They said their superiors were the first to run; they said their ammunition had been sabotaged; they said the ambulances had been transformed into accommodations for the officers' lady friends; they said: *"Nous avons été vendus,"* or, *"On nous a vendu,"* over and over until you could have made a popular song of these words and music of defeat. After their testimony was given, some of them added (not the young, but those who had fought before) in sober, part-embittered, part-vainglorious voices: "I'm ashamed to be a Frenchman," or "I'm ashamed of being French today," and then gravely took their places with the others.

There was one man at least who didn't say any of these things, probably because he had something else on his mind. He was a dark, short, rather gracefully made man, not thirty yet, with hot handsome eyes and a clefted chin. Even when he came back without his uniform and without the victory, a certain sense of responsibility, of authority, remained because he had been the chauffeur of the mail bus before the war. He didn't sit talking in the *bistrot* about what he had seen and where he had been, but he got the black beard off his face as quickly as he could, and bought a pair of new shoes, and went back to work in stubborn-lipped, youthful, almost violent pride. Except one night he did tell the story: he told it only once, about two months after he got back, and not to his own people or the people of the village but as if by chance to two commercial travelers for rival fruit-juice firms who were just beginning to circulate again from town to town in the unoccupied zone. They sat at the Café Central together, the three of them, drinking wine; the men perhaps talking about the anachronism of horse-and-mule-drawn cannon in Flanders and the beasts running amok under the enemy planes, or saying still what they had all believed: that the French line was going to hold somewhere, that it wasn't going to break in the end.

"At first we thought it would hold at the Oise," one of the traveling men was saying. "We kept on retreating, saying the new front must be at the Oise, and believing it too, and then when we dropped below the Oise, we kept saying it would hold at the Seine, and believing it; and even when we were south of Paris we kept on believing about some kind of line holding on the Loire—"

"I still don't know why we stopped retreating," said the other commercial traveler. He sat looking soberly at his glass. "We can't talk about the Italians any more. I still don't see why we didn't retreat right down to Senegal. I don't see what stopped us," he said. And the quiet-mouthed little bus driver began telling them about what happened on the Fourteenth of July.

It seems that in some of the cities the enemy hadn't taken or had withdrawn from, processions formed on the Fourteenth and passed through the streets in silence, the flagstaffs they carried draped with black, and their heads bowed. In some of the villages the mayor, dressed for mourning, laid a wreath on the monument to the last war's dead while the peasants knelt about him in the square.

"I was in Pontcharra on the Fourteenth," said one of the traveling salesmen, "and when the mayor put the wreath down and the bugle called out like that for the dead, all the peasants uncovered themselves, but the military didn't even stand at attention."

"By that time none of the privates were saluting their officers in the street anywhere you went," said the other salesman, but the bus driver didn't pay any attention to what they said. He went on telling them that he'd been taken prisoner near Rennes on the seventeenth of June, and there he saw the air tracts the Boche planes had showered down the week before. The tracts said: "Frenchmen, prepare your coffins! Frenchwomen, get out your ball dresses! We're going to dance the soles off your shoes on the Fourteenth of July!" He told the commercial travelers exactly what use they made of the tracts in the public places there. He was more than three weeks in the prison camp, and on the night of the twelfth of July he and a *copain* made their escape. They went in uniform, on borrowed bicycles. They kept to the main road all night, wheeling along as free and unmolested in the dark as two young men cycling home from a dance, with their hearts light, and the stars out over them, and the night air mild. At dawn they took to the side roads, and toward eight o'clock of the new day they saw a house standing a little in advance of the village that lay ahead.

"We'll ask there," the bus driver said, and they pushed their cycles in off the road and laid them down behind a tree. The house, they could see then, was the schoolhouse, with a sign for *filles* over one door and for *garçons* over the other. The *copain* said there would be nobody there, but the bus driver had seen the woman come to the window and look at them, and he walked up to the door.

The desks were empty because of what had happened and the time of year, but it must have been the schoolmistress who was standing in the middle of the room between the benches: a young woman with fair, wavy hair, eying them fearlessly and even sharply as they came. The bus driver and his *copain* said good morning, and they saw at once the lengths of three-colored stuff in her hands and the work she had been doing. They looked around them and saw the four French flags clustered in each corner of the classroom and the great loops of bunting that were draped along the walls. The first thing the bus driver thought was that she ought to be warned, she ought to be told, and then when he looked at her face again he knew she knew as much or more than they.

"You ought to keep the door locked," he said, and the schoolmistress looked at him almost in contempt.

"I don't care who comes in," she said, and she went on folding the bunting over in the lengths she wanted to cut it to drape across the farthest wall.

"So the village is occupied?" the bus driver said, and he jerked his head toward the window.

"Yes," she said, but she went on cutting the tricolor bunting.

"There's one thing," said the *copain,* looking a little bleakly at them. "If you give yourself up at least you don't get shot," he said.

But the schoolmistress had put her scissors down and she said to the bus driver:

"You'll have to get rid of your uniforms before there's any chance of your getting through." She glanced around the classroom as though the demands of action had suddenly made it strange to her. "Take them off and put them in the cupboard there," she said, "and cover yourselves over in this stuff while you wait," and she heaped the blue and white and red lengths up on the desks. "In case they might come in," she said. She took her hat and filet off the hook as she said: "I'll come back with other clothes for you."

"If there would be any way of getting something to eat," the bus driver said, and because he asked this the tide of courage seemed to rise even higher in her.

"Yes," she said. "I'll bring back food for you."

"And a bottle of *pinard,*" said the *copain,* but he didn't say it very loud.

When she was gone they took their uniforms off and they wrapped the bunting around them, doing it for her and modesty's sake, and then they sat down at the first form's desks, swathed to their beards in red, white, and blue. Even if the Boche had walked into the schoolhouse then, there probably wasn't any military regulation made to deal with what they would have found, the bus driver said: just two Frenchmen in their underwear sitting quietly inside the color of their country's flag. But whether he said the other thing to her as soon as she brought the bread and sausage and wine and the scraps of other men's clothing back, he didn't know. Sometimes when he thought of it afterwards he wasn't quite sure he had ever got the actual words out, but then he remembered the look on her face as she stood by the tree where the bicycles had lain and watched them pedaling toward the village just ahead, and he knew he must have said it. He knew he must have wiped the sausage grease and the wine off his mouth with the back of his hand and said: "A country isn't defeated as long as its women aren't," or "until its women are," or "as long as the women of a country aren't defeated, it doesn't matter if its army is," perhaps saying it just before they shook hands with her and cycled away.

That was the morning of the thirteenth, and they rode all day in the heat, two what-might-have-been peasants cycling slowly hour after hour across the hushed, summery, sunny land. The war was over for them; for this country the war was over. There was no sound or look of it in the meadows or the trees or grain. The war was finished, but the farmhouse they stopped at that evening would not take them in.

"Have you got your bread tickets with you?" the peasant

said, and even the white-haired sows behind his legs eyed them narrowly with greed.

"We're prisoners escaped, we've got a bit of money," the bus driver said. "We'll pay for our soup, and maybe you'll let us sleep in the loft."

"And when the Boches come in for the milk they'll shoot me and the family for having taken you in!" he said, and the bus driver stood looking at him bitterly a moment before he began to swear. When he had called him the names he wanted to, he said:

"Look here, we were soldiers—perhaps you haven't got that yet? We haven't been demobilized, we were taken prisoner, we escaped. We were fighting a little war up there."

"If you'd fought it better the Boches wouldn't have got this far," the peasant said. He said it in cunning and triumph, and then he closed the door.

They slept the night at the next farm, eating soup and bread and drinking red wine in the kitchen, and when they had paid for it they were shown up to the loft. But they were not offered the side on which the hay lay; the farmer was thinking of next winter and he told them they could lie down just as well on the boards. They slept heavily and well, and it was very light when they woke in the morning, and so that day, the day of the Fourteenth, they did not get far. By six that night they were only another hundred and thirty kilometers on, and then the *copain*'s tire went flat. But a little town stood just ahead, and they pushed their bicycles toward it through the summer evening, and down the wide-laid, treeless street that had been road a moment before and would be road again in a moment once it had passed the houses. They hadn't seen the uniform yet, but they knew the Germans must be there; even on the square in the heart of town they saw no sign. But still there was that unnatural quiet, that familiar uneasiness on the air, so they pushed their wheels through the open doors of the big garage, past the dry and padlocked gas pumps, and stood them up against the inside wall. There, in the half-security and semidark of the garage, they looked around them: twenty or more cars stood one beside the other, halted as if forever because of the lack of fluid to flow through their veins, and the little Bibendum man astride the air hose on wheels was smoking his cigar the way he would never smoke it again. Over their heads the glass panes of the roof were still painted blue; the military and staff cars parked in the shadowy silence still bore their green and khaki camouflage. The war was over, everything had stopped, and out beyond the wide-open automobile doorway they saw the dance platform that had been erected in the square, dark, heavy, leafy branches twined through the upright beams and the balustrade, and the idle people standing looking. There were no flags up, only this rather dismal atmosphere of preparation, and the bus driver and his *copain* remembered it was today.

"It's a national holiday and we haven't had a drink yet," the *copain* said. He stood there in the garage with his hands in the pockets of the trousers that didn't belong to him, staring bleakly out across the square. Even when the two German soldiers who were putting the electric wiring up in the temporary construction came into view, his face did not alter. He simply went on saying: "We haven't had the *apéritif* all day."

The bus driver took a packet of cigarettes out of his jacket pocket and put one savagely on his lip. As he lit it, he looked in hot, bitter virulence out to where the Germans were hanging the strings of bulbs among the fresh dark leaves.

"Frenchmen, prepare your coffins!" he said, and then he gave a laugh. "They've only made one mistake so far, just one," he said, and as he talked the cigarette jerked up and down in fury on his lip. "They've got the dance floor and the decorations all right, and they've probably got the music and maybe the refreshments too. So far so good," he said. "But they haven't got the partners. That's what's going to be funny. That's what's going to be really funny," he said.

He sat there in the Café Central some time in September telling it to the two commercial travelers, perhaps because he had had more to drink than usual telling them the story, or perhaps because it had been weighing heavy on his heart long enough. He told them about the dinner the garage owner gave him and his *copain:* civet and fried potatoes and salad and four kinds of cheese, and Armagnac with the coffee. He said they could scarcely get it all down, and then he opened a bottle of champagne for them. That's the kind of man the garage owner was. And during the dinner or afterwards, with the wine inside him, it seems the bus driver had said it again. He said something about as long as the women of a nation weren't defeated the rest of it didn't matter, and just as he said it the music struck up in the dance pavilion outside.

The place the garage owner offered them for the night was just above the garage itself, a species of storeroom with three windows overlooking the square. First he repaired the *copain*'s tire for him, and behind him on the wall as he worked they could read the newspaper cutting he had pinned up, perhaps in some spirit of derision. It exhorted all Frenchmen to accept quietly and without protest the new regulations concerning the circulation of private and public vehicles.

"Without protest!" said the garage owner, taking the dripping red tube out of the basin of water and pinching the leak between his finger and thumb. "I'll have to close the place up, and they ask me to do it without protest!" He stood rubbing the sandpaper gently around where the imperceptible hole in the rubber was. "We weren't ready for war and yet we declared it just the same," he said, "and now we've asked for peace and we aren't ready for that either," and when he had finished with the tire he showed them up the stairs.

"I'll keep the light off," he said, "in case it might give them the idea of coming up and having a look," but they didn't need any light, for the illumination from the dance pavilion in the square shone in through the windows and lit the rows of storage batteries and the cases of spare parts and spark plugs with an uncanny and partial brilliancy. From outside they heard the music playing: the exact waltz time and the quick, entirely martial version of swing.

"Somebody ought to tell them they're wasting their time," the bus driver said, jerking one shoulder toward the windows. He could have burst out laughing at the sight of them, some with white gloves on even, waiting out there to the strains of music for what wasn't going to come.

The garage owner shook out the potato sacks of waste on the floor and gave them the covers to lie down on, and then he took one look out the window at the square and grinned and said good night and went downstairs. The *copain* was tired and he lay down at once on the soft rags on the floor and drew a blanket up over him, but the bus driver stood awhile to the side of the window, watching the thing below. A little group of townspeople was standing around the platform where the variously colored lights hung, and the band was playing in one corner of the pavilion underneath the leaves. No one was dancing, but the German soldiers were hanging around in expectation, some standing on the steps of the platform, and some leaning on the garnished rails.

"For a little while there wasn't a woman anywhere," the bus driver told the commercial travelers. "There was this crowd of people from the town, perhaps thirty or forty of them, looking on, and maybe some others further back in the dark where you couldn't see them, but that was all," he said, and then he stopped talking.

"And then what happened?" said one of the traveling men after a moment, and the bus driver sat looking in silence at his glass.

"They had a big long table spread out with things to eat on it," he went on saying in a minute, and he didn't look up. "They had fruit tarts, it looked like, and sweet chocolate, and bottles of lemonade and beer. They had as much as you wanted of everything," he said, "and perhaps once you got near enough to start eating and drinking, then the other thing just followed naturally afterward, or that's the way I worked it out," he said. "Or maybe if you've had a dress a long time that you wanted to wear and you hadn't had the chance of putting it on and showing it off because all the men were away; I mean if you were a woman. I worked it out that maybe the time comes when you want to put it on so badly that you put it on just the same whatever's happened, or maybe if you're one kind of woman any kind of uniform looks all right to you after a certain time. The music was good, it was first class," he said, but he didn't look up. "And here was all this food spread out, and the corks popping off the bottles, and the lads in uniform great big fellows handing out chocolates to all the girls—"

The three of them sat at the table without talking for a while after the bus driver's voice had ceased, and then one of the traveling men said:

"Well, that was just one town."

"Yes, that was just one town," said the bus driver, and when he picked up his glass to drink, something as crazy as tears was standing in his eyes.

GREATER LOVE

.

by James Jones

"Here's that detail roster," Corporal Quentin Thatcher said.

"Thanks," the first sergeant said. He did not look up, or stop working.

"Would you do me a favor?"

"Probably not," the First said. He went on working.

"I wish you wouldn't send Shelb down to the beach on this unloading detail. They've been bombing the Slot three or four times every day since the new convoy got in."

"Pfc Shelby Thatcher," the First said distinctly, without stopping working, "just because he's the kid brother of the compny clerk, does not rate no special privileges in my outfit. The 2nd Platoon is due for detail by the roster; you typed it out. Pfc Shelby Thatcher is in the 2nd Platoon."

"So is Houghlan in the 2nd Platoon. But I notice he never pulls any these details."

"Houghlan is the Compny Commander's dog robber."

"I know it."

"See the chaplain, kid," the First said, looking up for the first time. His wild eyes burned the skin of Quentin Thatcher's face. "That ain't my department."

"I thought maybe you would do it as a favor."

"What are you going to do when we really get into *com*bat, kid? up there on the *line?*"

"I'm going to be in the 2nd Platoon," Quentin said. "Where I can look out for my brother Shelb."

"Not unless I say so, you ain't." The First grinned at him evilly. "And I ain't saying so." He stared at Quentin a moment with those wild old soldier's eyes. Then he jerked his head toward the typing table across the mud floor of the tent. "Now get the hell back to work and don't bother me. I'm busy."

"Damn you," Quentin said deliberately. "Damn you to hell. You don't even know what it is, to love somebody."

"For two cents I'd send you back to straight duty today," the First said calmly, "and see how you like it. Only I'm afraid it would kill you."

"That suits me fine," Quentin said. He reached in his pocket and tossed two pennies onto the field desk. "I quit."

"You can't quit," the First grinned malevolently. "I won't let you. You're an ass, Thatcher, but you can type and I need a clerk."

"Find another one."

"After I spent all this time training you? Anyway, there ain't a platoon sergeant in the compny would have you. And I still got hopes maybe someday you'll make a soldier. Though I wouldn't know the hell why. Now get the hell out of here and take them papers over to the supply room like I told you, before I throw you over there with them bodily."

"I'm going. But you don't scare me a bit. And the last thing on this earth I'd ever want to be is a soldier."

The First laughed. Quentin took his own sweet time collecting the papers. The two pennies, lying on the field desk, he ignored.

*　　*　　*

The pennies were still there the next morning when Quentin came out of the orderly tent for a break. He watched the First legging it off down the road toward Regiment, then he walked across to where the four men were sitting on water cans in the tracky mud in front of the supply tent like four sad crows on a fence. They had only got back from the detail an hour before.

"Any news yet?" his brother Shelb asked him.

"Not a bit," Quentin said. "Nothing."

The waiting was beginning to get into all of them. The division had been here a month now, and both the 35th and 161st had gone up to relieve Marine outfits on the hills two weeks ago.

"Where was the first sergeant going, Quentin?" Al Zwermann asked hopefully. "He looked like he was in a hurry." Al Zwermann's brother Vic was in C Company of the 35th.

"Just to Regiment," Quentin said. "See about some kind of a detail."

"Not another detail!" Gorman growled.

"Sure. Ain't you heard?" Joe Martuscelli said sourly. "They done transferred the whole Regiment into the Quartermaster."

"You don't think it might be the order to move, then?" Zwermann asked.

"Not from what I heard over the phone. From what he said over the phone it was just another detail of some kind."

"A fine clerk," Gorman growled. "Why the hell dint you ask him what kind of a detail, you jerk?"

"Go to hell," Quentin said. "Why the hell didn't you ask him? You don't ask that man things."

"How'd the unloading go?"

"The unloading went fine," Shelb grinned. "They only bombed twice, and I stole a full fifth of bourbon off an officer's orderly on one of the transports."

"Yeah," Martuscelli said sourly. "A full fifth. And he has to save it all for his precious big brother."

"You think you'll have time to help drink it, Quent?" Shelb said, getting up, "before the First gets back?"

"Sometimes I don't think we'll any of us ever get to see any action," Gorman growled.

"To hell with the First," Quentin said.

"I'll go get it then," Shelb grinned.

"A hell of a fine way to treat your own squad," Martuscelli said sourly, watching him leave.

"I took a bust from corpul to transfer into this outfit," Gorman growled. "Because it was shipping out. They put me in Cannon Company and I took another bust from pfc to get in a rifle compny. All because I wanted to see action."

"We all enlisted," Martuscelli said sourly.

"All I ask is they give me a rifle," Gorman growled. "None of your 155s for this soldier. Just a rifle, a bayonet and a knife. That's all. Gimme that and I'm ready." He thought a second, then added inconclusively, "Maybe couple grenades."

"You talk like my brother Vic," Zwermann said.

Somebody grunted. On the road that had not been a road a month ago a couple of jeeps hammered by, fighting the mud that came clear up to their belly plates. From where the men sat, the rows of coconut trees wheeled away in every direction like spokes from a hub. The sun was bright and clear in the sea air under the tall trees of the grove. It was a fine summery morning. Whenever the wind veered you could hear the sound of the firing from back in the hills.

"Vic's up there now," Zwermann said wonderingly.

"Well, when do we go up," Quentin said suddenly, committing himself, "I'm putting in for straight duty. With the 2nd Platoon. Soon's we get our orders to move."

"What the hell for?" Gorman asked, startled.

"Because I want to," Quentin said.

"If you do, you're nuts," Martuscelli said sourly.

"Ha," Gorman growled. "He won't. You know where he'll be when we go in, don't you? He'll be sitting under a hill on the first sarnt's lap punching his typewriter. That's where."

"You think so?" Quentin said.

"I know so. You don't think the First is going to let his protégé get where it's dangerous, do you?"

"I'm putting in to the Company Commander," Quentin said. "Not to the first sergeant."

"So what, clerk? You think that'll make any difference?"

"Don't worry about the clerks," Quentin said. "There's a lot things you don't know about soldiering, too."

"What do you want to do it for, Quentin?" Zwermann said.

"Oh, a lot of things," Quentin said vaguely, "but mainly so I'll be able to look after Shelb."

"I'm glad my brother's in Africa," Martuscelli said sourly.

"I'm gladder yet," Gorman growled. "I ain't got one."

"Vic can take care of himself," Zwermann said. "Better than me." He was looking away from them.

"In a war," Gorman growled, *"every* man's got to take care of himself. That's my philosophy."

"That's a hell of a thing to say!" Quentin said. Then he began to laugh, feeling a wild need to do something—he didn't know what—and there was nothing to do.

"What're you laughing at, clerk?" Gorman said stiffly.

"Because," Quentin said, stopping himself. "I'm laughing because here comes Shelb with the bottle, and here comes the First back from Regiment just in time to spoil everything."

"What'll I do with it?" Shelb said.

"Well, don't just stand there," Martuscelli said savagely. "Hide the damn' thing." He grabbed the bottle desperately and stuck it down between two of the stacked water cans.

"If he finds it," Gorman said bitterly, "I know where it'll go."

"Thatcher!" the First bellowed. He was raging.

"Yes, sir," Shelb said resignedly.

"Not you," the First raged, "damn it."

"What do you want?" Quentin said.

"Go down and get Sergeant Merdith. Tell him to get his men together and report to me. The 2nd Platoon is going out on a detail."

There was a dull pause of adjustment.

"But hell, First," Martuscelli protested. "We just now got back from one."

* * *

The First said, "And you're just now going out on another one. Ain't you heard? There's a war on. The 1st and 3rd Platoons and the Weapons Platoon already out. Who you think I'm going to send? the cook force?"

"What kind of a detail is it, Sergeant?" Zwermann asked.

"How the hell do I know! You think they tell me anything? All they tell me is how many men. And how soon." He ran his fingernails through his hair. "You're going up in the hills," he said, "with a shavetail from the Graves Registration Corps. You're going up to dig up casualties and carry them down to the graveyard so the Quatermaster Salvage can come in and clean up."

"That's great," Martuscelli said.

"Well," the First raged, "what the hell're you waiting for, Thatcher? Get a move on. The truck's on its way."

"Sergeant," Quentin said, "I'd like to have permission to go along on this detail."

"What do you think this is, Thatcher? A vacation resort? There's work to be done."

"I've done everything you had laid out for me."

The First looked at him shrewdly. "Okay," he said. "Go. *Now get the hell down there and get Sergeant Merdith.*"

"Right," Quentin said, and took off.

Behind him, he heard the First say, "The rest of you men can wait here. But first, Martuscelli, I want that bottle. Maybe it'll teach you not to be so slow the next time. You men know better than to have whisky in camp. It's against Army Regulations."

There were four trucks with the GRC second lieutenant. The detail rode in the first two. They wound away down through the endless coconut grove, breasting the mud like swimmers, the two empty trucks lumbering along behind.

"I always wondered how they got them down to the cemetery," Martuscelli said.

"Well, now you know," Gorman growled.

It took them an hour to get through the belt of jungle in low gear. Then they came up out of it into the hills like submarines surfacing and ground on for another hour up the hills before they stopped at one that had a crumbling line of slit trenches along the rearward slope.

"Okay, everybody out," the GRC lieutenant said briskly, climbing out of the cab of the first truck. "Each man get a shovel."

The drivers dropped the tailgates and the detail clambered down and went immediately to the lip of the hill. Beyond the crest was a wide saddle that led up to the next hill. The saddle was littered with all kinds of equipment—packs, entrenching tools, helmets, rifles, bayonets, abandoned stretchers, even stray shoes and empty C ration cans. It gave the impression that everyone had suddenly dropped everything in a mad rush to cover ground.

"If any of you are interested in tactics," the GRC lieutenant said, pointing to a faint haze of smoke three miles to the east, "that's the present line of the 35th Infantry over there. Three days ago the 35th was here, and jumped off across this saddle."

The men looked at the distant hills, then at the far-off line of smoke from which sporadic sounds of firing came faintly, then at the saddle below them. There were a few half-muttered comments.

"Okay, fellows," the GRC lieutenant said briskly. "First, I want to warn you about duds and unexploded grenades. Don't touch them. There's nothing to worry about as long as nobody gets wise, but the Ordnance hasn't been in here yet.

"Now," he said. "I want you to spread out. We're only covering the saddle today. Make a line and whenever you see a grave, stop. Some of them, as you see, are marked with bayoneted rifles stuck in the ground. Others are marked with just helmets on sticks. Still others aren't marked at all, so be watchful. We don't want to miss any.

"If there are dog tags on them, make sure one is fastened securely to them and give the other to me. If there's only one, leave it on them, and come get me and I'll note the information. If there's no dog tags, just forget it.

"It's best to work in threes or fours. Two men can't handle one very well, as advanced as the decomposition is by now. And there's no rush, men. We've got all day to cover the area and we want to do a good job. Someday after the war they'll be shipped home to their families.

"There are shelter-halfs to roll them in in the last two trucks. The best way is to work shovels in under the head, the knees and the buttocks; that's why it's best for three to work together on one; and then roll them up out of the hole with one concerted movement onto the shelter-half which you have already placed alongside. That way you don't get any on you, and you also keep them from coming apart as much as possible.

"Now. Any questions?" the GRC lieutenant said briskly. "No? Okay then, let's go to work," he said, and he sat down on the running board of the first truck and lighted a cigarette.

The line spread out and moved forward down the crest out onto the saddle and began breaking up into little huddles of moving shovels from which there began to come strained exclamations followed by weak laughter and curses.

As each mound was opened, the smell, strange and alien as the smell of the jungle, burst up out of it like a miniature explosion and then fell heavily back to spread like mercury until it met and joined the explosions from other mounds to form a thick carpet over the whole saddle that finally overflowed and began to drip down into the jungled valleys.

"Just like a treasure hunt back home in the Y.M.C.A.," Martuscelli muttered sourly, sweating heavily.

"You don't reckon I'll ever look like that, do you?" Gorman growled, grinning.

"If you do," Shelb said, "I won't speak to you."

"What his best friends wouldn't tell him," Quentin laughed wildly.

"Well, I hope you're happy now, clerk," Gorman growled. "You finally got to come along and find out what straight duty in a rifle company's like. You still putting in for it?"

"Sure," Quentin said. "Wouldn't miss it."

Al Zwermann, of them all, was the only one who did not say anything, but nobody noticed. They were all too busy trying to carry off the collective fantasy that they were unmoved.

It was Quentin's turn to feel for the tags at the sixth mound, and when he brought them out and cut one off and read it he was somehow not surprised at all. The tag read:

ZWERMANN VICTOR L
12120653 T43 B

and Quentin put it in the handkerchief with the other five and straightened up and wiped his hand off and heard his voice saying toughly, "Well, let's get him out."

"Let me see that tag, will you, Quentin?" Zwermann said.

"What tag?" he heard his voice say. "This one?"

"I've seen all the others. Let me see that one."

"I don't even know which one it was, now, Al."

"Quentin, let me see that tag!"

Shelb, Martuscelli and Gorman were still standing at the head, knees and buttocks with their shovels. They had all known Vic back at Schofield, and Vic's battalion of the 35th had come over on the same transport with them. Quentin noticed there was an odd, distant look on all their faces except Zwermann's and it made him think of those slugs in the garden with their eyes on the ends of two horns and when they got scared or worried they pulled in the horns.

"Well," Martuscelli said with a voice that had been pulled in along with the horns, "we might as well get him out of there."

"Don't touch him," Zwermann said, still holding the tag.

"But, Al," Quentin said, "we got to get him out of there, Al. We can't leave him there," he said reasonably. "That's against orders."

"I said don't touch him, damn you!" Zwermann yelled. He picked up one of the shovels and started for Martuscelli and Gorman and Shelb, who were still holding theirs and standing all together like three hens in the rain. "You're not going to put any shovels on *him*, damn you!"

They let go of their shovels and stepped back guiltily, still all together like three hens in the rain. Zwermann stopped and brandished the shovel at them and then flung it over the edge of the saddle into the jungle.

"Nobody's going to touch *him* with shovels!" he yelled.

* * *

The four of them backed off slowly, back up the saddle toward the hill where the GRC lieutenant and Sergeant Merdith were watching. The men working at the other mounds near them began to back off placatingly in the same way, still holding their shovels, collecting the men at the further mounds as they moved, until the whole line that had descended into the saddle was slowly backing up out of the saddle.

"Nobody's going to touch *him!* I'll shoot the first man that touches *him!* Nobody's going to see *him!*"

The line went on backing placatingly out of the saddle, and Zwermann stood holding them off as if at gun point and cursing, his bald head shining in the afternoon sun.

"My Lord," the GRC lieutenant said dismally, when they were hidden behind the number one truck. "I wouldn't've had this happen for anything. What do you suppose he's going to do?"

They stood, milling a little like nervous sheep, listening to Zwermann moving around down on the saddle. Then they heard him staggering up the slope to the number two truck, where he dropped something heavily onto the iron floor and then clambered in. Then there was silence. It was Sergeant Merdith who finally peered over the hood.

Zwermann was sitting on the bench of the truck, glaring out at them. He had gotten his brother out of the hole by himself and wrapped him up in the shelter-half and carried him up and put him instinctively, without thinking, in the same truck he himself had ridden out in.

"Let's just leave him alone," the GRC lieutenant said. "He'll be all right now."

Sheepishly they straggled back down onto the saddle and went back to work. When they had the rest of the corpses wrapped and stacked in the two empty trucks, as many men as could squeezed into the first truck. Only an unlucky handful rode home in the second truck. Zwermann sat on the bench, holding a shovel, and glared at them forbiddingly all the way down.

At the cemetery on the Point there was a moment of unpleasant suspense when the handful of GRC men, who had taken over with the swift efficiency of long practice, prepared to unload the number two truck. But Zwermann only glared at them with a kind of inarticulate fury and seemed to feel he had relieved himself of some obscure obligation and did not protest. He climbed down and started off to walk the mile and a half back to the bivouac.

"Somebody better go with him," the GRC lieutenant said apprehensively. "He's liable to wander off in the jungle or something. I'm still responsible for you men till I deliver you back to your outfit."

"We'll go," Quentin said, "the four of us. We're sort of his buddies."

"Then you're responsible for him, Corporal," the GRC lieutenant said after them. "You and these other men."

When they caught up to him, Zwermann glared at them with the ferocious suspicion of a man who has learned not to trust strangers. But he did not protest their walking behind him.

That night, instead of waiting till they got marching orders, Quentin Thatcher put in to the Company Commander personally to go back to straight duty with the 2nd Platoon immediately. His request was immediately rejected, emphatically and with finality.

* * *

Five days later the Regiment moved out, and Quentin marched with the Company Headquarters at the head of the company column beside the First, who carried a Listerine bottle full of whisky and took frequent gargles for his sore throat without offering Quentin any for his. The 2nd Platoon was somewhere in the rear.

Their battalion hiked seven miles the first day and bivouacked that night in the jungle, dead beat. The next day they crossed an Engineers' bridge and started up a steep hill that rose abruptly up out of the jungle from the riverbank. The noise of the firing did not sound any closer than it had back down on the beach.

Then they came up over the crest of the hill and found themselves in combat. The noise that had sounded faint in the jungle beat about their ears and fell upon them with both drumming fists. It seemed a little unfair for no one to have warned them.

The hilltop was alive with men, but none of them noticed the new arrivals except to curse them for being in the way. The men cursed one another ferociously and ran back and forth, with boxes of ammo and C rations. Over on the next hill the men in Quentin's battalion could see the little black figures of the 3rd Battalion toiling doggedly up the slope toward other little black figures at the top.

Their first reaction was to tiptoe back down the hill and get the hell out of the way before they disturbed somebody or were run over: or at least to go back down and come up properly this time, in squad column with scouts out. They stood around awkwardly, trying to see, waiting for someone to tell them what they were supposed to do, feeling like poor relations at the family reunion.

Quentin found himself standing beside Fred Beeson, the supply sergeant, who had insisted on coming to see the fun.

"I thought they'd have a better system of supply than this in combat," Beeson said excitedly. "Didn't you?"

"Yeah," Quentin said, wondering what had become of the First. He looked around to see if he could see Shelb. His eyes found the First, over on the right. The big man was kneeling over some cases of grenades and hacking at them with his bayonet as if he were using a machete, deftly splitting box after box open around the middle.

"Hey, hey! let's go!" the First, who still had his Listerine bottle, whooped, drunkenly happy. "Let's go, let's go. Here's grenades. Who wants grenades?" he hollered, pulling the black containers out of the racked boxes and forward-passing them like footballs at arms raised out of the crowd.

"Let's go, you men!" he roared at them. "What the hell you guys waiting for?"

"Yeah," somebody said indecisively, "what we waiting for?"

They started fixing bayonets, as if each man had thought of it first, individually by himself, and then they were walking down the hill with the Company Commander in the lead, as if that were the most nearly normal thing to do, under the circumstances.

"Get your eggs here!" the First howled at them happily as they passed. "Nice fresh yard eggs!"

Quentin found himself in motion between the mess sergeant and two of the cooks. They had also come along to see the fun. Wondering again where Shelb was, he looked around and discovered he was surrounded by fun-seeking members of the cook force.

"This is better'n slingin' hash any day," one of them grinned at him excitedly.

"Yeah," Quentin said. *We're in combat,* he thought; and then repeated it: *we're in combat.* Was this all there was to it?

Ahead of them the hill sloped down, long and gradual and quite bare, to a brushy creek at the bottom. Ahead was the steep hill where the black figures of the 3rd Battalion were still toiling doggedly, but closer to the top now.

* * *

As Quentin watched them, he saw one marionette at the top throw something down at another marionette below him. The second marionette turned without hesitation and jumped out from the side of the hill as a man jumps out from a ladder. He fell maybe seven yards before he hit again and began to roll. From where he had jumped something burst black like a cannon cracker. The second marionette stopped rolling and got up and began to toil doggedly back up toward the top again. The first marionette had disappeared over the crest.

Then Quentin's company was at the bottom, fighting through the brush and starting up the slope, and Quentin could not see the men at the top any more.

Mortar shells were beginning to drop down here and there around Quentin's company, and that was when Quentin noticed that the explosions did not make any noise. Men around him were beginning to shuck out of their combat packs and leave them where they fell.

Quentin shucked out of his own pack, wishing momentarily that he knew where Shelb was. He looked around.

He could not see Shelb, but way off to the left he saw Gorman a second, climbing doggedly. Then somebody came between. Gorman had no pack. Gorman's face looked peculiar, as if somebody had poulticed it with plastic wood. The heel.

The silent mortar shell explosions were getting thicker, and the 3rd Battalion was puffing hard and digging holes along the military crest, in the shelter of the real crest of the hill. As the uneven line passed through between the holes on toward the real crest, the diggers glared up at them furiously without stopping digging. Then Quentin's company was over the crest and going down the second hill toward the jungle that came halfway up, only this time there was nobody in front of them and everything changed weirdly and seemed to shift its gears. Quentin felt as if a light bulb had been turned off in his mind. He was all alone in the silence of the dark locked closet.

He was also getting very tired.

Two strangers who were walking beside him on his left suddenly quit and lay down to rest. Quentin closed over automatically, wishing he had guts enough to quit and lay down to rest. That Gorman. Quentin's legs ached, and a dull rage began to grow in him at this obvious laziness that would only leave more dirty work for him and Shelb to do.

A mortar shell burst silently in front of him and he saw three more strange men he did not know lie down to rest. Quentin felt like kicking them, but he closed over further left and went around. Smoke burned his eyes. One of the strangers yelled something at him. The other two strangers were asleep already. Quentin went on. There sure were a lot of strangers with the company today.

It was when he closed over that he saw Shelb for the first time since at breakfast. Shelb was walking with Joe Martuscelli and Al Zwermann and Gorman, off to Quentin's left. Quentin had difficulty telling them apart; they all four seemed to be wearing the same poulticed face. As he opened his mouth to yell at them through the silence, a mortar shell geysered silently in front of them and three of them jerked, and lay down to rest. Only Shelb went on walking.

Quentin was outraged. *Who do they think they are? They're no better than I am. Or Shelb is. Is everybody going to quit but me and Shelb?*

Joe Martuscelli sat back up and looked at Quentin dully. Shakily, he got to his feet with his rifle, holding his left arm close in to his side, and started on.

Sure, Quentin thought furiously, *that damn' Martuscelli, he always was a goldbrick. Looks like me and Shelb will have to do it all.*

Then Shelby, who had moved perhaps ten yards, dropped his rifle and put his hands to his face and fell down.

Why, damn him! Quentin thought outragedly. *I thought at least he would stick with me. What do they want me to do? win this war all by myself?*

Shelb did not move and Martuscelli stumbled past him and went on. Shelb lay as he had fallen, face down and shoulders limp, his lax hands still up by his face.

Well, I'm damned, Quentin thought disgustedly, *if he hasn't fainted dead away.* Embarrassment for his brother made him suddenly hate him for failing in the clutch. *Gone yellow. Can't take it. Ought to go and kick him up.*

"Hey!" the man on his right said. "There's one. I see one."

"Where?" Quentin said.

"There," the man said. "Right there. See him?"

"No," Quentin said. The man was a big man and right beside him but his voice came from a long way off.

"Well, I see him," the big man said. He raised his rifle and fired the whole clip into the jungle. "Must of missed him," he said. "Come on."

"Okay," Quentin said. Then he stopped. Fifteen yards away on the edge of the jungle was a dark blob of wood on the side of a tree. Somehow his eyes had fastened themselves upon it and recognized it for a helmet. He was astounded.

"What is it?" the man beside him said.

"Shh," Quentin said craftily. He dropped down to a kneeling position. No shooting from the offhand this time; he was taking no chances. The big man beside him stopped, trying to see what it was, and Quentin chuckled to himself.

As he took up the slack and started the squeeze, the helmet moved. Slowly and carefully it raised itself and a face appeared over his sights. Quentin was astonished. He touched her off and in firing was even more astonished to see the same plastic-wood poultice on this face, too.

Ha, he's afraid, he thought savagely; and all the hate and fear of the past two hours compressed itself into his forefinger vindictively.

The recoil slammed his shoulder and he kept both eyes open like he had been taught and saw the face open redly like a thrown tomato. A piece of bridgework popped out of the mouth.

"I got him!" Quentin yelled. "I got him!"

"Good work," the big man said. "Congratulations."

"Come on!" Quentin said. He jumped up to run to the tree. A mortar shell, a ninety, burst close by and slammed him right back down. He lay there stunned by the concussion, reminded that there were other Japanese. He had forgotten the war.

"Come on," the big man beside him said. "Get up. You ain't hurt. Get up!" A big hand grabbed Quentin by the shoulder and hoisted him back up.

* * *

His chin was bleeding from a cut where it had hit a rock but it did not seem important. He wiped it off and started to walk on toward the jungle. The big man stayed close beside him. All around them groups of men were entering the jungle.

The dead Japanese lay sprawled out on his back. The bullet had gone in just below his nose and smashed the teeth. Thick gluelike blood had filled the mouth and run out at both corners to hang in strings down to the ground.

"He looks awful dead," Quentin said, looking at the other man. Slowly, he recognized him; it was the First. But his face looked different.

"Your face looks different," Quentin said.

"So does yours," the First said.

"It does?" Quentin said. He felt of his face. "I need a shave," he said. He picked up the piece of bridgework that had popped out of the Jap's mouth and stuck it between his helmet and the liner strap and struck a pose for the First.

"The immortal infantryman," the First said. "How about his wallet?"

"I forgot!"

Quentin fished it out of the grimy shirt pocket. There was a picture. It showed a Japanese woman holding a baby and smiling toothily. There was Japanese writing in up-and-down lines on the back. There was no money.

"Tough luck," the First grinned.

"Mine by right of conquest," Quentin said. "I guess you won't be so damn' wise about clerks now, will you?"

"Nope," the First said. "I guess not."

"You and Gorman."

"Want a little drink?" the First said.

"Sure," Quentin said. The rifle fire was getting heavier down below in the jungle. He wiped his mouth. "Hear that? Come on." He turned down toward the firing, then turned back. "Did you see that damn Shelb poop out back there on the hill?"

"No," the First said. "I didn't see him."

"He was right beside us."

"I didn't see him," the First said, impassively. "I saw a lot a guys get hit though."

"You don't have to kid me," Quentin said. "I know you saw him. Wait'll I get my hands on him! I'll beat his damned head in!" He moved away between the trees down the hill toward the firing, looking for more Japs to kill.

"He'll never make a soldier. Come on, First, let's go," he said eagerly to the man moving slowly behind him. "Come on, damn it, let's go."

"I'm coming," the First said, watching up in the trees. "Go ahead. I'm right beside you. Go ahead, you're doing fine."

"He ought to be shot," Quentin said.

"Watch the trees," the First said. "You're doing fine."

ZONE OF INTERIOR

·

by James Ross

I still remember the afternoon, late in September, 1945, when
Lieutenant Bell, the adjutant, found his travel orders in the
mail that had been lying unopened on his desk all day.

"I've made it!" he said, and he let out a whoop that woke up
everybody in headquarters office.

We crowded around his desk. The magic paper was made
out in triplicate, and advised that the lieutenant proceed to
Antwerp for immediate return to the Zone of Interior, an
Army term for the United States.

Then the lieutenant shook hands all around, put on his cap,
and headed for the bar at the Hotel des Ardennes. He was the
first officer from our outfit to make it home on points.

It was half past four by then, so we knocked off work. Corporal Peters, charge of quarters for the night, went outside and
took the flag down. He brought it inside and came on over to
my desk.

"Hold the end of it there, and I'll show you how to make George Washington's hat," Corporal Peters said.

Just then the door at the back swung open and Master Sergeant Fat Otis came into the room. He was puffing a little from climbing the stairs.

"Say, Jordan, where's my jeep?" he called to the motor sergeant.

"Major Dort borrowed it," Jordan said. "Promised he'd have it back by evening chow."

"He'd better," Fat Otis said. Then he noticed us folding the flag. "Corporal, you've got that wrong."

So Peters unrolled it, holding the end with the field of stars while Fat did it over. Fat's hands looked stubby, but his touch was quick and sure. When Fat had finished, he held the folded flag over his head. From the side it looked like he was wearing an old-fashioned, three-cornered hat.

"Now I ask you, men," Fat said. "Who could tell George and myself apart?"

"Me, for one," Peters said. "George Washington's a dead man."

Fat put the flag on the adjutant's desk.

"Where's Bell anyway?" he asked.

We told him that the lieutenant was going back to the States. Fat shook his head.

"Here's where the guy goes back to driving a truck," he said. "He'll never have it so good again. Few officers will."

Sergeant Fat Otis—nobody called him Fat to his face—did not fraternize with the officers. Maybe because his girl back home had jilted him for a colonel with a desk job in Washington. The sergeant was a college man himself, but he had flunked out of OCS because of an argument with his commanding officer. Now he was the ranking noncom in battalion headquarters, where even the privates had it soft.

Our office took up the second floor of a brownstone house in the Rue de la Casquette, in Liége. Ten of us lived in a squad room which opened on a balcony, with stairs leading down to the office. Sergeant Otis had a room with private bath on the ground floor. His valet was an ex-tailor, a German prisoner named Paul. The sergeant's working day was about five minutes long. Each morning he lined up the work for the rest of us, including officers—when we had an officer that knew how to do anything.

Lieutenant Bell hadn't done anything much except hang around the office, getting in everybody's way. But sometimes an officer from Chanor Base—a roving inspector—would visit Liége; and at such times it was best to have one of our own officers lurking somewhere in the background. This gave the office an air of grim respectability, besides furnishing the fall guy if one became necessary. So Fat began looking around for someone to replace Lieutenant Bell.

Finally, on payday, Major Dort came into the office to get his money. Fat asked him if he had any particular officer in mind that he would like to have made into an adjutant. The major said that anything Fat decided to do would be okay with him. And that was the truth, because Fat had considerable dirt on the major.

That afternoon, Fat put on his glasses, opened the safe and got out the qualification cards of the officers under Major Dort's command. Fat studied the cards for a couple of hours, shaking his head a lot. Then he called up a Lieutenant Androskofsky, who was stationed at St. Hubert. Androskofsky said that he couldn't spell his own name, or even remember it half the time. So he felt that he was not qualified to be an adjutant. Fat let him off. Nobody else he called that afternoon felt qualified either. To hear them tell it, every officer in the command was blind, deaf, ruptured and crazy—though none of them was crazy enough to answer the telephone again that week.

Fat finally decided to put the screws on a Captain Simpkins, who was stationed at Verviers, and had once been professor of mechanical bookkeeping in a West Virginia business college. That was the morning when Second Lieutenant Angus Ramsey came in from Bastogne, where he commanded a company of German POWs. Ramsey was a little fellow, and when he walked he seemed to shrink from taking the next step. None of us paid any attention to him until he stumbled on the carpet at Fat's desk, caught his left foot in a wire wastebasket and fell flat on his back.

"Pardon me!" Lieutenant Ramsey said.

Fat leaned over and took the wastebasket from the lieutenant's shoe.

"What can I do for you, sir?" Fat asked, his voice matter-of-fact, as if he were used to officers lying around on the floor.

Lieutenant Ramsey got up with enough dignity to make us feel like a pack of fools for snickering at his fall.

"I'd like to see Major Dort," he said, stooping to pick up his cap.

"Major Dort's inspecting," Fat said. "What do you want to see him about?"

Lieutenant Ramsey's eyes were brown, and seemed too large for the rest of his face. He stood in front of Fat's desk and twisted his cap in his hands. "I want to go home," he said.

Fat stared at Lieutenant Ramsey. "You do, eh?" he said.

"I've got to go home. My girl's fixing to get married on me," Lieutenant Ramsey said.

"You want an emergency furlough?" Fat asked.

"I've got enough points to get a discharge, only I can't prove it. My records was lost in Germany," the lieutenant said.

"That's too bad," Fat said. "What makes you think you could change her mind if you got home?"

"Because she don't love him. They've wore her down. It's her family wants her to marry anything in pants, just so it's not me," Lieutenant Ramsey said. He was not talking to us, except incidentally.

"What's the objection to you?" Fat asked.

"I've got bad blood in me from both sides of the house. I had two uncles hung for murder," Lieutenant Ramsey said.

Fat was studying the lieutenant's face.

"I wrote Evelyn to put off the wedding. She says she can't do it," Lieutenant Ramsey said. He seemed to be lost in meditation.

"She might not be joking about it, either," Fat said in a voice so pleasant that I knew he was getting fed up with what he considered a case of indecent exposure. "You ever hear tell of the military wedding, where they use the impressive teething-ring-and-shotgun ceremony to hitch the happy couple?"

*   *   *

Lieutenant Ramsey started a little, and he squeezed his cap into a compact, though lopsided ball. He had the look of a worried schoolboy, but his voice was full of ice when he said, "Sergeant, you'll have to apologize for that."

Fat's face turned red, then almost black. After a minute he said, "Very well, sir. I apologize."

"Stand up, soldier, when you apologize to me," Lieutenant Ramsey said.

Fat stood up slowly, "Sir, I am sorry that I spoke lightly of Miss Evelyn Somebody," he said. "I know nothing about this lady's reputation. Did not know of her existence until the lieutenant's visit this morning." Then Fat saluted. Lieutenant Ramsey returned the salute, relaxing his grip on his cap at the last moment and batting himself in the eye. The cap fluttered to the floor.

"That's all, Sergeant," Lieutenant Ramsey said. He got his cap and made it to the door.

Fat Otis sat down again. He put a cigarette in his mouth,

but he didn't light it. Finally he said, "There's no file here on Ramsey. Does anybody know anything about him?"

"I heard he didn't have much education for an officer. Just a grade-school education," said Private Bud Tinsley, a typist.

"He's from a little city in Tennessee. That's the only information I ever heard him turn loose of before today," said Private Zero Mallard, who was also classified as a typist.

"He's around thirty-five, I'd say," Fat Otis said, licking his lips, which seemed quite thin in a face otherwise plump. "He's old enough to know better than to chew me out."

"Oh, he's all right. Just has a lot on his mind," I said.

"He's a rank-happy moron," Fat said. . . .

Still it might have blown over, if it hadn't been for Sergeant Jordan. It was his day off and he hadn't been around since breakfast. Somewhere, however, he'd heard about the lieutenant and Fat having a brush.

It was late that afternoon when Jordan got back to the office and noticed Fat Otis sitting there with his feet propped on the desk.

"Get them feet on the ground, soldier!" Jordan roared. "Assume the kneeling position and—"

"Shut up, Private Jordan," Fat Otis said.

Everything got still in the room. It was getting dark, too, but you could see the bloom of youth and cognac fading from Jordan's face.

"I thought I was a sergeant," Jordan said.

"No, you're a private," Fat Otis said. "Get those stripes off your sleeves before tomorrow, Private Jordan."

Fat turned to the desk on his left. He said, "Here, Tinsley. Type a letter to Chanor Base. 'Request that Jordan, Edward E., ASN four two double-O six one, be reduced from present grade of sergeant to grade of private. Reason for reduction: Negligence of duty. Dort, Major, Q.M.C., Commanding.' I'll sign Dort's name. Get it in the mail tonight."

Jordan pulled off his field jacket. He got a razor blade and began cutting the chevrons off his sleeves.

Next morning Fat Otis telephoned Bastogne and relieved Lieutenant Ramsey of his command.

* * *

At five that afternoon, Major Dort came in from the golf course, which he inspected every day when the weather was good and he had a caddie. Fat told him that Lieutenant Ramsey had finished on top in the race for adjutant. The major twirled his swagger stick. He was a slight, red-eyed man, who only lacked about an inch of having a chin.

"Ramsey's a little peculiar," Major Dort said.

"He'll make an ideal adjutant," Fat said. "But he's putting up a kick about it."

"Is that a fact?" the major asked. "Tell Ramsey he'll report here for duty on Wednesday morning, or move his gear to the guardhouse."

"I've already told him," Fat said absently.

The new adjutant came to work on Wednesday morning. He wore combat boots, a pair of pants with shrapnel wounds, a combat jacket and a helmet liner. I guess he forgot his gas mask and rifle. Fat gave the lieutenant a smart salute, then he told him he'd better go out and get a haircut. That afternoon Fat gave him a rapid outline of office routine.

But the lieutenant had leaned heavily on his company clerk in the past. So we found a manual called *The Army Clerk,* and gave it to him. He began to study, always hiding the book when Fat came in.

One afternoon Major Dort came by to spot-check the outgoing mail. The clerks, Privates Bud Tinsley and Zero Mallard, were fast typists, but they punctuated at random and had unique ideas about spelling. Fat usually corrected their work before it got as far as the adjutant's desk. But this time Fat just handed the folder to Lieutenant Ramsey, saying he was to make whatever corrections he thought necessary before taking the letters in to Major Dort, who would sign them that day.

The lieutenant read a couple of the letters. You could see his lips moving. Then he took the folder of letters into the major's office, closing the door behind him. That didn't keep us from hearing, about two minutes later, the opening remarks of a lecture delivered by the major, covering the elements of spelling, grammar, sentence structure and punctuation. The lecture itself was punctuated verbally by short snatches of heartfelt cussing.

After that, on days too rainy for golf, the major got his exercise by walking to the office and chewing out Lieutenant Ramsey.

The lieutenant got thin and suspicious. He never spoke unless it was urgent.

*　　*　　*

Then one morning he got a letter that livened him up. After he'd read it a couple of times, he turned to Fat and said, "Sergeant, I believe I'll put in for that emergency furlough. You want to type the letter for me, so it'll be worded right?"

"Tinsley and Mallard are the typists here," Fat told him coldly. "You're supposed to be an adjutant yourself, and able to dictate your own letters."

Lieutenant Ramsey began to study the palm of his right hand.

"A man is supposed to have an I.Q.—or an AGCT rating— of at least one hundred and ten before he can qualify as an officer," Fat went on. His voice was bitter; his own I.Q. was one hundred and fifty.

"Well, I got my commission in the Battle of the Bulge," Lieutenant Ramsey explained, "after everybody with a high I.Q. had been killed."

Then the lieutenant got up and walked over to Fat's desk. His voice was almost hoarse when he said, "You've got me wrong, Sergeant Otis. I've worried about that time I made you apologize. I'm sorry. I was just too touchy that day."

Lieutenant Ramsey held out his hand. Fat shook hands with him, but didn't get up.

"Forget it," Fat told the lieutenant. "I'll fix your letter."

"Oh, Tinsley can do it," the lieutenant said.

"No. I'll take care of it myself."

But the letter didn't go out that night, nor the next morning. I know because I was acting mail clerk then, in place of Peters, who was away in England on a furlough. When I collected the mail next afternoon, I reminded Fat about the letter.

"What of it?" he said.

"I thought maybe you'd forgotten it."

"I didn't forget it," Fat said. "You want to get on my list, too?"

"No," I said.

"Then draw your nose in," he said.

Lieutenant Ramsey came in then, and I didn't say anything else. Corporal Peters came in on the Paris train that same afternoon. He'd picked up a couple of revolvers at Loot Alley in London, and was showing Fat a German Luger. Fat was fond of weapons, and he was a very good shot. They dickered a bit, then Fat got it for twelve hundred francs, *belgique*. He was putting the Luger into a desk drawer when he looked up and caught Lieutenant Ramsey watching him.

"I like a pistol myself," Lieutenant Ramsey said.

Fat had a cigar box full of medals he'd won for marksmanship. "Ever fire the revolver for record?" he asked.

The lieutenant nodded.

"How'd you make out?" Fat asked.

"I got a fifty," Lieutenant Ramsey said.

"Out of a possible what?" Fat asked.

"Out of a possible fifty," Lieutenant Ramsey said.

"That's pretty good," Fat said.

"I was lucky," Lieutenant Ramsey said. A few minutes later he went out.

"I'll say he's been lucky!" Fat said.

"Who? Him? When was he ever lucky?" Corporal Peters asked.

"When he got his commission," Fat said. "And anybody's lucky that makes ten straight bulls with a service revolver. Myself—I'll never believe he did it."

"He ain't smart enough to make up a lie without he's got reinforcements," Peters said. "Besides that, he just looks like a dead shot to me."

"Nuts. He's too jumpy to hit the side of a barn," Fat Otis said.

The lieutenant got jumpier, waiting for an answer to the furlough request that he thought had been sent in to base headquarters. Fat advised him not to get excited, since a little red tape is normal in the Army. Then, the first week in November, Major Dort went home on points. He had done very little for the lieutenant, aside from assaulting him verbally on afternoons when it rained, but the major's departure seemed to upset Lieutenant Ramsey.

"I've got to find my records," he told us that morning, after the major had gone. "I'll never get home for Christmas if they don't do something about finding my records."

"Oh, we'll be hearing on your furlough any day now," Fat told him.

The lieutenant's face brightened a bit at that. "Anyway, I'm straightening things out with the girl friend," he said.

"You mean she'll wait for you, sir?" Fat asked.

Lieutenant Ramsey was sitting in a swivel chair, all huddled up inside a field jacket that would have made a good tent for a childless couple that only wanted to do light housekeeping. He nodded.

"She's promised not to marry this Mister Clontz—he's a

gentleman I'm unacquainted with—if I'll turn over a new leaf. She said she had turned to him out of pure despair, instead of love. I guess it was all my fault," Lieutenant Ramsey said, turning away from us, toward the windows that faced the street. When he spoke again it was very slow, like each word had to be brought from a long way off.

"At one time I was very profane—a gambler and a drunkard, always fighting. I knew plenty of ladies, such as they were. Then I found my girl. She was nice—better educated than me, but not stuck up. All of a sudden I didn't want to drink, or even talk rough. I saved my money to build us a house. Her family didn't like me. They said all the Ramseys had a murdering streak. Well, the war got started. I joined up. Went home on a furlough, knowing I'd be shipped soon. We wanted to get married. But Evelyn was scared 'cause the family made such a fuss.

"So I went out and got drunk. Had a fight with the sheriff and two deputies. Not mad or anything—just had to work off steam. Like to killed the sheriff. They let me off. But you see how it was. Everybody said, 'Well, the Ramseys are a tribe of killers. It's in the blood.' "

The lieutenant took a deep breath, sighed, and went on: "We patched it up. But then the war got over and she got to asking why I couldn't get home when so many others could. Folks back home don't understand what it is for your records to get lost in the Army. So now I've gone ahead and promised her I'd be home for Christmas, one way or another. I want to show Evelyn that I'm a changed man."

"You mean that you're harmless now, sir?" Fat said.

Lieutenant Ramsey blinked and sat up straight. "Well, I've got myself under control now," he said.

"You're nervous, though," Fat Otis said.

Lieutenant Ramsey was now the only officer in headquarters company. That put him in command, but only on paper. Fat

Otis had the ring with the keys. He signed Ramsey's name to the mail, paid off on payday, and conferred with the brass from higher echelons. He kept the safe's combination inside his head, and the only telephone in the office was firmly rooted to his desk.

* * *

One morning the lieutenant decided to call Brussels and find out what had happened to his furlough request. Fat advised him to suffer in silence.

"But it's already November! I've got to get home by Christmas," Lieutenant Ramsey said, "What'll I do?"

"Why don't you sit down somewhere and just take your medicine?" Fat asked, his voice quiet and poisonous.

"I don't get you," Lieutenant Ramsey said.

"No, I've got you," Fat told him. "That's the hell of it."

They squared off with their eyes. But Lieutenant Ramsey soon threw in the sponge. "Sergeant Otis," he said slowly. "I don't believe you ever sent that letter in."

"I never told you I did," Fat said.

"You told me you would," Lieutenant Ramsey said.

"I changed my mind," Fat said.

"What have you got against me?" Lieutenant Ramsey asked.

"Your rank," Fat told him. "You've got a rankness that I don't much like."

Lieutenant Ramsey called Brussels anyway, but it didn't do any good. The European Theater of Operations was short of officers and all furloughs had been canceled until officer replacements could arrive from the States. These replacements were expected at "an early date." That's an Army way of saying six months from now, or maybe never.

Lieutenant Ramsey thought that over, then said that he'd have to take his case to Brussels and talk it over with the brass.

He asked Fat for one of the jeeps. But Fat wouldn't give him the key for either of the jeeps.

So Lieutenant Ramsey finally decided to take the three-o'clock train to Brussels. He told Tinsley to make out a set of travel orders, saying that he'd pick them up about two o'clock. The lieutenant went to his hotel to pack.

* * *

When Tinsley got back from lunch that afternoon, he started typing the travel orders. Then the telephone rang. Fat answered it.

"Nineteenth Labor Supervision Center. Sergeant Otis speaking. . . . We're understaffed, sir. . . . Well, in that case. . . . For tonight? Just a moment, sir." Fat put his hand over the mouthpiece for a minute, then he said, "Hello, Colonel. I find that we do have an officer available for duty tonight. Lieutenant Ramsey, sir."

Tinsley stopped typing. He began to file his nails.

It was a little after two o'clock when Lieutenant Ramsey came in. I was on the balcony on my way to the squad room on some pretext or other—but I stopped at the head of the stairs to see what would happen. Ramsey carried a small canvas bag and wore his trench coat. "You finish the travel orders?" he asked Tinsley.

Tinsley opened his mouth, but Fat beat him to the draw.

"I'm afraid you'll have to call off your trip, sir," Fat said. "The provost marshal called up just now. We have to furnish an officer for MP patrol tonight. You're it."

"I'm not due yet! I just pulled it last Monday night!" Lieutenant Ramsey said.

"I can't spare an officer from any of the companies," Fat said. "You'll go on duty at eighteen hundred. Don't forget to wear your side arms."

Lieutenant Ramsey looked up and down the room, with a kind of helpless anger in his eyes. Then he went to his desk, picked up a bottle of red ink, and threw it hard for a bull's-eye against the knob of the squad-room door. He pivoted and ran quickly out of the room.

"He's a dead shot," Corporal Peters said.

I walked to the squad-room door, stopping outside long enough to stare at the floor, where the ink had made a sluggish puddle. . . .

I was charge of quarters that night, and went to early chow. All the others, except for Fat, went to the G.I. movie after supper. Fat came back to the office and sat down at Lieutenant Ramsey's desk. After a while he got out a cigarette. It was raining outside. The street lights flickered damply like the reflections from fireflies on a lake.

"It's getting cold outside," Fat said; and I noticed how tired he looked.

"Listen, Fat, you'd better let the lieutenant alone," I said.

"Don't call me Fat," he said.

"I forgot," I said. "But Ramsey's going nuts."

"I know it. I get to thinking about it sometimes at night, wondering what makes me work on him," Fat said. "But in the morning, there he is again. It makes me uneasy as hell."

"Then ship him home," I said.

"I don't know what to do," Fat said. After a while he went downstairs to his room.

I slept on a cot in the office that night. It was still raining next morning when I went upstairs to call the others for breakfast. Lieutenant Ramsey was sitting at his desk when I got back to the office. His cap and trench coat were soaked. He was asleep. I sneezed. Lieutenant Ramsey woke up.

"Good morning," I said.

He nodded without looking at me. There was a service revolver lying on the desk blotter before him, yet I noticed that the lieutenant was still wearing the side arms that he must have worn on the MP patrol. I folded the CQ's cot and took it into the office that had been Major Dort's. I stood the cot in a corner and walked to the window. Raindrops were bouncing in the street below. I heard somebody come into the other office. The footsteps sounded light, like Fat's.

"Good morning, sir," I heard Fat say.

It was quiet in there for at least a minute, then Lieutenant Ramsey said, "You know, there's not enough room here for you and me both. Can you shoot a pistol, Sergeant?"

Fat Otis said that he could.

"All right," Lieutenant Ramsey said. "Take your pick. They're both the same, and both of them are loaded." His voice was calm. "You afraid of me, Sergeant?"

"No," Fat said. One of them scraped a chair across the floor.

"I want to see who's the best man," Lieutenant Ramsey said.

"All right, Ramsey," Fat said. "You've been tiptoeing around here, trusting in love and women—"

"Get that holster you've got over there in your desk someplace," Lieutenant Ramsey said.

"I guess you've penned a farewell note to your mountain flower," Fat said. "I'll mail it for you."

"We'll draw from the holster," Lieutenant Ramsey said.

"All the double-crossing in this lousy world comes straight out of these big loving hearts," Fat Otis said. "I'm going to put a slug through yours right now."

"I'll blow out your brains," Lieutenant Ramsey replied.

One of them said something else that I didn't catch. But I heard their footsteps, slow and measured. Then a gun went off. Something thudded against the floor. I heard somebody sigh.

It was quiet so suddenly that I had to break it up. I ran into the room.

Sergeant Otis lay face down in front of his desk. Lieutenant Ramsey was standing beside him. The lieutenant's eyes were bloodshot, and he looked dazed, like a man trying to remember his own name.

"Corporal," he said, speaking very slowly, "Sergeant Otis has been shot to death. Note his absence on the morning report."

Sergeant Otis was buried at three o'clock the next afternoon in the American Cemetery at Henri-Chapelle. A bugler played taps for him, and a rifle squad fired a round of blanks over his grave.

Lieutenant Ramsey's court-martial was held in Brussels the following week. I had to go as a witness. A sharp-faced major from Quartermaster was officer for the defense. He asked if I had seen the lieutenant shoot Sergeant Otis. I said that I had not. Then he asked if I had seen any person whatsoever shoot Sergeant Otis at any time whatsoever. I said no. The major rested his case.

But they convicted Lieutenant Ramsey anyway. They found him guilty of carelessly discharging a firearm. He was fined one hundred dollars and given a reprimand. At the same time it was recommended that he be returned to the Zone of Interior for recuperation and rehabilitation—or for separation from the service if he so desired.

We never saw him in Liége again. About a month later, I heard that his name was on a roster of military personnel that had sailed from Antwerp, December 1st, on a Victory ship that might have been called *The Pyrrhus,* for all I know.

FLYING HOME

·

by Ralph Ellison

When Todd came to, he saw two faces suspended above him in a sun so hot and blinding that he could not tell if they were black or white. He stirred, feeling a pain that burned as though his whole body had been laid open to the sun which glared into his eyes. For a moment an old fear of being touched by white hands seized him. Then the very sharpness of the pain began slowly to clear his head. Sounds came to him dimly. *He done come to.* Who are they? he thought. *Naw he ain't, I coulda sworn he was white.* Then he heard clearly,

"You hurt bad?"

Something within him uncoiled. It was a Negro sound.

"He's still out," he heard.

"Give 'im time. . . . Say, son, you hurt bad?"

Was he? There was that awful pain. He lay rigid, hearing their breathing and trying to weave a meaning between them and his being stretched painfully upon the ground. He watched them warily, his mind traveling back over a painful distance. Jagged scenes, swiftly unfolding as in a movie trailer, reeled through his mind, and he saw himself piloting a tail-spinning plane and landing and falling from the cockpit and trying to stand. Then, as in a great silence, he remembered the sound of crunching bone and, now, looking up into the anxious faces of an old Negro man and a boy from where he lay in the same field, the memory sickened him and he wanted to remember no more.

"How you feel, son?"

Todd hesitated, as though to answer would be to admit an inacceptable weakness. Then, "It's my ankle," he said.

"Which one?"

"The left."

With a sense of remoteness he watched the old man bend and remove his boot, feeling the pressure ease.

"That any better?"

"A lot. Thank you."

He had the sensation of discussing someone else, that his concern was with some far more important thing, which for some reason escaped him.

"You done broke it bad," the old man said. "We have to get you to a doctor."

He felt that he had been thrown into a tailspin. He looked at his watch; how long had he been here? He knew there was but one important thing in the world, to get the plane back to the field before his officers were displeased.

"Help me up," he said. "Into the ship."

"But it's broke too bad. . . ."

"Give me your arm!"

"But, son . . ."

Clutching the old man's arm he pulled himself up, keeping his left leg clear, thinking, "I'd never make him understand," as the leather-smooth face came parallel with his own.

"Now, let's see."

He pushed the old man back, hearing a bird's insistent shrill. He swayed, giddily. Blackness washed over him, like infinity.

"You best sit down."

"No, I'm OK."

"But, son. You jus' gonna make it worse. . . ."

It was a fact that everything in him cried out to deny, even against the flaming pain in his ankle. He would have to try again.

"You mess with that ankle they have to cut your foot off," he heard.

Holding his breath, he started up again. It pained so badly that he had to bite his lips to keep from crying out and he allowed them to help him down with a pang of despair.

"It's best you take it easy. We gon' git you a doctor."

Of all the luck, he thought. Of all the rotten luck, now I have done it. The fumes of high-octane gasoline clung in the heat, taunting him.

"We kin ride him into town on old Ned," the boy said.

Ned? He turned, seeing the boy point toward an ox team, browsing where the buried blade of a plow marked the end of a furrow. Thoughts of himself riding an ox through the town, past streets full of white faces, down the concrete runways of the airfield made swift images of humiliation in his mind. With a pang he remembered his girl's last letter. "Todd," she had written, "I don't need the papers to tell me you had the intelligence to fly. And I have always known you to be as brave as anyone else. The papers annoy me. Don't you be contented to prove over and over again that you're brave or skillful just because you're black, Todd. I think they keep beating that dead horse because they don't want to say why you boys are not yet fighting. I'm really disappointed, Todd. Anyone with brains can learn to fly, but then what. What about using it, and who will you use it for? I wish, dear, you'd write about this. I

sometimes think they're playing a trick on us. It's very humili-
ating. . . ." He whipped cold sweat from his face, thinking,
What does she know of humiliation? She's never been down
South. *Now* the humiliation would come. When you must have
them judge you, knowing that they never accept your mistakes
as your own, but hold it against your whole race—that was
humiliation. Yes, and humiliation was when you could never
be simply yourself; when you were always a part of this old
black ignorant man. Sure, he's all right. Nice and kind and
helpful. But he's not you. Well, there's one humiliation I can
spare myself.

"No," he said, "I have orders not to leave the ship. . . ."

"Aw," the old man said. Then turning to the boy, "Teddy,
then you better hustle down to Mister Graves and get him to
come. . . ."

"No, wait!" he protested before he was fully aware. Graves
might be white. "Just have him get word to the field, please.
They'll take care of the rest."

He saw the boy leave, running.

"How far does he have to go?"

"Might' nigh a mile."

He rested back, looking at the dusty face of his watch. But
now they know something has happened, he thought. In the
ship there was a perfectly good radio, but it was useless. The
old fellow would never operate it. That buzzard knocked me
back a hundred years, he thought. Irony danced within him
like the gnats circling the old man's head. With all I've learned
I'm dependent upon this "peasant's" sense of time and space.
His leg throbbed. In the plane, instead of time being measured
by the rhythms of pain and a kid's legs, the instruments would
have told him at a glance. Twisting upon his elbows he saw
where dust had powdered the plane's fuselage, feeling the
lump form in his throat that was always there when he
thought of flight. It's crouched there, he thought, like the

abandoned shell of a locust. I'm naked without it. Not a machine, a suit of clothes you wear. And with a sudden embarrassment and wonder he whispered, "It's the only dignity I have. . . ."

He saw the old man watching, his torn overalls clinging limply to him in the heat. He felt a sharp need to tell the old man what he felt. But that would be meaningless. If I tried to explain why I need to fly back, he'd think I was simply afraid of white officers. But it's more than fear . . . a sense of anguish clung to him like the veil of sweat that hugged his face. He watched the old man, hearing him humming snatches of a tune as he admired the plane. He felt a furtive sense of resentment. Such old men often came to the field to watch the pilots with childish eyes. At first it had made him proud; they had been a meaningful part of a new experience. But soon he realized they did not understand his accomplishments and they came to shame and embarrass him, like the distasteful praise of an idiot. A part of the meaning of flying had gone, then, and he had not been able to regain it. If I were a prize-fighter I would be more human, he thought. Not a monkey doing tricks, but a man. They were pleased simply that he was a Negro who could fly, and that was not enough. He felt cut off from them by age, by understanding, by sensibility, by technology and by his need to measure himself against the mirror of other men's appreciation. Somehow he felt betrayed, as he had when as a child he grew to discover that his father was dead. Now, for him, any real appreciation lay with his white officers; and with them he could never be sure. Between ignorant black men and condescending whites, his course of flight seemed mapped by the nature of things away from all needed and natural landmarks. Under some sealed orders, couched in ever more technical and mysterious terms, his path curved swiftly away from both the shame the old man symbolized and the cloudy terrain of white man's regard. Flying blind, he knew but one point of landing and there he would receive his wings. After that the enemy would appreciate his skill and he would assume his deepest meaning, he thought sadly, neither from those who condescended nor from those who praised without understanding, but from the enemy who would recognize his manhood and skill in terms of hate. . . .

He sighed, seeing the oxen making queer, prehistoric shadows against the dry brown earth.

"You just take it easy, son," the old man soothed. "That boy won't take long. Crazy as he is about airplanes."

"I can wait," he said.

"What kinda airplane you call this here'n?"

"An Advanced Trainer," he said, seeing the old man smile. His fingers were like gnarled dark wood against the metal as he touched the low-slung wing.

" 'Bout how fast can she fly?"

"Over two hundred an hour."

"Lawd! That's so fast I bet it don't seem like you moving!"

Holding himself rigid, Todd opened his flying suit. The shade had gone and he lay in a ball of fire.

"You mind if I take a look inside? I was always curious to see . . ."

"Help yourself. Just don't touch anything."

He heard him climb upon the metal wing, grunting. Now the questions would start. Well, so you don't have to think to answer. . . .

He saw the old man looking into the cockpit, his eyes bright as a child's.

"You must have to know a lot to work all these here things."

He was silent, seeing him step down and kneel beside him.

"Son, how come you want to fly way up there in the air?"

Because it's the most meaningful act in the world . . . because it makes me less like you, he thought.

But he said: "Because I like it, I guess. It's as good a way to fight and die as I know."

"Yeah? I guess you right," the old man said. "But how long you think before they gonna let you all fight?"

He tensed. This was the question all Negroes asked, put with the same timid hopefulness and longing that always opened a greater void within him than that he had felt beneath the plane the first time he had flown. He felt lightheaded. It came to him suddenly that there was something sinister about the conversation, that he was flying unwillingly into unsafe and uncharted regions. If he could only be insulting and tell this old man who was trying to help him to shut up!

"I bet you one thing . . ."

"Yes?"

"That you was plenty scared coming down."

He did not answer. Like a dog on a trail the old man seemed to smell out his fears and he felt anger bubble within him.

"You sho' scared *me*. When I seen you coming down in that thing with it a-rollin' and a-jumpin' like a pitchin' hoss, I thought sho' you was a goner. I almost had me a stroke!"

He saw the old man grinning. "Ever'thin's been happening round here this morning, come to think of it."

"Like what?" he asked.

"Well, first thing I know, here come two white fellers looking for Mister Rudolph, that's Mister Graves' cousin. That got me worked up right away. . . ."

"Why?"

"Why? 'Cause he done broke outta the crazy house, that's why. He liable to kill somebody," he said. "They oughta have him by now though. Then here *you* come. First I think it's one of them white boys. Then doggone if you don't fall outa there. Lawd, I'd done heard about you boys but I haven't never *seen* one o' you-all. Cain't tell you how it felt to see somebody what look like me in a airplane!"

The old man talked on, the sound streaming around Todd's thoughts like air flowing over the fuselage of a flying plane. You were a fool, he thought, remembering how before the spin the sun had blazed, bright against the billboard signs beyond the town, and how a boy's blue kite had bloomed beneath him, tugging gently in the wind like a strange, odd-shaped flower. He had once flown such kites himself and tried to find the boy at the end of the invisible cord. But he had been flying too high and too fast. He had climbed steeply away in exultation. Too steeply, he thought. And one of the first rules you learn is that if the angle of thrust is too steep the plane goes into a spin. And then, instead of pulling out of it and going into a dive you let a buzzard panic you. A lousy buzzard!

"Son, what made all that blood on the glass?"

"A buzzard," he said, remembering how the blood and feathers had sprayed back against the hatch. It had been as though he had flown into a storm of blood and blackness.

"Well, I declare! They's lots of 'em around here. They after dead things. Don't eat nothing what's alive."

"A little bit more and he would have made a meal out of me," Todd said grimly.

"They bad luck all right. Teddy's got a name for 'em, calls 'em 'jimcrows,' " the old man laughed.

"It's a damned good name."

"They the damnedest birds. Once I seen a hoss all stretched out like he was sick, you know. So I hollers, 'Gid up from there, suh!' Just to make sho! An, doggone, son, if I don't see two ole jimcrows come flying right up outa that hoss's insides! Yessuh! The sun was shinin' on 'em and they couldn't a been no greasier if they'd been eating barbecue!"

Todd thought he would vomit, his stomach quivered.

"You made that up," he said.

"Nawsuh! Saw him just like I see you."

"Well, I'm glad it was you."

"You see lots a funny things down here, son."

"No, I'll let you see them," he said.

"By the way, the white folks round here don't like to see you boys up there in the sky. They ever bother you?"

"No."

"Well, they'd like to."

"Someone always wants to bother someone else," Todd said. "How do you know?"

"I just know."

"Well," he said defensively, "no one has bothered us."

Blood pounded in his ears as he looked away into space. He tensed, seeing a black spot in the sky and strained to confirm what he could not clearly see.

"What does that look like to you?" he asked excitedly.

"Just another bad luck, son."

Then he saw the movement of wings with disappointment. It was gliding smoothly down, wings outspread, tail feathers gripping the air, down swiftly—gone behind the green screen of trees. It was like a bird he had imagined there, only the sloping branches of the pines remained, sharp against the pale stretch of sky. He lay barely breathing and stared at the point where it had disappeared, caught in a spell of loathing and admiration. Why did they make them so disgusting and yet teach them to fly so well? *It's like when I was up in heaven* he heard, starting.

The old man was chuckling, rubbing his stubbed chin.

"What did you say?"

"Sho', I died and went to heaven . . . maybe by time I tell you about it they be done come after you."

"I hope so," he said wearily.

"You boys ever sit around and swap lies?"

"Not often. Is this going to be one?"

"Well, I ain't so sho', on account of it took place when I was dead."

The old man paused, "That wasn't no lie 'bout the buzzards, though."

"All right," he said.

"Sho' you want to hear 'bout heaven?"

"Please," he answered, resting his head upon his arm.

"Well, I went to heaven and right away started to sproutin' me some wings. Six foot ones, they was. Just like them the white angels had. I couldn't hardly believe it. I was so glad that I went off on some clouds by myself and tried 'em out. You know, 'cause I didn't want to make a fool outa myself the first thing. . . ."

It's an old tale, Todd thought. Told me years ago. Had forgotten. But at least it will keep him from talking about buzzards.

He closed his eyes, listening.

". . . First thing I done was to git up on a low cloud and jump off. And doggone, boy, if them wings didn't work! First I tried the right; then I tried the left; then I tried 'em both together. Then, Lawd, I started to move on out among the folks. I let 'em see me. . . ."

He saw the old man gesturing flight with his arms, his face full of mock pride as he indicated an imaginary crowd, thinking, *It'll be in the newspapers,* as he heard, ". . . so I went and found me some colored angels—somehow I didn't believe I was an angel 'til I seen a real black one, ha, yes! Then I was sho'—but they tole me I better come down 'cause us colored folks had to wear a special kin'a harness when we flew. That was how come *they* wasn't flyin'. Oh yes, an' you had to be extra strong for a black man even, to fly with one of them harnesses. . . ."

This is a new turn, Todd thought, what's he driving at?

"So I said to myself, I ain't gonna be bothered with no harness! Oh naw! 'Cause if God let you sprout wings you oughta have sense enough not to let nobody make you wear something what gits in the way of flyin'. So I starts to flyin'. Hecks, son," he chuckled, his eyes twinkling, "you know I had to let eve'ybody know that old Jefferson could fly good as anybody else. And I could too, fly smooth as a bird! I could even loop-the-loop—only I had to make sho' to keep my long white robe down roun' my ankles. . . ."

Todd felt uneasy. He wanted to laugh at the joke, but his body refused, as of an independent will. He felt as he had as a child when after he had chewed a sugar-coated pill which his mother had given him, she had laughed at his efforts to remove the terrible taste.

". . . Well," he heard. "I was doing all right 'til I got to speeding. Found out I could fan up a right strong breeze, I could fly so fast. I could do all kin'sa stunts too. I started flying up to the stars and divin' down and zooming roun' the moon. Man, I like to scare the devil outa some ole white angels. I was raisin' hell. Not that I meant any harm, son. But I was just feeling good. It was so good to know I was free at last. I accidently knocked the tips offa some stars and they tell me I caused a storm and a coupla lynchings down here in Macon County—though I swear I believe them boys what said that was making up lies on me. . . ."

He's mocking me, Todd thought angrily. He thinks it's a joke. Grinning down at me . . . His throat was dry. He looked at his watch; why the hell didn't they come? Since they had to, why? *One day I was flying down one of them heavenly streets.* You got yourself into it, Todd thought. Like Jonah in the whale.

"Justa throwin' feathers in everybody's face. An' ole Saint Peter called me in. Said, 'Jefferson, tell me two things, what you doin' flyin' without a harness; an' how come you flyin' so fast?' So I tole him I was flyin' without a harness 'cause it got in my way, but I couldn'ta been flyin' so fast, 'cause I wasn't usin' but one wing. Saint Peter said, 'You wasn't flyin' with but *one* wing?' 'Yessuh,' I says, scared-like. So he says, 'Well, since you got sucha extra fine pair of wings you can leave off yo' harness awhile. But from now on none of that there one-wing flyin', 'cause you gittin' up too damn much speed!"

And with one mouth full of bad teeth you're making too damned much talk, thought Todd. Why don't I send him after the boy? His body ached from the hard ground and seeking to shift his position he twisted his ankle and hated himself for crying out.

"It gittin' worse?"

"I . . . I twisted it," he groaned.

"Try not to think about it, son. That's what I do."

He bit his lip, fighting pain with counter pain as the voice resumed its rhythmical droning. Jefferson seemed caught in his own creation.

". . . After all that trouble I just floated roun' heaven in slow motion. But I forgot like colored folks will do and got to flyin' with one wing agin. This time I was restin' my ole broken arm and got to flyin' fast enough to shame the devil. I was comin' so fast, Lawd, I got myself called befo' ole Saint Peter agin. He said, 'Jeff, didn't I warn you 'bout that speedin'?' 'Yessuh,' I says, 'but it was an accident.' He looked at me sad-like and shook his head and I knowed I was gone. He said, 'Jeff, you and that speedin' is a danger to the heavenly community. If I was to let you keep on flyin', heaven wouldn't be nothin' but uproar. Jeff, you got to go!' Son, I argued and pleaded with that old white man, but it didn't do a bit of good. They rushed me straight to them pearly gates and gimme a parachute and a map of the state of Alabama. . . ."

Todd heard him laughing so that he could hardly speak, making a screen between them upon which his humiliation glowed like fire.

"Maybe you'd better stop awhile," he said, his voice unreal.

"Ain't much more," Jefferson laughed. "When they gimme

241

the parachute ole Saint Peter ask me if I wanted to say a few words before I went. I felt so bad I couldn't hardly look at him, specially with all them white angels standin' around. Then somebody laughed and made me mad. So I tole him, 'Well, you done took my wings. And you puttin' me out. You got charge of things so's I can't do nothin' about it. But you got to admit just this: While I was up here I was the flyinest sonofabitch what ever hit heaven!"

At the burst of laughter Todd felt such an intense humiliation that only great violence would wash it away. The laughter which shook the old man like a boiling purge set up vibrations of guilt within him which not even the intricate machinery of the plane would have been adequate to transform and he heard himself screaming, "Why do you laugh at me this way?"

He hated himself at that moment, but he had lost control. He saw Jefferson's mouth fall open, "What—?"

"Answer me!"

His blood pounded as though it would surely burst his temples and he tried to reach the old man and fell, screaming, "Can I help it because they won't let us actually fly? Maybe we are a bunch of buzzards feeding on a dead horse, but we can hope to be eagles, can't we? *Can't we?*"

He fell back, exhausted, his ankle pounding. The saliva was like straw in his mouth. If he had the strength he would strangle this old man. This grinning, gray-headed clown who made him feel as he felt when watched by the white officers at the field. And yet this old man had neither power, prestige, rank nor technique. Nothing that could rid him of this terrible feeling. He watched him, seeing his face struggle to express a turmoil of feeling.

"What you mean, son? What you talking 'bout . . . ?"

"Go away. Go tell your tales to the white folks."

"But I didn't mean nothing like that . . . I . . . I wasn't tryin' to hurt your feelings. . . ."

"Please. Get the hell away from me!"

"But I didn't, son. I didn't mean all them things a-tall."

Todd shook as with a chill, searching Jefferson's face for a trace of the mockery he had seen there. But now the face was somber and tired and old. He was confused. He could not be sure that there had ever been laughter there, that Jefferson had ever really laughed in his whole life. He saw Jefferson reach out to touch him and shrank away, wondering if anything except the pain, now causing his vision to waver, was real. Perhaps he had imagined it all.

"Don't let it get you down, son," the voice said pensively.

He heard Jefferson sigh wearily, as though he felt no more than he could say. His anger ebbed, leaving only the pain.

"I'm sorry," he mumbled.

"You just wore out with pain, was all. . . ."

He saw him through a blur, smiling. And for a second he felt the embarrassed silence of understanding flutter between them.

"What you was doin' flyin' over this section, son? Wasn't you scared they might shoot you for a crow?"

Todd tensed. Was he being laughed at again? But before he could decide the pain shook him and a part of him was lying calmly behind the screen of pain that had fallen between them, recalling the first time he had ever seen a plane. It was as though an endless series of hangars had been shaken ajar in the air base of his memory and from each, like a young wasp emerging from its cell, arose the memory of a plane.

*　　*　　*

The first time I ever saw a plane I was very small and planes were new in the world. I was four-and-a-half and the only plane that I had ever seen was a model suspended from the ceiling of the automobile exhibit at the State Fair. But I did not know that it was only a model. I did not know how large a real plane was, nor how expensive. To me it was a fascinating toy, complete in itself, which my mother said could only be owned by rich little white boys. I stood rigid with admiration, my head straining backwards as I watched the gray little plane describing arcs above the gleaming tops of the automobiles. And I vowed that, rich or poor, some day I would own such a toy. My mother had to drag me out of the exhibit, and not even the merry-go-round, the Ferris wheel, or the racing horses could hold my attention for the rest of the Fair. I was too busy imitating the tiny drone of the plane with my lips, and imitating with my hands the motion, swift and circling, that it made in flight.

After that I no longer used the pieces of lumber that lay about our back yard to construct wagons and autos . . . now it was used for airplanes. I built bi-planes, using pieces of board for wings, a small box for the fuselage, another piece of wood for the rudder. The trip to the Fair had brought something new into my small world. I asked my mother repeatedly when the Fair would come back again. I'd lie in the grass and watch the sky and each flighting bird became a soaring plane. I would have been good a year just to have seen a plane again. I became a nuisance to everyone with my questions about airplanes. But planes were new to the old folks, too, and there was little that they could tell me. Only my uncle knew some of the answers. And better still, he could carve propellers from pieces of wood that would whirl rapidly in the wind, wobbling noisily upon oiled nails.

I wanted a plane more than I'd wanted anything; more than I wanted the red wagon with rubber tires, more than the train that ran on a track with its train of cars. I asked my mother over and over again:

"Mamma?"

"What do you want, boy?" she'd say.

"Mamma, will you get mad if I ask you?" I'd say.

"What do you want now, I ain't got time to be answering a lot of fool questions. What you want?"

"Mamma, when you gonna get me one . . . ?" I'd ask.

"Get you one what?" she'd say.

"You know, Mamma; what I been asking you. . . ."

"Boy," she'd say, "if you don't want a spanking you better come on 'n tell me what you talking about so I can get on with my work."

"Aw, Mamma, you know. . . ."

"What I just tell you?" she'd say.

"I mean when you gonna buy me a airplane."

"AIRPLANE! Boy, is you crazy? How many times I have to tell you to stop that foolishness. I done told you them things cost too much. I bet I'm gon' wham the living daylight out of you if you don't quit worrying me 'bout them things!"

But this did not stop me, and a few days later I'd try all over again.

Then one day a strange thing happened. It was spring and for some reason I had been hot and irritable all morning. It was a beautiful spring. I could feel it as I played barefoot in the back-yard. Blossoms hung from the thorny black locust trees like clusters of fragrant white grapes. Butterflies flickered in the sunlight above the short new dew-wet grass. I had gone in the house for bread and butter and coming out I heard a steady unfamiliar drone. It was unlike anything I had ever heard before. I tried to place the sound. It was no use. It was a sensation like that I had when searching for my father's watch, heard ticking unseen in a room. It made me feel as though I had forgotten to perform some task that my mother had ordered . . . then I located it, overhead. In the sky, flying quite low and about a hundred yards off was a plane! It came so slowly that it seemed barely to move. My mouth hung wide; my bread and butter fell into the dirt. I wanted to jump up and down and cheer. And when the idea struck I trembled with excitement: "Some little white boy's plane's done flew away and all I got to do is stretch out my hands and it'll be mine!" It was a little plane like that at the Fair, flying no higher than the eaves of our roof. Seeing it come steadily forward I felt the world grow warm with promise. I opened the screen and climbed over it and clung there, waiting. I would catch the plane as it came over and swing down fast and run into the house before anyone could see me. Then no one could come to claim the plane. It droned nearer. Then when it hung like a silver cross in the blue directly above me I stretched out my hand and grabbed. It was like sticking my finger through a soap bubble. The plane flew on, as though I had simply blown my breath after it. I grabbed again, frantically, trying to catch the tail. My fingers clutched the air and disappointment surged tight and hard in my throat. Giving one last desperate grasp, I strained forward. My fingers ripped from the screen. I was falling. The ground burst hard against me. I drummed the earth with my heels and when my breath returned, I lay there bawling.

My mother rushed through the door.

"What's the matter, chile! What on earth is wrong with you?"

"It's gone! It's gone!"

"What gone?"

"The airplane . . ."

"Airplane?"

"Yessum, jus' like the one at the Fair. . . . I . . . I tried to stop it an' it kep' right on going. . . ."

"When, boy?"

"Just now," I cried through my tears.

"Where it go, boy, what way?"

"Yonder, there . . ."

She scanned the sky, her arms akimbo and her checkered apron flapping in the wind as I pointed to the fading plane. Finally she looked down at me, slowly shaking her head.

"It's gone! It's gone!" I cried.

"Boy, is you a fool?" she said. "Don't you see that there's a real airplane 'stead of one of them toy ones?"

"Real . . . ?" I forgot to cry. "Real?"

"Yass, real. Don't you know that thing you reaching for is bigger'n a auto? You here trying to reach for it and I bet it's flying 'bout two hundred miles higher'n this roof." She was disgusted with me. "You come on in this house before somebody else sees what a fool you done turned out to be. You must think these here li'l ole arms of your'n is mighty long. . . ."

I was carried into the house and undressed for bed and the doctor was called. I cried bitterly, as much from the disappointment of finding the plane so far beyond my reach as from the pain.

When the doctor came I heard my mother telling him about the plane and asking if anything was wrong with my mind. He explained that I had had a fever for several hours. But I was kept in bed for a week and I constantly saw the plane in my sleep, flying just beyond my fingertips, sailing so slowly that it seemed barely to move. And each time I'd reach out to grab it I'd miss and through each dream I'd hear my grandma warning:

> *"Young man, young man*
> *Yo' arm's too short*
> *To box with God. . . ."*

"Hey, son!"

At first he did not know where he was and looked at the old man pointing, with blurred eyes.

"Ain't that one of you-all's airplanes coming after you?"

As his vision cleared he saw a small black shape above a distant field, soaring through waves of heat. But he could not be sure and with the pain he feared that somehow a horrible recurring fantasy of being split in twain by the whirling blades of a propeller had come true.

"You think he sees us?" he heard.

"See? I hope so."

"He's coming like a bat outa hell!"

Straining, he heard the faint sound of a motor and hoped it would soon be over.

"How you feeling?"

"Like a nightmare," he said.

"Hey, he's done curved back the other way!"

"Maybe he saw us," he said. "Maybe he's gone to send out the ambulance and ground crew." And, he thought with despair, maybe he didn't even see us.

"Where did you send the boy?"

"Down to Mister Graves," Jefferson said. "Man what owns this land."

"Do you think he phoned?"

Jefferson looked at him quickly.

"Aw sho'. Dabney Graves is got a bad name on accounta them killings but he'll call though. . . ."

"What killings?"

"Them five fellers . . . ain't you heard?" he asked with surprise.

"No."

"Everybody knows 'bout Dabney Graves, especially the colored. He done killed enough of us."

Todd had the sensation of being caught in a white neighborhood after dark.

"What did they do?" he asked.

"Thought they was men," Jefferson said. "An' some he owed money, like he do me. . . ."

"But why do you stay here?"

"You black, son."

"I know, but . . ."

"You have to come by the white folks, too."

He turned away from Jefferson's eyes, at once consoled and accused. And I'll have to come by them soon, he thought with despair. Closing his eyes, he heard Jefferson's voice as the sun burned blood red upon his lids.

"I got nowhere to go," Jefferson said, "an' they'd come after me if I did. But Dabney Graves is a funny fellow. He's all the time making jokes. He can be mean as hell, then he's liable to turn right around and back the colored against the white folks. I seen him do it. But me, I hates him for that more'n anything else. 'Cause just as soon as he gits tired helping a man he don't care what happens to him. He just leaves him stone cold. And then the other white folks is double hard on anybody he done helped. For him it's just a joke. He don't give a hilla beans for nobody—but hisself. . . ."

Todd listened to the thread of detachment in the old man's voice. It was as though he held his words at arm's length before him to avoid their destructive meaning.

"He'd just as soon do you a favor and then turn right around and have you strung up. Me, I stays outa his way 'cause down here that's what you gotta do."

If my ankle would only ease for a while, he thought. The closer I spin toward the earth the blacker I become, flashed through his mind. Sweat ran into his eyes and he was sure that he would never see the plane if his head continued whirling. He tried to see Jefferson, what it was that Jefferson held in his hand? It was a little black man, another Jefferson! A little black Jefferson that shook with fits of belly-laughter while the other Jefferson looked on with detachment. Then Jefferson looked up from the thing in his hand and turned to speak but Todd was far away, searching the sky for a plane in a hot dry land on a day and age he had long forgotten. He was going mysteriously with his mother through empty streets where black faces peered from behind drawn shades and someone was rapping at a window and he was looking back to see a hand and a frightened face frantically beckoning from a cracked door and his mother was looking down the empty perspective of the street and shaking her head and hurrying him along and at first it was only a flash he saw and a motor was droning as through the sun-glare he saw it gleaming silver as it circled and he was seeing a burst like a puff of white smoke and hearing his mother yell, Come along, boy, I got no time for them fool airplanes, I got no time, and he saw it a second time, the plane flying high, and the burst appeared suddenly and fell slowly, billowing out and sparkling like fireworks and he was watching and being hurried along as the air filled with a flurry of white pin-wheeling cards that caught in the wind and scattered over the rooftops and into the gutters and a woman was running and snatching a card and reading it and screaming and he darted into the shower, grabbing as in winter he grabbed for snowflakes and bounding away at his mother's, Come on here, boy! Come on, I say! and he was watching as she took the card away seeing her face grow puzzled and turning taut as her voice quavered, "Niggers Stay From The Polls," and died to a moan of terror as she saw the eyeless sockets of a white hood staring at him from the card and above he saw the plane spiraling gracefully, agleam in the sun like a fiery sword. And seeing it soar he was caught, transfixed between a terrible horror and a horrible fascination.

The sun was not so high now, and Jefferson was calling and gradually he saw three figures moving across the curving roll of the field.

"Look like some doctors, all dressed in white," said Jefferson.

They're coming at last, Todd thought. And he felt such a release of tension within him that he thought he would faint. But no sooner did he close his eyes than he was seized and he was struggling with three white men who were forcing his arms into some kind of coat. It was too much for him, his arms were pinned to his sides and as the pain blazed in his eyes, he realized that it was a straitjacket. What filthy joke was this?

"That oughta hold him, Mister Graves," he heard.

His total energies seemed focused in his eyes as he searched their faces. That was Graves, the other two wore hospital uniforms. He was poised between two poles of fear and hate as he heard the one called Graves saying,

"He looks kinda purty in that there suit, boys. I'm glad you dropped by."

"This boy ain't crazy, Mister Graves," one of the others said. "He needs a doctor, not us. Don't see how you led us way out here anyway. It might be a joke to you, but your cousin Rudolph liable to kill somebody. White folks or niggers don't make no difference. . . ."

Todd saw the man turn red with anger. Graves looked down upon him, chuckling.

"This nigguh belongs in a straitjacket, too, boys. I knowed that the minit Jeff's kid said something 'bout a nigguh flyer. You all know you cain't let the nigguh git up that high without his going crazy. The nigguh brain ain't built right for high altitudes. . . ."

Todd watched the drawling red face, feeling that all the unnamed horror and obscenities that he had ever imagined stood materialized before him.

"Let's git outa here," one of the attendants said.

Todd saw the other reach toward him, realizing for the first time that he lay upon a stretcher as he yelled,

"Don't put your hands on me!"

They drew back, surprised.

"What's that you say, nigguh?" asked Graves.

He did not answer and thought that Graves' foot was aimed at his head. It landed in his chest and he could hardly breathe. He coughed helplessly, seeing Graves' lips stretch taut over his yellow teeth and tried to shift his head. It was as though a half-dead fly was dragging slowly across his face and a bomb seemed to burst within him. Blasts of hot, hysterical laughter tore from his chest, causing his eyes to pop and he felt that the veins in his neck would surely burst. And then a part of him stood behind it all, watching the surprise in Graves' red face and his own hysteria. He thought he would never stop, he would laugh himself to death. It rang in his ears like Jefferson's laughter and he looked for him, centering his eyes desperately upon his face, as though somehow he had become his sole salvation in an insane world of outrage and humiliation. It brought a certain relief. He was suddenly aware that although his body was still contorted it was an echo that no longer rang in his ears. He heard Jefferson's voice with gratitude.

"Mister Graves, the Army done tole him not to leave his airplane."

"Nigguh, Army or no, you gittin' off my land! That airplane can stay 'cause it was paid for by taxpayers' money. But you gittin' off. An' dead or alive, it don't make no difference to me."

Todd was beyond it now, lost in a world of anguish.

"Jeff," Graves said, "you and Teddy come and grab holt. I want you to take this here black eagle over to that nigguh airfield and leave him."

Jefferson and the boy approached him silently. He looked away, realizing and doubting at once that only they could release him from his overpowering sense of isolation.

They bent for the stretcher. One of the attendants moved toward Teddy.

"Think you can manage it, boy?"

"I think I can, suh," Teddy said.

"Well, you better go behind then, and let yo' pa go ahead so's to keep that leg elevated."

He saw the white men walking ahead as Jefferson and the boy carried him along in silence. Then they were pausing and he felt a hand wiping his face, then he was moving again. And it was as though he had been lifted out of his isolation, back into the world of men. A new current of communication flowed between the man and boy and himself. They moved him gently. Far away he heard a mockingbird liquidly calling. He raised his eyes, seeing a buzzard poised unmoving in space. For a moment the whole afternoon seemed suspended and he waited for the horror to seize him again. Then like a song within his head he heard the boy's soft humming and saw the dark bird glide into the sun and glow like a bird of flaming gold.

BRASSARD, MOURNING, OFFICIAL

A STORY

·

by Miller Harris

He walked through the train until he found a girl he thought he'd like to sit next to, threw the manila envelope down and, smiling so she'd know he wasn't Monty Woolley, warned her not to let anyone sit on it. Then he went back to the baggage car to see if Sergeant McCormick was comfortable. He unfastened the flag from the Sergeant's casket and folded it in the prescribed fashion until it was the size and shape of a cocked hat. He placed it in its cover and returned to the coach.

The manila envelope still held his seat.

"You're a good girl," he said to the girl.

"Thank you," she said, and resumed looking out the window. The train began to move through West Philadelphia. He looked the girl over. Not bad, he thought. Maybe she'll have lunch with me. If she stops looking out the window.

"Where're you bound for?" he asked.

"Harrisburg. And you?" It looked like lunch.

"Lancaster."

"Oh, do you live in Lancaster?" she asked.

"Nope. Put all the 'do you knows' back in your file. I've never been to Lancaster and I've never been to Harrisburg. Know anybody on Leyte?" he asked and immediately regretted it. "I guess that sounds like hell, doesn't it? Very bitter. Very warlike. I am twenty-seven years old. I have been everywhere, seen everything, done everything. Know anybody on Leyte?" He nodded toward the autumn fields of Pennsylvania Dutchland. "Nice out."

"Yes, it's lovely. And so is your uniform. What are you dressed as?" she asked.

"That's a rather personal question. I didn't comment on your clothes. I never said you looked lovely."

"How could I possibly look anything but faded sitting next to a peacock? Whatever are you dressed as?"

"A ghoul."

"What do you mean, a ghoul?"

"I mean I am dressed as a ghoul. What did it sound like I meant?" He smiled his no-malice smile.

"That's ridiculous—a ghoul!"

"This peacock regalia—you must be very young not to know it—is the uniform of the United States Marine Corps."

"I thought Marines wore those awful green uniforms."

"They also wear these awful blue ones. With the high neckline. Revealing almost no bosom. Definitely the Old Look."

"And the black armband?"

"Brassard, mourning, official."

"Oh," she said. She said it as if he had just announced that his twin brother had been bayoneted publicly in a Tokyo square.

"That 'oh' sounded sympathetic," he said.

"Was that wrong?"

"It was wrong. I'm in mourning for a guy I never knew.

Sergeant Thomas Joseph McCormick, USMC, deceased. He's in the baggage car."

"I'd like to say I understand and then we could talk about something else," she said, "but I don't understand in the least."

"I'm a ghoul. I told you that. I'm a graverobber."

"Go on."

"If you were married—it's out of the question, of course—but if you were married, and your husband got blown into a million little pieces, or maybe just had his head torn off, five thousand miles from home, would you be satisfied to leave him where he was? Supposing that to bring him home cost nothing (it costs a great deal)—supposing that it bothered nobody (it bothers me)—would it mean anything to you to have him home?"

"I guess I'd want him to stay where he fell."

"You're a good girl, and 'fell' is a good girl's word. The Sergeant got his at Pearl Harbor. His mother wants him home. So they dug him up. After six years they woke him up and shipped him home. I'm escorting him from Philly to his new grave. A brand new grave. Look, Mac, clean sheets."

*   *   *

The train was stopping. "We're stopping," he said. "Do you know what I'm supposed to do when we stop? I'm supposed to run up to the baggage car and see that they don't throw Mac off at the wrong stop. And if anybody's looking I'm supposed to drape the flag over his casket. And in Lancaster I'm supposed to give the flag to his mother and say, 'This flag is offered by a grateful nation in memory of faithful service performed by your loved one.' It ought to be pretty effective, don't you think?"

"Is this your first trip?" she asked. He could tell she didn't know what to make of him.

"First trip."

"Will you only have to make this one?" She sounded worried about him.

"Just this one trip. Just this one trip once a week for two years."

"You're kidding!"

"Oh, I'll miss some weeks. Next boatload is coming in from Europe. Not many Marines got to Europe. Not many died there. Not many coming back." The train pulled away from the platform. He looked out. "I don't see Mac. I guess we can assume he's where I left him. Flat on his back."

"Actually you're not as callous as you'd have me believe." She was a nice girl.

"Actually, I'm not," he admitted. "Do you want to know the truth? I have a recurring dream, awake. I take Mac to his mother. My God, that's this afternoon, isn't it? I take him to his mother, and she says who are you? And I tell her. And she says what are you doing here? And I tell her. And she says why did they kill my boy? And I say I don't know, but I'm sorry they did. And she says why did they kill my boy and not you? And I say I guess I was luckier. And she says what makes you better than my boy? And all I can say is I'm sorry they killed her boy. And she starts crying and beating her fists on my chest and when I make my little speech and give her the flag she throws it on the ground and screams that no rag is going to replace her boy."

"That's dramatic enough," the girl said, "but she'll probably be perfectly lovely. She'll ask you to stay to supper and—"

"Then why didn't she leave him alone? Why didn't she leave him at Pearl, this perfectly lovely mother?"

"Maybe it's part of her religion. Or maybe it's superstition or family custom. Maybe the empty space in the family plot is to her as depressing as his empty room at home. Maybe she's sentimental. Maybe she's—"

"Maybe she's nuts. Maybe she gets a bang out of weeping in

cemeteries. Maybe she wants him where everybody can see him, where she can sport him like a badge in her lapel, where all her friends can be reminded what she gave."

"You know," the girl spoke softly, "I think you don't like this duty."

"Why didn't she leave him alone?"

"That isn't what you mean. You mean why didn't she leave you alone." She stood up and slipped by him. "How about some lunch?" she said.

"Not hungry," he said. He slid over next to the window as she went down the aisle to the diner. Then suddenly he got up and followed her, the nice girl.

THE RAM
IN THE THICKET

.

by Wright Morris

In this dream Mr. Ormsby stood in the yard—at the edge of
the yard where the weeds began—and stared at a figure that
appeared to be on a rise. This figure had the head of a bird
with a crown of bright, exotic plumage, only partially concealed by a paint-daubed helmet. Mr. Ormsby felt the urgent
need to identify this strange bird. Feathery wisps of plumage
shot through the crown of the helmet like a pillow leaking
sharp spears of yellow straw. The face beneath it was inde-
scribably solemn, with eyes so pale they were like openings on
the sky. Slung over the left arm, casually, was a gun, but the
right arm, the palm upward, extended toward a cloud of hovering birds. They came and went, like bees after honey, and
there were so many and all so friendly, that Mr. Ormsby extended his own hand toward them. No birds came, but in his
upturned palm he felt the dull throb of the alarm clock, which
he held tenderly, a living thing, until it ran down.

In the morning light the photograph at the foot of his bed

seemed startling. The boy stood alone on a rise, and he held, very casually, a gun. The face beneath the helmet had no features, but Mr. Ormsby would have known him just by the stance, by the way he held the gun, like some women hold their arms when their hands are idle, parts of their body that for the moment are not much use. Without the gun it was as if some part of the boy had been amputated; the way he stood, even the way he walked was not quite right.

Mr. Ormsby had given the boy a gun because he had never had a gun himself, not because he wanted him to shoot anything. The boy didn't want to kill anything either, and during the first year he found it hard to: the rattle of the BBs in the barrel of the gun frightened the birds before he could shoot them. And that was what had made him a *hunter*. He had to stalk everything in order to hit it, and after all that trouble you naturally try to hit what you're shooting at. He didn't seem to realize that after he hit it it might be dead. It seemed natural for a boy like that to join the Navy, and let God strike Mr. Ormsby dead to hear him say so, nothing ever seemed more natural to him than the news that the boy had been killed. Mother had steeled herself for the worst, the moment the boy enlisted, but Mr. Ormsby had not been prepared to feel what he felt. Mother need never know it unless he slipped up and talked in his sleep.

He turned slowly on the bed, careful to keep the springs quiet, and as he lowered his feet he scooped his socks from the floor. As a precaution Mother had slept the first few months of their marriage in her corset—as a precaution and as an aid to self-control. In the fall they had ordered twin beds. Carrying his shoes—today, of all days, would be a trial for Mother—he tiptoed to the closet and picked up his shirt and pants. There was simply no reason, as he had explained to her twenty years ago, why she should get up when he could just as well get a bite for himself. He had made that suggestion when the boy was just a baby and she needed her strength. Even as it was she didn't come out of it any too well. The truth was, Mother was so thorough about everything she did that her breakfasts usually took an hour or more. When he did it himself he was out of the kitchen in ten, twelve minutes and without leaving any pile of dishes around. By himself he could quick-rinse them in a little hot water, but with Mother there was the dishpan and all of the suds. Mother had the idea that a meal simply wasn't a meal without setting the table and using half the dishes in the place. It was easier to do it himself, and except for Sunday, when they had brunch, he was out of the house an hour before she got up. He had a bite of lunch at the store and at four o'clock he did the day's shopping since he was right downtown anyway. There was a time he called her up and inquired as to what she thought she wanted, but since he did all the buying he knew that better himself. As secretary for the League of Women Voters she had enough on her mind in times like these without cluttering it up with food. Now that he left the store an hour early he usually got home in the midst of her nap or while she was taking her bath. As he had nothing else to do he prepared the vegetables and dressed the meat, as Mother had never shown much of a flair for meat. There had been a year— when the boy was small and before he had taken up that gun— when she had made several marvelous lemon meringue pies. But feeling as she did about the gun—and she told them both how she felt about it—she didn't see why she should slave in the kitchen for people like that. She always spoke to them as *they*—or as *you* plural—from the time he had given the boy the gun. Whether this was because they were both men, both culprits, or both something else, they were never entirely separate things again. When she called, *they* would both answer, and though the boy had been gone two years he still felt him *there,* right beside him, when Mother said *you.*

For some reason Mr. Ormsby could not understand—although the rest of the house was neat as a pin—the room they *lived* in was always a mess. Mother refused to let the cleaning woman set her foot in it. Whenever she left the house she locked the door. Long, long ago he had said something, and she had said something, and she had said she wanted one room in the house where she could relax and just let her hair down. That had sounded so wonderfully human, so unusual for Mother, that he had been completely taken with it. As a matter of fact he still didn't know what to say. It was the only room in the house—except for the screened-in porch in the summer—where he could take off his shoes and open his shirt on his underwear. If the room was *clean,* it would be clean like all of the others, and that would leave him nothing but the basement and the porch. The way the boy took to the out-of-doors—he stopped looking for his cuff links, began to look for pins—was partially because he couldn't find a place in the house to sit down. They had just redecorated the house—the boy at that time was just a little shaver—and Mother had spread newspapers over everything. There hadn't been a chair in the place—except the straight-backed ones at the table—that hadn't been, that *wasn't,* covered with a piece of newspaper. Anyone who had ever scrunched around on a paper knew what that was like. It was at that time that he had got the idea of having his pipe in the basement, reading in the bedroom, and the boy had taken to the out-of-doors. Because he had always wanted a gun himself, and because the boy was alone, with no kids around to play with, he had brought him home a thousand-shot BB gun by the name of Daisy—funny that he should remember the name—and five thousand BBs in a draw-string bag.

That gun had been a mistake—he began to shave himself in tepid, lukewarm water rather than let it run hot, which would bang the pipes and wake Mother up. When the telegram came that the boy had been killed Mother hadn't said a word, but she made it clear whose fault it was. There was never any doubt, *any* doubt, as to just whose fault it was.

He stopped thinking while he shaved, attentive to the mole at the edge of his mustache, and leaned to the mirror to avoid dropping suds on the rug. There had been a time when he had wondered about an Oriental throw rug in the bathroom, but over twenty years he had become accustomed to it. As a matter of fact he sort of missed it whenever they had guests with children and Mother remembered to take it up. Without the rug he always felt just a little uneasy in the bathroom; it led him to whistle or turn on the water and let it run. If it hadn't been for that he might not have noticed as soon as he did that Mother did the same thing whenever anybody was in the house. She turned on the water and let it run until she was through with the toilet, then she would flush it before she turned the water off. If you happen to have old-fashioned plumbing, and have lived with a person for twenty years, you can't help noticing little things like that. He had got to be a little like that himself: since the boy had gone he used the one in the basement or waited until he got down to the store. As a matter of fact it was more convenient, didn't wake Mother up, and he could have his pipe while he was sitting there.

With his pants on, but carrying his shirt—for he might get it soiled preparing breakfast—he left the bathroom and tiptoed down the stairs.

Although the boy had gone, was gone, that is, Mother still liked to preserve her slipcovers and the kitchen linoleum. It was a good piece, well worth preserving, but unless there were guests in the house and the papers were taken up, Mr. Ormsby forgot it was there. Right now he couldn't tell you what color the linoleum was. Stooping to see what the color might be—it proved to be blue, Mother's favorite color—he felt the stirring in his bowels. Usually this occurred while he was rinsing the dishes after his second cup of coffee or after the first long draw on his pipe. He was not supposed to smoke in the morning, but it was more important to be regular that way than irregular with his pipe. Mother had been the first to realize this—not in so many words—but she would rather he did anything than not be able to do *that*.

He measured out a pint and a half of water, put it over a medium fire, and added just a pinch of salt. Then he walked to the top of the basement stairs, turned on the light, and at the bottom turned it off. He dipped his head to pass beneath a sagging line of wash, the sleeves dripping, and with his hands out, for the corner was dark, he entered the cell.

The basement toilet had been put in to accommodate the help, who had to use something, and Mother would not have them on her Oriental rug. Until the day he dropped some money out of his pants and had to strike a match to look for it, he had never noticed what kind of a stool it was. Mother had picked it up secondhand—she had never told him where— because she couldn't see buying something new for a place always in the dark. It was very old, with a chain pull, and operated on a principle that invariably produced quite a splash. But, in spite of that, he preferred it to the one at the store and very much more than the one upstairs. This was rather hard to explain since the seat was pretty cold in the winter and the water sometimes nearly froze. But it was private like no other place in the house. Considering that the house was as good as empty, that was a strange thing to say, but it was the only way to say how he felt. If he went off for a walk like the boy, Mother would miss him, somebody would see him, and he wouldn't feel right about it anyhow. All he wanted was a dark, quiet place and the feeling that for five minutes, just five minutes, nobody would be looking for him. Who would ever believe five minutes like that were so hard to come by? The closest he had ever been to the boy—after he had given him the gun—was the morning he had found him here on the stool. It was then that the boy had said, *et tu, Brutus,* and they had both laughed so hard they had had to hold their sides. The boy had put his head in a basket of wash so Mother wouldn't hear. Like everything the boy said there were two or three ways to take it, and in the dark Mr. Ormsby could not see his face. When he stopped laughing the boy said, *Well, Pop, I suppose one flush ought to do,* but Mr. Ormsby had not been able to say anything. To be called Pop made him so weak that he had to sit right down on the stool, just like he was, and support his head in his hands. Just as he had never had a name for the boy, the boy had never had a name for him —none, that is, that Mother would permit him to use. Of all the names Mother couldn't stand, Pop was the worst, and he agreed with her; it was vulgar, common, and used by strangers to intimidate old men. He agreed with her, completely—until he heard the word in the boy's mouth. It was only natural that the boy would use it if he ever had the chance—but he never dreamed that any word, especially *that* word, could mean what it did. It made him weak, he had to sit down and pretend he was going about his business, and what a blessing it was that the place was dark. Nothing more was said, ever, but it remained their most important conversation—so important they were afraid to try and improve on it. Days later he remembered what the boy had actually said, and how shocking it was but without any *sense* of shock. A blow so sharp that he had no sense of pain, only a knowing, as he had under gas, that he had been worked on. For two, maybe three minutes, there in the dark, they had been what Mother called them, they were *they*—and they were there in the basement because they were so much alike. When the telegram came, and when he knew what he would find, he had brought it there, had struck a match, and read what it said. The match filled the cell with light and he saw—he couldn't help seeing—piles of tinned goods in the space beneath the stairs. Several dozen cans of tuna fish and salmon, and since *he* was the one that had the points, bought the groceries, there was only one place Mother could have got such things. It had been a greater shock than the telegram—that was the honest-to-God's truth and anyone who knew Mother as well as he did would have felt the same. It was unthinkable, but there it was—and there were more on top of the water closet, where he peered while precariously balanced on the stool. Cans of pineapple, crabmeat, and tins of Argentine beef. He had been stunned, the match had burned down and actually scorched his fingers, and he nearly killed himself when he forgot and stepped off the seat. Only later in the morning—after he had sent flowers to ease the blow for Mother—did he realize how such a thing *must* have occurred. Mother knew so many influential people, and they gave her so much that they had very likely given her all of this stuff as well. Rather than turn it down and needlessly alienate people, influential people, Mother had done the next best thing. While the war was on she refused to serve it, or profiteer in any way —and at the same time not alienate people foolishly. It had been an odd thing, certainly, that he should discover all of that by the same match that he read the telegram. Naturally, he never breathed a word of it to Mother, as something like that, even though she was not superstitious, would really upset her. It was one of those things that he and the boy would keep to themselves.

It would be like Mother to think of putting it in here, the very last place that the cleaning woman would look for it. The new cleaning woman would neither go upstairs nor down, and did whatever she did somewhere else. Mr. Ormsby lit a match to see if everything was all right—hastily blew it out when he saw that the can pile had increased. He stood up, then hurried up the stairs without buttoning his pants as he could hear the water boiling. He added half a cup, then measured three heaping tablespoons of coffee into the bottom of the double boiler, buttoned his pants. Looking at his watch he saw that it was seven thirty-five. As it would be a hard day—sponsoring a boat was a man-size job—he would give Mother another ten minutes or so. He took two bowls from the cupboard, set them on blue pottery saucers, and with the grapefruit knife in his hand walked to the icebox.

As he put his head in the icebox door—in order to see he had to—Mr. Ormsby stopped breathing and closed his eyes. What had been dying for some time was now dead. He leaned back, inhaled, leaned in again. The floor of the icebox was covered with a fine assortment of jars full of leftovers Mother simply could not throw away. Some of the jars were covered with little oilskin hoods, some with saucers, and some with wax paper snapped on with a rubber band. It was impossible to tell, from the outside, which one it was. Seating himself on the floor he removed them one at a time, starting at the front and working toward the back. As he had done this many times before, he got well into the problem, near the middle, before troubling to sniff anything. A jar that might have been carrots —it was hard to tell without probing—was now a furry marvel of green mold. It smelled only mildly, however, and Mr. Ormsby remembered that this was penicillin, the life giver. A spoonful of cabbage—it had been three months since they had had cabbage—had a powerful stench but was still not the one he had in mind. There were two more jars of mold; the one screwed tight he left alone as it had a frosted look and the top of the lid bulged. The culprit, however, was not that at all, but in an open saucer on the next shelf—part of an egg—Mr. Ormsby had beaten the white himself. He placed the saucer on the sink and returned all but two of the jars to the icebox: the cabbage and the explosive-looking one. If it smelled he took it out, otherwise Mother had to see for herself as she refused to take *their* word for these things. When he was just a little shaver the boy had walked into the living room full of Mother's guests and showed them something in a jar. Mother had been horrified—but she naturally thought it a frog or something and not a bottle out of her own icebox. When one of the ladies asked the boy where in the world he had found it, he naturally said, *In the icebox.* Mother had never forgiven him. After that she forbade him to look in the box without permission, and the boy had not so much as peeked in it since. He would eat only what he found on the table, or ready to eat in the kitchen—or what he found at the end of those walks he took everywhere.

With the jar of cabbage and furry mold Mr. Ormsby made a trip to the garage, picked up the garden spade, walked around behind. At one time he had emptied the jars and merely buried the contents, but recently, since the war that is, he had buried it all. Part of it was a question of time—he had more work to do at the store—but the bigger part of it was to put an end to the jars. Not that it worked out that way—all Mother had to do was open a new one—but it gave him a real satisfaction to bury them. Now that the boy and his dogs were gone there was simply no one around the house to eat up all the food Mother saved.

There were worms in the fork of earth he had turned and he stood looking at them—*they* both had loved worms—when he remembered the water boiling on the stove. He dropped everything and ran, ran right into Emil Ludlow, the milkman, before he noticed him. Still on the run he went up the steps and through the screen door into the kitchen—he was clear to the stove before he remembered the door would slam. He started back, but too late, and in the silence that followed the BANG he stood with his eyes tightly closed, his fists clenched. Usually he remained in this condition until a sign from Mother—a thump on the floor or her voice at the top of the stairs. None came, however, only the sound of the milk bottles that Emil Ludlow was leaving on the porch. Mr. Ormsby gave him time to get away, waited until he heard the horse walking, then he went out and brought the milk in. At the icebox he remembered the water—why it was he had come running in the first place—and he left the door open and hurried to the stove. It was down to half a cup but not, thank heavens, dry. He added a full pint, then put the milk in the icebox; took out the butter, four eggs, and a Flori-gold grapefruit. Before he cut the grapefruit he looked at his watch and, seeing that it was ten minutes to eight, an hour before train time, he opened the stairway door.

"Ohhh, Mother!" he called, and then he returned to the grapefruit.

* * *

"*Ad astra per aspera,*" she said, and rose from the bed. In the darkness she felt about for her corset, then let herself go completely for the thirty-five seconds it required to get it on. This done, she pulled the cord to the light that hung in the attic, and as it snapped on, in a firm voice she said, "*Fiat lux.*" Light having been made, Mother opened her eyes.

As the bulb hung in the attic, the closet remained in an afterglow, a twilight zone. It was not light, strictly speaking, but it was all Mother wanted to see. Seated on the attic stairs she trimmed her toenails with a pearl-handled knife that Mr. Ormsby had been missing for several years. The blade was not so good any longer and using it too freely had resulted in ingrown nails on both of her big toes. But Mother preferred it to scissors, which were proven, along with bathtubs, to be one of the most dangerous things in the home. *Even more than the battlefield, the most dangerous place in the world. Dry feet and hands before turning on lights, dry between toes.*

Without stooping she slipped into her sabots and left the closet, the light burning, and with her eyes dimmed, but not closed, went down the hall. Locking the bathroom door she stepped to the basin and turned on the cold water, then she removed several feet of paper from the toilet-paper roll. This took time, as in order to keep the roller from squeaking it had to be removed from its socket in the wall, then returned. One piece she put in the pocket of her kimono, the other she folded into a wad and used as a blotter to dab up spots on the floor. Turning up the water she sat down on the stool—then she got up to get a pencil and pad from the table near the window. On the first sheet she wrote—

Ars longa, vita brevis
Wildflower club, sun. 4 P.M.

She tore this off and filed it, tip showing, right at the front of her corset. On the next page—

ROGER—
Ivory Snow
Sani-Flush on thurs.

As she placed this on top of the toilet-paper roll she heard him call "First for breakfast." She waited until he closed the stairway door, then she stood up and turned on the shower. As it rained into the tub and splashed behind her in the basin, she lowered the lid, flushed the toilet. Until the water closet had filled, stopped gurgling, she stood at the window watching a squirrel cross the yard from tree to tree. Then she turned the shower off and noisily dragged the shower curtain, on its metal rings, back to the wall. She dampened her shower cap in the basin and hung it on the towel rack to dry, dropping the towel that was there down the laundry chute. This done, she returned to the basin and held her hands under the running water, now cold, until she was awake. With her index finger she massaged her gums—*there is no pyorrhea among the Indians*—and then, with the tips of her fingers, she dampened her eyes.

She drew the blind, and in the half-light the room seemed to be full of lukewarm water, greenish in color. With a piece of Kleenex, she dried her eyes, then turned it to gently blow her nose, first the left side, then with a little more blow on the right. There was nothing to speak of, nothing, so she folded the tissue, slipped it into her pocket. Raising the blind, she faced the morning with her eyes softly closed, letting the light come in as prescribed—gradually. Eyes wide, she then stared for a full minute at the yard full of grackles, covered with grackles, before she actually saw them. Running to the door, her head in the hall, her arm in the bathroom wildly pointing, she tried to whisper, loud-whisper to him, but her voice cracked.

"Roger," she called, a little hoarsely. "The window—run!"

She heard him turn from the stove and skid on the newspapers, bump into the sink, curse, then get on again.

"Blackbirds?" he whispered.

"Grackles!" she said, for the thousandth time she said *Grackles.*

"They're pretty!" he said.

"Family—" she said, ignoring him, "family *Icteridae* American."

"Well—" he said.

"Roger!" she said. "Something's burning."

She heard him leave the window and on his way back to the stove, on the same turn, skid on the papers again. She left him there and went down the hall to the bedroom, closed the door, and passed between the mirrors once more to the closet. From five dresses—*any woman with more than five dresses, at this time, should have the vote taken away from her*—she selected the navy blue sheer with pink lace yoke and kerchief, short bolero. At the back of the closet—but in order to see she had to return to the bathroom, look for the flashlight in the drawer full of rags and old tins of shoe polish—were three shelves, each supporting ten to twelve pairs of shoes, and a large selection of slippers were piled on the floor. On the second shelf were the navy blue pumps—*we all have one weakness, but between men and shoes you can give me shoes*—navy blue pumps with a Cuban heel and a small bow. She hung the dress from the neck of the floor lamp, placed the shoes on the bed. From beneath the bed she pulled a hat box—the hat was new. Navy straw with shasta daisies, pink geraniums, and a navy blue veil with pink and white fuzzy dots. She held it out where it could be seen in the mirror, front and side, without seeing herself—*it's not every day that one sponsors a boat.* Not every day, and she turned to the calendar on her night table, a bird calendar featuring the natural-color male goldfinch for the month of June. Under the date of June 23 she printed the words, FAMILY ICTERIDAE—YARDFUL, and beneath it—

Met Captain Sudcliffe and gave him U.S.S. *Ormsby*

When he heard Mother's feet on the stairs Mr. Ormsby cracked her soft-boiled eggs and spooned them carefully into her heated cup. He had spilled his own on the floor when he had run to look at the black—or whatever color they were—birds. As they were very, very soft he had merely wiped them up. As he buttered the toast—the four burned slices were on the back porch airing—Mother entered the kitchen and said, "Roger—*more* toast?"

"I was watching blackbirds," he said.

"Grack-les," she said. "Any bird is a *black*bird if the males are largely or entirely black."

Talk about male and female birds really bothered Mr. Ormsby. Although she was a girl of the old school Mother never hesitated, *anywhere,* to speak right out about male and female birds. A cow was a cow, a bull was a bull, but to Mr. Ormsby a bird was a bird.

"Among the birdfolk," said Mother, "the menfolk, so to

speak, wear the feathers. The female has more serious work to do."

"How does that fit the blackbirds?" said Mr. Ormsby.

"Every rule," said Mother, "has an exception."

There was no denying the fact that the older Mother got the more distinguished she appeared. As for himself, what he saw in the mirror looked very much like the Roger Ormsby that had married Violet Ames twenty years ago. As the top of his head got hard the bottom tended to get a little soft, but otherwise there wasn't much change. But it was hard to believe that Mother was the pretty little pop-eyed girl—he had thought it was her corset that popped them—whose nipples had been like buttons on her dress. Any other girl would have looked like a you-know—but there wasn't a man in Media County, or anywhere else, who ever mentioned it. A man could think what he would think, but he was the only man who really knew what Mother was like. And how little she was like *that*.

"Three-seven-four East One-One-Six," said Mother.

That was the way her mind worked, all over the place on one cup of coffee—birds one moment, Mrs. Dinardo the next.

He got up from the table and went after Mrs. Dinardo's letter—Mother seldom had time to read them unless he read them to her. Returning, he divided the rest of the coffee between them, unequally: three-quarters for Mother, a swallow of grounds for himself. He waited a moment, wiping his glasses, while Mother looked through the window at another blackbird. "Cowbird," she said, *"Molothrus ater."*

" 'Dear Mrs. Ormsby,' " Mr. Ormsby began. Then he stopped to scan the page, as Mrs. Dinardo had a strange style and was not much given to writing letters. " 'Dear Mrs. Ormsby,' " he repeated, " 'I received your letter and I Sure was glad to know that you are both well and I know you often think of me I often think of you too—' " He paused to get his breath—Mrs. Dinardo's style was not much for pauses—and to look at Mother. But Mother was still with the cowbird. " 'Well, Mrs. Ormsby,' " he continued, " 'I haven't a thing in a room that I know of the people that will be away from the room will be only a week next month. But come to See me I may have Something if you don't get Something.' " Mrs. Dinardo, for some reason, always capitalized the letter S which along with everything else didn't make it easier to read. " 'We are both well and he is Still in the Navy Yard. My I do wish the war was over it is So long. We are So tired of it do come and See us when you give them your boat. Wouldn't a Street be better than a boat? If you are going to name Something why not a Street? Here in my hand is news of a boat Sunk what is wrong with Ormsby on a Street? Well 116 is about the Same we have the river and its nice. If you don't find Something See me I may have Something. Best Love, Mrs. Myrtle Dinardo.' "

It was quite a letter to get from a woman that Mother had known, known Mother, that is, for nearly eighteen years. Brought in to nurse the boy—he could never understand why a woman like Mother, with her figure—but anyhow, Mrs. Dinardo was brought in. Something in her milk, Dr. Paige said, when it was as plain as the nose on your face it was nothing in the milk, but something in the boy. He just refused, plain refused, to nurse with Mother. The way the little rascal would look at her, but not a sound out of him but gurgling when Mrs. Dinardo would scoop him up and go upstairs to their room—the only woman—other woman, that is, that Mother ever let step inside of it. She had answered an ad that Mother had run, on Dr. Paige's suggestion, and they had been like *that* from the first time he saw them together.

"I'll telephone," said Mother.

On the slightest provocation Mother would call Mrs. Dinardo by long distance—she had to come down four flights of stairs to answer—and tell her she was going to broadcast

over the radio or something. Although Mrs. Dinardo hardly
knew one kind of bird from another, Mother sent her printed
copies of every single one of her bird-lore lectures. She also
sent her hand-pressed flowers from the garden.

"I'll telephone," repeated Mother.

"My own opinion—" began Mr. Ormsby, but stopped when
Mother picked up her egg cup, made a pile of her plates, and
started toward the sink. "I'll take care of that," he said. "Now
you run along and telephone." But Mother walked right by
him and took her stand at the sink. With one hand—with the
other she held her kimono close about her—she let the water
run into a large dish pan. Mr. Ormsby had hoped to avoid this;
now he would have to first rinse, then dry, every piece of silver
and every dish they had used. As Mother could only use one
hand it would be even slower than usual.

"We don't want to miss our local," he said. "You better run
along and let me do it."

"Cold water," she said, "for the eggs." He had long ago
learned not to argue with Mother about the fine points of
washing pots, pans, or dishes with bits of egg. He stood at the
sink with the towel while she went about trying to make suds
with a piece of stale soap in a little wire cage. As Mother
refused to use a fresh piece of soap, nothing remotely like suds
ever appeared. For this purpose, he kept a box of Gold Dust
Twins concealed beneath the sink, and when Mother turned
her back he slipped some in.

"There now," Mother said, and placed the rest of the dishes
in the water, rinsed her fingers under the tap, paused to sniff at
them.

"My own opinion—" Mr. Ormsby began, but stopped when
Mother raised her finger, the index finger with the scar from
the wart she once had. They stood quiet, and Mr. Ormsby
listened to the water drip in the sink—the night before he had
come down in his bare feet to shut it off. All of the taps

dripped now and there was just nothing to do about it but put a rag or something beneath it to break the ping.

"Thrush!" said Mother. "Next to the nightingale the most popular of European songbirds."

"Very pretty," he said, although he simply couldn't hear a thing. Mother walked to the window, folding the collar of her kimono over her bosom and drawing the tails into a hammock beneath her behind. Mr. Ormsby modestly turned away. He quick-dipped one hand into the Gold Dust—drawing it out as he slipped it into the dishpan and worked up a suds.

As he finished wiping the dishes she came in with a bouquet for Mrs. Dinardo and arranged it, for the moment, in a tall glass.

"According to her letter," Mrs. Ormsby said, "she isn't too sure of having something—Roger!" she said. "You're dripping."

Mr. Ormsby put his hands over the sink and said, "If we're going to be met right at the station I don't see where you're going to see Mrs. Dinardo. You're going to be met at the station and then you're going to sponsor the boat. My own opinion is that after the boat we come on home."

"I know that street of hers," said Mother. "There isn't a wildflower on it!"

On the wall above the icebox was a pad of paper and a blue pencil hanging by a string. As Mother started to write the point broke off, fell behind the icebox.

"Mother," he said, "you ever see my knife?"

"Milkman," said Mother. "If we're staying overnight we won't need milk in the morning."

In jovial tones Mr. Ormsby said, "I'll bet we're right back here before dark." That was all, that was *all* that he said. He had merely meant to call her attention to the fact that Mrs. Dinardo said—all but said—that she didn't have a room for them. But when Mother turned he saw that her mustache was showing, a sure sign that she was mad.

"Well—now," Mother said and lifting the skirt of her kimono swished around the cabinet, and then he heard her on the stairs. From the landing at the top of the stairs she said, "In that case I'm sure there's no need for *my* going. I'm sure the Navy would just as soon have you. After all," she said, "it's *your* name on the boat!"

"Now, Mother," he said, just as she closed the door, *not* slammed it, just closed it as quiet and nice as you'd please. Although he had been through this a thousand times it seemed he was never ready for it, never knew when it would happen, never felt anything but nearly sick. He went into the front room and sat down on the chair near the piano—then got up to arrange the doily at the back of his head. Ordinarily he could leave the house and after three or four days it would blow over, but in all his life—their life—there had been nothing like this. The government of the United States—he got up again and called, "OHHhhhh, Mother!"

No answer.

He could hear her moving around upstairs, but as she often went back to bed after a spat, just moving around didn't mean much of anything. He came back into the front room and sat down on the milk stool near the fireplace. It was the only seat in the room not protected with newspapers. The only thing the boy ever sat on when he had to sit on something. Somehow, thinking about that made him stand up. He could sit in the lawn swing, in the front yard, if Mother hadn't told everybody in town why it was that he, Roger Ormsby, would have to take the day off—not to sit in the lawn swing, not by a long shot. Everybody knew—Captain Sudcliffe's nice letter had appeared on the first page of the *Graphic,* under a picture of Mother leading a bird-lore hike in the Poconos. This picture bore the

title LOCAL WOMAN HEADS DAWN BUSTERS, and marked
Mother's appearance on the national bird-lore scene. But it
was not one of her best pictures—it dated from way back in
the twenties and those hipless dresses and round, bucket hats
were not Mother's type. Until they saw that picture, and the
letter beneath it, some people had forgotten that Virgil was
missing, and most of them seemed to think it was a good idea
to swap him for a boat. The U.S.S. *Ormsby* was a permanent
sort of thing. Although he was born and raised in the town
hardly anybody knew very much about Virgil, but they all
were pretty familiar with his boat. "How's that boat of yours
coming along?" they would say, but in more than twenty years
nobody had ever asked him about *his* boy. Whose boy? Well,
that was just the point. Everyone agreed Ormsby was a fine
name for a boat.

It would be impossible to explain to Mother, maybe to anybody for that matter, what this U.S.S. *Ormsby* business meant
to him. "The" boy and "the" *Ormsby*—it was a pretty strange
thing that they both had the definite article, and gave him the
feeling he was facing a monument.

"Oh Rog-gerrr!" Mother called.

"Coming," he said, and made for the stairs.

From the bedroom Mother said, "However I might feel personally, I do have my *own* name to think of. I am not one of
these people who can do as they please—Roger, are you listening?"

"Yes, Mother," he said.

"—with their life."

As he went around the corner he found a note pinned to the
door.

> Bathroom window up
> Cellar door down
> Is it blue or brown for Navy?

He stopped on the landing and looked up the stairs.

"Did you say something?" she said.

"No, Mother—" he said, then he added, "it's blue. For the Navy, Mother, it's blue."

1948

THE GERMAN REFUGEE

·

by Bernard Malamud

Oskar Gassner sits in his cotton-mesh undershirt and summer bathrobe at the window of his stuffy, hot, dark hotel room on West Tenth Street while I cautiously knock. Outside, across the sky, a late-June green twilight fades in darkness. The refugee fumbles for the light and stares at me, hiding despair but not pain.

I was in those days a poor student and would brashly attempt to teach anybody anything for a buck an hour, although I have since learned better. Mostly I gave English lessons to recently arrived refugees. The college sent me, I had acquired a little experience. Already a few of my students were trying their broken English, theirs and mine, in the American market place. I was then just twenty, on my way into my senior year in college, a skinny, life hungry kid, eating himself waiting for the next world war to start. I was a goddamn cheat. Here I was palpitating to get going, and across the ocean Adolf Hitler, in black boots and a square mustache, was tearing up and spitting out all the flowers. Will I ever forget what went on with Danzig that summer?

Times were still hard from the Depression but anyway I made a little living from the poor refugees. They were all over uptown Broadway in 1939. I had four I tutored—Karl Otto Alp, the former film star; Wolfgang Novak, once a brilliant economist; Friedrich Wilhelm Wolff, who had taught medieval history at Heidelberg; and after the night I met him in his disordered cheap hotel room, Oskar Gassner, the Berlin critic and journalist, at one time on the *Acht Uhr Abenblatt.* They were accomplished men. I had my nerve associating with them, but that's what a world crisis does for people, they get educated.

Oskar was maybe fifty, his thick hair turning gray. He had a big face and heavy hands. His shoulders sagged. His eyes, too, were heavy, a clouded blue; and as he stared at me after I had identified myself, doubt spread in them like underwater currents. It was as if, on seeing me, he had again been defeated. I had to wait until he came to. I stayed at the door in silence. In such cases I would rather be elsewhere but I had to make a living. Finally he opened the door and I entered. Rather, he released it and I was in. "Bitte," he offered me a seat and didn't know where to sit himself. He would attempt to say something and then stop, as though it could not possibly be said. The room was cluttered with clothing, boxes of books he had managed to get out of Germany, and some paintings. Oskar sat on a box and attempted to fan himself with his meaty hand. "Zis heat," he muttered, forcing his mind to the deed. "Impozzible. I do not know such heat." It was bad enough for me but terrible for him. He had difficulty breathing. He tried to speak, lifted a hand, and let it drop like a dead duck. He breathed as though he were fighting a battle; and maybe he won because after ten minutes we sat and slowly talked.

Like most educated Germans Oskar had at one time studied

English. Although he was certain he couldn't say a word he managed to put together a fairly decent, if sometimes comical English sentence. He misplaced consonants, mixed up nouns and verbs, and mangled idioms, yet we were able at once to communicate. We conversed in English, with an occasional assist by me in pidgin-German or Yiddish, what he called "Jiddish." He had been to America before, last year for a short visit. He had come a month before *Kristallnacht,* when the Nazis shattered the Jewish store windows and burnt all the synagogues, to see if he could find a job for himself; he had no relatives in America and getting a job would permit him quickly to enter the country. He had been promised something, not in journalism, but with the help of a foundation, as a lecturer. Then he returned to Berlin, and after a frightening delay of six months was permitted to emigrate. He had sold whatever he could, managed to get some paintings, gifts of Bauhaus friends, and some boxes of books out by bribing two Dutch border guards; he had said goodbye to his wife and left the accursed country. He gazed at me with cloudy eyes. "We parted amicably," he said in German, "my wife was gentile. Her mother was an appalling anti-Semite. They returned to live in Stettin." I asked no questions. Gentile is gentile, Germany is Germany.

His new job was in the Institute for Public Studies, in New York. He was to give a lecture a week in the fall term, and during next spring, a course, in English translation, in "The Literature of the Weimar Republic." He had never taught before and was afraid to. He was in that way to be introduced to the public, but the thought of giving the lecture in English just about paralyzed him. He didn't see how he could do it. "How is it pozzible? I cannot say two words. I cannot pronounziate. I will make a fool of myself." His melancholy deepened. Already in the two months since his arrival, and a round of diminishingly expensive hotel rooms, he had had two English tutors, and I was the third. The others had given him up, he said, because his progress was so poor, and he thought he also depressed them. He asked me whether I felt I could do something for him, or should he go to a speech specialist, someone, say, who charged five dollars an hour, and beg his assistance? "You could try him," I said, "and then come back to me." In those days I figured what I knew, I knew. At that he managed a smile. Still, I wanted him to make up his mind or it would be no confidence down the line. He said, after a while, he would stay with me. If he went to the five-dollar professor it might help his tongue but not his stomach. He would have no money left to eat with. The Institute had paid him in advance for the summer but it was only three hundred dollars and all he had.

He looked at me dully. *"Ich weiss nicht wie ich weiter machen soll."*

I figured it was time to move past the first step. Either we did that quickly or it would be like drilling rock for a long time.

"Let's stand at the mirror," I said.

He rose with a sigh and stood there beside me, I thin, elongated, red-headed, praying for success, his and mine; Oskar, uneasy, fearful, finding it hard to face either of us in the faded round glass above his dresser.

"Please," I said to him, "could you say 'right'?"

"Ghight," he gargled.

"No—right. You put your tongue here." I showed him where as he tensely watched the mirror. I tensely watched him. "The tip of it curls behind the ridge on top, like this."

He placed his tongue where I showed him.

"Please," I said, "now say right."

Oskar's tongue fluttered. "Rright."

"That's good. Now say 'treasure'—that's harder."

"Tgheasure."

"The tongue goes up in front, not in the back of the mouth. Look."

He tried, his brow wet, eyes straining, "Trreasure."

"That's it."

"A miracle," Oskar murmured.

I said if he had done that he could do the rest.

We went for a bus ride up Fifth Avenue and then walked for a while around Central Park Lake. He had put on his German hat, with its hatband bow at the back, a broad-lapeled wool suit, a necktie twice as wide as the one I was wearing, and walked with a small-footed waddle. The night wasn't bad, it had got a bit cooler. There were a few large stars in the sky and they made me sad.

"Do you sink I will succezz?"

"Why not?" I asked.

Later he bought me a bottle of beer.

II

To many of these people, articulate as they were, the great loss was the loss of language—that they could not say what was in them to say. You have some subtle thought and it comes out like a piece of broken bottle. They could, of course, manage to communicate but just to communicate was frustrating. As Karl Otto Alp, the ex-film star who became a buyer for Macy's, put it years later, "I felt like a child, or worse, often like a moron. I am left with myself unexpressed. What I know, indeed, what I am, becomes to me a burden. My tongue hangs useless." The same with Oskar it figures. There was a terrible sense of useless tongue, and I think the reason for his trouble with his other tutors was that to keep from drowning in things unsaid he wanted to swallow the ocean in a gulp: Today he would learn English and tomorrow wow them with an impeccable Fourth of July speech, followed by a successful lecture at the Institute for Public Studies.

We performed our lessons slowly, step by step, everything in its place. After Oskar moved to a two-room apartment in a house on West 85th Street, near the Drive, we met three times a week at 4:30, worked an hour and a half, then, since it was too hot to cook, had supper at the 72nd Street Automat and conversed on my time. The lessons we divided into three parts: diction exercises and reading aloud; then grammar, because Oskar felt the necessity of it, and composition correction; with conversation, as I said, thrown in at supper. So far as I could see, he was coming along. None of these exercises was giving him as much trouble as they apparently had in the past. He seemed to be learning and his mood lightened. There were moments of elation as he heard his accent flying off. For instance when sink became think. He stopped calling himself "hopelezz," and I became his "bezt teacher," a little joke I liked.

Neither of us said much about the lecture he had to give early in October, and I kept my fingers crossed. It was somehow to come out of what we were doing daily, I think I felt, but exactly how, I had no idea; and to tell the truth, though I didn't say so to Oskar, the lecture frightened me. That and the ten more to follow during the fall term. Later, when I learned that he had been attempting with the help of the dictionary to write in English and had produced "a complete disahster," I suggested maybe he ought to stick to German and we could afterwards both try to put it into passable English. I was cheating when I said that because my German is meager, enough to read simple stuff but certainly not good enough for serious translation; anyway, the idea was to get Oskar into production and worry about translating later. He sweated with it, from enervating morning to exhausted night, but no matter what language he tried, though he had been a professional writer for a generation and knew his subject cold, the lecture refused to move past page one.

It was a sticky, hot July and the heat didn't help at all.

III

I had met Oskar at the end of June and by the seventeenth of July we were no longer doing lessons. They had foundered on the "impozzible" lecture. He had worked on it each day in frenzy and growing despair. After writing more than a hundred opening pages he furiously flung his pen against the wall, shouting he could no longer write in that filthy tongue. He cursed the German language. He hated the damned country and the damned people. After that what was bad became worse. When he gave up attempting to write the lecture, he stopped making progress in English. He seemed to forget what he already knew. His tongue thickened and the accent returned in all its fruitiness. The little he had to say was in handcuffed and tortured English. The only German I heard him speak was in a whisper to himself. I doubt he knew he was talking it. That ended our formal work together, though I did drop in every other day or so to sit with him. For hours he sat motionless in a large green velours armchair, hot enough to broil in, and through tall windows stared at the colorless sky above 85th Street, with a wet depressed eye.

Then once he said to me, "If I do not this legture prepare, I will take my life."

"Let's begin, Oskar," I said. "You dictate and I'll write. The ideas count, not the spelling."

He didn't answer so I stopped talking.

He had plunged into an involved melancholy. We sat for hours, often in profound silence. This was alarming to me, though I had already had some experience with such depression. Wolfgang Novak, the economist, though English came more easily to him, was another. His problems arose mainly, I think, from physical illness. And he felt a greater sense of the lost country than Oskar. Sometimes in the early evening I persuaded Oskar to come with me for a short walk on the Drive. The tail end of sunsets over the Palisades seemed to appeal to him. At least he looked. He would put on full regalia —hat, suit coat, tie, no matter how hot or what I suggested— and we went slowly down the stairs, I wondering whether he would ever make it to the bottom. He seemed to me always suspended between two floors.

We walked slowly uptown, stopping to sit on a bench and watch night rise above the Hudson. When we returned to his room, if I sensed he had loosened up a bit, we listened to music on the radio; but if I tried to sneak in a news broadcast, he said to me, "Please, I can not more stand of world misery." I shut off the radio. He was right, it was a time of no good news. I squeezed my brain. What could I sell him? Was it good news to be alive? Who could argue the point? Sometimes I read aloud to him—I remember he liked the first part of *Life on the Mississippi*. We still went to the Automat once or twice a week, he perhaps out of habit, because he didn't feel like going any- where—I to get him out of his room. Oskar ate little, he toyed with a spoon. His dull eyes looked as though they had been squirted with a dark dye.

* * *

Once after a momentary cooling rainstorm we sat on news- papers on a wet bench overlooking the river and Oskar at last began to talk. In tormented English he conveyed his intense and everlasting hatred of the Nazis for destroying his career, uprooting his life after half a century, and flinging him like a piece of bleeding meat to the hawks. He cursed them thickly, the German nation, an inhuman, conscienceless, merciless people. "They are pigs mazquerading as peacogs," he said. "I feel certain that my wife, in her heart, was a Jew hater." It was a terrible bitterness, an eloquence almost without vocabulary. He became silent again. I hoped to hear more about his wife but decided not to ask.

Afterwards in the dark Oskar confessed that he had attempted suicide during his first week in America. He was living, at the end of May, in a small hotel, and had one night filled himself with barbiturates; but his phone had fallen off the table and the hotel operator had sent up the elevator boy who found him unconscious and called the police. He was revived in the hospital.

"I did not mean to do it," he said, "it was a mistage."

"Don't ever think of it again," I said, "it's total defeat."

"I don't," he said wearily, "because it is so arduouz to come back to life."

"Please, for any reason whatever."

Afterwards when we were walking, he surprised me by saying, "Maybe we ought to try now the legture onze more."

We trudged back to the house and he sat at his hot desk, I trying to read as he slowly began to reconstruct the first page of his lecture. He wrote, of course, in German.

IV

He got nowhere. We were back to nothing, to sitting in silence in the heat. Sometimes, after a few minutes, I had to take off before his mood overcame mine. One afternoon I came unwillingly up the stairs—there were times I felt momentary surges of irritation with him—and was frightened to find Oskar's door ajar. When I knocked no one answered. As I stood there, chilled down the spine, I realized I was thinking about the possibility of his attempting suicide again. "Oskar?" I went into the apartment, looked into both rooms and the bathroom, but he wasn't there. I thought he might have drifted out to get something from a store and took the opportunity to look quickly around. There was nothing startling in the medicine chest, no pills but aspirin, no iodine. Thinking, for some reason, of a gun, I searched his desk drawer. In it I found a thin-paper airmail letter from Germany. Even if I had wanted to, I couldn't read the handwriting, but as I held it in my hand I did make out a sentence: *"Ich bin dir siebenundzwanzig Jahre treu gewesen."* There was no gun in the drawer. I shut it and stopped looking. It had occurred to me if you want to kill yourself all you need is a straight pin. When Oskar returned he said he had been sitting in the public library, unable to read.

Now we are once more enacting the changeless scene, curtain rising on two speechless characters in a furnished apartment, I, in a straightback chair, Oskar in the velours armchair that smothered rather than supported him, his flesh gray, the big gray face, unfocused, sagging. I reached over to switch on the radio but he barely looked at me in a way that begged no. I then got up to leave but Oskar, clearing his throat, thickly asked me to stay. I stayed, thinking, was there more to this than I could see into? His problems, God knows, were real enough, but could there be something more than a refugee's displacement, alienation, financial insecurity, being in a strange land without friends or a speakable tongue? My speculation was the old one; not all drown in this ocean, why does he? After a while I shaped the thought and asked him, was there something below the surface, invisible? I was full of this thing from college, and wondered if there mightn't be some unknown quantity in his depression that a psychiatrist maybe might help him with, enough to get him started on his lecture.

He meditated on this and after a few minutes haltingly said he had been psychoanalyzed in Vienna as a young man. "Just the jusual drek," he said, "fears and fantazies that afterwaards no longer bothered me."

"They don't now?"

"Not."

"You've written many articles and lectures before," I said. "What I can't understand, though I know how hard the situation is, is why you can never get past page one."

He half lifted his hand. "It is a paralysis of my will. The whole legture is clear in my mind but the minute I write down a single word—or in English or in German—I have a terrible fear I will not be able to write the negst. As though someone has thrown a stone at a window and the whole house—the whole idea, zmashes. This repeats, until I am dezperate."

He said the fear grew as he worked that he would die before he completed the lecture, or if not that, he would write it so disgracefully he would wish for death. The fear immobilized him.

"I have lozt faith. I do not—not longer possezz my former value of myself. In my life there has been too much illusion."

I tried to believe what I was saying: "Have confidence, the feeling will pass."

"Confidenze I have not. For this and alzo whatever else I have lozt I thank the Nazis."

V

It was by then mid-August and things were growing steadily worse wherever one looked. The Poles were mobilizing for war. Oskar hardly moved. I was full of worries though I pretended calm weather.

He sat in his massive armchair with sick eyes, breathing like a wounded animal.

"Who can write aboud Walt Whitman in such terrible times?"

"Why don't you change the subject?"

"It mages no differenze what is the subject. It is all uzelezz."

I came every day, as a friend, neglecting my other students and therefore my livelihood. I had a panicky feeling that if things went on as they were going they would end in Oskar's suicide; and I felt a frenzied desire to prevent that. What's more, I was sometimes afraid I was myself becoming melancholy, a new talent, call it, of taking less pleasure in my little pleasures. And the heat continued, oppressive, relentless. We thought of escape into the country but neither of us had the money. One day I bought Oskar a second-hand fan—wondering why we hadn't thought of that before—and he sat in the breeze for hours each day, until after a week, shortly after the Soviet-Nazi non-aggression pact was signed, the motor gave out. He could not sleep at night and sat at his desk with a wet towel on his head, still attempting to write his lecture. He wrote reams on a treadmill, it came out nothing. When he slept out of exhaustion he had fantastic frightening dreams of the Nazis inflicting tortures on him, sometimes forcing him to look upon the corpses of those they had slain. In one dream he told me about, he had gone back to Germany to visit his wife. She wasn't home and he had been directed to a cemetery. There, though the tombstone read another name, her blood seeped out of the earth above her shallow grave. He groaned aloud at the memory.

Afterwards he told me something about her. They had met as students, lived together, and were married at twenty-three. It wasn't a very happy marriage. She had turned into a sickly woman, physically unable to have children. "Something was wrong with her interior strugture."

Though I asked no questions, Oskar said, "I offered her to come with me here but she refused this."

"For what reason?"

"She did not think I wished her to come."

"Did you?" I asked.

"Not," he said.

He explained he had lived with her for almost twenty-seven

years under difficult circumstances. She had been ambivalent about their Jewish friends and his relatives, though outwardly she seemed not a prejudiced person. But her mother was always a violent anti-Semite.

"I have nothing to blame myself," Oskar said.

He took to his bed. I took to the New York Public Library. I read some of the German poets he was trying to write about, in English translation. Then I read *Leaves of Grass* and wrote down what I thought one or two of them had got from Whitman. One day, towards the end of August, I brought Oskar what I had written. It was in good part guessing but my idea wasn't to write the lecture for him. He lay on his back, motionless, and listened utterly sadly to what I had written. Then he said, no, it wasn't the love of death they had got from Whitman—that ran through German poetry—but it was most of all his feeling for Brudermensch, his humanity.

"But this does not grow long on German earth," he said, "and is soon deztroyed."

I said I was sorry I had got it wrong, but he thanked me anyway.

I left, defeated, and as I was going down the stairs, heard the sound of someone sobbing. I will quit this, I thought, it has gotten to be too much for me. I can't drown with him.

I stayed home the next day, tasting a new kind of private misery too old for somebody my age, but that same night Oskar called me on the phone, blessing me wildly for having read those notes to him. He had got up to write me a letter to say what I had missed, and it ended by his having written half the lecture. He had slept all day and tonight intended to finish it up.

"I thank you," he said, "for much, alzo including your faith in me."

"Thank God," I said, not telling him I had just about lost it.

VI

Oskar completed his lecture—wrote and rewrote it—during the first week in September. The Nazis had invaded Poland, and though we were greatly troubled, there was some sense of release; maybe the brave Poles would beat them. It took another week to translate the lecture, but here we had the assistance of Friedrich Wilhelm Wolff, the historian, a gentle, erudite man, who liked translating and promised his help with future lectures. We then had about two weeks to work on Oskar's delivery. The weather had changed, and so, slowly, had he. He had awakened from defeat, battered, after a wearying battle. He had lost close to twenty pounds. His complexion was still gray; when I looked at his face I expected to see scars, but it had lost its flabby unfocused quality. His blue eyes had returned to life and he walked with quick steps, as though to pick up a few for all the steps he hadn't taken during those long hot days he had lain torpid in his room.

We went back to our former routine, meeting three late afternoons a week for diction, grammar, and the other exercises. I taught him the phonetic alphabet and transcribed long lists of words he was mispronouncing. He worked many hours trying to fit each sound into place, holding half a matchstick between his teeth to keep his jaws apart as he exercised his tongue. All this can be a dreadfully boring business unless you think you have a future. Looking at him I realized what's meant when somebody is called "another man."

The lecture, which I now knew by heart, went off well. The director of the Institute had invited a number of prominent people. Oskar was the first refugee they had employed and there was a move to make the public cognizant of what was then a new ingredient in American life. Two reporters had come with a lady photographer. The auditorium of the Institute was crowded. I sat in the last row, promising to put up my hand if he couldn't be heard, but it wasn't necessary. Oskar, in a blue suit, his hair cut, was of course nervous, but you couldn't see it unless you studied him. When he stepped up to the lectern, spread out his manuscript, and spoke his first English sentence in public, my heart hesitated; only he and I, of everybody there, had any idea of the anguish he had been through. His enunciation wasn't at all bad—a few s's for th's, and he once said bag for back, but otherwise he did all right. He read poetry well—in both languages—and though Walt Whitman, in his mouth, sounded a little as though he had come to the shores of Long Island as a German immigrant, still the poetry read as poetry:

> And I know the spirit of God is the brother of my
> own,
> And that all the men ever born are also my brothers,
> and the women my sisters and lovers,
> And that the kelson of creation is love . . .

Oskar read it as though he believed it. Warsaw had fallen but the verses were somehow protective. I sat back conscious of two things: how easy it is to hide the deepest wounds; and the pride I felt in the job I had done.

VII

Two days later I came up the stairs into Oskar's apartment to find a crowd there. The refugee, his face beet-red, lips bluish, a trace of froth in the corners of his mouth, lay on the floor in his limp pajamas, two firemen on their knees, working over him with an inhalator. The windows were open and the air stank.

A policeman asked me who I was and I couldn't answer. "No, oh no."

I said no but it was unchangeably yes. He had taken his life —gas—I hadn't even thought of the stove in the kitchen.

"Why?" I asked myself. "Why did he do it?" Maybe it was the fate of Poland on top of everything else, but the only answer anyone could come up with was Oskar's scribbled note that he wasn't well, and had left Martin Goldberg all his possessions. I am Martin Goldberg.

I was sick for a week, had no desire to inherit or investigate, but I thought I ought to look through his things before the court impounded them, so I spent a morning sitting in the depths of Oskar's armchair, trying to read his correspondence. I had found in the top drawer a thin packet of letters from his wife and an airmail letter of recent date from his anti-Semitic mother-in-law.

She writes in a tight script it takes me hours to decipher, that her daughter, after Oskar abandons her, against her own mother's fervent pleas and anguish, is converted to Judaism by a vengeful rabbi. One night the Brown Shirts appear, and though the mother wildly waves her bronze crucifix in their faces, they drag Frau Gassner, together with other Jews, out of the apartment house, and transport them in lorries to a small border town in conquered Poland. There, it is rumored, she is shot in the head and topples into an open tank ditch, with the naked Jewish men, their wives and children, some Polish soldiers, and a handful of gypsies.

DEFENDER
OF THE FAITH

.

by Philip Roth

In May of 1945, only a few weeks after the fighting had ended in Europe, I was rotated back to the States, where I spent the remainder of the war with a training company at Camp Crowder, Missouri. We had been racing across Germany so swiftly during the late winter and spring that when I boarded the plane that drizzly morning in Berlin, I couldn't believe our destination lay to the west. My mind might inform me otherwise, but there was an inertia of the spirit that told me we were flying to a new front where we would disembark and continue our push eastward—eastward until we'd circled the globe, marching through villages along whose twisting, cobbled streets crowds of the enemy would watch us take possession of what up till then they'd considered their own. I had changed enough in two years not to mind the trembling of the old people, the crying of the very young, the uncertain fear in the eyes of the once-arrogant. After two years I had been fortunate enough to develop an infantryman's heart which, like his feet, at first aches and swells, but finally grows horny enough for him to travel the weirdest paths without feeling a thing.

Captain Paul Barrett was to be my C.O. at Camp Crowder. The day I reported for duty he came out of his office to shake my hand. He was short, gruff, and fiery, and indoors or out he wore his polished helmet liner down on his little eyes. In Europe he had received a battlefield commission and a serious chest wound, and had been returned to the States only a few months before. He spoke easily to me, but was, I thought, unnecessarily abusive towards the troops. At the evening formation, he introduced me.

"Gentlemen," he called. "Sergeant Thurston, as you know, is no longer with this Company. Your new First Sergeant is Sergeant Nathan Marx here. He is a veteran of the European theater and consequently will take no shit."

I sat up late in the orderly room that evening, trying half-heartedly to solve the riddle of duty rosters, personnel forms, and morning reports. The CQ slept with his mouth open on a mattress on the floor. A trainee stood reading the next day's duty roster, which was posted on the bulletin board directly inside the screen door. It was a warm evening and I could hear the men's radios playing dance music over in the barracks.

The trainee, who I knew had been staring at me whenever I looked groggily into the forms, finally took a step in my direction.

"Hey, Sarge—we having a G.I. party tomorrow night?" A G.I. party is a barracks-cleaning.

"You usually have them on Friday nights?"

"Yes," and then he added mysteriously, "that's the whole thing."

"Then you'll have a G.I. party."

He turned away and I heard him mumbling. His shoulders were moving and I wondered if he was crying.

"What's your name, soldier?" I asked.

He turned, not crying at all. Instead his green-speckled eyes, long and narrow, flashed like fish in the sun. He walked over to me and sat on the edge of my desk.

He reached out a hand. "Sheldon," he said.

"Stand on your own two feet, Sheldon."

Climbing off the desk, he said, "Sheldon Grossbart." He smiled wider at the intimacy into which he'd led me.

"You against cleaning the barracks Friday night, Grossbart? Maybe we shouldn't have G.I. parties—maybe we should get a maid." My tone startled me: I felt like a Charlie McCarthy, with every top sergeant I had ever known as my Edgar Bergen.

"No, Sergeant." He grew serious, but with a seriousness that seemed only to be the stifling of a smile. "It's just G.I. parties on Friday night, of all nights . . ."

He slipped up to the corner of the desk again—not quite sitting, but not quite standing either. He looked at me with those speckled eyes flashing and then made a gesture with his hand. It was very slight, no more than a rotation back and forth of the wrist, and yet it managed to exclude from our affairs everything else in the orderly room, to make the two of us the center of the world. It seemed, in fact, to exclude everything about the two of us except our hearts. "Sergeant Thurston was one thing," he whispered, an eye flashing to the sleeping CQ, "but we thought with you here, things might be a little different."

"We?"

"The Jewish personnel."

"Why?" I said, harshly.

He hesitated a moment, and then, uncontrollably, his hand went up to his mouth. "I mean . . ." he said.

"What's on your mind?" Whether I was still angry at the "Sheldon" business or something else, I hadn't a chance to tell —but clearly I was angry.

". . . we thought you . . . Marx, you know, like Karl

Marx. The Marx brothers. Those guys are all . . . M-A-R-X, isn't that how you spell it, Sergeant?"

"M-A-R-X."

"Fishbein said—" He stopped. "What I mean to say, Sergeant—" His face and neck were red, and his mouth moved but no words came out. In a moment, he raised himself to attention, gazing down at me. It was as though he had suddenly decided he could expect no more sympathy from me than from Thurston, the reason being that I was of Thurston's faith and not his. The young man had managed to confuse himself as to what my faith really was, but I felt no desire to straighten him out. Very simply, I didn't like him.

When I did nothing but return his gaze, he spoke, in an altered tone. "You see, Sergeant," he explained to me, "Friday nights, Jews are supposed to go to services."

"Did Sergeant Thurston tell you you couldn't go to them when there was a G.I. party?"

"No."

"Did he say you had to stay and scrub the floors?"

"No, Sergeant."

"Did the Captain say you had to stay and scrub the floors?"

"That isn't it, Sergeant. It's the other guys in the barracks." He leaned toward me. "They think we're goofing off. But we're not. That's when Jews go to services, Friday night. We have to."

"Then go."

"But the other guys make accusations. They have no right."

"That's not the Army's problem, Grossbart. It's a personal problem you'll have to work out yourself."

"But it's un*fair.*"

I got up to leave. "There's nothing I can do about it," I said.

Grossbart stiffened in front of me. "But this is a matter of *religion,* sir."

"Sergeant."

"I mean 'Sergeant,' " he said, almost snarling.

"Look, go see the chaplain. The I.G. You want to see Captain Barrett, I'll arrange an appointment."

"No, no. I don't want to make trouble, Sergeant. That's the first thing they throw up to you. I just want my rights!"

"Damn it, Grossbart, stop whining. You have your rights. You can stay and scrub floors or you can go to *shul*—"

The smile swam in again. Spittle gleamed at the corners of his mouth. "You mean church, Sergeant."

"I mean *shul*, Grossbart!" I walked past him and outside. Near me I heard the scrunching of a guard's boots on gravel. In the lighted windows of the barracks the young men in T-shirts and fatigue pants were sitting on their bunks, polishing their rifles. Suddenly there was a light rustling behind me. I turned and saw Grossbart's dark frame fleeing back to the barracks, racing to tell his Jewish friends that they were right —that like Karl and Harpo, I was one of them.

*   *   *

The next morning, while chatting with the Captain, I recounted the incident of the previous evening, as if to unburden myself of it. Somehow in the telling it seemed to the Captain that I was not so much explaining Grossbart's position as defending it.

"Marx, I'd fight side by side with a nigger if the fellow proved to me he was a man. I pride myself," the Captain said looking out the window, "that I've got an open mind. Consequently, Sergeant, nobody gets special treatment here, for the good *or* the bad. All a man's got to do is prove himself. A man fires well on the range, I give him a weekend pass. He scores high in PT, he gets a weekend pass. He *earns* it." He turned from the window and pointed a finger at me. "You're a Jewish fellow, am I right, Marx?"

"Yes, sir."

"And I admire you. I admire you because of the ribbons on

your chest, not because you had a hem stitched on your dick before you were old enough to even know you had one. I judge a man by what he shows me on the field of battle, Sergeant. It's what he's got *here,"* he said, and then, though I expected he would point to his heart, he jerked a thumb towards the buttons straining to hold his blouse across his belly. "Guts," he said.

"Okay, sir, I only wanted to pass on to you how the men felt."

"Mr. Marx, you're going to be old before your time if you worry about how the men feel. Leave that stuff to the chaplain —pussy, the clap, church picnics with the little girls from Joplin, that's all his business, not yours. Let's us train these fellas to shoot straight. If the Jewish personnel feels the other men are accusing them of goldbricking . . . well, I just don't know. Seems awful funny how suddenly the Lord is calling so loud in Private Grossman's ear he's just got to run to church."

"Synagogue," I said.

"Synagogue is right, Sergeant. I'll write that down for handy reference. Thank you for stopping by."

* * *

That evening, a few minutes before the company gathered outside the orderly room for the chow formation, I called the CQ, Corporal Robert LaHill, in to see me. LaHill was a dark burly fellow whose hair curled out of his clothes wherever it could. He carried a glaze in his eyes that made one think of caves and dinosaurs. "LaHill," I said, "when you take the formation, remind the men that they're free to attend church services *whenever* they are held, provided they report to the orderly room before they leave the area."

LaHill didn't flicker; he scratched his wrist, but gave no indication that he'd heard or understood.

"LaHill," I said, *"church.* You remember? Church, priest, Mass, confession . . ."

He curled one lip into a ghastly smile; I took it for a signal that for a second he had flickered back up into the human race.

"Jewish personnel who want to attend services this evening are to fall out in front of the orderly room at 1900." And then I added, "By order of Captain Barrett."

A little while later, as a twilight softer than any I had seen that year dropped over Camp Crowder, I heard LaHill's thick, inflectionless voice outside my window: "Give me your ears, troopers. Toppie says for me to tell you that at 1900 hours all Jewish personnel is to fall out in front here if they wants to attend the Jewish Mass."

* * *

At seven o'clock, I looked out of the orderly-room window and saw three soldiers in starched khakis standing alone on the dusty quadrangle. They looked at their watches and fidgeted while they whispered back and forth. It was getting darker, and alone on the deserted field they looked tiny. When I walked to the door I heard the noises of the G.I. party coming from the surrounding barracks—bunks being pushed to the wall, faucets pounding water into buckets, brooms whisking at the wooden floors. In the windows big puffs of cloth moved round and round, cleaning the dirt away for Saturday's inspection. I walked outside and the moment my foot hit the ground I thought I heard Grossbart, who was now in the center, call to the other two, "Ten-*hut!*" Or maybe when they all three jumped to attention, I imagined I heard the command.

At my approach, Grossbart stepped forward. "Thank you, sir," he said.

"Sergeant, Grossbart," I reminded him. "You call officers 'sir.' I'm not an officer. You've been in the Army three weeks —you know that."

He turned his palms out at his sides to indicate that, in

truth, he and I lived beyond convention. "Thank you, any-way," he said.

"Yes," the tall boy behind him said. "Thanks a lot."

And the third whispered, "Thank you," but his mouth barely fluttered so that he did not alter by more than a lip's movement, the posture of attention.

"For what?" I said.

Grossbart snorted, happily. "For the announcement before. The Corporal's announcement. It helped. It made it . . ."

"Fancier." It was the tall boy finishing Grossbart's sentence.

Grossbart smiled. "He means formal, sir. Public," he said to me. "Now it won't seem as though we're just taking off, gold-bricking, because the work has begun."

"It was by order of Captain Barrett," I said.

"Ahh, but you pull a little weight . . ." Grossbart said. "So we thank you." Then he turned to his companions. "Sergeant Marx, I want you to meet Larry Fishbein."

The tall boy stepped forward and extended his hand. I shook it. "You from New York?" he asked.

"Yes."

"Me too." He had a cadaverous face that collapsed inward from his cheekbone to his jaw, and when he smiled—as he did at the news of our communal attachment—revealed a mouth-ful of bad teeth. He blinked his eyes a good deal, as though he were fighting back tears. "What borough?" he asked.

I turned to Grossbart. "It's five after seven. What time are services?"

"*Shul,*" he smiled, "is in ten minutes. I want you to meet Mickey Halpern. This is Nathan Marx, our Sergeant."

The third boy hopped forward. "Private Michael Halpern." He saluted.

"Salute officers, Halpern." The boy dropped his hand, and in his nervousness checked to see if his shirt pockets were buttoned on the way down.

"Shall I march them over, sir?" Grossbart asked, "or are you coming along?"

From behind Grossbart, Fishbein piped up. "Afterwards they're having refreshments. A Ladies' Auxiliary from St. Louis, the rabbi told us last week."

"The chaplain," whispered Halpern.

"You're welcome to come along," Grossbart said.

To avoid his plea, I looked away, and saw, in the windows of the barracks, a cloud of faces staring out at the four of us.

"Look, hurry out of here, Grossbart."

"Okay, then," he said. He turned to the others. "Double time, *march!*" and they started off, but ten feet away Grossbart spun about, and running backwards he called to me, "Good *shabus,* sir." And then the three were swallowed into the Missouri dusk.

Even after they'd disappeared over the parade grounds, whose green was now a deep twilight blue, I could hear Grossbart singing the double-time cadence, and as it grew dimmer and dimmer it suddenly touched some deep memory—as did the slant of light—and I was remembering the shrill sounds of a Bronx playground, where years ago, beside the Grand Concourse, I had played on long spring evenings such as this. Those thin fading sounds . . . It was a pleasant memory for a young man so far from peace and home, and it brought so very many recollections with it that I began to grow exceedingly tender about myself. In fact, I indulged myself to a reverie so strong that I felt within as though a hand had opened and was reaching down inside. It had to reach so very far to touch me. It had to reach past those days in the forests of Belgium and the dying I'd refused to weep over; past the nights in those German farmhouses whose books we'd burned to warm us, and which I couldn't bother to mourn; past those endless stretches when I'd shut off all softness I might feel for my fellows, and managed even to deny myself the posture of a conqueror—the swagger that I, as a Jew, might well have worn as my boots whacked against the rubble of Münster, Braunschweig, and finally Berlin.

But now one night noise, one rumor of home and time past, and memory plunged down through all I had anesthetized and came to what I suddenly remembered to be myself. So it was not altogether curious that in search of more of me I found myself following Grossbart's tracks to Chapel No. 3 where the Jewish services were being held.

I took a seat in the last row, which was empty. Two rows in front sat Grossbart, Fishbein, and Halpern, each holding a little white dixie cup. Fishbein was pouring the contents of his cup into Grossbart's, and Grossbart looked mirthful as the liquid drew a purple arc between his hand and Fishbein's. In the glary yellow light, I saw the chaplain on the pulpit chanting the first line of the responsive reading. Grossbart's prayerbook remained closed on his lap; he swished the cup around. Only Halpern responded in prayer. The fingers of his right hand were spread wide across the cover of the book, and his cap was pulled down low onto his brow so that it was round like a *yarmulke* rather than long and pointed. From time to time, Grossbart wet his lips at the cup's edge; Fishbein, his long yellow face, a dying light bulb, looked from here to there, leaning forward at the neck to catch sight of the faces down the row, in front—then behind. He saw me and his eyelids beat a tattoo. His elbow slid into Grossbart's side, his neck inclined towards his friend, and then, when the congregation responded, Grossbart's voice was among them. Fishbein looked into his book now too; his lips, however, didn't move.

Finally it was time to drink the wine. The chaplain smiled down at them as Grossbart swigged in one long gulp, Halpern sipped, meditating, and Fishbein faked devotion with an empty cup.

At last the chaplain spoke: "As I look down amongst the

congregation—" he grinned at the word, "this night, I see many new faces, and I want to welcome you to Friday night services here at Camp Crowder. I am Major Leo Ben Ezra, your chaplain. . . ." Though an American, the chaplain spoke English very deliberately, syllabically almost, as though to communicate, above all, to the lip-readers in the audience. "I have only a few words to say before we adjourn to the refreshment room where the kind ladies of the Temple Sinai, St. Louis, Missouri, have a nice setting for you."

Applause and whistling broke out. After a momentary grin, the chaplain raised his palms to the congregation, his eyes flicking upward a moment, as if to remind the troops where they were and Who Else might be in attendance. In the sudden silence that followed, I thought I heard Grossbart's cackle— "Let the goyim clean the floors!" Were those the words? I wasn't sure, but Fishbein, grinning, nudged Halpern. Halpern looked dumbly at him, then went back to his prayerbook, which had been occupying him all through the rabbi's talk. One hand tugged at the black kinky hair that stuck out under his cap. His lips moved.

The rabbi continued. "It is about the food that I want to speak to you for a moment. I know, I know, I know," he intoned, wearily, "how in the mouths of most of you the *trafe* food tastes like ashes. I know how you gag, some of you, and how your parents suffer to think of their children eating foods unclean and offensive to the palate. What can I tell you? I can only say close your eyes and swallow as best you can. Eat what you must to live and throw away the rest. I wish I could help more. For those of you who find this impossible, may I ask that you try and try, but then come to see me in private where, if your revulsion is such, we will have to seek aid from those higher up."

A round of chatter rose and subsided; then everyone sang

"Ain Kelohanoh"; after all those years I discovered I still knew the words.

Suddenly, the service over, Grossbart was upon me. "Higher up? He means the General?"

"Hey, Shelly," Fishbein interrupted, "he means God." He smacked his face and looked at Halpern. "How high can you go!"

"Shhh!" Grossbart said. "What do you think, Sergeant?"

"I don't know. You better ask the chaplain."

"I'm going to. I'm making an appointment to see him in private. So is Mickey."

Halpern shook his head. "No, no, Sheldon . . ."

"You have rights, Mickey. They can't push us around."

"It's okay. It bothers my mother, not me . . ."

Grossbart looked at me. "Yesterday he threw up. From the hash. It was all ham and God knows what else."

"I have a cold—that was why," Halpern said. He pushed his *yarmulke* back into a cap.

"What about you, Fishbein?" I asked. "You kosher too?"

He flushed, which made the yellow more gray than pink. "A little. But I'll let it ride. I have a very strong stomach. And I don't eat a lot anyway . . ." I continued to look at him, and he held up his wrist to re-enforce what he'd just said. His watch was tightened to the last hole and he pointed that out to me. ". . . so I don't mind."

"But services are important to you?" I asked him.

He looked at Grossbart. "Sure, sir."

"Sergeant."

"Not so much at home," said Grossbart, coming between us, "but away from home it gives one a sense of his Jewishness."

"We have to stick together," Fishbein said.

I started to walk towards the door; Halpern stepped back to make way for me.

"That's what happened in Germany," Grossbart was saying, loud enough for me to hear. "They didn't stick together. They let themselves get pushed around."

I turned. "Look, Grossbart, this is the Army, not summer camp."

He smiled. "So?" Halpern tried to sneak off, but Grossbart held his arm. "So?" he said again.

"Grossbart," I asked, "how old are you?"

"Nineteen."

"And you?" I said to Fishbein.

"The same. The same month even."

"And what about him?" I pointed to Halpern, who'd finally made it safely to the door.

"Eighteen," Grossbart whispered. "But he's like he can't tie his shoes or brush his teeth himself. I feel sorry for him."

"I feel sorry for all of us, Grossbart, but just act like a man. Just don't overdo it."

"Overdo what, sir?"

"The sir business. Don't overdo that," I said, and I left him standing there. I passed by Halpern but he did not look up. Then I was outside, black surrounded me—but behind I heard Grossbart call, "Hey, Mickey, *liebschen,* come on back. Refreshments!"

Liebschen! My grandmother's word for me!

* * *

One morning, a week later, while I was working at my desk, Captain Barrett shouted for me to come into his office. When I entered, he had his helmet liner squashed down so that I couldn't even see his eyes. He was on the phone, and when he spoke to me, he cupped one hand over the mouthpiece.

"Who the fuck is Grossbart?"

"Third platoon, Captain," I said. "A trainee."

"What's all this stink about food? His mother called a goddam congressman about the food . . ." He uncovered the mouthpiece and slid his helmet up so I could see the curl of his bottom eyelash. "Yes, sir," he said into the phone. "Yes, sir. I'm still here, sir. I'm asking Marx here right now . . ."

He covered the mouthpiece again and looked back to me. "Lightfoot Harry's on the phone," he said, between his teeth. "This congressman calls General Lyman who calls Colonel Sousa who calls the Major who calls me. They're just dying to stick this thing on me. What's a matter," he shook the phone at me, "I don't feed the troops? What the hell is this?"

"Sir, Grossbart is strange . . ." Barrett greeted that with a mockingly indulgent smile. I altered my approach. "Captain, he's a very orthodox Jew and so he's only allowed to eat certain foods."

"He throws up, the congressman said. Every time he eats something his mother says he throws up!"

"He's accustomed to observing the dietary laws, Captain."

"So why's his old lady have to call the White House!"

"Jewish parents, sir, they're apt to be more protective than you expect. I mean Jews have a very close family life. A boy goes away from home, sometimes the mother is liable to get very upset. Probably the boy *mentioned* something in a letter and his mother misinterpreted."

"I'd like to punch him one right in the mouth. There's a goddam war on and he wants a silver platter!"

"I don't think the boy's to blame, sir. I'm sure we can straighten it out by just asking him. Jewish parents worry—"

"*All* parents worry, for Christ sake. But they don't get on their high horse and start pulling strings—"

I interrupted, my voice higher, tighter than before. "The home life, Captain, is so very important . . . but you're right, it may sometimes get out of hand. It's a very wonderful thing, Captain, but because it's so close, this kind of thing—"

He didn't listen any longer to my attempt to present both myself and Lightfoot Harry with an explanation for the letter.

He turned back to the phone. "Sir?" he said. "Sir, Marx here tells me Jews have a tendency to be pushy. He says he thinks he can settle it right here in the Company . . . Yes, sir . . . I *will* call back, sir, soon as I can . . ." He hung up. "Where are the men, Sergeant?"

"On the range."

With a whack on the top, he crushed his helmet over his eyes, and charged out of his chair. "We're going for a ride."

* * *

The Captain drove and I sat beside him. It was a hot spring day and under my newly starched fatigues it felt as though my armpits were melting down onto my sides and chest. The roads were dry and by the time we reached the firing range, my teeth felt gritty with dust though my mouth had been shut the whole trip. The Captain slammed the brakes on and told me to get the hell out and find Grossbart.

I found him on his belly, firing wildly at the 500 feet target. Waiting their turns behind him were Halpern and Fishbein. Fishbein, wearing a pair of rimless G.I. glasses I hadn't seen on him before, gave the appearance of an old peddler who would gladly have sold you the rifle and cartridges that were slung all over him. I stood back by the ammo boxes, waiting for Grossbart to finish spraying the distant targets. Fishbein straggled back to stand near me.

"Hello, Sergeant Marx."

"How are you?" I mumbled.

"Fine, thank you. Sheldon's really a good shot."

"I didn't notice."

"I'm not so good, but I think I'm getting the hang of it now . . . Sergeant, I don't mean to, you know, ask what I shouldn't . . ." The boy stopped. He was trying to speak intimately but the noise of the shooting necessitated that he shout at me.

"What is it?" I asked. Down the range I saw Captain Barrett standing up in the jeep, scanning the line for me and Grossbart.

"My parents keep asking and asking where we're going. Everybody says the Pacific. I don't care, but my parents . . . If I could relieve their minds I think I could concentrate more on my shooting."

"I don't know where, Fishbein. Try to concentrate anyway."

"Sheldon says you might be able to find out—"

"I don't know a thing, Fishbein. You just take it easy, and don't let Sheldon—"

"*I'm* taking it easy, Sergeant. It's at home—"

Grossbart had just finished on the line and was dusting his fatigues with one hand. I left Fishbein's sentence in the middle.

"Grossbart, the Captain wants to see you."

He came toward us. His eyes blazed and twinkled. "Hi!"

"Don't point that goddam rifle!"

"I wouldn't shoot you, Sarge." He gave me a smile wide as a pumpkin as he turned the barrel aside.

"Damn you, Grossbart—this is no joke! Follow me."

I walked ahead of him and had the awful suspicion that behind me Grossbart was *marching*, his rifle on his shoulder, as though he were a one-man detachment.

At the jeep he gave the Captain a rifle salute. "Private Sheldon Grossbart, sir."

"At ease, Grossman." The captain slid over to the empty front seat, and crooking a finger, invited Grossbart closer.

"Bart, sir. Sheldon Gross*bart*. It's a common error." Grossbart nodded to me—*I* understand, he indicated. I looked away, just as the mess truck pulled up to the range, disgorging a half dozen K.P.'s with rolled-up sleeves. The mess sergeant screamed at them while they set up the chow line equipment.

"Grossbart, your mama wrote some congressman that we don't feed you right. Do you know that?" the Captain said.

"It was my father, sir. He wrote to Representative Franconi that my religion forbids me to eat certain foods."

"What religion is that, Grossbart?"

"Jewish."

"Jewish, *sir,*" I said to Grossbart.

"Excuse me, sir. 'Jewish, sir.'"

"What have you been living on?" the Captain asked. "You've been in the Army a month already. You don't look to me like you're falling to pieces."

"I eat because I have to, sir. But Sergeant Marx will testify to the fact that I don't eat one mouthful more than I need to in order to survive."

"Marx," Barrett asked, "is that so?"

"I've never seen Grossbart eat, sir," I said.

"But you heard the rabbi," Grossbart said. "He told us what to do, and I listened."

The Captain looked at me. "Well, Marx?"

"I still don't know what he eats and doesn't eat, sir."

Grossbart raised his rifle, as though to offer it to me. "But, Sergeant—"

"Look, Grossbart, just answer the Captain's questions!" I said sharply.

Barrett smiled at me and I resented it. "All right, Grossbart," he said, "What is it you want? The little piece of paper? You want out?"

"No, sir. Only to be allowed to live as a Jew. And for the others, too."

"What others?"

"Fishbein, sir, and Halpern."

"They don't like the way we serve either?"

"Halpern throws up, sir. I've seen it."

"I thought *you* throw up."

"Just once, sir. I didn't know the sausage was sausage."

"We'll give menus, Grossbart. We'll show training films about the food, so you can identify when we're trying to poison you."

Grossbart did not answer. Out before me, the men had been organized into two long chow lines. At the tail end of one I spotted Fishbein—or rather, his glasses spotted me. They winked sunlight back at me like a friend. Halpern stood next to him, patting inside his collar with a khaki handkerchief. They moved with the line as it began to edge up towards the food. The mess sergeant was still screaming at the K.P.'s, who stood ready to ladle out the food, bewildered. For a moment I was actually terrorized by the thought that somehow the mess sergeant was going to get involved in Grossbart's problem.

"Come over here, Marx," the Captain said to me. "Marx, you're a Jewish fella, am I right?"

I played straight man. "Yes, sir."

"How long you been in the Army? Tell this boy."

"Three years and two months."

"A year in combat, Grossbart. Twelve goddam months in combat all through Europe. I admire this man," the Captain said, snapping a wrist against my chest. But do you hear him peeping about the food? Do you? I want an answer, Grossbart. Yes or no."

"No, sir."

"And why not? He's a Jewish fella."

"Some things are more important to some Jews than other things to other Jews."

Barrett blew up. "Look, Grossbart, Marx here is a good man, a goddam *hero*. When you were sitting on your sweet ass in high school, Sergeant Marx was killing Germans. Who does more for the Jews, you by throwing up over a lousy piece of sausage, a piece of firstcut meat—or Marx by killing those Nazi bastards? If I was a Jew, Grossbart, I'd kiss this man's feet. He's a goddam hero, you know that? And *he* eats what we give him. Why do you have to cause trouble is what I want to know! What is it you're buckin' for, a discharge?"

"No, sir."

"I'm talking to a *wall!* Sergeant, get him out of my way." Barrett pounced over to the driver's seat. "I'm going to see the chaplain!" The engine roared, the jeep spun around, and then, raising a whirl of dust, the Captain was headed back to camp.

For a moment, Grossbart and I stood side by side, watching the jeep. Then he looked at me and said, "I don't want to start trouble. That's the first thing they toss up to us."

When he spoke I saw that his teeth were white and straight, and the sight of them suddenly made me understand that Grossbart actually did have parents: that once upon a time someone had taken little Sheldon to the dentist. He was someone's son. Despite all the talk about his parents, it was hard to believe in Grossbart as a child, an heir—as related by blood to anyone, mother, father, or, above all, to me. This realization led me to another.

"What does your father do, Grossbart?" I asked, as we started to walk back towards the chow line.

"He's a tailor."

"An American?"

"Now, yes. A son in the Army," he said, jokingly.

"And your mother?" I asked.

He winked. "A *ballabusta*—she practically sleeps with a dustcloth in her hand."

"She's also an immigrant?"

"All she talks is Yiddish, still."

"And your father too?"

"A little English. 'Clean,' 'Press,' 'Take the pants in . . .' That's the extent of it. But they're good to me . . ."

"Then, Grossbart—" I reached out and stopped him. He turned towards me and when our eyes met his seemed to jump back, shiver in their sockets. He looked afraid. "Grossbart, then you were the one who wrote that letter, weren't you?"

It took only a second or two for his eyes to flash happy again. "Yes." He walked on, and I kept pace. "It's what my father *would* have written if he had known how. It was his name, though. *He* signed it. He even mailed it. I sent it home. For the New York postmark."

I was astonished, and he saw it. With complete seriousness, he thrust his right arm in front of me. "Blood is blood, Sergeant," he said, pinching the blue vein in his wrist.

"What the hell *are* you trying to do, Grossbart? I've seen you eat. Do you know that? I told the Captain I don't know what you eat, but I've seen you eat like a hound at chow."

"We work hard, Sergeant. We're in training. For a furnace to work, you've got to feed it coal."

"If you wrote the letter, Grossbart, then why did you say you threw up all the time?"

"I was really talking about Mickey there. But he would never write, Sergeant, though I pleaded with him. He'll waste away to nothing if I don't help. Sergeant, I used my name, my father's name, but it's Mickey and Fishbein too I'm watching out for."

"You're a regular Messiah, aren't you?"

We were at the chow line now.

"That's a good one, Sergeant." He smiled. "But who knows? Who can tell? Maybe you're the Messiah . . . a little bit. What Mickey says is the Messiah is a collective idea. He went to Yeshivah, Mickey, for a while. He says *together* we're the Messiah. Me a little bit, you a little bit . . . You should hear that kid talk, Sergeant, when he gets going."

"Me a little bit, you a little bit. You'd like to believe that, wouldn't you, Grossbart? That makes everything so clean for you."

"It doesn't seem too bad a thing to believe, Sergeant. It only means we should all give a little, is all . . ."

I walked off to eat my rations with the other noncoms.

*　　*　　*

Two days later a letter addressed to Captain Barrett passed over my desk. It had come through the chain of command— from the office of Congressman Franconi, where it had been received, to General Lyman, to Colonel Sousa, to Major Lamont, to Captain Barrett. I read it over twice while the Captain was at the officers' mess. It was dated May 14th, the day Barrett had spoken with Grossbart on the rifle range.

Dear Congressman:

First let me thank you for your interest in behalf of my son, Private Sheldon Grossbart. Fortunately, I was able to speak with Sheldon on the phone the other night, and I think I've been able to solve our problem. He is, as I mentioned in my last letter, a very religious boy, and it was only with the greatest difficulty that I could persuade him that the religious thing to do—what God Himself would want Sheldon to do—would be to suffer the pangs of religious remorse for the good of his country and all mankind. It took some doing, Congressman, but finally he saw the light. In fact, what he said (and I wrote down the words on a scratch pad so as never to forget), what he said was, "I guess you're right, Dad. So many millions of my fellow Jews gave up their lives to the enemy, the least I can do is live for a while minus a bit of my heritage so as to help end this struggle and regain for all the children of God dignity and humanity." That, Congressman, would make any father proud.

By the way, Sheldon wanted me to know—and to pass on to you—the name of a soldier who helped him reach this decision: SERGEANT NATHAN MARX. Sergeant Marx is a combat veteran who is Sheldon's First Sergeant. This man has helped Sheldon over some of the first hurdles he's had to face in the Army, and is in part responsible for Sheldon's changing his mind about the dietary laws. I know Sheldon would appreciate any recognition Marx could receive.

Thank you and good luck. I look forward to seeing your name on the next election ballot.

Respectfully,

SAMUEL E. GROSSBART

Attached to the Grossbart communiqué was a communiqué addressed to General Marshall Lyman, the post commander, and signed by Representative Charles E. Franconi of the House of Representatives. The communiqué informed General Lyman that Sergeant Nathan Marx was a credit to the U.S. Army and the Jewish people.

What was Grossbart's motive in recanting? Did he feel he'd gone too far? Was the letter a strategic retreat—a crafty attempt to strengthen what he considered our alliance? Or had he actually changed his mind, via an imaginary dialogue between Grossbart *père* and *fils?* I was puzzled, but only for a few days—that is, only until I realized that whatever his reasons, he had actually decided to disappear from my life: he was going to allow himself to become just another trainee. I saw him at inspection but he never winked; at chow formations but he never flashed me a sign; on Sundays, with the other trainees, he would sit around watching the noncoms' softball team, for whom I pitched, but not once did he speak an unnecessary or unusual word to me. Fishbein and Halpern retreated from sight too, at Grossbart's command I was sure. Apparently he'd seen that wisdom lay in turning back before he plunged us over into the ugliness of privilege undeserved. Our separation allowed me to forgive him our past encounters, and, finally, to admire him for his good sense.

Meanwhile, free of Grossbart, I grew used to my job and my administrative tasks. I stepped on a scale one day and discovered I had truly become a noncombatant: I had gained seven pounds. I found patience to get past the first three pages of a book. I thought about the future more and more, and wrote letters to girls I'd known before the war—I even got a few answers. I sent away to Columbia for a Law School catalogue. I continued to follow the war in the Pacific, but it was not my war and I read of bombings and battles like a civilian. I thought I could see the end in sight and sometimes at night I dreamed that I was walking on streets of Manhattan—Broadway, Third Avenue, and 116th Street, where I had lived those three years I'd attended Columbia College. I curled myself around these dreams and I began to be happy.

And then one Saturday when everyone was away and I was alone in the orderly room reading a month-old copy of *The Sporting News,* Grossbart reappeared.

"You a baseball fan, Sergeant?"

I looked up. "How are you?"

"Fine," Grossbart said. "They're making a soldier out of me."

"How are Fishbein and Halpern?"

"Coming along," he said. "We've got no training this afternoon. They're at the movies."

"How come you're not with them?"

"I wanted to come over and say hello."

He smiled—a shy, regular-guy smile, as though he and I well knew that our friendship drew its sustenance from unexpected visits, remembered birthdays, and borrowed lawnmowers. At first it offended me, and then the feeling was swallowed by the general uneasiness I felt at the thought that everyone on the post was locked away in a dark movie theater and I was here alone with Grossbart. I folded my paper.

"Sergeant," he said, "I'd like to ask a favor. It is a favor and I'm making no bones about it."

He stopped, allowing me to refuse him a hearing—which, of course, forced me into a courtesy I did not intend. "Go ahead."

"Well, actually it's two favors."

I said nothing.

"The first one's about these rumors. Everybody says we're going to the Pacific."

"As I told your friend Fishbein, I don't know. You'll just have to wait to find out. Like everybody else."

"You think there's a chance of any of us going East?"

"Germany," I said, "maybe."

"I meant New York."

"I don't think so, Grossbart. Offhand."

"Thanks for the information, Sergeant," he said.

"It's not information, Grossbart. Just what I surmise."

"It certainly would be good to be near home. My parents . . . you know." He took a step towards the door and then turned back. "Oh the other thing. May I ask the other?"

"What is it?"

"The other thing is—I've got relatives in St. Louis and they say they'll give me a whole Passover dinner if I can get down there. God, Sergeant, that'd mean an awful lot to me."

I stood up. "No passes during basic, Grossbart."

"But we're off from now till Monday morning, Sergeant. I could leave the post and no one would even know."

"I'd know. You'd know."

"But that's all. Just the two of us. Last night I called my aunt and you should have heard her. 'Come, come,' she said. 'I got gefilte fish, *chrain,* the works!' Just a day, Sergeant, I'd take the blame if anything happened."

"The captain isn't here to sign a pass."

"You could sign."

"Look, Grossbart—"

"Sergeant, for two months practically I've been eating *trafe* till I want to die."

"I thought you'd made up your mind to live with it. To be minus a little bit of heritage."

He pointed a finger at me. "You!" he said. "That wasn't for you to read!"

"I read it. So what."

"That letter was addressed to a congressman."

"Grossbart, don't feed me any crap. You *wanted* me to read it."

"Why are you persecuting me, Sergeant?"

"Are you kidding!"

"I've run into this before," he said, "but never from my own!"

"Get out of here, Grossbart! Get the hell out of my sight!"

He did not move. "Ashamed, that's what you are. So you take it out on the rest of us. They say Hitler himself was half a Jew. Seeing this, I wouldn't doubt it!"

"What are you trying to do with me, Grossbart? What are you after? You want me to give you special privileges, to change the food, to find out about your orders, to give you weekend passes."

"You even talk like a goy!" Grossbart shook his fist. "Is this a weekend pass I'm asking for? Is a Seder sacred or not?"

Seder! It suddenly occurred to me that Passover had been celebrated weeks before. I confronted Grossbart with the fact.

"That's right," he said. "Who says no? A month ago, and *I* was in the field eating hash! And now all I ask is a simple favor —a Jewish boy I thought would understand. My aunt's willing to go out of her way—to make a Seder a month later—" He turned to go, mumbling.

"Come back here!" I called. He stopped and looked at me. "Grossbart, why can't you be like the rest? Why do you have to stick out like a sore thumb? Why do you beg for special treatment?"

"Because I'm a Jew, Sergeant. I *am* different. Better, maybe not. But different."

"This is a war, Grossbart. For the time being *be* the same."

"I refuse."

"What?"

"I refuse. I can't stop being me, that's all there is to it." Tears came to his eyes. "It's a hard thing to be a Jew. But now I see what Mickey says—it's a harder thing to stay one." He raised a hand sadly toward me. "Look at you."

"Stop crying!"

"Stop this, stop that, stop the other thing! You stop, Sergeant. Stop closing your heart to your own!" And wiping his face with his sleeve, he ran out the door. "The least we can do for one another . . . the least . . ."

An hour later I saw Grossbart headed across the field. He wore a pair of starched khakis and carried only a little leather ditty bag. I went to the door and from the outside felt the heat of the day. It was quiet—not a soul in sight except over by the mess hall four K.P.'s sitting round a pan, sloped forward from the waists, gabbing and peeling potatoes in the sun.

"Grossbart!" I called.

He looked toward me and continued walking.

"Grossbart, get over here!"

He turned and stepped into his long shadow. Finally he stood before me.

"Where are you going?" I said.

"St. Louis. I don't care."

"You'll get caught without a pass."

"So I'll get caught without a pass."

"You'll go to the stockade."

"I'm in the stockade." He made an about-face and headed off.

I let him go only a step: "Come back here," I said, and he followed me into the office, where I typed out a pass and signed the Captain's name and my own initials after it.

He took the pass from me and then, a moment later, he reached out and grabbed my hand. "Sergeant, you don't know how much this means to me."

"Okay. Don't get in any trouble."

"I wish I could show you how much this means to me."

"Don't do me any favors. Don't write any more congressmen for citations."

Amazingly, he smiled. "You're right. I won't. But let me do something."

"Bring me a piece of that gefilte fish. Just get out of here."

"I will! With a slice of carrot and a little horseradish. I won't forget."

"All right. Just show your pass at the gate. And don't tell *anybody.*"

"I won't. It's a month late, but a good Yom Tov to you."

"Good Yom Tov, Grossbart," I said.

"You're a good Jew, Sergeant. You like to think you have a hard heart, but underneath you're a fine decent man. I mean that."

Those last three words touched me more than any words from Grossbart's mouth had the right to. "All right, Grossbart. Now call me 'sir' and get the hell out of here."

He ran out the door and was gone. I felt very pleased with myself—it was a great relief to stop fighting Grossbart. And it had cost me nothing. Barrett would never find out, and if he did, I could manage to invent some excuse. For a while I sat at my desk, comfortable in my decision. Then the screen door flew back and Grossbart burst in again. "Sergeant!" he said.

Behind him I saw Fishbein and Halpern, both in starched khakis, both carrying ditty bags exactly like Grossbart's.

"Sergeant, I caught Mickey and Larry coming out of the movies. I almost missed them."

"Grossbart, did I say tell no one?"

"But my aunt said I could bring friends. That I should, in fact."

"I'm the Sergeant, Grossbart—not your aunt!"

Grossbart looked at me in disbelief; he pulled Halpern up by his sleeve. "Mickey, tell the Sergeant what this would mean to you."

"Grossbart, for God's sake, spare us—"

"Tell him what you told me, Mickey. How much it would mean."

Halpern looked at me and, shrugging his shoulders, made his admission. "A lot."

Fishbein stepped forward without prompting. "This would mean a great deal to me and my parents, Sergeant Marx."

"No!" I shouted.

Grossbart was shaking his head. "Sergeant, I could see you denying me, but how you can deny Mickey, a Yeshivah boy, that's beyond me."

"I'm not denying Mickey anything. You just pushed a little too hard, Grossbart. *You* denied him."

"I'll give him my pass, then," Grossbart said. "I'll give him my aunt's address and a little note. At least let him go."

In a second he had crammed the pass into Halpern's pants' pocket. Halpern looked at me, Fishbein too. Grossbart was at the door, pushing it open. "Mickey, bring me a piece of gefilte fish at least." And then he was outside again.

The three of us looked at one another and then I said, "Halpern, hand that pass over."

He took it from his pocket and gave it to me. Fishbein had now moved to the doorway, where he lingered. He stood there with his mouth slightly open and then pointed to himself. "And me?" he asked.

His utter ridiculousness exhausted me. I slumped down in my seat and felt pulses knocking at the back of my eyes. "Fishbein," I said, "you understand I'm not trying to deny you anything, don't you? If it was my Army I'd serve gefilte fish in the mess hall. I'd sell kugel in the PX, honest to God."

Halpern smiled.

"You understand, don't you, Halpern?"

"Yes, Sergeant."

"And you, Fishbein? I don't want enemies. I'm just like you —I want to serve my time and go home. I miss the same things you miss."

"Then, Sergeant," Fishbein interrupted, "why don't you come too?"

"Where?"

"To St. Louis. To Shelley's aunt. We'll have a regular Seder. Play hide-the-matzoh." He gave a broad, black-toothed smile.

I saw Grossbart in the doorway again, on the other side of the screen.

"Pssst!" He waved a piece of paper. "Mickey, here's the address. Tell her I couldn't get away."

Halpern did not move. He looked at me and I saw the shrug moving up his arms into his shoulders again. I took the cover off my typewriter and made out passes for him and Fishbein. "Go," I said, "the three of you."

I thought Halpern was going to kiss my hand.

* * *

That afternoon, in a bar in Joplin, I drank beer and listened with half an ear to the Cardinal game. I tried to look squarely at what I'd become involved in, and began to wonder if perhaps the struggle with Grossbart wasn't much my fault as his. What was I that I had to *muster* generous feelings? Who was I to have been feeling so grudging, so tight-hearted? After all, I wasn't being asked to move the world. Had I a right, then, or a reason, to clamp down on Grossbart, when that meant clamping down on Halpern, too? And Fishbein, that ugly agreeable soul, wouldn't he suffer in the bargain also? Out of the many recollections that had tumbled over me these past few days, I heard from some childhood moment my grandmother's voice: "What are you making a *tsimas?*" It was what she would ask my mother when, say, I had cut myself with a knife and her daughter was busy bawling me out. I would need a hug and a kiss and my mother would moralize! But my grandmother knew—mercy overrides justice. I should have known it, too. Who was Nathan Marx to be such a pennypincher with kindness? Surely, I thought, the Messiah himself—if he should ever come—won't niggle over nickels and dimes. God willing, he'll hug and kiss.

The next day, while we were playing softball over on the Parade Grounds, I decided to ask Bob Wright, who was noncom in charge over at Classification and Assignment, where he thought our trainees would be sent when their cycle ended in two weeks. I asked casually, between innings, and he said, "They're pushing them all into the Pacific. Shulman cut the orders on your boys the other day."

The news shocked me, as though I were father to Halpern, Fishbein, and Grossbart.

* * *

That night I was just sliding into sleep when someone tapped on the door. "What is it?"

"Sheldon."

He opened the door and came in. For a moment I felt his presence without being able to see him. "How was it?" I asked, as though to the darkness.

He popped into sight before me. "Great, Sergeant." I felt my springs sag; Grossbart was sitting on the edge of the bed. I sat up.

"How about you?" he asked. "Have a nice weekend?"

"Yes."

He took a deep paternal breath. "The others went to sleep . . ." We sat silently for a while, as a homey feeling invaded my ugly little cubicle: the door was locked, the cat out, the children safely in bed.

"Sergeant, can I tell you something? Personal?"

I did not answer and he seemed to know why. "Not about me. About Mickey. Sergeant, I never felt for anybody like I feel for him. Last night I heard Mickey in the bed next to me. He was crying so, it could have broken your heart. Real sobs."

"I'm sorry to hear that."

"I had to talk to him to stop him. He held my hand, Sergeant—he wouldn't let it go. He was almost hysterical. He kept saying if he only knew where we were going. Even if he knew it *was* the Pacific, that would be better than nothing. Just to know."

Long ago, someone had taught Grossbart the sad law that only lies can get the truth. Not that I couldn't believe in Halpern's crying—his eyes *always* seemed red-rimmed. But, fact or not, it became a lie when Grossbart uttered it. He was entirely strategic. But then—it came with the force of indictment—so was I! There are strategies of aggression, but there are strategies of retreat, as well. And so, recognizing that I, myself, had not been without craft and guile, I told him what I knew. "It is the Pacific."

He let out a small gasp, which was not a lie. "I'll tell him. I wish it was otherwise."

"So do I."

He jumped on my words. "You mean you think you could do something? A change maybe?"

"No, I couldn't do a thing."

"Don't you know anybody over at C & A?"

"Grossbart, there's nothing I can do. If your orders are for the Pacific then it's the Pacific."

"But Mickey."

"Mickey, you, me—everybody, Grossbart. There's nothing to be done. Maybe the war'll end before you go. Pray for a miracle."

"But—"

"Good night, Grossbart." I settled back, and was relieved to feel the springs upbend again as Grossbart rose to leave. I could see him clearly now; his jaw had dropped and he looked like a dazed prizefighter. I noticed for the first time a little paper bag in his hand.

"Grossbart"—I smiled—"my gift?"

"Oh, yes, Sergeant. Here, from all of us." He handed me the bag. "It's egg roll."

"Egg roll?" I accepted the bag and felt a damp grease spot on the bottom. I opened it, sure that Grossbart was joking.

"We thought you'd probably like it. You know, Chinese egg roll. We thought you'd probably have a taste for—"

"Your aunt served egg roll?"

"She wasn't home."

"Grossbart, she invited you. You told me she invited you and your friends."

"I know. I just reread the letter. *Next* week."

I got out of bed and walked to the window. It was black as far off as I could see. "Grossbart," I said. But I was not calling him.

"What?"

"What are you, Grossbart? Honest to God, what are you?"

I think it was the first time I'd asked him a question for which he didn't have an immediate answer.

"How can you do this to people?" I asked.

"Sergeant, the day away did us all a world of good. Fishbein, you should see him, he *loves* Chinese food."

"But the Seder," I said.

"We took second best, Sergeant."

Rage came charging at me. I didn't sidestep—I grabbed it, pulled it in, hugged it to my chest.

"Grossbart, you're a liar! You're a schemer and a crook! You've got no respect for anything! Nothing at all! Not for me, for the truth, not even for poor Halpern! You use us all—"

"Sergeant, Sergeant, I feel for Mickey, honest to God, I do. I *love* Mickey. I try—"

"You try! You feel!" I lurched towards him and grabbed his shirt front. I shook him furiously. "Grossbart, get out. Get out and stay the hell away from me! Because if I see you, I'll make your life miserable. *You understand that?*"

"Yes."

I let him free, and when he walked from the room I wanted to spit on the floor where he had stood. I couldn't stop the fury from rising in my heart. It engulfed me, owned me, till it seemed I could only rid myself of it with tears or an act of violence. I snatched from the bed the bag Grossbart had given me and with all my strength threw it out the window. And the next morning, as the men policed the area around the barracks, I heard a great cry go up from one of the trainees who'd been anticipating only this morning handful of cigarette butts and candy wrappers. "Egg roll!" he shouted. "Holy Christ, Chinese goddam egg roll!"

* * *

A week later when I read the orders that had come down from C & A I couldn't believe my eyes. Every single trainee was to be shipped to Camp Stoneham, California, and from there to the Pacific. Every trainee but one: Private Sheldon Grossbart was to be sent to Fort Monmouth, New Jersey. I read the mimeographed sheet several times. Dee, Farrell, Fishbein, Fuselli, Fylypowycz, Glinicki, Gromke, Gucwa, Halpern, Hardy, Helebrandt . . . right down to Anton Zygadlo, all were to be headed West before the month was out. All except Grossbart. He had pulled a string and I wasn't it.

I lifted the phone and called C & A.

The voice on the other end said smartly, "Corporal Shulman, sir."

"Let me speak to Sergeant Wright."

"Who is this calling, sir?"

"Sergeant Marx."

And to my surprise, the voice said, *"Oh."* Then: "Just a minute, Sergeant."

Shulman's *oh* stayed with me while I waited for Wright to come to phone. Why *oh?* Who was Shulman? And then, so simply, I knew I'd discovered the string Grossbart had pulled. In fact, I could hear Grossbart the day he'd discovered Shulman, in the PX, or the bowling alley, or maybe even at services. "Glad to meet you. Where you from? Bronx? Me too. Do you know so-and-so? And so-and-so? Me too! You work at C & A? Really? Hey, how's chances of getting East? Could you do something? Change something? Swindle, cheat, lie? We gotta help each other, you know . . . if the Jews in Germany . . ."

At the other end Bob Wright answered. "How are you, Nate? How's the pitching arm?"

"Good. Bob, I wonder if you could do me a favor." I heard clearly my own words and they so reminded me of Grossbart that I dropped more easily than I could have imagined into what I had planned. "This may sound crazy, Bob, but I got a kid here on orders to Monmouth who wants them changed. He had a brother killed in Europe and he's hot to go to the Pacific. Says he'd feel like a coward if he wound up stateside. I don't know, Bob, can anything be done? Put somebody else in the Monmouth slot?"

"Who?" he asked cagily.

"Anybody. First guy on the alphabet. I don't care. The kid just asked if something could be done."

"What's his name?"

"Grossbart, Sheldon."

Wright didn't answer.

"Yeah," I said, "he's a Jewish kid, so he thought I could help him out. You know."

"I guess I can do something," he finally said. "The Major hasn't been around here for weeks—TDY to the golf course. I'll try, Nate that's all I can say."

"I'd appreciate it, Bob. See you Sunday," and I hung up, perspiring.

And the following day the corrected orders appeared: Fishbein, Fuselli, Fylypowycz, Glinicki, Grossbart, Gucwa, Halpern, Hardy . . . Lucky Private Harley Alton was to go to Fort Monmouth, New Jersey, where for some reason or other, they wanted an enlisted man with infantry training.

After chow that night I stopped back at the orderly room to straighten out the guard duty roster. Grossbart was waiting for me. He spoke first.

"You son of a bitch!"

I sat down at my desk and while he glared down at me I began to make the necessary alterations in the duty roster.

"What do you have against me?" he cried. "Against my family? Would it kill you for me to be near my father, God knows how many months he has left to him."

"Why?"

"His heart," Grossbart said. "He hasn't had enough troubles in a lifetime, you've got to add to them. I curse the day I ever met you, Marx! Shulman told me what happened over there. There's no limit to your anti-Semitism, is there! The damage you've done here isn't enough. You have to make a special phone call. You really want me dead!"

I made the last few notations in the duty roster and got up to leave. "Good night, Grossbart."

"You owe me an explanation!" He stood in my path.

"Sheldon, you're the one who owes explanations."

He scowled. "To *you?*"

"To me, I think so, yes. Mostly to Fishbein and Halpern."

"That's right, twist things around. I owe nobody nothing, I've done all I could do for them. Now I think I've got the right to watch out for myself."

"For each other we have to learn to watch out, Sheldon. You told me yourself."

"You call this watching out for me, what you did?"

"No. For all of us."

I pushed him aside and started for the door. I heard his furious breathing behind me, and it sounded like steam rushing from the engine of his terrible strength.

"You'll be all right," I said from the door. And, I thought, so would Fishbein and Halpern be all right, even in the Pacific, if only Grossbart could continue to see in the obsequiousness of the one, the soft spirituality of the other, some profit for himself.

I stood outside the orderly room, and I heard Grossbart weeping behind me. Over in the barracks, in the lighted windows, I could see the boys in their T-shirts sitting on their bunks talking about their orders, as they'd been doing for the past two days. With a kind of quiet nervousness, they polished shoes, shined belt buckles, squared away underwear, trying as best they could to accept their fate. Behind me, Grossbart swallowed hard, accepting his. And then, resisting with all my will an impulse to turn and seek pardon for my vindictiveness, I accepted my own.

THE TIME OF FRIENDSHIP

.

by Paul Bowles

The trouble had been growing bigger each year, ever since the end of the war. From the beginning, although aware of its existence, Fräulein Windling had determined to pay it no attention. At first there were only whispered reports of mass arrests. People said: "Many thousands of Moslems have been sent to prison in France." Soon some of her own friends had begun to disappear, like young Bachir and Omar ben Lakhdar, the postmaster of Timimoun, who suddenly one morning were gone, or so she was told, for when she returned the following winter they were not there, and she never had seen them since. The people simply made their faces blank when she tried to talk about it. After the hostilities had begun in earnest, even though the nationalists had derailed the trains and disrupted the trans-Saharan truck service on several occasions, still it was possible to get beyond the disturbed region to her oasis. There in the south the fighting was far away, and the long hours of empty desert that lay between made it seem much farther, almost as though it had been across the sea. If the men of her oasis should ever be infected by the virus of discontent from the far-off north—and this seemed to her almost inconceivable—then in spite of the fact that she was certain that war could bring them nothing but unhappiness, she would have no recourse but to hope for their victory. It was their own land they would be fighting for, their own lives they would be losing in order to win the fight. In the meantime people did not talk; life was hard but peaceful. Each one was aware of the war that was going on in the north, and each one was glad it was far away.

Summers, Fräulein Windling taught in the Freiluftschüle in Bern, where she entertained her pupils with tales of the life led by the people in the great desert in Africa. In the village where she lived, she told them, everything was made by the people themselves out of what the desert had to offer. They lived in a world of objects fashioned out of baked earth, woven grass, palmwood and animal skins. There was no metal. Although she did not admit it to the children, this was no longer wholly true, since recently the women had taken to using empty oil tins for carrying water, instead of the goathide bags of a few years before. She had tried to discourage her friends among the village women from this innovation, telling them that the tins could poison the water; they had agreed, and gone on using them. "They are lazy," she decided. "The oil tins are easier to carry."

When the sun went down and the cool air from the oasis below with its sting of woodsmoke rose to the level of the hotel, she would smell it inside her room and stop whatever she was doing. Then she would put on her burnoose and climb the stairs to the roof. The blanket she lay on while she sunbathed each morning would be there, and she would stretch out on it facing the western sky, and feel the departed sun's heat still strong underneath her body. It was one of the pleasures of the day, to watch the light changing in the oasis below, when dusk and the smoke from the evening fires slowly blotted out the valley. There always came a moment when all that was left was the faint outline, geometric and precise, of the mass of mud prisms that was the village, and a certain clump of high date palms that stood outside its entrance. The houses themselves were no longer there, and eventually the highest palm disappeared; and unless there was a moon all that remained to be seen was the dying sky, the sharp edges of the rocks on the hammada, and a blank expanse of mist that lay over the valley but did not reach as far up the cliffs as the hotel.

Perhaps twice each winter a group of the village women would invite Fräulein Windling to go with them up into the vast land of the dunes to look for firewood. The glare here was cruel. There was not even the trace of a twig or a stem anywhere on the sand, yet as they wandered along the crests barefoot the women could spot the places where roots lay buried beneath the surface, and then they would stoop, uncover them, and dig them up. "The wind leaves a sign," they told her, but she was never certain of being able to identify the sign, nor could she understand how there might be a connection between the invisible roots in the sand and the wind in the air above. "What we have lost, they still possess," she thought.

Her first sight of the desert and its people had been a transfiguring experience; indeed, it seemed to her now that before coming here she had never been in touch with life at all. She believed firmly that each day she spent here increased the aggregate of her resistance. She coveted the rugged health of the natives, when her own was equally strong, but because she was white and educated, she was convinced that her body was intrinsically inferior.

All the work in the hotel was done by one quiet, sad-faced man named Boufelja. He had been there when she had first arrived many years ago; for Fräulein Windling he had come to be as much a part of the place as the cliffs across the valley. She often sat on her table by the fireplace after lunch, playing cards by herself, until the logs no longer gave out heat. There were two very young French soldiers from the fort opposite, who ate in the hotel dining-room. They drank a great amount of wine, and it annoyed her to see their faces slowly turning red as they sat there. At first the soldiers had tipped their caps to her as they went out, and they had stopped their laughing long enough to say, *"Bonjour, madame,"* to her, but now they no longer did. She was happy when they had left, and savored the moment before the fire burned out, while it still glowed under the gusts of wind that wandered down the wide chimney.

Almost always the wind sprang up early in the afternoon, a steady, powerful blowing that roared through the thousands of palms in the oasis below and howled under each door in the hotel, covering the more distant village sounds. This was the hour when she played solitaire, or merely sat, watching the burnt-out logs as they fell to pieces before her eyes. Later she would go along the terrace, a high, bright place like the deck of a great ship sailing through the desert afternoon, hurrying into her room for an instant to get her sweater and cane, and start out on a walk. Sometimes she went southward following the river valley, along the foot of the silent cliffs and through the crooked gorges, to an abandoned village built in a very hot place at a turn in the canyon. The sheer walls of rock behind it sent back the heat, so that the air burned her throat as she breathed it in. Or she went farther, to where the cliff dwellings were, with their animals and symbols incised in the rock.

Returning along the road that led to the village, deep in the green shade of the thickest part of the palm forest, she was regularly aware of the same group of boys sitting at the turn of the road, at a place just before it led up the hill to the shops and the village. They squatted on the sand behind the feathery branches of a giant tamarisk, quietly talking. When she came up to them she greeted them, and they always replied, remained silent a moment until she had passed by, and then resumed their conversation. As far as she could tell, there was never any reference to her by word, and yet this year it sometimes seemed to her that once she had gone by, their inflection had subtly altered, as though there had been a modulation into another key. Did their attitude border on derision? She did not know, but since this was the first time during all her years in the desert that the idea had ever suggested itself to her, she put it resolutely out of her mind. "A new generation requires a new technique if one is to establish contact," she thought. "It is for me to find it." Nevertheless she was sorry that there was no other way of getting into the village save along this main road where they invariably gathered. Even the slight tension caused by having to go past them marred the pleasure of her walks.

One day she realized with a slight shock of shame that she did not even know what the boys looked like. She had seen them only as a group from a distance; when she drew near enough to say good-day to them, she always had her head down, watching the road. The fact that she had been afraid to look at them was unacceptable; now, as she came up to them, she stared into the eyes of one after the other, carefully. Nodding gravely, she went on. Yes, they were insolent faces, she thought—not at all like the faces of their elders. The respectful attitudes into which they had been startled were the crudest sort of shamming. But the important thing to her was that she had won: she was no longer preoccupied with having to pass by them every day. Slowly she even grew to recognize each boy.

There was one, she noted, younger than the others, who always sat a little apart from them, and it was this shy one who stood talking to Boufelja in the hotel kitchen early one morning when she went in. She pretended not to notice him. "I am going to my room to work on the machine for about an hour," she told Boufelja. "You can come then to make up the room," and she turned to go out. As she went through the doorway she glanced at the boy's face. He was looking at her, and he did not turn away when his eyes met hers. "How are you?" she said. Perhaps half an hour later, when she was typing her second letter, she raised her head. The boy was standing on the terrace looking at her through the open door. He squinted, for the wind was strong; behind his head she saw the tops of the palms bending.

"If he wants to watch, let him watch," she said to herself, deciding to pay him no attention. After a while he went away. While Boufelja served her lunch, she questioned him about the boy. "Like an old man," said Boufelja. "Twelve years old but very serious. Like some old, old man." He smiled, then shrugged. "It's the way God wanted him to be."

"Of course," she said, remembering the boy's alert, unhappy face. "A young dog that everyone has kicked," she thought, "but he hasn't given up."

In the days that followed, he came often to the terrace and stood watching her while she typed. Sometimes she waved to him, or said: "Good morning." Without answering he would take a step backward, so that he was out of her range. Then he would continue to stand where he was. His behavior irked her, and one day when he had done this, she quickly got up and went to the door. "What is it?" she asked him, trying to smile as she spoke.

"I didn't do anything," he said, his eyes reproachful.

"I know," she answered. "Why don't you come in?"

The boy looked swiftly around the terrace as if for help; then he bowed his head and stepped inside the door. Here he stood waiting, his head down, looking miserable. From her luggage she brought out a bag of hard candy, and handed him a piece. Then she put a few simple questions to him, and found that his French was much better than she had expected. "Do the other boys know French as well as you?" she asked him.

"*Non, madame,*" he said, shaking his head slowly. "My father used to be a soldier. Soldiers speak good French."

She tried to keep her face from expressing the disapproval she felt, for she despised everything military. "I see," she said with some asperity, turning back to her table and shuffling the papers. "Now I must work," she told him, immediately adding in a warmer voice, "but you come back tomorrow, if you like." He waited an instant, looking at her with unchanged wistfulness. Then slowly he smiled, and laid the candy wrapper, folded into a tiny square, on the corner of her table. "*Au revoir, madame,*" he said, and went out of the door. In the silence she heard the scarcely audible thud of his bare heels on the earth floor of the terrace. "In this cold," she thought. "Poor child! If I ever buy anything for him it will be a pair of sandals."

Each day thereafter, when the sun was high enough to give substance to the still morning air, the boy would come stealthily along the terrace to her door, stand a few seconds, and then say in a lost voice that was all the smaller and more hushed for the great silence outside: "*Bonjour, madame.*" She would tell him to come in, and they would shake hands gravely, he afterward raising the backs of his fingers to his lips, always with the same slow ceremoniousness. She sometimes tried to fathom his countenance as he went through this ritual, to see if by any chance she could detect a shade of mockery there; instead she saw an expression of devotion so convincing that it startled her, and she looked away quickly. She always kept a bit of bread or some biscuits in a drawer of the wardrobe; when she had brought the food out and he was eating it, she would ask him for news about the families in his quarter of the village. For discipline's sake she offered him a piece of candy only every other day. He sat on the floor by the doorway, on a torn old camel blanket, and he watched her constantly, never turning his head away from her.

She wanted to know what he was called, but she was aware of how secretive the inhabitants of the region were about names, seldom giving their true ones to strangers; this was a peculiarity she respected because she knew it had its roots in their own prehistoric religion. So she forbore asking him, sure that the time would come when he trusted her enough to give it of his own volition. And the moment happened one morning unexpectedly, when he had just recounted several legends involving the great Moslem king of long ago, whose name was Solomon. Suddenly he stopped, and forcing himself to gaze steadily at her without blinking, he said: "And my name too is Slimane, the same as the king."

She tried to teach him to read, but he did not seem able to learn. Often just as she felt he was about to connect two loose ends of ideas and perhaps at last make a contact which would enable him to understand the principle, a look of resignation and passivity would appear in his face, and he would willfully cut off the stream of effort from its source, and remain sitting, merely looking at her, shaking his head from side to side to show that it was useless. It was hard not to lose patience with him at such moments.

The following year she decided not to go on with the lessons, and to use Slimane instead as a guide, bearer and companion, a role which she immediately saw was more suited to his nature than that of pupil. He did not mind how far they went or how much equipment he had to carry; on the contrary, to him a long excursion was that much more of an event, and whatever she loaded onto him he bore with the air of one upon whom an honor is conferred. It was probably her happiest season in the desert, that winter of comradeship when together they made the countless pilgrimages down the valley.

As the weeks passed the trips grew in scope, and the hour of departure was brought forward until it came directly after she had finished her breakfast. All day long, trudging in the open sun and in the occasional shade of the broken fringe of palms that skirted the riverbed, she conversed passionately with him. Sometimes she could see that he felt like telling her what was in his head, and she let him speak for as long as his enthusiasm lasted, often reviving it at the end with carefully chosen questions. But usually it was she who did the speaking as she walked behind him. Pounding the stony ground with her steel-tipped stick each time her right foot went down, she told him in great detail the story of the life of Hitler, showing why he was hated by the Christians. This she thought necessary since Slimane had been under a different impression, and indeed had imagined that the Europeans thought as highly of the vanished leader as did he and the rest of the people in the village. She talked a good deal about Switzerland, casually stressing the cleanliness, honesty and good health of her countrymen in short parables of daily life. She told him about Jesus, Martin Luther and Garibaldi, taking care to keep Jesus distinct from the Moslem prophet Sidna Aissa, since even for the sake of argument she could not agree for an instant with the Islamic doctrine according to which the Savior was a Moslem. Slimane's attitude of respect bordering on adoration with regard to her never altered unless she inadvertently tangled with the subject of Islam; then, no matter what she said (for at that point it seemed that automatically he was no longer within hearing) he would shake his head interminably and cry: "No, no, no, no! Nazarenes know nothing about Islam. Don't talk, madame, I beg you, because you don't know what you're saying. No, no, no!"

Long ago she had kept the initial promise to herself that she would buy him sandals; this purchase had been followed by others. At fairly regular intervals she had taken him to Benaissa's store to buy a shirt, a pair of baggy black cotton trousers of the kind worn by the Chaamba camel-drivers, and ultimately a new white burnoose, despite the fact that she knew the entire village would discuss the giving of so valuable an object. She also knew that it was only the frequent bestowing of such gifts that kept Slimane's father from forbidding him to spend his time with her. Even so, according to reports brought by Slimane, he sometimes objected. But Slimane himself, she was sure, wanted nothing, expected nothing.

It was each year when March was drawing to a close that the days began to be painfully hot and even the nights grew breathless; then, although it always required a strenuous effort of the will to make herself take the step which would bring about renewed contact with the outside world, she would devote two or three days to washing her clothing and preparing for the journey. When the week set for her departure had come, she went over to the fort and put in a call to the café at Kerzaz, asking the proprietor to tell the driver of the next northbound truck to take the detour that would enable her to catch him at a point only about three kilometers from the village.

She and Slimane had come back to the hotel on the afternoon of their last excursion down the valley; Fräulein Windling stood on the terrace looking out at the orange mountains of sand behind the fort. Slimane had taken the packs into the room and put them down. She turned and said: "Bring the big tin box." When he had pulled it out from under the bed he carried it to her, dusting it off with the sleeve of his shirt, and she led the way up the stairs to the roof. They sat down on the blanket; the glow of the vanished sun's furnace heated their faces. A few flies still hovered, now and then attacking their necks. Slimane handed her the biscuit tin and she gave him a fistful of chocolate-covered cakes. "So many all at once?"

"Yes," she said. "You know I'm going home in four days."

He looked down at the blanket a moment before replying. "I know," he murmured. He was silent again. Then he cried out aggrievedly: "Boufelja says it's hot here in the summer. It's not hot! In our house it's cool. It's like the oasis where the big pool is. You would never be hot there."

"I have to earn money. You know that. I want to come back next year."

He said sadly: "Next year, madame! Only Moulana knows how next year will be."

Some camels growled as they rolled in the sand at the foot of the fort; the light was receding swiftly. "Eat your biscuits," she told him, and she ate one herself. "Next year we'll go to Abadla with the caid, *incha' Allah.*"

He sighed deeply. "Ah, madame!" he said. She noted, at first with a pang of sympathy and then, reconsidering, with disapproval, the anguish that lent his voice its unaccustomed intensity. It was the quality she least liked in him, this faintly theatrical self-pity. "Next year you'll be a man," she told him firmly. Her voice grew less sure, assumed a hopeful tone. "You'll remember all the things we talked about?"

She sent him a postcard from Marseille, and showed her classes photographs they had taken of one another, and of the caid. The children were impressed by the caid's voluminous turban. "Is he a Bedouin?" asked one.

When she left the embassy office she knew that this was the last year she would be returning to the desert. There was not only the official's clearly expressed unfriendliness and suspicion: for the first time he had made her answer a list of questions which she found alarming. He wanted to know what subjects she taught in the Freiluftschüle, whether she had ever been a journalist, and exactly where she proposed to be each day after arriving in the Sahara. She had almost retorted: I go where I feel like going. I don't make plans. But she had merely named the oasis. She knew that Frenchmen had no respect for elderly Swiss ladies who wore woolen stockings; this simply made them more contemptible in her eyes. However, it was they who controlled the Sahara.

The day the ship put into the African port it was raining. She knew the gray terraced ramps of the city were there in the gloom ahead, but they were invisible. The ragged European garments of the dock workers were soaked with rain. Later, the whole rain-sodden city struck her as grim, and the people passing along the streets looked unhappy. The change, even from the preceding year, was enormous; it made her sad to sit in the big, cold café where she went for coffee after dinner, and so she returned to her hotel and slept. The next day she got on the train for Perrégaux. The rain fell most of the day. In Perrégaux she took a room in a hotel near the station, and stayed in it, listening to the rain rattle down the gutter by her window. "This place would be a convenient model for Hell," she wrote to a friend in Basel before going to sleep that night. "A full-blown example of the social degeneracy achieved by forced cultural hybridism. Populace debased and made hostile by generations of merciless exploitation. I take the southbound narrow-gauge train tomorrow morning for a happier land, and trust that my friend the sun will appear at some point during the day. *Seien Sie herzlich gegrüsst von Ihrer Maria.*"

As the train crawled southward, up over the high plateau land, the clouds were left behind and the sun took charge of the countryside. Fräulein Windling sat attentively by the smeared window, enveloped in an increasing sadness. As long as it had been raining, she had imagined the rain as the cause of her depression: the gray cloud light gave an unaccustomed meaning to the landscape by altering forms and distances. Now she understood that the more familiar and recognizable the contours of the desert were to become, the more conscious she would be of having no reason to be in it, because it was her last visit.

Two days later, when the truck stopped to let her out, Boufelja stood in the sun beside the boulders waving; one of the men of the village was with him to help carry the luggage. Once the truck had gone and its cloud of yellow dust had fled across the hammada, the silence was there; it seemed that no sound could be louder than the crunch of their shoes on the ground.

"How is Slimane?" she asked. Boufelja was noncommittal. "He's all right," he said. "They say he tried to run away. But he didn't get very far." The report might be true, or it might be false; in any case she determined not to allude to it unless Slimane himself mentioned it first.

She felt an absurd relief when they came to the edge of the cliffs and she saw the village across the valley. Not until she had made the rounds of the houses where her friends lived, discussed their troubles with them and left some pills here and some candy there, was she convinced that no important change had come to the oasis during her absence. She went to the house of Slimane's parents: he was not there. "Tell him to come and see me," she said to his father as she left the house.

On the third morning after her arrival Slimane appeared, and stood there in the doorway smiling. Once she had greeted him and made him sit down and have coffee with her, she plied him with questions about life in the village while she had been in Europe. Some of his friends had gone to become patriots, he said, and they were killing the French like flies. Her heart sank, but she said nothing. As she watched him smiling she was able to exult in the reflection that Slimane had been reachable, after all; she had proved that it was possible to make true friends of the younger people. But even while she was saying, "How happy I am to see you, Slimane," she remembered that their time together was now limited, and an expression of pain passed over her face as she finished the phrase. "I shall not say a word to him about it," she decided. If he, at least, still had the illusion of unbounded time lying ahead, he would some-how retain his aura of purity and innocence, and she would feel less anguish during the time they spent together.

One day they went down the valley to see the caid, and discussed the long-planned trip to Abadla. Another day they started out at dawn to visit the tomb of Moulay Ali ben Said, where there was a spring of hot water. It was a tiny spot of oasis at the edge of a ridge of high dunes; perhaps fifty palms were there around the decayed shrine. In the shade of the rocks below the walls there was a ruined cistern into which the steaming water dribbled. They spread blankets on the sand nearby, at the foot of a small tamarisk, and took out their lunch. Before starting to eat, they drank handfuls of the water, which Slimane said was famed for its holiness. The palms rat-tled and hissed in the wind overhead.

"Allah has sent us the wind to make us cool while we eat," Slimane said when he had finished his bread and dates.

"The wind has always been here," she answered carelessly, "and it always will be here."

He sat up straight. "No, no!" he cried. "When Sidna Aissa has returned for forty days there will be no more Moslems and the world will end. Everything, the sky and the sun and the moon. And the wind too. Everything." He looked at her with an expression of such satisfaction that she felt one of her occa-sional surges of anger against him.

"I see," she said. "Stand over by the spring a minute. I want to take your picture." She had never understood why it was that the Moslems had conceded Jesus even this Pyrrhic vic-tory, the coda to all creation: its inconsistency embarrassed her. Across the decayed tank she watched Slimane assume the traditional stiff attitude of a person about to be photographed, and an idea came into her head. For Christmas Eve, which would come within two weeks, she would make a crèche. She would invite Slimane to eat with her by the fireplace, and when midnight came she would take him in to see it.

She finished photographing Slimane; they gathered up the equipment and set out against the hot afternoon wind for the village. The sand sometimes swept by, stinging their faces with its invisible fringe. Fräulein Windling led the way this time, and they walked fast. The image of the crèche, illumined by candles, occurred to her several times on the way back over the rocky erg; it made her feel inexpressibly sad, for she could not help connecting it with the fact that everything was ending. They came to the point north of the village where the empty erg was cut across by the wandering river valley. As they climbed slowly upward over the fine sand, she found herself whispering: "It's the right thing to do." "*Right* is not the word," she thought, without being able to find a better one. She was going to make a crèche because she loved Christmas and wanted to share it with Slimane. They reached the hotel shortly after sunset, and she sent Slimane home in order to sit and plan her project on paper.

It was only when she began actually to put the crèche together that she realized how much work it was going to be. Early the next morning she asked Boufelja to find her an old wooden crate. Before she had been busy even a half-hour, she heard Slimane talking in the kitchen. Quickly she pushed everything under the bed and went out onto the terrace.

"Slimane," she said. "I'm very busy. Come in the afternoon." And that afternoon she told him that since she was going to be working every morning until after the day of the Christ Child, they would not be making any more long trips during that time. He received the information glumly. "I know," he said. "You are getting ready for the holy day. I understand."

"When the holy day comes, we will have a feast," she assured him.

"If Allah wills."

"I'm sorry," she said, smiling.

He shrugged. "Good-by," he told her.

Afternoons they still walked in the oasis or had tea on the roof, but her mornings she spent in her room sewing, hammering and sculpting. Once she had the platform constructed, she had to model the figures. She carried a great mass of wet clay from the river to her room. It was two days before she managed to make a Virgin whose form pleased her. From an old strip of muslin she fashioned a convincing tent to house the Mother and the Child in its nest of tiny white chicken feathers. Shredded tamarisk needles made a fine carpet for the interior of the tent. Outside she poured sand, and then pushed the clay camels' long legs deep into it; one animal walked behind the other over the dune, and a Wise Man sat straight on top of each, his white *djellaba* falling in long pointed folds to either side of the camel's flanks. The Wise Men would come carrying sacks of almonds and very small liqueur chocolates wrapped in colored tinfoil. When she had the crèche finished, she put it on the floor in the middle of the room and piled tangerines and dates in front of it. With a row of candles burning behind it, and one candle on each side in front, it would look like a Moslem religious chromolithograph. She hoped the scene would be recognizable to Slimane; he might then be more easily persuaded of its poetic truth. She wanted only to suggest to him that the god with whom he was on such intimate terms was the god worshipped by the Nazarenes. It was not an idea she would ever try to express in words.

An additional surprise for the evening would be the new flash-bulb attachment to her camera, which Slimane had not yet seen. She intended to take a good many pictures of the crèche and of Slimane looking at it; these she would enlarge to show her pupils. She went and bought a new turban for Slimane; he had been wearing none for more than a year now.

This was a man's turban, and very fine: ten meters of the softest Egyptian cotton.

The day before Christmas she overslept, duped by the heavy sky. Each winter the oasis had a few dark days; they were rare, but this was one of them. While she still lay there in bed, she heard the roar of the wind, and when she got up to look out the window she found no world outside—only a dim rose-gray fog that hid everything. The swirling sand sprayed ceaselessly against the glass; it had formed in long drifts on the floor of the terrace. When she went for breakfast, she wore her bur-noose with the hood up around her face. The blast of the wind as she stepped out onto the terrace struck her with the impact of a solid object, and the sand gritted on the concrete floor under her shoes. In the dining-room Boufelja had bolted the shutters; he greeted her enthusiastically from the gloom inside, glad of her presence.

"A very bad day for your festival, alas, mademoiselle!" he observed as he set her coffee pot on the table.

"Tomorrow's the festival," she said. "It begins tonight."

"I know. I know." He was impatient with Nazarene feasts because the hours of their beginnings and ends were observed in so slipshod a manner. Moslem feasts began precisely, either at sundown or an hour before sunup, or when the new moon was first visible in the western sky at twilight. But the Nazarenes began their feasts whenever they felt like it.

She spent the morning in her room writing letters. By noon the air outside was darker with still more sand; the wind shook the hotel atop its rock as if it would hurl it over the tips of the palms below into the riverbed. Several times she rose and went to the window to stare out at the pink emptiness beyond the terrace. Storms made her happy, although she wished this one could have come after Christmas. She had imagined a pure desert night—cold, alive with stars, and the dogs yapping from the oasis. It might yet be that; there was still time, she thought, as she slipped her burnoose over her head to go in to lunch.

With the wind, the fireplace was an unsure blessing: besides the heat it gave, it provided the only light in the dining-room, but the smoke that belched from it burned her eyes and throat. The shutters at the windows rattled and pounded, covering the noise of the wind itself.

She got out of the dining-room as soon as she had finished eating, and hurried back to her room to sit through the slowly darkening afternoon, as she continued with her letter-writing and waited for the total extinction of daylight, Slimane was coming at eight. There would be enough time to carry everything into the dining-room before that, and to set the crèche up in the dark unused wing into which Boufelja was unlikely to go. But when she came to do it, she found that the wind's force was even greater than she had imagined. Again and again she made the trip between her room and the dining-room, carrying each object carefully wrapped in her burnoose. Each time she passed in front of the kitchen door she expected Boufelja to open it and discover her. She did not want him there when she showed the crèche to Slimane; he could see it tomorrow at breakfast.

Protected by the noise of the gale she succeeded in transporting all the parts to the far dark corner of the dining-room without alerting Boufelja. Long before dinner time the crèche was in readiness, awaiting only the lighting of the candles to be brought alive. She left a box of matches on the table beside it, and hurried back to her room to arrange her hair and change her clothing. The sand had sifted through her garments and was now everywhere; it showered from her underwear and stuck like sugar to her skin. Her watch showed a few minutes after eight when she went out.

Only one place had been laid at table. She waited, while the blinds chattered and banged, until Boufelja appeared carrying the soup tureen.

"What a bad night," he said.

"You forgot to prepare for Slimane," she told him. But he was not paying attention. "He's stupid!" he exclaimed, beginning to ladle out the soup.

"Wait!" she cried. "Slimane's coming. I mustn't eat until he comes."

Still Boufelja misunderstood. "He wanted to come into the dining-room," he said. "And he knows it's forbidden at dinner time."

"But I invited him!" She looked at the lone soup plate on the table. "Tell him to come in, and set another place."

Boufelja was silent. He put the ladle back into the tureen. "Where is he?" she demanded, and without waiting for him to reply she went on. "Didn't I tell you he was going to have dinner with me tonight?" For suddenly she suspected that in her desire for secrecy she might indeed have neglected to mention the invitation to Boufelja.

"You didn't say anything," he told her. "I didn't know. I sent him home. But he'll be back after dinner."

"Oh, Boufelja!" she cried. "You know Slimane never lies."

He looked down at her with reproach on his face. "I didn't know anything about mademoiselle's plans," he said aggrievedly. This made her think for a swift instant that he had discovered the crèche, but she decided that if he had he would have spoken of it.

"Yes, yes, I know. I should have told you. It's my fault."

"That's true, mademoiselle," he said. And he served the remaining courses observing a dignified silence which she, still feeling some displeasure with him, did not urge him to break. Only at the end of the meal, when she had pushed back her chair from the table and sat studying the pattern of the flames in the fireplace, did he decide to speak. "Mademoiselle will take coffee?"

"I do want some," she said, trying to bring a note of enthusiasm into her voice. *"Bien,"* murmured Boufelja, and he left her alone in the room. When he returned carrying the coffee, Slimane was with him, and they were laughing, she noted, quite as though there had been no misunderstanding about dinner. Slimane stood by the door an instant, stamping his feet and shaking the sand from his burnoose. As he came forward to take her hand, she cried: "Oh, Slimane, it's my fault! I forgot to tell Boufelja. It's terrible!"

"There is no fault, madame," he said gravely. "This is a festival."

"Yes, this is a festival," she echoed. "And the wind's still blowing. Listen!"

Slimane would not take coffee, but Boufelja, ceding to her pressure, let her pour him out a cup, which he drank standing by the fireplace. She suspected him of being secretly pleased that Slimane had not managed to eat with her. When he had finished his coffee, he wished them good-night and went off to bed in his little room next to the kitchen.

They sat a while watching the fire, without talking. The wind rushed past in the emptiness outside, the blinds hammered. Fräulein Windling was content. Even if the first part of the celebration had gone wrong, the rest of the evening could still be pleasant.

She waited until she was sure that Boufelja had really gone to bed, and then she reached into her bag and brought out a small plastic sack full of chocolate creams, which she placed on the table.

"Eat," she said carelessly, and she took a piece of candy herself. With some hesitation Slimane put out his hand to take the sack. When he had a chocolate in his mouth, she began to speak. She intended to tell him the story of the Nativity, a subject she already had touched upon many times during their excursions, but only in passing. This time she felt she should tell him the entire tale. She expected him to interrupt when he discovered that it was a religious story, but he merely kept his noncommittal eyes on her and chewed mechanically, showing that he followed her by occasionally nodding his head. She became engrossed in what she was saying, and began to use her arms in wide gestures. Slimane reached for another chocolate and went on listening.

She talked for an hour or more, aware as from a distance of her own eloquence. When she told him about Bethlehem she was really describing Slimane's own village, and the house of Joseph and Mary was the house down in the *ksar* where Slimane had been born. The night sky arched above the Oued Zousfana and its stars glared down upon the cold hammada. Across the erg on their camels came the Wise Men in their burnooses and turbans, pausing at the crest of the last great dune to look ahead at the valley where the dark village lay. When she had finished, she blew her nose.

Slimane appeared to be in a state bordering on trance. She glanced at him, expected him to speak, but as he did not, she looked more closely at him. His eyes had an obsessed, vacant expression, and although they were still fixed on her face, she would have said that he was seeing something much farther away than she. She sighed, not wanting to make the decision to rouse him. The possibility she would have liked to entertain, had she not been so conscious of its unlikelihood, was that the boy somehow had been captivated by the poetic truth of the story, and was reviewing it in his imagination. "Certainly it could not be the case," she decided; it was more likely that he had ceased some time back to listen to her words, and was merely sitting there, only vaguely aware that she had come to the end of her story.

Then he spoke. "You're right. He was the King of Men."

Fräuline Windling caught her breath and leaned forward, but he went on. "And later Satan sent a snake with two heads. And Jesus killed it. Satan was angry with Him. He said: 'Why did you kill my friend? Did it hurt you, perhaps?' And Jesus said: 'I knew where it came from.' And Satan put on a black burnoose. That's true," he added, as he saw the expression of what he took to be simple disbelief on her face.

She sat up very straight and said: "Slimane, what are you talking about? There are no such stories about Jesus. Nor about Sidna Aissa either." She was not sure of the accuracy of this last statement; it was possible, she supposed, that such legends did exist among these people. "You know those are just stories that have nothing to do with the truth."

He did not hear her because he had already begun to talk. "I'm not speaking of Sidna Aissa," he said firmly. "He was a Moslem prophet. I'm talking about Jesus, the prophet of the Nazarenes. Everyone knows that Satan sent Him a snake with two heads."

She listened to the wind for an instant. "Ah," she said, and took another chocolate; she did not intend to carry the argument further. Soon she dug into her bag again and pulled out the turban, wrapped in red and white tissue paper.

"A present for you," she said, holding it out to him. He seized it mechanically, placed it on his lap and remained staring down at it. "Aren't you going to open it?" she demanded.

He nodded his head twice and tore open the paper. When he saw the pile of white cotton he smiled. Seeing his face at last come to life, she jumped up. "Let's put it on you!" she exclaimed. He gave her one end, which she pulled taut by walking all the way to the door. Then with his hand holding the other end to his forehead, he turned slowly round and round, going toward her all the time, arranging the form of the turban as it wound itself about his head. "Magnificent!" she cried. He went over to the row of black windows to look at himself.

"Can you see?" she asked.

"Yes, I can see the sides of it," he told her. "It's very beautiful."

She walked back toward the center of the room. "I'd like to take your picture, Slimane," she said, seeing an immediate look of puzzlement appear in his face. "Would you do me a favor? Go to my room and get the camera."

"At night? You can take a picture at night?"

She nodded, smiling mysteriously. "And bring me the yellow box on the bed."

Keeping the turban on his head, he got into his burnoose, took her flashlight and went out, letting the wind slam the door. She hoped the sound had not wakened Boufelja; for an instant she listened while there was no sound but the roar of air rushing through the corridor outside. Then she ran to the dark wing of the room and struck a match. Quickly she lighted all the candles around the crèche, straightened a camel in the sand, and walked back around the corner to the fireplace. She would not have thought the candles could give so much light. The other end of the room was now brighter than the end where she stood. In a moment the door burst open and Slimane came back in, carrying the camera slung over his shoulder. He put it down carefully on the table. "There was no yellow box on the bed," he told her. Then his glance caught the further walls flickering with the unfamiliar light, and he began to walk toward the center of the room. She saw that this was the moment. "Come," she said, taking his arm and pulling him gently around the corner to where the crèche was finally visible, bright with its multiple shuddering points of light. Slimane said nothing; he stopped walking and stood completely still. After a moment of silence, she plucked tentatively at his arm. "Come and see," she urged him. They continued to walk toward the crèche; as they came up to it she had the impression that if she had not been there he would have reached out his hand and touched it, perhaps would have lifted the tiny gold-clad infant Jesus out of His bed of feathers. But he stood quietly, looking at it. Finally he said: "You brought all this from Switzerland?"

"Of course not!" It was a little disappointing that he should not have recognized the presence of the desert in the picture, should not have sensed that the thing was of his place, and not an importation. "I made it all here," she said. She waited an instant. "Do you like it?"

"Ah, yes," he said with feeling. "It's beautiful. I thought it came from Switzerland."

To be certain that he understood the subject-matter, she began to identify the figures one by one, her voice taking on such an unaccustomed inflection of respect that he glanced up at her once in surprise. It was almost as if she too were seeing it for the first time. "And the Wise Men are coming down out of the erg to see the child."

"Why did you put all those almonds there?" asked Slimane, touching some with his forefinger.

"They're gifts for the little Jesus."

"But what are you going to do with them?" he pursued.

"Eat them, probably later," she said shortly. "Take one if you like. You say there was no yellow box on the bed?" She wanted to take the photographs while the candles were still of equal height.

"There was nothing but a sweater and some papers, madame."

She left him there by the crèche, crossed the room and put on her burnoose. The darkness in the corridor was complete; there was no sign that Boufelja had awakened. She knew her room was in great disorder, and she played the beam of the flashlight around the floor before entering. In the welter of displaced things that strewed the little room there seemed small chance of finding anything. The feeble ray illumined one by one the meaningless forms made by the piling of disparate objects one on the other; the light moved over the floor, along the bed, behind the flimsy curtain of the armoire. Suddenly she stopped and turned the beam under the bed. The box was in front of her face; she had put it with the crèche.

"I mustn't fall," she thought, running along the corridor. She forced herself to slow her pace to a walk, entered the dining-room and shut the door after her carefully. Slimane was on his knees in the middle of the room, a small object of some sort in his hand. She noted with relief that he was amusing himself. "I'm sorry it took me so long," she exclaimed. "I'd forgotten where I'd put it." She was pulling her burnoose off over her head; now she hung it on a nail by the fireplace, and taking up the camera and the yellow box, she walked over to join him.

Perhaps a faint glimmer of guilt in his expression as he glanced up made her eyes stray along the floor toward another object lying nearby, similar to the one he held in his hand. It was one of the Wise Men, severed at the hips from his mount. The Wise Man in Slimane's hand was intact, but the camel had lost its head and most of its neck.

"Slimane! What are you doing?" she cried with undisguised anger. "What have you done to the crèche?" She advanced around the corner and looked in its direction. There was not really much more than a row of candles and a pile of sand that had been strewn with tangerine peel and date stones; here and there a carefully folded square of lavender or pink tinfoil had been planted in the sand. All three of the Wise Men had been enlisted in Slimane's battle on the floor, the tent ravaged in the campaign to extricate the almonds piled inside, and the treasure sacks looted of their chocolate liqueurs. There was no sign anywhere of the infant Jesus or his gold-lamé garment. She felt tears come into her eyes. Then she laughed shortly, and said: "Well, it's finished. Yes?"

"Yes, madame," he said calmly. "Are you going to make the photograph now?" He got to his feet and laid the broken camel on the platform in the sand with the other debris.

Fräulein Windling spoke evenly, "I wanted to take a picture of the crèche."

He waited an instant, as if he were listening to a distant sound. Then he said "Should I put on my burnoose?"

"No." She began to take out the flash-bulb attachment. When she had it ready, she took the picture before he had time to strike a pose. She saw his astonishment at the sudden bright light prolong itself into surprise that the thing was already done, and then become resentment at having been caught off his guard; but pretending to have seen nothing, she went on snapping covers shut. He watched her as she gathered up her things. "Is it finished?" he said, disappointed. "Yes," she replied. "It will be a very good picture."

"Incha' Allah."

She did not echo his piety. "I hope you've enjoyed the festival," she told him.

Slimane smiled widely. "Ah yes, madame. Very much. Thank you."

She let him out into the camel-square and turned the lock in the door. Quickly she went back into her room, wishing it were a clear night like other nights, when she could stand out on the terrace and look at the dunes and stars, or sit on the roof and hear the dogs, for in spite of the hour she was not sleepy. She cleared her bed of all the things that lay on top of it, and got in, certain that she was going to lie awake for a long time. For it had shaken her, the chaos Slimane had made in those few minutes of her absence. Across the seasons of their friendship she had come to think of him as being very nearly like herself, even though she knew he had not been that way when she first had met him. Now she saw the dangerous vanity at the core of that fantasy: she had assumed that somehow his association with her had automatically been for his ultimate good, that inevitably he had been undergoing a process of improvement as a result of knowing her. In her desire to see him change, she had begun to forget what Slimane was really like. "I shall never understand him," she thought helplessly, sure that just because she felt so close to him she would never be able to observe him dispassionately.

"This is the desert," she told herself. Here food is not an adornment; it is meant to be eaten. She had spread out food and he had eaten it. Any argument which attached blame to that could only be false. And so she lay here accusing herself. "It has been too much head and high ideals," she reflected, "and not enough heart." Finally she traveled on the sound of the wind into sleep.

At dawn when she awoke she saw that the day was going to be another dark one. The wind had dropped. She got up and shut the window. The early morning sky was heavy with clouds. She sank back into bed and fell asleep. It was later than usual when she rose, dressed, and went into the dining-room. Boufelja's face was strangely expressionless as he wished her good morning. She supposed it was the memory of last night's misunderstanding, still with him—or possibly he was annoyed at having had to clean up the remains of the crèche. Once she had sat down and spread her napkin across her lap, he unbent sufficiently to say to her: "Happy festival."

"Thank you. Tell me, Boufelja," she went on, changing her inflection. "When you brought Slimane back in after dinner last night, do you know where he had been? Did he tell you?"

"He's a stupid boy," said Boufelja. "I told him to go home and eat and come back later. You think he did that? Never. He walked the whole time up and down in the courtyard here, outside the kitchen door, in the dark."

"I understand!" exclaimed Fräulein Windling triumphantly. "So he had no dinner at all."

"I had nothing to give him," he began, on the defensive.

"Of course not," she said sternly. "He should have gone home and eaten."

"Ah, you see?" grinned Boufelja. "That's what I told him to do."

In her mind she watched the whole story being enacted: Slimane aloofly informing his father that he would be eating at the hotel with the Swiss lady, the old man doubtless making some scornful reference to her, and Slimane going out. Unthinkable, once he had been refused admittance to the dining-room, for him to go back and face the family's ridicule. "Poor boy," she murmured.

"The commandant wants to see you," said Boufelja, making one of his abrupt conversational changes. She was surprised, since from one year to the next the captain never gave any sign of being aware of her existence; the hotel and the fort were like two separate countries. "Perhaps for the festival," Boufelja suggested, his face a mask. "Perhaps," she said uneasily.

When she had finished her breakfast, she walked across to the gates of the fort. The sentry seemed to be expecting her. One of the two young French soldiers was in the compound painting a chair. He greeted her, saying that the captain was in his office. She went up the long flight of stairs and paused an instant at the top, looking down at the valley in the unaccustomed gray light, noting how totally different it looked from its usual self, on this dim day.

A voice from inside called out: *"Entrez, s'il vous plait!"* She opened the door and stepped in. The captain sat behind his desk; she had the unwelcome sensation of having played this same scene on another occasion, in another place. And she was suddenly convinced that she knew what he was going to say. She seized the back of the empty chair facing the desk. "Sit down, Mademoiselle Windling," he said, rising halfway out of his seat, waving his arm, and sitting again quickly.

There were several topographical maps on the wall behind him, marked with lavender and green chalk. The captain looked at his desk and then at her, and said in a clear voice: "It is an unfortunate stroke of chance that I should have to call you here on this holiday." Fräulein Windling sat down in the chair; leaning forward, she seemed about to rest her elbow on his desk, but instead crossed her legs and folded her arms tight. "Yes?" she said, tense, waiting for the message. It came immediately, for which she was conscious, even then, of being grateful to him. He told her simply that the entire area had been closed to civilians; this order applied to French nationals as well as to foreigners, so she must not feel discriminated against. The last was said with a wry attempt at a smile. "This means that you will have to take tomorrow morning's truck," he continued. "The driver has already been advised of your journey. Perhaps another year, when the disturbances are over. . . ." ("Why does he say that?" she thought, "when he knows it's the end, and the time of friendship is finished?") He rose and extended his hand.

She could not remember going out of the room and down the long stairway into the compound, but now she was standing outside the sentry gate beside the wall of the fort, with her hand on her forehead. "Already," she thought. "It came so soon." And it occurred to her that she was not going to be given time to make amends to Slimane, so that it was really true she was never going to understand him. She walked up to the parapet to look down at the edge of the oasis for a moment, and then went back to her room to start packing. All day long she worked in her room, pulling out boxes, forcing herself to be aware only of the decisions she was making as to what was to be taken and what was to be left behind once and for all.

At lunchtime Boufelja hovered near her chair. "Ah, mademoiselle, how many years we have been together, and now it is finished!" "Yes," she thought, but there was nothing to do about it. His lamentations made her nervous and she was short with him. Then she felt guilt-stricken and said slowly, looking directly at him: "I am very sad, Boufelja." He sighed, "Ay, mademoiselle, I know!"

By nightfall the pall of clouds had been blown away across the desert, and the western sky was partly clear. Fräulein Windling had finished all her packing. She went out onto the terrace, saw the dunes pink and glowing, and climbed the steps to the roof to look at the sunset. Great skeins of fiery storm-cloud streaked the sky. Mechanically she let her gaze follow the meanders of the river valley as it lost itself in the darkening hammada to the south. "It is in the past," she reminded herself; this was already the new era. The desert out there looked the same as it always had looked. But the sky, ragged, red and black, was like a handbill that had just been posted above it, announcing the arrival of war.

It was a betrayal, she was thinking, going back down the steep stairs, running her hand along the familiar rough mud wall to steady herself, and the French of course were the culprits. But beyond that she had the irrational and disagreeable conviction that the countryside itself had connived in the betrayal, that it was waiting to be transformed by the struggle. She went into her room and lit the small oil lamp; sitting down, she held her hands over it to warm them. At some point there had been a change: the people no longer wanted to go on living in the world they knew. The pressure of the past had become too great, and its shell had broken.

In the afternoon she had sent Boufelja to tell Slimane the news, and to ask him to be at the hotel at daybreak. During dinner she discussed only the details of departure and travel; when Boufelja tried to pull the talk in emotional directions, she did not reply. His commiseration was intolerable; she was not used to giving voice to her despair. When she got to her room she went directly to bed. The dogs barked half the night.

It was cold in the morning. Her hands ached as she gathered up the wet objects from around the washbowl on the table, and somehow she drove a sliver deep under the nail of her thumb. She picked some of it out with a needle, but the greater part remained. Before breakfast she stepped outside.

Standing in the wasteland between the hotel and the fort, she looked down at the countryside's innocent face. The padlocked gasoline pump, triumphant in fresh red and orange paint, caught the pure early sunlight. For a moment it seemed the only living thing in the landscape. She turned around. Above the dark irregular mass of palm trees rose the terraced village, calm under its morning veil of woodsmoke. She shut her eyes for an instant, and then went into the hotel.

She could feel herself sitting stiffly in her chair while she drank her coffee, and she knew she was being distant and formal with Boufelja, but it was the only way she could be certain of being able to keep going. Once he came to tell her that Slimane had arrived bringing the donkey and its master for her luggage. She thanked him and set down the coffee cup. "More?" said Boufelja. "No," she answered. "Drink another, mademoiselle," he urged her. "It's good on a cold morning." He poured it and she drank part of it. There was a knocking at the gate. One of the young soldiers had been sent with a jeep to carry her out to the truck-stop on the trail.

"I can't!" she cried, thinking of Slimane and the donkey. The young soldier made it clear that he was not making an offer, but giving an order. Slimane stood beside the donkey outside the gate. While she began to speak with him the soldier shouted: "Does he want to come, the *gosse?* He can come too, if he likes." Slimane ran to get the luggage and Fräulein Windling rushed inside to settle her bill. "Don't hurry," the soldier called after her. "There's plenty of time."

Boufelja stood in the kitchen doorway. Now for the first time it occurred to her to wonder what was going to become of him. With the hotel shut he would have no work. When she had settled her account and given him a tip which was much larger than she could afford, she took both his hands in hers and said: *"Mon cher* Boufelja, we shall see one another very soon."

"Ah, yes," he cried, trying to smile. "Very soon, mademoiselle."

She gave the donkey-driver some money, and got into the jeep beside the soldier. Slimane had finished bringing the luggage and stood behind the jeep, kicking the tires. "Have you got everything?" she called to him. "Everything?" She would have liked to see for herself, but she was loath to go back into the room. Boufelja had disappeared; now he came hurrying out, breathless, carrying a pile of old magazines. "It's all right," she said. "No, no! I don't want them." The jeep was already moving ahead down the hill. In what seemed to her an unreasonably short time they had reached the boulders. When Fräulein Windling tried to lift out her briefcase the pain of the sliver under her nail made the tears start to her eyes, and she let go with a cry. Slimane glanced at her, surprised. "I hurt my hand," she explained. "It's nothing."

The bags had been piled in the shade. Sitting on a rock near the jeep, the soldier faced Fräulein Windling; from time to time he scanned the horizon behind her for a sign of the truck. Slimane examined the jeep from all sides; eventually he came to sit nearby. They did not say very much to one another. She was not sure whether it was because of the soldier with them, or because her thumb ached so constantly, but she sat quietly waiting, not wanting to talk.

It was a long time before the far-off motor made itself heard. When the truck was still no more than a puff of dust between sky and earth, the soldier was on his feet watching; an instant later Slimane jumped up. "It is coming, madame," he said. Then he bent over, putting his face very close to hers. "I want to go with you to Colomb-Bechar," he whispered. When she did not respond, because she was seeing the whole story of their friendship unrolled before her, from its end back to its beginning, he said louder, with great urgency: "Please, madame."

Fräulein Windling hesitated only an instant. She raised her head and looked carefully at the smooth brown face that was so near. "Of course, Slimane," she said. It was clear that he had not expected to hear this; his delight was infectious, and she smiled as she watched him run to the pile of bags and begin carrying them out into the sunlight to align them in the dust beside the edge of the trail.

Later, when they were rattling along the hammada, she in front beside the driver and Slimane squatting in the back with a dozen men and a sheep, she considered her irresponsible action in allowing him to make this absurd trip with her all the way to Colomb-Bechar. Still, she knew she wanted to give this ending to their story. A few times she turned partially around in her seat to glance at him through the dirty glass. He sat there in the smoke and dust, laughing like the others, with the hood of his burnoose hiding most of his face.

It had been raining in Colomb-Bechar; the streets were great puddles to reflect the clouded sky. At the garage they found a surly Negro boy to help them carry the luggage to the railway station. Her thumb hurt a little less.

"It's a cold town," Slimane said to her as they went down the main street. At the station they checked the bags and then went outside to stand and watch a car being unloaded from an open freight train: the roof of the automobile was still white with snow from the high steppes. The day was dark, and the wind rippled the surface of the water in the flooded empty lots.

Fräulein Windling's train would not be leaving until late in the afternoon. They went to a restaurant and ate a long lunch.

"You really will go back home tomorrow?" she asked him anxiously at one point, while they were having fruit. "You know we have done a very wicked thing to your father and mother. They will never forgive me." A curtain seemed to draw across Slimane's face. "It doesn't matter," he said shortly.

After lunch they walked in the public garden and looked at the eagles in their cages. A fine rain had begun to be carried on the wind. The mud of the paths grew deeper. They went back to the center of the town and sat down on the terrace of a large, shabby modern café. The table at the end was partly sheltered from the wet wind; they faced an empty lot strewn with refuse. Nearby, spread out like the bones of a camel fallen on the trail, were the rusted remains of an ancient bus. A long, newly felled date palm lay diagonally across the greater part of the lot. Fräulein Windling turned to look at the wet orange fiber of the stump, and felt an idle pity for the tree. "I'm going to have a Coca-Cola," she declared. Slimane said he, too, would like one.

They sat there a long time. The fine rain slanted through the air outside the arcades and hit the ground silently. She had expected to be approached by beggars, but none arrived, and now that the time had come to leave the café and go to the station she was thankful to see that the day had passed so easily. She opened her pocketbook, took out three thousand francs, and handed them to Slimane, saying: "This will be enough for everything. But you must buy your ticket back home today. When you leave the railway station. Be very careful of it."

Slimane put the money inside his garments, rearranged his burnoose, and thanked her. "You understand, Slimane," she said, detaining him with her hand, for he seemed about to rise from the table. "I'm not giving you any money now, because I need what I have for my journey. But when I get to Switzerland I shall send you a little, now and then. Not much. A little."

His face was swept by panic; she was perplexed.

"You haven't got my address," he told her.

"No, but I shall sent it to Boufelja's house," she said, thinking that would satisfy him. He leaned toward her, his eyes intense. "No, madame," he said with finality. "No. I have your address, and I shall send you mine. Then you will have it, and you can write to me."

It did not seem worth arguing about. For most of the afternoon her thumb had not hurt too much; now, as the day waned, it had begun to ache again. She wanted to get up, find the waiter, and pay him. The fine rain still blew; the station was fairly far. But she saw Slimane had something more to say. He leaped forward in his chair and looked down at the floor. "Madame," he began.

"Yes?" she said.

"When you are in your country and you think of me you will not be happy. It's true, so?"

"I shall be very sad," she answered, rising.

Slimane got slowly to his feet and was quiet for an instant before going on. "Sad because I ate the food out of the picture. That was very bad. Forgive me."

The shrill sound of her own voice exclaiming, "No!" startled her. "No!" she cried. "That was good!" She felt the muscles of her cheeks and lips twisting themselves into grimaces of weeping; fiercely she seized his arm and looked down into his face. *"Oh, mon pauvre petit!"* she sobbed, and then covered her face with both hands. She felt him gently touching her sleeve. A truck went by in the main street, shaking the floor.

With an effort she turned away and scratched in her bag for

a handkerchief. "Come," she said, clearing her throat. "Call the waiter."

They arrived at the station cold and wet. The train was being assembled; passengers were not allowed to go out onto the platform and were sitting on the floor inside. While Fräulein Windling bought her ticket Slimane went to get the bags from the checkroom. He was gone for a long time. When he arrived he came with his burnoose thrown back over his shoulders, grinning triumphantly, with three valises piled on his head. A man in ragged European jacket and trousers followed behind carrying the rest. As he came nearer she saw that the man held a slip of paper between his teeth.

The ancient compartment smelled of varnish. Through the window she could see, above some remote western reach of wasteland, a few strips of watery white sky. Slimane wanted to cover the seats with the luggage, so that no one would come into the compartment. "No," she said. "Put them in the racks." There were very few passengers in the coach. When everything was in place, the porter stood outside in the corridor and she noticed that he still held the slip of paper between his teeth. He counted the coins she gave him and pocketed them. Then quickly he handed the paper to Slimane, and was gone.

Fräulein Windling bent down a bit, to try and see her face in the narrow mirror that ran along the back of the seat. There was not enough light; the oil lantern above illumined only the ceiling, its base casting a leaden shadow over everything beneath. Suddenly the train jolted and made a series of crashing sounds. She took Slimane's head between her hands and kissed the middle of his forehead. "Please get down from the train," she told him. "We can talk here." She pointed to the window and began to pull up the torn leather strap that lowered it.

Slimane looked small on the dark platform, staring up at her as she leaned out. Then the train started to move. She thought surely it would go only a few feet and then stop, but it continued ahead, slowly. Slimane walked with it, keeping abreast of her window. In his hand was the paper the porter had given him. He held it up to her, crying: "Here is my address! Send it here!"

She took it, and kept waving as the train went faster, kept calling: "Good-bye!" He continued to walk quickly along beside the window, increasing his gait until he was running, until all at once there was no more platform. She leaned far out, looking backward, waving; straightway he was lost in the darkness and rain. A bonfire blazed orange by the track, and the smoke stung her nostrils. She pulled up the window, glanced at the slip of paper she had in her hand, and sat down. The train jolted her this way and that; she went on staring at the paper, although now it was in shadow; and she remembered the first day, long ago, when the child Slimane had stood outside the door watching her, stepping back out of her range of vision each time she turned to look at him. The words hastily printed for him on the scrap of paper by the porter were indeed an address, but the address was in Colomb-Bechar. "They said he tried to run away. But he didn't get very far." Each detail of his behavior as she went back over it clarified the pattern for her. "He's too young to be a soldier," she told herself. "They won't take him." But she knew they would.

Her thumb was hot and swollen; sometimes it seemed almost that its throbbing accompanied the side-to-side jolting of the coach. She looked out at the few remaining patches of colorless light in the sky. Sooner or later, she argued, he would have done it.

"Another year, perhaps," the captain had said. She saw her own crooked, despairing smile in the dark window-glass beside her face. Maybe Slimane would be among the fortunate ones, an early casualty. "If only death were absolutely certain in wartime," she thought wryly, "the waiting would not be so painful." Listing and groaning, the train began its long climb upwards over the plateau.

Tangier
1962

LITTLE BEAVER

.

by Charles Durden

"I still don't get it," Cpl. Thompson said to Addison Burke as they settled into the meager shade provided by the crumbling pagoda. "You're a civilian, right?"

"Last I heard," Burke answered as he wiped his sweaty hands on the sleeves of his jungle fatigues, then cranked the army-issue opener around the lip of the canned peaches.

"Which means," Cpl. Thompson surmised aloud, "that there ain't no good goddamn reason why you hafta be here." He leaned his M-16 against the bullet-pocked and faded pastel wall, removed his helmet, and shook his canteen. Reassured by the sound of the water sloshing, he unscrewed the cap and filled his mouth. A moment later he spat the water into the dry sand between his feet and made a face.

Burke tossed aside the olive-green top of the C-ration can and drank the juice, some of which immediately seeped into the cracked molar on the lower left side of his mouth. He winced with pain.

"So what don't you understand?" he asked. "Why I came or why I'm still here?"

"Yeah."

Burke laughed, spooned some of the peach slices into his mouth and passed the can to Cpl. Thompson. "I came because I got tired of writing obits. And I'm still here because I don't have enough money to go back."

Cpl. Thompson raised his ice-blue eyes from the peach slices to the face of Burke, whose eyes were hidden behind the dark-green tint of his aviator sunglasses. He wasn't sure what to make of the smile that played across Burke's full-lipped mouth.

Addison Burke, free-lance correspondent, was a mystery of significant proportions to Cpl. James Thompson, career soldier, and for the moment, designated bodyguard to the only member of the media ever to visit Charlie Company in the seven months since the corporal had arrived from a pleasant two-year tour of duty in Bavaria.

It occurred to the corporal that Burke was laughing at him, making fun of his inability to understand why any supposedly sane person would willingly come to this outhouse of humanity, this misbegotten crotch of creation. *And,* he added silently, still staring at Burke, *and* pay his own way. If that was true, Cpl. Thompson had his doubts about that part of Burke's story.

Burke removed his bush hat and wiped the sweat from his forehead with the damp sleeve of his jacket. A hundred fuckin' degrees, at least, he thought. And enough humidity to grow orchids. He smiled at the corporal's puzzlement. "You plan to eat any of those?" he inquired.

Cpl. Thompson slipped a switchblade knife from his pocket and flicked it open. The blade, long and slender like his bony fingers and lanky frame, was razor-sharp. He impaled two of the slices, carefully slid them into his thin-lipped mouth and handed the can back to Burke.

The radio nestled between the feet of the R.T.O. several meters away abruptly crackled with static, followed by a booming bass voice. "Red Ryder Six, this is Red Ryder. Radio check, over."

The R.T.O., a young black private first class named Richards who had wilted in the heat and was slumped against the base of a scrawny tree, roused himself to respond. "Red Ryder, this is Red Ryder Six. C.A.F.B."

Burke laughed softly. *Clear as a fucking bell.*

"Roger, Red Ryder Six . . . How's our friend, Little Beaver, holding up?"

The R.T.O. glanced at Burke and Burke shrugged. "Tell 'im I'm just fuckin' peachy."

"Little Beaver say this is just another walk in the park."

"Roger, Red Ryder Six. Keep 'im outta trouble. Red Ryder out."

PFC Richards replaced the receiver and resumed his sleepy-eyed observations of the young Vietnamese girl who had left the shade of a tree at the far end of the hamlet, where she appeared to be reweaving a torn basket and was slowly walking toward one of the hooches. So many Charlie Company patrols had passed through the area in the last few months that none of the farmers or their families seemed to notice them.

Cpl. Thompson swallowed his resentment of the captain's concern for this dumb-ass civilian and cleared his throat to get Burke's attention. "So how come you don't just call your paper and tell 'em you need money for a ticket home? I mean, they pay you to do this shit, right?"

"I don't work for anyone in particular. That's why I had to pay my own way here."

"You mean, you ain't got a regular job?"

"The 'job' is regular. I just don't get a paycheck every week. I don't always get a paycheck every month. Which is why I bought a one-way ticket. It was a lot cheaper and I wanted to hold on to as much cash as I could." He ate a few of the peach slices and handed the can back to the corporal.

"And you ain't got enough money left to buy a ticket out of here?" Cpl. Thompson asked in amazement.

The mystery was too much for him. A man worked a day, he was paid for a day. Or in the case of the U.S. Army, work a month, get paid for a month. But by the day, the week, or the month, payday was payday, predictable. For a moment he wondered if "free-lance" meant you worked for free, but that didn't make any more sense than being in Nam when you didn't have to be.

"Sometimes," Burke said, "no one wants what I write or any of the pictures I take, so I live off my reserves. At the moment, the 'reserves' are less than the price of a ticket to the World." In truth, he thought, the reserves wouldn't buy me a night with a bar girl in DaNang.

He smiled again and adjusted the strap of the beat-up F-2 Nikon. The mystery confounding Cpl. Thompson was nothing new. More times than he could remember, Burke had tried and failed to explain to the grunts why he was in Nam. His best response was always patience and a change of subject. "Listen, I can give you a good deal on a camera," he joked. "Maybe you could become a photojournalist in your spare time."

The corporal eyed the Nikon. In the farmlands of Iowa, from whence he had enlisted in the army five years earlier, a camera like the Nikon was as rare as a mortgage-free farm. "It looks kinda heavy," he finally said, as though he had seriously considered the idea and decided he had enough crap to carry around.

Burke removed the lens cover and focused on the face of the

corporal. Cpl. Thompson frowned. Burke snapped the picture and wound the film to the next frame. He loved the sound of the Nikon winding through a roll of film.

"I still don't get it," the corporal said with a heavy sigh. "You pay your own way to this hole in Hell so you can write stories and take pictures that maybe nobody wants to buy, and you ain't got enough money to fly home? What happens if you don't sell no more stuff?"

"Beats the shit out of me." Burke snapped two more shots of the corporal while he tried to explain the life of free-lancing to a farm boy from Iowa. "A free-lance writer or photographer writes stories or takes pictures and sells them to anyone who wants to buy. I do both. And sooner or later I'll sell some more of my stuff.

"I've sold pictures to UPI, stories to probably fifteen or twenty different newspapers, and I sold photo spreads with copy to three or four magazines. You ever see *Argosy?* Or *True?*"

"Sure, but I didn't see nothin' 'bout Vietnam in them."

"*Argosy* was three months ago. The pictures and story for *True* won't be out until September."

"How long you been here?" the corporal asked.

"Six months and a week." Burke let the Nikon hang from his neck while he ate half of the remaining peach slices, then passed the can back to the corporal and lit a cigarette.

"You seen anything worth the trip?"

"You and Sergeant Washington, all by yourselves, were worth the trip," Burke laughed. "Not to mention that horse's ass, Body Bag Kester."

Cpl. Thompson shook his head. "We heard you asked him if he knew that was his nickname. You must be crazy." He stabbed a peach slice and held it just below the level of his mouth, his eyes on Burke's face, his mind racing. "You look kinda crazy."

"It goes with the job," Burke answered, and ran his hands through his dirty-blond hair, which was ragged around the edges and well below his ears. He had been five-feet and ten-inches tall when he arrived in Saigon, and weighed one-hundred and sixty-two pounds. Six months of C-rations and heavy sweating had consumed close to fifteen pounds. And he suspected that he was at least an inch shorter, squashed by the weight of his equipment and the unrelenting heat.

Cpl. Thompson finished the peaches, one slice at a time, then once more rinsed his mouth with the tepid, foul-tasting water from his canteen and spat a stream between his feet. "Fuckin' halazone tablets. You'd think they'd at least give us fresh water."

"I always pour a little brandy in mine. . . ." He uncapped his canteen and passed it to the corporal. "Take a taste."

Cpl. Thompson eyed the canteen with some suspicion, then tipped it to his lips and swallowed. He made a face and handed it back to Burke. "Tastes like shit."

"But a smoother vintage." Burke swallowed three or four times and belched lightly.

"So, can I ask you somethin' else, 'bout your job?"

"Sure."

"What's them obits you was talkin' 'bout? Is that newspaper stuff?"

Burke giggled in disbelief. "You serious? You don't know what an obit is?"

"I don't read newspapers, 'cept *Stars and Stripes* once in a while." He was clearly offended by Burke's reaction. "Not all of us is college boys, y'know."

"An obit," Burke explained, "is short for obituary. It usually runs about three or four paragraphs, unless the person who died is famous. Or notorious.

"Most days I'd sit at my desk for four or five hours writing obits and rewriting press releases for the next day's edition."

He studied the corporal's face, searching for some indication of comprehension. Cpl. Thompson's face was almost as empty as Burke's last words to his fiancée: "Listen, I'm only going for six weeks, so there's nothing to make a big deal about, okay?"

"Let me get this straight," the corporal said, and tilted his head slightly, as though he needed a new angle on the mystery confronting him. "You had a job back in the World, right? Working for a big-city newspaper—"

"San Francisco."

"And you got paid every week . . . ?"

"Yeah, I was paid every week," Burke answered with a hint of frustration. This was the same old bullshit he'd heard from his editor, his girlfriend, his parents, and the parish priest. It always came down to *security.*

"And your job was writin' obits, which is a story about somebody that died. Right?" Burke nodded agreement. "So to get away from writin' stories about dead people you gave up a good job, probably a girl, and you come to Viet-fuckin'-Nam!?" The corporal allowed his disdain and dismay to mingle while he slowly shook his head from side to side. "Man, Nam ain't nothin' but stories 'bout dead people." Then, abruptly and without warning, he cackled. "Man comes to Nam to get away from dead people!" His laughter expanded, building upon itself, until he was howling, tears streaming from his eyes.

Burke's face froze, iced over in cold anger. Then, slowly, he felt his face warming. The "fool's flush," he called it. He was embarrassed, pure and simple. He'd been had and he could, he realized quickly, lose his cool and blow it all. That wouldn't do.

At various times in the last six months he'd been on a riverboat in the Delta when the VC caught them in a crossfire . . . he'd been out for days at a time with long-range recon grunts, some truly crazy motherfuckers, and once they were saved

from certain death by an equally crazy chopper pilot . . .
he'd spent the night at the Rock Pile within sight of the DMZ,
and a week with the Marines at Kai Shan. . . . He had come
face-to-face with pure terror more than once and had never
given any sign that he wasn't fearless *and* unflappable.

Most important of all, none of the grunts with whom he had
struck up a relationship had been killed, miracle of miracles.
He hadn't had to write one goddamn obit since he had landed
in Saigon.

And now, out of nowhere, on a patrol that he had guessed
would be little more than an opportunity to shoot pictures and
pick up some names for a series of so-called "home towners,"
here was some fucking farm boy from Iowa laughing at him
because simple wisdom and equally simple logic said he was a
fool on a fool's errand. He had come to the Valley of the
Shadow of Death to get away from writing about dead people.

Sgt. Elroy Washington, the very large, very black, and wonderfully patient platoon sergeant in charge of the patrol
strolled up as Cpl. Thompson regained a modicum of compo-
sure. The howling had diminished to cackling bursts.

"Thompson, what the fuck is so funny?" Sgt. Washington
asked. "This here *re*-porter tellin' you stories 'bout how many
Donut Dollies he screwed in Saigon?"

Cpl. Thompson, still grinning, gained control of himself and
scrambled to his feet. "Sarge, you ain't goin' to believe this
shit. Listen to this . . ." Cpl. Thompson giggled a couple of
times.

Burke, annoyed, started walking toward the rice paddies
that bordered the hamlet, which in truth wasn't even a hamlet.
It wasn't, to Burke's eye, anything more than another short
string of hooches fashioned from bamboo and stolen sheets of
rusty tin with dirt floors and thatched roofs.

"Listen." The corporal started the story again. "Little Beaver here was tellin' me how it was he paid his own way here because he got tired of writin' *obits.* . . ."

Burke, at the edge of the nearest paddy, turned and raised his Nikon, focusing on Sgt. Washington and Cpl. Thompson. Fuck 'em, they were perfect for stories about hometown boys in Nam. He didn't have to like them, or win their approval, or ever see them again if he didn't chose to. He only needed their names, ranks, military units, and hometowns. Take the pictures, write the story, fill in the blanks. Do one for each of the twelve on this patrol, sell four or five, and he'd have enough money to last another month.

"Can you picture that, Sarge? Can you see yourself buyin' a ticket, a *one-way* ticket, to fuckin' Nam so you don't have to write stories 'bout dead people?"

Washington grinned and Cpl. Thompson erupted in another burst of laughter that was lost in the louder, more insistent hammering of an automatic weapon. Burke, in that frozen instant between the recognition of the sound, the disintegration of Cpl. Thompson's chest, and the surge of adrenaline through his own system, thought it might be a .50 caliber.

One round of the incoming fire pierced a fragmentation grenade that Cpl. Thompson had hung on his pack strap. The fragments shredded Sgt. Washington's face and upper body.

Burke was still backing up, methodically focusing and snapping pictures, when he tripped and fell backward into the rice paddy and sank to the bottom.

* * *

"It has been seven months since I last wrote an obit," Burke typed the next afternoon. He was seated at a table on the riverside patio of the press center in DaNang. *"Today I'm writing ten of them. Ten stories about ten American boys who died in a hamlet not much larger than a football stadium, twenty-five miles from nowhere in the Republic of Vietnam."*

With a slightly trembling hand, Burke picked up the glass of warm beer at the side of his battered typewriter and sipped. Then, with the same trembling hand, he lit a cigarette and reread his opening paragraph.

It's a start, he thought. A good start to a good story. And this is what I came here to do, he reminded himself. Write stories about this weird war where battles are fought with an enemy you almost never see and nothing but the futility of this shit is *C.A.F.B.*

* * *

Two hours and four beers later he was still sitting, still staring at the page on which he had written nothing more because he was still trying to understand how he had survived, why he had been spared, and when he could possibly hope to scrape together enough money to buy a ticket back to the World.

THE VILLAGE

.

by Jim Pitzen

The village was ancient. It lay nestled in a peaceful valley in the Central Highlands, midway between Hanoi and Saigon and just forty kilometers from the South China Sea.

The first houses built upon these same sites had been houses of mud walls mixed with rice-straw binder and thatched rice-straw roofs (as were these houses).

The first time that the village was destroyed in war (it had been destroyed many times before that by flood) was during the War of the Two Villages, or the War Between the North and the South. The village had been destroyed by war many other times by the Chinese, the Cambodians, the Chinese, the Thailanders, the Huns, the Chinese, the French, and the Japanese.

The people of the village had become so good at having their village destroyed by war that they knew exactly how to go about it. First they would hide all the food and plows and scythes. They would drive all the water buffalo into the jungle.

Then, gathering all the people of the village except for one old and worthless grandmother who was too weak to travel, they would disappear into the jungle. The village had been destroyed so many times and the people of the village had become so good at having it destroyed that the village actually did not exist anymore; in fact it had never existed, and neither had the people who were so good at disappearing. It was all an illusion, but it did not matter because the soldiers who were coming to destroy it and who had always come to destroy it were an illusion also; and all the wars, and all their causes that had ever destroyed the village were also illusions. In fact everything was an illusion except for the jungle, which was an orderly place where things existed to be killed and eaten. All humankind and all the possessions and passions of humankind (including war) were illusions. Human beings had created themselves in their own minds (they were fabrications of their own imaginations) and their minds were such disorderly places that they had forgotten how or why they had created themselves so they were doomed to wander about trying to uncreate themselves.

The jungle and the mosquitoes and the leeches were orderly because they had not been created but had always been and always would be, and they fit in their natural place and knew it and did not try to be anything else. The jungle and the mosquitoes and the leeches watched with amusement the imaginary soldiers destroying the illusory village over and over and over again, and they sucked the imaginary blood of the imaginary soldiers just to keep up the illusion.

* * *

"Cheechee, cheechee," the monkey called.

The slightly built, blond soldier jumped awake, at first frightened, then guilty. He'd been sleeping on guard again. At dawn, too, the worst time. He squirmed around. The soaked jungle fatigues had given him a swimming-suit itch all over except on his bare brown arms where the mosquitoes feasted. He wiped them off, killing fifteen or twenty on each arm.

Fucking mosquitoes, he thought, fucking monsoon. The mosquitoes buzzed and the rain dripped from the huge-leafed banana tree above him. His jungle boot reached out and nudged Hardje's foot.

Hardje awoke instantly. His thumb checked the safety on his M-16. He wiped the mosquitoes from his bare brown arms. He whispered, "What?"

Tyler whispered back, "Almost dawn."

Hardje sat up, shivered; his wet jungle fatigues clung to him.

Light began to grow in the east and spread slowly. Tyler whispered, "You need a shave."

"So fucking what," Hardje said.

They sat and listened to the elephant grass grow; green, six feet tall, taller, and still growing. The rain hissed. Monkeys called. Parrots began to quarrel.

Hardje grunted and said, "They're not going to hit us. They'd of done it by now."

Tyler wiped at the mosquitoes and nodded. "Listen to the parrots."

Hardje wiped the mosquitoes from his arms and stood up slowly, groaning at the stiffness in his muscles. "Son of a bitch," he said.

Tyler grinned and said, "I fell asleep again. Just at dawn. Dammit. I can't stay awake at dawn."

Hardje shrugged. "Neither can anyone else."

The parrots and monkeys called.

* * *

Hardje started to wipe the mosquitoes from his arm, changed his mind, and scratched his neck instead. He said, "Well, leech time."

He pulled down his pants (nobody wore underwear anymore because of jock itch) and removed his shirt. His rear end and legs glowed white next to his mahogany arms and chest and back. The leeches, black and two inches long, clung to him, one on each inner thigh, two more at the beltline, one on his back just beneath the shoulder blade. Red pockmarks scattered over his skin traced the leeches that had gone before.

"Mosquito dope?" Tyler asked.

The mosquito dope, G.I. Gin, made the leeches curl up, writhing, and let go, but the alcohol made the bites burn like fire.

"Fuck it," Hardje answered. He began slowly pulling off a leech, one of the two at his beltline. The reddened, irritated skin lifted with the leech, its suction-cup mouth clinging. Then the leech let go suddenly. Bright blood trickled down Hardje's lower stomach and disappeared into the reddish-brown pubic hair. He threw the leech down and stamped it into the ground.

"Fucking things," Hardje said. "Fucking valley."

With a steady hand he pulled off three more leeches, tossing them into the tall grass. "How in hell do they get in your pants?" he said. "I had my pants tucked into my boots, and my belt was so fucking tight I couldn't breathe."

Tyler shrugged and wiped the mosquitoes from his arms.

Hardje looked over his shoulder. "Get that bastard, will you?" Tyler stood and pulled the leech from Hardje's back.

"Rain's letting up," Hardje said.

Tyler nodded.

"You leech yourself yet?" Hardje asked.

Tyler shook his head no.

"Talkative bastard, ain't you," Hardje said.

Tyler nodded and began to strip as Hardje started to dress.

The rain had stopped but would continue to fall from the canopy of trees covering them like a tent.

"Sun's gonna shine," Hardje said. "Gonna get hotter than hell."

He took his entrenching tool and scraped the rotting vegetation from a small spot on the ground. As the leaves turned over, an exposed leech curled and uncurled. "Rotten bastard," Hardje said. He ground it into the mud beneath his heel. "It ain't natural. We're half a mile from the river, and these bastards are all over."

Tyler plucked a blood-engorged leech from near his groin and looked around. He impaled the leech on one of the bright green, three-inch-long thorns that covered the trunk of a nearby tree. He grinned as the leech squirmed and bled.

"What are you grinning about?" Hardje said. "It's your blood."

"I only had one," Tyler said. He pulled his pants up, trapping several mosquitoes.

"Of course," Hardje said. "You ain't as sweet as I am."

Tyler dug into a side pocket of his backpack and retrieved an empty C-ration can with holes punched in the bottom. He set it on the small patch of ground Hardje had cleared. He reached into another pocket of his backpack and brought out a small wad of C.4, a plastic explosive for blowing bunkers and tunnels. He rolled it into a tight wad the size of a walnut and dropped it into the C-ration-can stove. He opened a can of beans and franks almost all the way around with his P-38 can opener, pried the lid back and, using it as a handle, set the can carefully on the stove. He pulled a plastic bag from his shirt pocket, unrolled it, and took out a book of matches. The C.4 flared wildly and burned out in five seconds; the beans and franks bubbled. Tyler lifted the can off the stove, sat down on the wet ground, and began eating with a plastic spoon. He watched Hardje open a can of ham and lima beans and shuddered as he set them on the stove.

"You ever seen wood ticks?" he asked Hardje.

Hardje nodded. "I'm from Minnesota."

"Lima beans look like big gray wood ticks on a dog's neck."

Hardje grinned. "Next time you get a can of wood ticks,

give 'em to me. I'll eat 'em." He took a big bite, chewed, swallowed, and belched.

Tyler shook his head sadly and said, "No couth. That's your problem. You ain't got no couth."

Swenson, coming up from the next position to the south, parted the elephant grass. "Saddle up," he said. "We're moving out in fifteen. Pass the word."

He turned and disappeared as Hardje began to move toward Cadwell's position to the north. Tyler chopped a hole in the ground and threw the empty cans in it. He put away his stove and lit a Camel, sitting down alongside his pack. He wiped the mosquitoes from his arms. The thin material of his jungle fatigues was already dry except for the seat of the pants and the spots where the trees had dripped. He couldn't see the sun but knew it must be out. Steam was rising from the ground in pillars. He flicked the ember from his cigarette, sliced the paper with his thumbnail, scattered the tobacco, and rolled the paper into a tiny ball that he ground beneath his heel. He checked the safety on his M-16, thought about another cigarette, changed his mind, and sat.

Hardje appeared out of the steam, his uniform soaked from the wet grass. He dropped to one knee, wiped the mosquitoes from his arm, and said, "Guess who got point?"

Tyler stared at him in disbelief. "Christ. You just had it last week."

Hardje nodded and sat down. They sat not talking. Finally Tyler said, "Bastards."

Hardje nodded again. They sat. Swenson shouted, "Everyone pull back to the trail."

The trail was not on any map. It was, possibly, just a game trail, but it wandered more or less in the right direction, following the monsoon-swollen river, crossing and recrossing it, down out of the highlands toward the east and the An Loa Valley twenty kilometers away, toward the South China Sea.

* * *

The yellow clay floor of the trail was slippery and sticky. The clay built up on the cleats of Hardje's canvas jungle boots, making him three inches taller. With every step, his feet slid and skidded. The sweat poured out. He wiped the mosquitoes off his arms and checked the safety on his M-16.

Point position. The first man in the company. The lead man. The first man to hit the shit. Point position. Life-expectancy: three days.

Hardje moved slowly down the trail. The jungle was quiet. He watched the ground, the trail, the trees. Watched for trip wires, slender threads attached to booby-trapped mortar rounds, to grenades. Watched for punji stakes, splinters of bamboo smeared in human feces, guaranteed infection if one scratched your skin. Watched for snipers who tied themselves to the tree tops. Watched for ambush. Watched for pit vipers, for cobras. Watched. Sweat burned his eyes. His stomach felt tight, wanted to vomit. The trail wound through the jungle. Hardje stopped, looked back, caught Swenson's attention. He pointed at the punji stakes hidden in the tall grass. Swenson nodded. Hardje wiped the mosquitoes from his arms, moved on. Up a slight rise, then down to the yellow river that tore at its banks. He hesitated, watched the other bank, sick with fear. A perfect ambush spot. He watched, sweat burning his eyes. He checked the safety on his M-16 and plunged into the water. Waist-high water deepened to his armpits near the tall, curved bank on the far side. Then he was across, scrambling up the slippery bank, holding his breath, into the jungle. Nothing. No Charlie. He went back to the bank and waved the company across.

Hardje moved down the trail and sat on a rotting log. The training manual said that an infantry company should be able to march four miles an hour. It had taken him half an hour to go half a mile, yet he felt that he was moving too fast.

The company gathered on the trail behind him. He saw Tyler and waved. The company commander signaled him to move out. He groaned and cursed under his breath but stood up and began the cautious movement once more, watching.

Tyler wiped the mosquitoes from his arms and watched Hardje move out of sight around a bend in the trail. Tyler felt guilty that he wasn't on point. It had been three weeks. He also felt angry about his guilt. He knew Hardje was the best point man in the company. But still, it was past his turn. On and on the argument went as he moved with the company.

The saturated ground steamed in the 120-degree heat. This week's marching song, the song Tyler used to blot out all thought, started to run through his mind. "When Johnnie Comes Marching Home Again." Last week it had been "Up, Up and Away."

The company moved down the trail, one hundred men, eighteen to twenty years old, one hundred thousand thoughts about dying and being paralyzed and having arms and legs blown away and being bitten by snakes and spiders and centipedes and being stung by scorpions. Thinking of people back home. Thinking how glad they were that Hardje was on point. One hundred men with sweat-soaked uniforms, with huge backpacks that occasionally clinked and clunked.

Hardje paused to watch a dark purple butterfly on a black flower, and the company slowed and stopped behind him. He moved on down the trail and they followed.

Hardje paused as a mottled green and yellow, eighteen-foot constrictor slithered across the trail. He grinned as he thought about Tyler's snake phobia. He'd tell Tyler about this one tonight. He wiped the mosquitoes from his arms. Sweat washed the blood away. He checked the safety on his M-16 and moved on. The company followed.

The steaming trail dropped abruptly back down to another river crossing. Hardje stopped, checked his watch. Ten o'clock. He remembered a deer-hunting trip in the snow, how the buck's bloody entrails steamed as he plunged his stinging hands in the body cavity to remove them. He stared at the opposite bank. Stared. Sliding down the bank into the river, up to his waist, to his armpits, then across and scrambling up the other bank and back into the jungle. The company followed, cursing and grumbling and clinking and clanking.

Down the yellow trail. A trail that grew wider as other foot trails joined it from the hills (or took off from it into the hills). Hardje knew these small trails meant that Charlie used the path for disbursing the weapons and food that came in by sea. He moved down the trail watching each step, watching ahead. He stopped on the edge of a small clearing. Rice paddies and dikes, half a mile across, and on the far side, a small village. He signaled for the company to halt, watched as the company commander worked his way through the men who had collapsed alongside the trail. Hardje wiped the mosquitoes from his arms. He saw a huge, hairy tarantula the size of his hand walk across the trail, lifting high two or three legs at a time and planting them carefully, as if it didn't like the mud. Hardje shuddered.

The C.O. said from ten feet away, "What's up, Norway?"

Hardje pointed with his chin.

The C.O. looked around the rice paddy, at the village. He cursed softly. "Son of a bitch. This isn't on the map. How many houses?"

Hardje replied, "Fifteen. Maybe more."

The C.O. nodded. "Well, move out to the first dike and wait for the company to catch up. We'll have to search and destroy the vil. I'll try and get battalion headquarters on the horn."

Hardje waded up to his waist in the shitty-smelling water. He fingered the safety of his M-16, crouched, and waded toward the dike. He heard the company entering the water behind him but kept his eyes glued on the houses and the trees, expecting to die at any time. When the men all reached the dike and crouched down, the word came down the line: "Take it."

As one man, the company rose, clambered over the dike, slid into the next lower paddy, waded, and clambered over the next dike, slid into the next lower rice paddy, and waded.

Hardje and Tyler flicked the safeties off their M-16s and leaped into the first house and halfway across the dirt floor. They stood, holding their breath. Nothing happened. Quiet. There were only two more rooms. Two black, open doorways. They stood staring, waiting for the other to choose a door. Then from the door on the left came the most unearthly wail that either man had ever heard. Their knees sagged. They wanted to vomit, to run, but hadn't the strength to do either. They looked at each other and, rifles ready, entered the room.

When their eyes adjusted to the dark, they saw on a bed of rice-straw mats an incredibly old woman. (They couldn't tell if she was man, woman, or monkey, but they somehow knew.)

She was not much larger than a two-year-old child, shriveled, shrunken, sightless, toothless, nearly hairless, her feet and hands curled up like claws. As they stood, staring, she once again emitted the hideous, shrieking moan. Tyler turned to run but Hardje grabbed him, steadied him. They stared at each other, at her.

The two men stretched Hardje's poncho out alongside the old woman, slid her onto it, and carried her out of the crypt-like blackness of the room, through the main room of the house and into the sunlight. They called for a medic and told the radio operator to call in a Med-Evac chopper because the woman was in pain.

Actually she had been moaning not in pain but because the other people who did not live in the village and who did not disappear when the soldiers did not come out of the jungle had taken from her finger the brass ring that had belonged to her great-great-great-grandmother. The people who did not disappear took the ring because they felt that the soldiers who were not coming to the village that wasn't there would think it was gold and would steal it. So the grandmother was really moaning about her missing ring, and she never moaned again because she died when the sunlight hit her, though the men in the company never knew it because the medic refused even to look at her because she was so ugly. They loaded the old woman on the helicopter and she was never again seen in the village by the people who didn't live there nor by the nonexistent soldiers.

* * *

The knot of men watched the chopper pound away toward the south and Landing Zone Linda. The C.O. said, "All right, break it up. One grenade would get you all. Let's finish searching the vil. When you're done we'll burn what will burn and blow the walls with C.4."

The men carried all military-looking items to the hard-packed yard of the house that had been cleared by Hardje and Tyler. The most dangerous-looking items were a crossbow; an old curve-bladed sword; a long-barreled French muzzle-loader; and a small bronze statue of a gargoyle-faced dog with a dragon's tail, which had a star at the end.

Tyler leaned back in the shade of a coconut palm. He checked the safety on his M-16 and laid it across his lap. He opened a can of C-ration beef stew. Hardje wiped the mosquitoes from his arms and leaned back against the wall of the house and began eating his canned scrambled eggs, white bread, and peanut butter.

Each man swallowed a pink salt tablet, a large orange malaria tablet, and a small white malaria tablet and began to eat, more with resignation than with relish.

"I hate this shit," Hardje said conversationally.

Tyler shrugged. "It doesn't matter," he said. He belched. He looked to the west, at the bank of clouds that was crowding the mountains. "Be raining in an hour. This place'll never burn. We'll have to blow it all."

Hardje nodded. He finished the cold eggs and tossed the can over his shoulder, through the glassless window and into the house, where it clunked across the hard floor. Hardje lit a cigarette with a Zippo lighter, sighed. "Well," he said, "I suppose we might as well start."

Tyler nodded and pitched his garbage after Hardje's. He lit a cigarette and stood up. Grabbing his entrenching tool from his pack, he stepped to the house and began chopping the soil away from the foundation. When he judged the area was large enough, he packed C.4 against the foundation, stuck a blasting cap in it, and packed the mud back around the C.4. He strung electrical wire, which was connected to the blasting cap, over to the front yard where the others were waiting with other wires. Hardje wired them all to one main wire and began wading across the rice paddy to the closest dike, unrolling wire as he went.

When all the charges were set and all the wires strung and all the men down behind the rice paddy dike, the C.O. ordered, "Fire the hole!"

Hardje turned back once to look at the village. The cloud of dust still hung in the air. Just then, as if someone had turned on a switch, the rain started again and Hardje turned and plunged once more down the trail, under the dark canopy of leaves, looking carefully for booby traps and snipers and ambushes, and the company behind him followed with clinking, clunking packs.

Down the muddy trail under the dripping trees. Measuring time not in hours or minutes but in aching, weary steps. Shoulders slumping beneath the straps of heavy packs. Step by step, one step at a time, pick up a heavy foot and swing it forward, slog it down into the mud, a few thousand steps and a mile and a few muddy miles and a few more muddy miles and it was nearly dark and the C.O. signaled to set up a perimeter.

Hardje and Tyler readied their position without a word. Hardje chopped the tall grass, clearing firing lanes. Tyler set out trip flares and Claymore mines. Tyler pulled his stove from his pack and asked Hardje if he had any C.4 left. Hardje, standing in the gathering darkness, wiped the mosquitoes from his arms and nodded. "In the side pocket," he said.

As Tyler reached for the pack, his hand brushed Hardje's M-16. It tipped, falling. Tyler grabbed for it. His finger touched the trigger. Hardje had forgotten to check the safety back in the village because the old woman had unnerved him. The shell exploded. Hardje bent over. Looked at Tyler. Sat down.

Tyler said, "No."

He jumped to Hardje's side, asked, "Where?"

He saw Hardje's hands clutching his lower stomach. He unbuckled Hardje's belt, pulled his pants down, his shirt up. There was a tiny hole, not much larger than a leech scar. A stream of blood trickled down and lost itself in reddish-brown pubic hair.

"It doesn't look bad," Tyler said. "It really doesn't."

Hardje's eyes glazed over.

Tyler frantically rolled him over on his stomach. Steaming red entrails with globs of yellow fat poured out a hole the size of his fist in the middle of Hardje's back. The blood burned Tyler's hands as he tried to stuff the guts back in.

Mosquitoes drawn by the blood swarmed.

A leech slowly, sinuously slithered beneath Tyler's belt and snuggled up in the wet warmth of his groin. Tyler wiped the mosquitoes from his unfeeling arms as he cried.

THE VILLAGE

* * *

The people who did not live in the village that wasn't there heard the steel blades of the phantom helicopter chopping through the monsoon with Hardje's imaginary corpse. They looked up and saw its spectral shape slipping through the shadows of the clouds, and they stirred their rice.

THE GHOST SOLDIERS

·

by Tim O'Brien

I was shot twice. The first time, out by Tri Binh, it knocked me
against the pagoda wall, and I bounced and spun around and
ended up on Teddy Thatcher's lap. Lucky thing, because
Teddy was the medic. He tied on a compress and told me to
take a nap, then he ran off toward the fighting. For a long time
I lay there all alone, listening to the battle, thinking, *I've been
shot, I've been shot.* Winged, grazed, creased: all those Gene
Autry movies I'd seen as a kid. In fact, I even laughed. Except
then I started to think I might bleed to death. It was the fear,
mostly, but I felt awful wobbly, and then I had a sinking sensation, ears all plugged up, as if I'd gone deep under water.
Thank God for Teddy Thatcher. Every so often, maybe four
times altogether, he trotted back to check me out. Which took
guts. It was a wild fight, lots of noise, guys running and laying
down fire, regrouping, running again, no front or rear, real
chaos, but Teddy took the risks. "Easy does it," he said. "Just
a side wound—no problem unless you're pregnant. You preg-

nant, buddy?" He ripped off the compress, applied a fresh one, and told me to clamp it in place with my fingers. "Press hard," he said. "Don't worry about the baby; too late to save it." Teddy wiped the blood off his hands. "No more house calls, pal. Gotta run." Then he took off. It was almost dark before the fighting petered out and the chopper came to take me and two dead guys away. "Adios, amigo," Teddy said in his fake Mexican accent. "Happy trails to you." I was barely feeling up to it, but I said, "Oh, Cisco," and Teddy wrapped his arms around me and kissed my neck and said, "Oh, Pancho!" Then the bird took off. On the ride in to Chu Lai, I kept waiting for the pain to come. I squeezed my fists tight and bit down, but actually I couldn't feel much. A throb, that's all. Even in the hospital it wasn't bad.

When I got back to Delta Company twenty-six days later, in mid-March, Teddy Thatcher was dead, and a new medic named Jorgenson had replaced him. Jorgenson was no Teddy. Incompetent and wimpy and scared. So when I got shot the second time, in the butt, along the Song Tra Bong, it took the son of a bitch almost ten minutes to work up the courage to crawl over to me. By then I was gone with the pain. Later I found out I'd almost died of shock. Jorgenson didn't know about shock, or if he knew, the fear made him forget. To make it worse, the guy bungled the patch job, and a couple of weeks later my ass started to rot away. You could actually peel off chunks of meat with your fingernail.

It was borderline gangrene. I spent a month flat on my belly —couldn't play cards, couldn't sleep. I kept seeing Jorgenson's scared-green face. Those buggy eyes, the way his lips twitched, that silly excuse for a mustache. After the rot cleared up, once I could think straight, I devoted a lot of time to figuring ways to get back at him.

*   *   *

Getting shot should be an experience from which you can draw a little pride. I'm not talking macho crap; I'm not saying you should strut around with your Purple Hearts on display. All I mean is that you should be able to *talk* about it: the stiff thump of the bullet, the way it knocks the air out of you and makes you cough, the sound of the shot when it comes about ten decades later, the dizzy feeling, the disbelief, the smell of yourself, the stuff you think about and say and do right afterward, the way your eyes focus on a tiny pebble or a blade of grass and how you think, man, that's the last thing I'll ever see, *that* pebble, *that* blade of grass, which makes you want to cry. Pride isn't the right word; I don't know the right word. All I know is, you shouldn't feel embarrassed. Humiliation shouldn't be part of it.

Diaper rash, the nurses called it. They sprinkled me with talcum powder and patted my ass and said "Git-cha-goo, git-cha-goo." Male nurses, too. That was the worst part. It made me hate Jorgenson the way some guys hated Charlie—ear-cutting hate, the kind atrocities are made of.

*   *   *

I guess the higher-ups decided I'd been shot enough. In early May, when I was released from the Ninety-first Evac Hospital, they transferred me over to headquarters company—S-4, the battalion supply section. Compared with the boonies, of course, it was cushy duty. Regular hours, movies, floor shows, the blurry slow motion of the rear. Fairly safe, too. The battalion fire base was built into a big hill just off Highway One, surrounded on all sides by flat paddy land, and between us and the paddies there were plenty of bunkers and sandbags and rolls of razor-tipped barbed wire. Sure, you could still die there—once a month or so we'd get hit with some mortar fire —but what the hell, you could die in the bleachers at Fenway Park, bases loaded, Yaz coming to the plate. Safety is relative; it's never permanent.

I wasn't complaining. Naturally there were times when I halfway wanted to head back to the field; I missed the adventure, the friendships, even the danger. A hard thing to explain to somebody who hasn't felt it. Danger, it makes things vivid. When you're afraid, really afraid, you taste your own spit, you see things you never saw before, you pay attention. On the other hand, though, I wasn't crazy. I'd already taken two bullets; the odds were deadly. So I just settled in, took it easy, counted myself lucky. I figured my war was over. If it hadn't been for the constant ache in my butt, I guess things would've worked out fine.

But Jesus, it *hurt*. Torn-up muscle, nerves like live electric wires: it was pain.

Pain, you know?

At night, for example, I had to sleep on my belly. Doesn't sound so terrible until you consider that I'd been a back-sleeper all my life. It got to where I was almost an insomniac. I'd lie there all fidgety and tight, then after a while I'd get angry. I'd squirm around on my cot, cussing, half nuts with hurt, then I'd start remembering stuff. Jorgenson. I'd think, Jesus Christ, I almost died. Shock—how could the bastard forget to treat for shock? Diaper rash, butt rot. I'd remember how long it took him to get to me, how his fingers were all jerky and nervous, the way his lips twitched under that ridiculous mustache.

The nights were miserable.

Sometimes I'd roam around the base. I'd head down to the wire and stare out at the darkness, out where the war was, all those ghosts, and I'd count ways to make Jorgenson suffer.

One thing for sure. You forget how much you use your butt until you can't use it anymore.

*   *   *

In July, Delta Company came in for stand-down. I was there on the helipad to meet the choppers. Curtis and Lemon and Azar slapped hands with me—jokes, dirty names, disguised affection—then I piled their gear in my jeep and drove them down to the Delta hootches. We partied until chow time. Afterward, we kept on partying. It was one of the rituals. Even if you weren't in the mood, you did it on principle.

By midnight it was story time.

"Morty Becker wasted his luck," said Lemon. "No lie," said Azar.

I smiled and waited. There was a tempo to how stories got told. Lemon peeled open a finger blister and sucked on it and wagged his head sadly.

"Go on," Azar said. "Tell it."

"Becker used up his luck. Pissed it away."

"On *nothin',*" Azar said.

Lemon nodded, started to speak, then stopped and got up and moved to the cooler and shoved his hands deep into the ice. He was naked except for his socks and his dog tags. In a way, I envied him—all of them. Those deep bush tans, the jungle sores and blisters, the stories, the in-it-togetherness. I felt close to them, yes, but I also felt separate.

Bending forward, Lemon scooped ice up against his chest, pressing it there for a moment, eyes closed; then he fished out a beer and snapped it open.

"It was out by My Khe," he said. "Remember My Khe? Bad-ass country, right? A blister of a day, hot-hot, and we're just sort of groovin' it, lyin' around, nobody bustin' ass or anything. I mean, listen, it's *hot.* We're poppin' salt tabs just to stay conscious. Finally somebody says, 'Hey, where's Becker?' The captain does a head count, and guess what? No Becker."

"Gone," Azar said. "Vanished."

"Ghosts."

"*Poof,* no fuckin' Becker."

"We send out two patrols—no dice. Not a trace." Lemon poured beer on his open blister, slowly licked the foam off. "By then it's getting dark. Captain's about ready to have a fit—you know how he gets, right?—and then, guess what? Take a guess."

"Becker shows," I said.

"You got it, man. Becker shows. We've almost chalked him up as MIA, and then, bingo, he shows."

"Soaking wet," Azar said.

"Hey—"

"Okay, it's your story, but *tell* it."

Lemon frowned. "Soaking wet," he said.

"Ha!"

"Turns out he went for a swim. You believe that? All by himself, the moron just takes off, hikes a couple klicks, finds himself a river, strips, hops in, no security, no *nothin'*. Dig it? He goes swimming."

Azar giggled. "A hot day."

"Not that hot," murmured Curtis Young. "Not that fuckin' hot."

"Hot, though."

"Get the picture?" Lemon said. "I mean, this is My Khe we're talking about. Doomsville, and the guy goes for a *swim.*"

"Yeah," I said. "Crazy."

I looked across the hootch. Thirty or forty guys were there, some drinking, some passed out, but I couldn't find Morty Becker among them.

Lemon grinned. He reached out and put his hand on my knee and squeezed.

"That's the kicker, man. No more Becker."

"No?"

"The kicker's this," Lemon said, "Morty Becker's luck gets all used up. See? On a lousy swim."

"And that's the truth. That's the truth," said Azar.

Lemon's hand still rested on my knee, very gently. The fingers were quivering a little.

"What happened?"

"Ah, shit."

"Go on, tell."

"Fatality," Lemon said. "Couple days later, maybe a week, Becker gets real dizzy. Pukes a lot, temperature zooms way up. Out of sight, you know? Jorgenson says he must've swallowed bad water on that swim. Swallowed a virus or something."

"Jorgenson," I said. "Where is my good buddy Jorgenson?"

"Hey, look—"

"Just tell me where to find him."

Lemon made a quick clicking sound with his tongue. "You want to *hear* this? Yes or no?"

"Sure, but where's—"

"Listen up. Becker gets sick, right? Sick, sick, sick. Never seen nobody so bad off, *never.* Sicko! Arms jerkin' all over hell, can't walk, can't talk, can't fart, can't nothin'. Like he's paralyzed. Can't move. Polio, maybe."

Curtis Young shook his head. "Not polio. You got it wrong."

"Maybe polio."

"No way," Curtis said. "Not polio."

"*Maybe,*" Lemon said. "I'm just saying what Jorgenson says. Maybe fuckin' polio. Or that elephant disease. Elephantiasshole or whatever."

"But not polio."

Azar smiled and snapped his fingers. "Either way," he said, "it goes to show. Don't throw away luck on little stuff. Save it up."

"That's the lesson, all right."

"Becker was due."

"There it is. Overdue. Don't fritter away your luck."

"Fuckin' polio."

Lemon closed his eyes.

We sat quietly. No need to talk, because we were thinking about the same things: about Mort Becker, the way luck worked and didn't work, how it was impossible to gauge the odds. Maybe the disease was lucky. Who knows? Maybe it saved Morty from getting shot.

"Where's Jorgenson?" I said.

"Ease off on that," Lemon whispered. "Let it go."

"Sure. No sweat, no sweat. But where's the son of a bitch hiding?"

*   *   *

Another thing: three times a day, no matter what, I had to stop whatever I was doing, go find a private place, drop my pants, bend over, and apply this antibacterial ointment to my ass. No choice—I had to do it. And the worst part was how the ointment left yellow stains on the seat of my trousers, big greasy splotches. Herbie's hemorrhoids, that was one of the jokes. There were plenty of other jokes too—plenty.

During the first full day of Delta's stand-down, I didn't run into Jorgenson once. Not at chow, not at the flicks, not during our long booze sessions in the hootch.

I didn't hunt him down, though. I just waited.

"Forget it," Lemon said. "Granted, the man messed up bad, real bad, but you got to take into account how green he was. Just a tenderfoot. Brand new. Remember?"

"I forget. Remind me."

"You survived."

I showed Lemon the yellow stain on my britches. "I'm in terrific shape. Real funny, right?"

"Not exactly," Lemon said.

But he was laughing. He started snapping a towel at my backside. I laughed—I couldn't help it—but I didn't see the big joke.

Later, after some dope, Lemon said: "The thing is, Jorgenson's doing all right. Better and better. People change, they adapt. I mean, okay, he's not a Teddy Thatcher, he won't win medals or anything, but the poor dude hangs in there, he knows his shit. Kept Becker alive."

"My sore ass."

Lemon nodded. He shrugged, leaned back, popped the hot roach into his mouth, chewed for a long time. "You've lost touch, man. Jorgenson . . . he's *with* us now."

"I'm not."

"No," he said. "I guess you're not."

"Good old loyalty."

"War."

"Friends in need, friends get peed on."

Lemon shook his head. "We're friends, Herbie. You and me. But look, you're not *out* there anymore, and Jorgenson is. If you'd just seen him the past couple of weeks—the way he handled Becker, then when Pinko hit the mine—I mean, the kid did some good work. Ask anybody. So . . . I don't know. If it was me, Herbie, I'd say screw it. Leave it alone."

"I won't hurt him."

"Right."

"I won't. Show him some ghosts, that's all."

* * *

In the morning I spotted Jorgenson. I was up on the helipad, loading the resupply choppers, and then, when the last bird took off, while I was putting on my shirt, I looked up, half-squinting, and there he was. In a way, it was a shock. His size, I mean. Even smaller than I remembered—a little squirrel of a guy, five and a half feet tall, skinny and mousy and sad.

He was leaning against my jeep, waiting for me.

"Herb," he said, "can we talk?"

At first I just looked at his boots.

Those boots: I remembered them from when I got shot. Out along the Song Tra Bong, a bullet in my ass, all that pain, and the funny thing was that what I remembered, now, were those new boots—no scuffs; smooth, unblemished leather. One of those last details, Jorgenson's boots.

"Herb?"

I looked at his eyes—a long, straight-on stare—and he blinked and made a stabbing motion at his nose and backed off a step. Oddly, I felt some pity for him. A bona fide card-carrying twit. The tiniest arms and wrists I'd ever seen—a sparrow's nervous system. He made me think of those sorry kids back in junior high who used to spend their time collecting stamps and butterflies, always off by themselves, no friends, no hope.

He took another half-step backward and said, very softly, "Look, I just wanted . . . I'm sorry, Herb."

I didn't move or look away or anything.

"Herb?"

"Talk, talk, talk."

"What can I say? It was—"

"Excuses?"

Jorgenson's tongue flicked out, then slipped away. He shook his head. "No, it was a bungle, and I don't . . . I was *scared.* All the noise and everything, the shooting, I'd never seen that before. I couldn't make myself move. After you got hit, I kept telling myself to move, move, but I couldn't *do* it. Like I was full of Novocain or something. You ever feel like that? Like you can't even move?"

"Anyway," I said.

"And then I heard how you . . . the shock, the gangrene. Man, I felt like . . . couldn't sleep, couldn't eat. Nightmares, you know? Kept seeing you lying out there, heard you screaming, and . . . it was like my legs were filled up with cement. I *couldn't.*"

His lip trembled, and he made a weird moaning sound—not quite a moan, feathery and high—and for a second I was afraid he might start crying. That would've ended it. I was a sucker for tears. I would've patted his shoulder, told him to forget it. Thank God he tried to shake my hand. It gave me an excuse to spit.

"Kiss it," I said.

"Herb, I can't go back and do it over."

"Lick it, kiss it."

But Jorgenson just smiled. Very tentatively, like an invalid, he kept pushing his hand out at me. He looked so mournful and puppy-doggish, so damned hurt, that I made myself spit again. I didn't feel like spitting—my heart wasn't in it—but somehow I managed, and Jorgenson glanced away for a second, still smiling a weary little smile, resigned-looking, as if to show how generous he was, how bighearted and noble.

It almost made me feel guilty.

I got into the jeep, hit the ignition, left him standing there.

Guilty, for Chrissake. Why should it end up with *me* feeling the guilt? I hated him for making me stop hating him.

* * *

Thing is, it had been a vow. *I'll get him, I'll get him*—it was down inside me like a stone. Except now I couldn't generate the passion. Couldn't feel anger. I still had to get back at him, but now it was a need, not a want. An obligation. To rev up some intensity, I started drinking a little—more than a little, a lot. I remembered the river, getting shot, the pain, how I kept calling out for a medic, waiting and waiting and waiting, passing out once, waking up, screaming, how the scream seemed to make new pain, the awful stink of myself, the sweating and shit and fear, Jorgenson's clumsy fingers when he finally got around to working on me. I remembered it all, every detail. *Shock,* I thought. *I'm dying of shock.* I tried to tell him that, but my tongue didn't connect with my brain. All I could do was go, "Ough! Ough!" I wanted to say, "You *jerk!* I'm *dying!* Treat for shock, treat for shock!" I remembered all that, and the hospital, and those giggling nurses. I even remembered the rage. Except I couldn't feel it anymore. Just a word—*rage*—spelled out in my head. No *feeling*. In the end, all I had were the facts. Number one: the guy had almost killed me. Number two: there had to be consequences. Only thing was, I wished I could've gotten some pleasure out of them.

I asked Lemon to give me a hand.

"No pain," I said. "Basic psy-ops, that's all. We'll just scare him. Mess with his head a little."

"Negative," Lemon said.

"Just show him some ghosts."

"Sick, man."

"Not all *that* sick." I stuck a finger in Lemon's face. "Sick is getting shot. Try it sometime, you'll see what genuine sick is."

"No," he said.

"Comrade-in-arms. Such crap."

"I guess."

Stiffly, like a stranger, Lemon looked at me for a long time. Then he moved across the hootch and lay down with a comic book and pretended to read. His lips were moving, but that didn't fool me a bit.

I had to get Azar in on it.

Azar didn't have Lemon's intelligence, but he had a better sense of justice.

"Tonight?" he said.

"Just don't get carried away."

"Me?"

Azar grinned and snapped his fingers. It was a tic. Snap, snap—whenever things got tight, whenever there was a prospect of action.

"Understand?"

"Roger-dodger," Azar said. "Only a game, right?"

*   *   *

We called the enemy "ghosts." "Bad night," we'd murmur. "Ghosts are out." To get spooked, in the lingo, meant not only to get scared but to get killed. "Don't get spooked," we'd say. "Stay cool, stay alive." The countryside was spooky: snipers, tunnels, ancestor worship, ancient papa-sans, incense. The land was haunted. We were fighting forces that didn't obey the laws of twentieth-century science. Deep in the night, on guard, it seemed that all of Nam was shimmering and swaying—odd shapes swirling in the dark; phantoms; apparitions; spirits in the abandoned pagodas; boogeymen in sandals. When a guy named Olson was killed, in February, everybody started saying, "The Holy Ghost took him." And when Ron Ingo hit the booby trap, in April, somebody said he'd been made into a deviled egg—no arms, no legs, just a poor deviled egg.

It was ghost country, and Charlie was the main ghost. The way he came out at night. How you never really saw him, just thought you did. Almost magical—appearing, disappearing. He could levitate. He could pass through barbed wire. He was invisible, blending with the land, changing shape. He could fly. He could melt away like ice. He could creep up on you without sound or footsteps. He was scary.

In the daylight, maybe, you didn't believe in all this stuff. You laughed, you made jokes. But at night you turned into a believer: no skeptics in foxholes.

*   *   *

Azar was wound up tight. All afternoon, while we made preparations, he kept chanting, "Halloween, Halloween." That, plus the finger snapping, almost made me cancel the whole operation. I went hot and cold. Lemon wouldn't speak to me, which tended to cool it off, but then I'd start remembering things. The result was a kind of tepid numbness. No ice, no heat. I went through the motions like a sleepwalker—rigidly, by the numbers, no real emotion, no heart. I rigged up my special effects, checked out the battle terrain, measured distances, gathered the ordnance and gear we'd need. I was professional enough about it, I didn't miss a thing, but somehow it felt as if I were gearing up to fight somebody else's war. I didn't have that patriotic zeal.

Who knows? If there'd been a dignified way out, I might've taken it.

During evening chow, in fact, I kept staring across the mess hall at Jorgenson, and when he finally looked up at me, a puzzled frown on his face, I came very close to smiling. Very, very close. Maybe I was fishing for something. A nod, a bow, one last apology—anything. But Jorgenson only gazed back at me. In a strange way, too. As if he didn't *need* to apologize again. Just a straight, unafraid gaze. No humility at all.

To top it off, my ex-buddy Lemon was sitting with him, and they were having this chummy-chummy conversation, all smiles and sweetness.

That's probably what cinched it.

I went back to my hootch, showered, shaved, threw my helmet against the wall, lay down awhile, fidgeted, got up, prowled around, applied some fresh ointment, then headed off to find Azar.

Just before dusk, Delta Company stood for roll call. Afterward the men separated into two groups. Some went off to drink or sleep or catch a movie; the others trooped down to the base perimeter, where, for the next eleven hours, they would pull night guard duty. It was SOP—one night on, one night off.

This was Jorgenson's night on.

I knew that in advance, of course. And I knew his bunker assignment: number six, a pile of sandbags at the southwest corner of the perimeter. That morning I'd scouted every inch of his position; I knew the blind spots, the ripples of land, the places where he'd take cover in case of trouble. I was ready. To guard against freak screw-ups, though, Azar and I tailed him down to the wire. We watched him lay out his bedroll, connect the Claymores to their firing devices, test the radio, light up a cigarette, yawn, then sit back with his rifle cradled to his chest like a teddy bear.

"A pigeon," Azar whispered. "Roast pigeon on a spit. I smell it cookin'."

"Remember, though. This isn't for real."

Azar shrugged. He touched me on the shoulder, not roughly but not gently either. "What's real?" he said. "Eight months in Fantasyland, it tends to blur the line. Honest to God, I sometimes can't remember what real *is*."

*   *   *

Psychology—that was one thing I knew. I never went to college, and I wasn't exactly a whiz in high school either, but all my life I've paid attention to how things operate inside the skull. Example: You don't try to scare people in broad daylight. You wait. Why? Because the darkness squeezes you inside yourself, you get cut off from the outside world, the imagination takes over. That's basic psychology. I'd pulled enough night guard to know how the fear factor gets multiplied as you sit there hour after hour, nobody to talk to, nothing to do but stare blank-eyed into the Big Black Hole. The hours pile up. You drift; your brain starts to roam. You think about dark closets, madmen, murderers hiding under the bed, all those childhood fears. Fairy tales with gremlins and trolls and one-eyed giants. You try to block it all out but you can't. You see ghosts. You blink and laugh and shake your head. Bullshit, you say. But then you remember the guys who died: Teddy, Olson, Ingo, maybe Becker, a dozen others whose faces you can't see anymore. Pretty soon you begin to think about the stories you've heard about Charlie's magic. The time some guys cornered two VC in a dead-end tunnel, no way out, but how, when the tunnel was fragged and searched, nothing was found but dead rats. A hundred stories. A whole bookful: ghosts swinging from the trees, ghosts wiping out a whole Marine platoon in twenty seconds flat, ghosts rising from the dead, ghosts behind you and in front of you and inside you. Your ears get ticklish. Tiny sounds get heightened and distorted, crickets become monsters, the hum of the night takes on a weird electronic tingle. You try not to breathe. You coil and tighten up and listen. Your knuckles ache, and your pulse ticks like an alarm clock. What's *that?* You jerk up. Nothing, you say, nothing. Unless . . . You check to be sure your weapon is loaded. Put it on full automatic. Count your grenades, make sure the pins are bent for quick throwing. Crouch lower. Listen, listen. And then, after enough time passes, things start to get bad.

* * *

"Come on, man," Azar said. "Let's *do* it." But I told him to be patient. "Waiting, that's half the trick," I said. "Give him time, let him simmer." So we went to the movies. *Barbarella* again, the sixth straight night. But it kept Azar happy—he was crazy about Jane Fonda. "Sweet Janie," he kept saying, over and over. "Sweet Janie boosts a man's morale." Then, with his hand, he showed me which part of his morale got boosted. An old joke. Everything was old. The movie, the heat, the booze, the war. I fell asleep during the second reel—a hot, angry sleep —and forty minutes later I woke up to a sore ass and a foul temper.

It wasn't yet midnight.

We hiked over to the EM club and worked our way through a six-pack. Lemon was there, at another table, but he pretended not to see me.

Around closing time, I made a fist and showed it to Azar. He smiled like a little boy. "Goody," he said. We picked up the gear, smeared charcoal on our faces, then moved down to the wire.

"Let's hurt him," Azar whispered. "Pain time for ol' Jorgy."

"No, man, listen to me—"

But Azar lifted his thumb and grinned and peeled away from me and began circling behind Bunker Six. For a second I couldn't move. Not fear, exactly; I don't know what it was. My boots felt heavy.

In a way, it was purely mechanical. I didn't think, I just shouldered the gear and crossed quietly over to a heap of boulders that overlooked Jorgenson's bunker.

I was directly behind him. Thirty-two meters away, exactly. My measurements were precise.

Even in the heavy darkness, no moon yet, I could make out Jorgenson's silhouette: a helmet, his shoulders, the rifle barrel. His back was to me. That was the heart of the psychology: he'd be looking out at the wire, the paddies, where the danger was; he'd figure his back was safe; only the chest and belly were vulnerable.

Quiet, quiet.

I knelt down, took out the flares, lined them up in front of me, unscrewed the caps, then checked my wristwatch. Still five minutes to go. Edging over to my left, I groped for the ropes, found them wedged in the crotch of two boulders. I separated them and tested the tension and checked the time again. One minute.

My head was light. Fluttery and taut at the same time. It was the feeling I remembered from the boonies, on ambush or marching at night through ghost country. Peril and doubt and awe, all those things and a million more. You wonder if you're dreaming. Unreal, unreal. As if molting, you seem to slip outside yourself. It's like you're in a movie. There's a camera on you, so you begin acting, following the script: "Oh, Cisco!" You think of all the films you've seen, Audie Murphy and Gary Cooper and Van Johnson and Roy Rogers, all of them, and certain lines of dialogue come back to you—"I been plugged!"—and then, when you get shot, you can't help falling back on them. "Jesus, Jesus," you say, half to yourself, half to the camera. "I been fuckin' *plugged!*" You expect it of yourself. On ambush, poised in the dark, you fight to control yourself. Not too much fidgeting; it wouldn't look good. You try to grin. Eyes open, be alert—old lines, old movies. It all swirls together, clichés mixing with your own emotions, and in the end you can't distinguish. . . .

It was time. I fingered one of the ropes, took a breath, then gave it a sharp jerk.

Instantly there was a clatter outside the wire.

I expected the noise, I was even tensed for it, but still my heart took a funny little hop. I winced and ducked down.

"Now," I murmured. "Now it starts." Eight ropes altogether. I had four, Azar had four. Each rope was hooked up to a homemade noisemaker out in front of Jorgenson's bunker— eight tin cans filled with rifle cartridges. Simple devices, but they worked.

I waited a moment, and then, very gently, I gave all four of my ropes a little tug. Delicate—nothing loud. If you weren't listening, listening hard, you might've missed it. But Jorgenson was listening. Immediately, at the first low rattle, his silhouette seemed to freeze. Then he ducked down and blended in with the dark.

There—another rattle. Azar this time.

We kept at it for ten minutes. Noise, silence, noise, silence. Stagger the rhythm. Start slowly, gradually build the tension.

Crouched in my pile of boulders, squinting down at Jorgenson's position, I felt a swell of immense power. It was the feeling Charlie must have: full control, mastery of the night. Like a magician, a puppeteer. Yank on the ropes, watch the silly wooden puppet jump and twitch. It made me want to giggle. One by one, in sequence, I pulled on each of the ropes, and the sound came bouncing back at me with an eerie, indefinite formlessness: a rattlesnake, maybe, or the creak of a closet door or footsteps in the attic—whatever you made of it.

"There now," I whispered, or thought. "There, there."

Jorgenson wasn't moving. Not yet. He'd be coiled up in his circle of sandbags, fists tight, blinking, listening.

Again I tugged on my ropes.

I smiled. Eyes closed, I could almost *see* what was happening down there.

Bang. Jorgenson would jerk up. Rub his eyes, bend forward. Eardrums fluttering like wings, spine stiff, muscles hard, brains like Jell-O. I could *see* it. Right now, at this instant, he'd glance up at the sky, hoping for a moon, a few stars. But no moon, no stars. He'd start talking to himself: "Relax, relax." Desperately he'd try to bring the night into focus, but the effort would only cause distortions: objects would seem to pick themselves up and twist and wiggle; trees would creep forward like an army on midnight maneuvers; the earth itself would begin to sway. Fun house country. Trick mirrors and trapdoors and pop-up monsters. Lord, I could *see* it! It was as if I were down there *with* him, *beside* him. "Easy," he was muttering, "easy, easy, easy," but it didn't get easier. His ears were stiff, his eyeballs were dried up and hard, like stones, and the ghosts were coming out.

* * *

"Creepy," Azar cackled. "Wet pants, goose bumps. We *got* him. Ghost town!" He held a beer out to me, but I shook my head.

We sat in the dim quiet of my hootch, boots off, smoking, listening to Mary Hopkin.

"So what next?"

"Wait," I said. "More of the same."

"Well, sure, but—"

"Shut up and *listen.*"

That high elegant voice. That melody. "Those were the days, my friend. . . ." Someday, when the war was over, I'd go to London and ask Mary Hopkin to marry me. "We'd sing and dance forever and a day. . . ." Nostalgic and mawkish, but so what? That's what Nam does to you. Turns you sentimental, makes you want to marry girls like Mary Hopkin. You learn, finally, that you'll die. You see the corpses, sometimes you even kick them, feel the boot against meat, and you always think, *Me, me.* "We'd fight and never lose, those were the days, oh yes. . . ." That's what war does to you.

Azar switched off the tape.

"Shit, man," he said. "Don't you got some *music?*"

* * *

And now, finally, the moon was out. It was a white moon, mobile, clouded, nearly full. We slipped back to our positions and went to work again with the ropes. Louder, now, more insistently. The moon added resonance. Starlight shimmied in the barbed wire; reflections, layerings of shadow. Slowly, slowly we dragged the tin cans closer to Jorgenson's bunker, and this, plus the moon, gave a sense of creeping peril, the slow tightening of a noose.

At 0300 hours, the very deepest part of the night, Azar set off the first trip flare.

There was a light popping sound out in front of Bunker Six. Then a sizzle. And then the night seemed to snap itself in half. The flare burned ten paces from the bunker: like the Fourth of July, white-hot magnesium, a thousand sparklers exploding in a single cluster.

As the flare died, I fired three more.

It was instant daylight. For a moment I was paralyzed—blinded, struck dumb.

Then Jorgenson moved. There was a short, squeaky cry—not even a cry, really, just a sound of terror—and then a blurred motion as he jumped up and ran a few paces and rolled and lay still. His silhouette was framed like a cardboard cutout against the burning flares.

He was weeping.

A soft, musical sound. Like a long hollow sigh. As the flares burned themselves out, the weeping became raspy and painful. I sympathized. I really did. In fact, I almost trotted over to console him: "I know, I know. Scary business. You just want to cry and cry and cry."

* * *

In the dark outside my hootch, even though I bent toward him, nose to nose, all I could see were Azar's white eyes.

"Enough," I told him.

"Oh, sure."

"Seriously."

"Serious?" he said. "That's too serious for me; I'm a fun lover. A party boy on Halloween."

When Azar smiled I saw the quick glitter of teeth, but then the smile went away, and I knew it was hopeless. I tried, though. I told him the score was even—no need to rub it in. I was firm. I explained, very bluntly, that it was my game, beginning to end, and now I wanted to end it. I even got belligerent.

Azar just peered at me, almost dumbly.

"Poor Herbie," he said.

Nothing dramatic. The rest was inflection and those electric white-white eyes.

* * *

An hour before dawn we moved up for the last phase. Azar was in command now. I tagged after him, thinking maybe I could keep a lid on.

"Don't take this personal," Azar whispered. "You know? It's just that I like to finish things."

I didn't look at him; I looked at my fingernails, at the moon. When we got down near the wire, Azar gently put his hand on my shoulder, guiding me over toward the boulder pile. He knelt down and inspected the ropes and flares, nodded, peered out at Jorgenson's bunker, nodded again, removed his helmet and sat on it.

He was smiling again.

"Herbie?" he whispered.

I ignored him. My lips had a waxy, cold feel, like polished rock. I kept running my tongue over them. I told myself to stop it and I did, but then a second later I was doing it again.

"You know something?" Azar said, almost to himself. "Sometimes I feel like a little kid again. Playing war, you know? I get into it. I mean, wow, I *love* this shit."

"Look, why don't we—"

"Shhhh."

Smiling, Azar put a finger to his lips, partly as a warning, partly as a nifty gesture.

We waited another twenty minutes. It was cold now, and damp. My bones ached. I had a weird feeling of brittleness, as if somebody could reach out and grab me and crush me like a Christmas tree ornament. It was the same feeling out along the Song Tra Bong, when I got shot: I tried to grin wryly, like Bogie or Gable, and I thought about all the zingers Teddy Thatcher and I would use—except now Teddy was dead. Except when I called out for a medic, loud, nobody came. I started whimpering. The blood was warm, like dishwater, and I could feel my pants filling up with it. God, I thought, all this blood; I'll be *hollow*. Then the brittle feeling came over me. I passed out, woke up, screamed, tried to crawl but couldn't. I felt alone. All around me there was rifle fire, voices yelling, and yet for a moment I thought I'd gone deaf: the sounds were in my head, they weren't real. I smelled myself. The bullet had smashed through the colon, and the stink of my own shit made me afraid. I was crying. Leaking to death, I thought—blood and crap leaking out—and I couldn't quit crying. When Jorgenson got to me, all I could do was go "Ough! Ough!" I tightened up and pressed and grunted, trying to stop the leak, but that only made it worse, and Jorgenson punched me and told me to cut it out, ease off. *Shock,* I thought. I tried to tell him that: "Shock, man! Treat for shock!" I was lucid, things were clear, but my tongue wouldn't make the right words. And I was squirming. Jorgenson had to put his knee on my chest, turn me over, and when he did that, when he ripped my pants open, I shouted something and tried to wiggle away. I was hollowed out and cold. It was the *smell* that scared me. He was pressing down on my back—sitting on me, maybe, holding me down—and I kept trying to buck him off, rocking and moaning, even when he stuck me with morphine, even when he used his shirt to wipe my ass, even when he plugged the hole. Shock, I kept thinking. And then, like magic, things suddenly clicked into slow motion. The morphine, maybe: I focused on those brand-new black boots of his, then on a pebble, then on a single wisp of dried grass—the last things I'd ever see. I couldn't look away, I didn't dare, and I couldn't stop crying.

Even now, in the dark, I felt the sting in my eyes.

Azar said, "Herbie."

"Sure, man, I'm solid."

Down below, the bunker was silent. Nothing moved. The place looked almost abandoned, but I knew Jorgenson was there, wide awake, and I knew he was waiting.

Azar went to work on the ropes.

It began gently, like a breeze: a soft, lush, sighing sound. The ghosts were out. I was blinking, shivering, hugging myself. You can *die* of fright; it's possible, it can happen. I'd heard stories about it, about guys so afraid of dying that they died. You freeze up, your muscles snap, the heart starts fluttering, the brain floats away. It can *happen.*

"Enough," I whispered. "Stop it."

Azar looked at me and winked. Then he yanked sharply on all four ropes, and the sound made me squeal and jerk up.

"Please," I said. "Call it quits, right now. Please, man."

Azar wasn't listening. His white eyes glowed as he shot off the first flare. "Please," I murmured, but then I watched the flare arc up over Jorgenson's bunker, very slowly, pinwheeling, exploding almost without noise, just a sudden red flash.

There was a short, anguished whimper in the dark. At first I thought it was Jorgenson, or maybe a bird, but then I knew it was my own voice. I bit down and folded my hands and squeezed.

Twice more, rapidly, Azar fired off red flares, and then he turned and looked at me and lifted his eyebrows.

"Herbie," he said softly, "you're a sad case. Sad, sad."

"Look, can't we—"

"Sad."

I was frightened—of him, of us—and though I wanted to do something, wanted to stop him, I crouched back and watched him pick up the tear-gas grenade, pull the pin, stand up, smile, pause, and throw. For a moment the night seemed to stop as if bewitched; then the gas puffed up in a smoky cloud that partly obscured the bunker. I was moaning. Even from thirty meters away, upwind. I could smell the gas: not really *smell* it, though. I could *feel* it, like breathing razor blades. CS gas, the worst. Chickenshit gas, we called it, because that was what it turned you into—a mindless, squawking chickenshit.

"Jesus, please," I moaned, but Azar lobbed over another one, waited for the hiss, then scrambled over to the rope we hadn't used yet. *"Please,"* I said. Azar grabbed the rope with both hands and pulled.

It was my idea. That morning I'd rigged it up: a sandbag painted white, a pulley system, a rope.

Show him a ghost.

Azar pulled, and out in front of Bunker Six, as if rising up from a grave, the white sandbag lifted itself up and hovered in the misty swirl of gas.

Jorgenson began firing. Just one round at first—a single red tracer that thumped into the sandbag and burned.

"Ooooooh!" Azar murmured. "Star light, star bright . . ."

Quickly, talking to himself, Azar hurled the last gas grenade, shot up another flare, then snatched the rope and made the white sandbag dance.

Jorgenson did not go nuts. Quietly, almost with dignity, he stood up and took aim and fired at the sandbag. I could see his profile against the red flares. His face seemed oddly relaxed. No twitching, no screams. With a strange, calm deliberation, he gazed out at the sandbag for several seconds, as if deciding something, and then he shook his head and smiled. Very slowly, he began marching out toward the wire. He did not crouch or run or crawl. He walked. He moved with a kind of graceful ease—resolutely, bravely, straight at the sandbag—firing with each step, stopping once to reload, then resuming his stately advance.

"Guts," Azar said.

Azar yanked on the rope and the sandbag bobbed and shimmied, but Jorgenson kept moving forward. When he reached the sandbag he stopped and turned, then he shouted my name, then he placed his rifle muzzle directly against the bag.

"Herbie!" he hollered, and he fired. The sandbag seemed to explode.

Azar dropped the rope.

"Show's over," he said. He looked down at me with pity. "Sad, sad, sad."

I was weeping. Distantly, as if from another continent, I heard Jorgenson pumping rounds into the sandbag.

"Disgusting," Azar said. "Herbie, Herbie. Saddest fucking case I ever seen."

Azar smiled. He looked out at Jorgenson, then at me. Those eyes—falcon eyes, ghost eyes. He moved toward me as if to help me up, but then, almost as an afterthought, he kicked me. My kneecap seemed to snap.

"Sad," he murmured, then he turned and headed off to bed.

*   *   *

"No big deal," I told Jorgenson. "Leave it alone. I'll live."

But he hooked my arm over his shoulder and helped me down to the bunker. My knee was hurting bad, but I didn't say anything. We sat facing each other.

It was almost full dawn now, a hazy silver dawn, and you could tell by the color and smells that rain wasn't far off.

For a while we didn't speak.

"So," he finally said.

"Right."

We shook hands, but neither of us put much emotion in it, and we didn't look at each other's eyes.

Jorgenson pointed out at the shot-up sandbag.

"That was a nice touch," he said. "No kidding, it had me . . . a nice touch. You've got a real sense of drama, Herbie. Someday you should go into the movies or something."

"I've thought about that."

"Another Hitchcock."

I nodded.

"*The Birds.* You ever see it?"

"Scary shit, man."

We sat for a while longer, then I started to get up, but my knee wasn't working right. Jorgenson had to give me a hand.

"Even?" he asked.

"Pretty much."

We touched—not a hug or anything, but something like that —then Jorgenson picked up his helmet, brushed it off, touched his funny little mustache, and looked out at the sandbag. His face was filthy. There were still tear splotches on his cheeks.

Up at the medic's hootch, he cleaned and bandaged my knee, then we went to chow. We didn't have much to say.

Chitchat, some jokes. Afterward, in an awkward moment, I said, "Let's kill Azar."

Jorgenson smiled. "Scare him to death, right?"

"Right," I said.

"What a movie!"

I shrugged. "Sure. Or just kill him."

ABOUT THE EDITOR

Robert Benard is an award-winning writer and anthologist whose books include *A Catholic Education* and *Do You Like it Here?* He makes his home in New York City.